THE GIRL ON THE SWING

ALI COOPER

Standing Stone Press

Published by Standing Stone Press February 2010

Printed and distributed by Lightning Source

ISBN 978-0-9564811-0-8

Many thanks are due to everyone who has helped with this book.

To Laraine Pengilley for editing and Robin Lewington for proof reading; Ralph, Charles and Chris for computer-related help; and Katy, Jon, Lynne and Yvonne for edit suggestions.

To Year Zero Writers, especially to Larry for technical advice and Dan for forming the group and inviting me to publish with them.

And to all my friends all over the world for their suggestions and encouragement.

In memory of Mum and Dad.

Chapter 1

It takes a while for my eyes to adjust then gradually I see it.

It is a garden of high summer. Where hollyhocks turn their faces to the sun. Where oriental poppies, full and red, grow taller than I have ever seen. Where roses twist and turn over timber archways. Where delphiniums reach from their hiding places to erupt in a surprise of iridescent blue.

I pause and half close my eyes while I digest the scene before me, then I return.

At the edge of the borders pinks spill out across pathways and white alyssum creeps between flagstones. There is a lawn sprinkled with daisies, ready to be picked and threaded into chains, and, in its centre, an old apple tree that groans as though pained by arthritic joints and aching limbs. On the lowest branch of this tree, a rope is looped, its ends knotted through a wooden seat. And here a young girl sits, swaying to and fro, kicking her legs as her lace-edged petticoats ripple in the breeze.

I have been the spectator but now I join the game. I feel the warmth of summer on my skin. I smell the sweetness of honeysuckle and the soporific lure of lavender. I feel the rope, rough against my fingers as I cling on tightly and urge my body to fly higher. I ignore the heat of the dress and pinafore and the tightness of the laced up boots. Instead I savour the joy of childhood and lose myself in a carefree moment.

I don't know how long I am there. I am in a place where time has no meaning. The motion makes me dizzy and I close my eyes for a second. The warmth drains away and is replaced by an autumnal chill. The scent of flowers dissolves into the moist air. When I open my eyes the garden has gone. In its place is a gravelled yard with artistically placed palms and agaves in Italianate pots. The collage of flowers has become an intense green backdrop of ornamental conifers.

The house, too, has changed. Casement windows have been obscured by an out of place lean-to conservatory, and bricks, previously a bright terracotta, are stained dark and ugly with the residues of mining and exhaust fumes. High on the wall, one thing remains the same; a clay plaque announces that the building is called Kimberley Place.

I stand on the grass verge, peering through a knothole in a tall wooden fence. I take a moment to return to the present. Then I hurry to my car and drive away, before anyone sees me, before a worried neighbour fears that I am a crazy person and calls the police.

But I know I am not mad. I used to live in this very house many years ago, in a previous lifetime, when I was the girl on the swing.

Stately arpeggios greet me as I open the front door. They are not fluid, rippling like water, but sombre footsteps, striding up and down the keyboard. I start, guiltily. I hadn't expected Richard to be home yet. I hang my jacket and scarf in the cloakroom and swap my outdoor shoes for a pair of ballerina-style pumps. The music continues. It takes more form now. Beethoven, I think, lost and mournful. That's all Richard seems to play these days.

In the morning room I try not to squeak my shoes on the polished floorboards. Beyond the shadows, Richard sits at the grand piano, man and music silhouetted in the backlight of the low, slanting afternoon sun that spears through the French windows. He doesn't acknowledge my presence but plays on, as I know he will, to the end of the piece. His concentration is intense. His fingers move over the keys as precisely as if they were cutting through a chest wall or cannulating a blood vessel and he will not pause until the last suture is in place.

At last the music comes to an end. Richard looks up as he lingers over the final resounding chord. His dark eyebrows rise questioningly.

'I've been out walking,' I say, as though I have to account for my movements. I don't tell him where I've been, or why. It isn't a secret exactly, but rather an indulgence that I keep covetously to myself, like a box of Belgian chocolates or a bath scented with exotic oils. Besides, if I told Richard the truth he'd only worry about me. And he already has enough to think about.

He is silent for a few moments, looking away from me as he rehearses words that I will not want to hear. 'I thought we could eat out tonight,' he suggests.

'Oh! Do you think we should?' My answer flies back abruptly, impulsively. I am surprised, frightened even, at the prospect. Apart from a couple of informal dinners at the homes of close friends, we haven't eaten out for months. Eating out is a celebration. And there's been nothing to celebrate.

He persists. 'It would save you having to cook. And I'm not on call. Perhaps we should take the opportunity.'

I hesitate, caught off guard. I fumble for a reason to stay in. I tell myself this is not the same as an excuse not to go out. 'There's steak in the fridge,' I say. 'And salad.'

Richard pretends he hasn't heard. 'It's difficult for me too.' He feels his way cautiously. 'But we have to carry on living. We have to resume a normal life before we forget how.' He doesn't look at me as he speaks; instead he busies himself folding away his music.

'I have a headache,' I lie. 'Perhaps another time.'

Richard stares at me now. He is a clever man, a doctor of medicine as, indeed, am I, but despite his qualifications and experience there are times when he doesn't know what to do, doesn't know what to say. On this occasion he doesn't even try. 'There are some journals I should read,' he says. 'I'll be in my study.' And with this he rises and walks past me without a glance. His footsteps resound decisively on the stairs.

The kitchen is an extensive room, too large for its purpose, too large for two people to be together. I take the skillet from

3

the hook and scan the spice rack, pondering the possibility of a marinade. Then I select a recipe book from the shelf and begin to turn the pages. I can allow myself to relax now. Slowly I breathe out as I hug the safety of the Aga rail. Set in an alcove close to the window, it is a warm reassuring place to be. I can turn my back on the cupboards full of dinner settings that will never be used, the ridiculously long family breakfast table and the cold unnecessary space that still remains, and pretend that I am in a farmhouse, essential and familiar, with a dog, alert on the rug and a cat sleeping on an old winged armchair. I glance at the pictures of exquisite food without digesting the words. The instructions to chop, grind, sauté and blanch scare me with their demands for perfection. Microscopic surgery would be easier. I close the book in defeat, remembering that I used to enjoy cooking – though I rarely seemed to have time to do it justice.

Tonight, I feel I must make an extra effort, having denied Richard the chance to go out. He doesn't understand how I feel. For a woman, providing food is a necessity, a reason for her to exist; eating out is a luxury. For a man, a meal in a restaurant is simply functional, it is a way of acquiring food and assuaging hunger. I think about what happened earlier this afternoon. For some reason that luxury is allowable.

It was over twenty years ago that I first discovered Kimberley Place. We had recently moved to Nottingham, Richard and I, we were newly married, newly qualified, taking up our first posts as junior doctors, getting used to the roles of husband and wife. It was by chance that I found it. I was lost. I'd turned off the M1 at the northern junction and, trying to circumnavigate road works, had wound my way around the outer edge of town. I remember how I pulled over, first to look at the map, then to ask the way. If I hadn't got out of the car I wouldn't have noticed it at all. But it was right outside that house that I stood on the footpath and tried to concentrate as a kindly old gentleman traced his finger across the road atlas that I held between us. There was a sparse hedge back then and I could easily see into the garden. I tried to focus on the directions the man was describing, but out of the corner of my eye I was aware of time slipping away, of decades, centuries of change unravelling. That was when it came to me, a flash of memory. It wasn't just the sight but the sounds and smells of the past, the whining of the branch as the swing pulled to and fro, the laughter of childhood. My laughter. I had been lost but now I was found.

'Will ee be all right?' The man's voice had pulled me back to the present. I'd nodded, smiled, thanked him for his help. Then, with a nostalgic glance at the modern garden beyond the hedge, I'd climbed into the car and driven home.

We lived in Wollaton back then. Our house was a semi-detached in a comfortable residential area, where calm crescents and cul-de-sacs gave onto avenues lined with cherry trees. I sigh to myself. I still hanker after the pink-blossomed, Japanese-scented springtime. When I arrived home that day I had plenty to busy myself with. I didn't think much about what had occurred. And that's how it would have stayed. How it always had before. Because, in the past, that sort of feeling had only ever happened with people I would never see again or places to which I would never return.

I might have forgotten about it, what with the rush of a new job, a new marriage and the surprise, not long after, of an unplanned, though not unwelcome, pregnancy. But chance took me there again six months later, when I made a social call just a couple of roads away. And I couldn't resist it, just a quick look. And this time I saw it all, the girl, the flowers, the garden. I was overwhelmed by the happiness of that child. Or was I? At the time I was overwhelmed with love for my own, as yet, unborn child. The two events became linked together. I remember feeling a pull, a yearning to live more of that life. I felt sure I would want to go back. But then Jamie was born and of course that changed

Chapter 2

Richard is leaving for work as I wake. Guilt sneaks up on me, punishing me for not having risen in time to cook his breakfast. While I was working it was different. We would rise according to our shifts, switch off our alarm clocks, shower in separate bathrooms so as not to risk disturbing one another's routines – in happier times I used to joke that we were like the royal family in this respect. Sometimes we would breakfast together at work if we had an early schedule, but we would always travel separately in case one or other of us had to stay late. In short, we were equal. But in the weeks I have not been working the balance of power has changed.

It is different from when I had Jamie because during those early years he was my life's work. Now I feel as though I should make up for my idleness with doting housewifely attention. So I reprimand myself as the front door clicks shut and Richard leaves. Yet, at the same time, I am relieved that I don't have to spend time making small talk. The clock shows that it is not yet seven-thirty. Perhaps he has an urgent appointment, a heart valve replacement or a lung excision. But I think not. Immersing – or rather drowning – himself in his work has been Richard's way of coping, just as I have sought refuge in the past.

A year ago, six months even, dozing and drifting leisurely into the day would have been a luxury; but these days, lingering in bed is not an option. I rise hastily and wrap myself in a towelling robe. I need to do things, any things. I need to grind beans for coffee and to carefully butter and eat my toast. I need to glance at the paper then make a list of things to do. I need to plan my day before I dare take a shower.

Prompted by the snap of the letterbox, I amble down the long thoroughfare of the hall. On either side, chequered floor tiles escape from under the runners of tasteful rugs. Richard wanted to leave it cold and bare but our footsteps echoed back and forth until we sounded like an army marching into the house. Eventually he was forced to give in to my pleas for something softer and more welcoming.

The front door is huge and ostentatious. In the jewelled light of its stained glass I stoop to pick up the scatter of envelopes from the mat. There are two white foolscaps for Richard – I recognise them as a magazine subscription and a bulletin from a pharmaceuticals company, there are the usual mail shots, inviting us to take out loans and have yet more double-glazing fitted, and for me there is an official-looking buff-coloured envelope. I know what this letter is and I know what it will say. I know it with such certainty that I don't even open the envelope. Instead, I place it on the kitchen work surface beneath the notice board before taking Richard's post up to his study.

The unopened letter will confirm my return to work the following Monday. It is not before time. The weeks at home have done nothing to heal me. On the contrary, they have only highlighted my unhappiness. Perhaps it would have been better if I had followed Richard's example and chosen to focus wholeheartedly on my work. I could have got on with my job like a professional. I think that, had I had the choice, this is what I would have preferred. However, other factors played a part. There was an inquiry pending in my department. It was only a formality really but, in view of the added burden of my 'domestic situation', I was persuaded by the clinical director to take some time off. Domestic situation. What a useless euphemism. I wish people would stop pussyfooting around and say the words they mean - disease, divorce, or, in this case, death.

Back in the kitchen, I check the calendar on the wall and see that I am due to meet my friend Clare for lunch. It doesn't count as eating out as we will rendezvous in the staff canteen at Nottingham General – Clare's place of work and mine too. Clare is a psychologist, a behavioural therapist. Patients find her easy to talk to. Indeed, I often find myself telling her more than I should. We are meeting at one, so I am left with five hours to fill. As I bite into my toast I ponder what I will do with the morning.

After breakfast, I stroll into the conservatory. This is the only part of the house in which I feel truly comfortable. We moved here twelve years ago, soon after Richard became a consultant. If it had been up to me we wouldn't have moved at all. I was content in our old home. It was cosy and familiar. We had enough room, I thought, especially as we knew our family would never be more than the three of us. When I think back to that house now it seems compact, at the time it felt vast. But Richard argued that we needed the space. With more responsibilities he needed an office at home, somewhere that didn't get used for Jamie's friends to sleep over or my parents to stay. Although he had a point, I see now that what he was doing was making a statement. Our new house in The Park was his way of announcing to the world that he had arrived.

Our house was built a hundred and fifty years ago. Like the others occupying the grounds of Nottingham Castle, it was intended as an elegant residence for Victorian gentlefolk. And that's how Richard sees it. But to me it is a monstrosity. I find it impossible to feel cosy in the cavernous rooms with their high ceilings moulded and decorated like royal icing on a wedding cake. And as for communicating with one another - calling to say dinner is ready or a friend is on the phone - our voices chase down draughty corridors until they are halted, abruptly, by huge heavy doors. I used to tease Richard that he could commit a murder in the attic while I was in the kitchen, completely oblivious. I think Richard had hopes that he – perhaps both of us – would run private clinics at home, as though it were Harley Street. But, even if the estate had allowed it, our specialties took us into surgery and with it the necessity of working in a hospital complex.

9

The idea never materialised.

As my breath mists on glass, I twist the curly wrought-iron handle of the latch and push a window open, breathing in the smell of moist grass and mouldering leaves from the garden. The conservatory makes living here almost worthwhile. It is like a miniature of those at Kew, with its steeply-pitched roof and ornate design. In it I grow bougainvillea and stephanotis, a vine whose grapes are too sour to eat (I have never got round to making wine) and citrus trees, their pots arranged as if in a grove. It is these I tend now. I stroke the shiny leaves, checking for the first signs of disease and peer at the tiled floor, looking for telltale sticky spots of honeydew. The plants are healthy enough. They are kept warm, watered and fed. But they are not fooled by the cold grey skies of the East Midlands; somehow they know they are not basking in Italy's golden sunlight. The fruits ripen too slowly, slipping from youth to old age without ever reaching the firm bloom of adulthood. Eventually, when they begin to shrivel or droop sadly towards the floor, I pick them. But they are soft and waxy, only good for flavouring a cake or squeezing into a salad.

Even if the plants are not all they could be there is another reason I like it in here. It is the way I can be inside and yet out. It is a liminal space that tames the elements, distorting them like a dream. Standing close to the glass, I can imagine I am in the garden. I can feel the sun on my face and pretend it is midsummer rather than the start of autumn. In a storm it is like walking into a Hitchcock thriller. Best of all, I like it in the rain. I love the way the water clatters on the roof, streaming, exploding, making the panes appear to melt. Sometimes it drums so hard I fear the roof will shatter, that glass and water will cascade down, splintering on the floor and draping the trees as though they are decorated for Christmas.

I take some cotton wool and dip it into the water in the can. Then I begin to polish the citrus leaves, one by one, cleaning away the dust so they gleam in the morning sun. I think about yesterday and Kimberley Place. It has become such an important part of my life these past few months that I feel the need to talk about it, to share my experience with someone else. Yet I know from my work just how prejudiced, how narrow-minded, some people can be when presented with something outside their own understanding. The fact is I know that I have lived before. Many times. Not just here in Nottingham but all over the country, all over the world. I am not insane nor some New Age believer in all things esoteric. On the contrary, I am a rational person, a scientist, a doctor of medicine. I do not claim gifts of second sight or, indeed, entertain any beliefs in the supernatural. My awareness of my past lives is simply the knowledge that they exist. It is something I live with – have lived with – for as long as I can remember. It is not something I have probed or even questioned but simply accepted, the knowledge that, when I least expect it, some sight, some sound, some place will trigger a memory of a life long ago.

When I was young it would happen often. Sometimes during waking hours, as it did yesterday, but more often the visions would come at night. In the darkest hours I would wake, with a start, from another lifetime and scurry into my parents' room to snuggle between them in their bed. Sometimes I would tell my mother what I had seen and she would reassure me and soothe me back to sleep. 'It's only a dream, Julia,' she would whisper warm breath into my ear. And I believed her. I thought, in my child-like egocentric world, that this happened to everyone. I thought the word dream meant a previous life. But sometimes the memories would be filled with violence and pain. My mother had an answer for that though. 'Maybe you dreamt someone else's dream,' she would say. And those words kept me safe until morning. The memories visited me less often as I grew older. Yet they were always there. As other children learned the difference between imagination and reality I learned to

11

separate the present from the past.

I finish cleaning the last leaf then I bend down and, one by one, grasp each pot, twisting it a quarter turn so that every part of every plant will receive an equal share of light, so that each will grow steadily upwards instead of reaching, begging for its homeland. I stand upright and turn to face the adjoining wall of the house. Creeping along wires pegged into the brickwork, the last leaves on the vine are turning red. Soon they will fall; I will cut back this season's growth and the remains of the plant will splay, skeletal, against the wall until next Easter. Last spring, a pair of robins built their nest amongst the twisted woody stems. We had to leave a window open so they could come and go, their beaks crammed with grubs, until the youngsters had fledged. At the time I thought it was a good omen. How wrong that turned out to be.

It is three months now since Jamie died. The nightmare of it replays constantly in my brain, as though on a never-ending loop. I remember how it was when I heard the news. Just like the whole world remembers where they were when Kennedy was assassinated, or John Lennon.

It was quite an ordinary day. Routine. Boring, even. I often wish it had been something more, a violent storm, perhaps, or a sizzling heat wave. I feel cheated that I did not sense, intuitively, that something was wrong (as surely a mother is supposed to do). I wish I could say that I felt a tug, a wrench, deep inside, at the moment he ceased to exist, that I was shocked yet not surprised when they told me. Perhaps, if I had felt those things, I would believe that I had somehow been there for him when his time came. But I have no such consolation.

It was a Thursday and I had spent the first half of the morning doing paperwork, tedious administration. Then I had performed some straightforward surgery – two tube ties and an investigative laparoscopy. I was still wearing my green theatre scrubs when they came to tell me. Two uniformed police officers, one male and one female. Not a good sign. But even then I didn't realise. I assumed they needed to question me about one of my patients, I never thought it would be personal. I approached them smiling. Professional face. 'Can I help you?'

The WPC asked if there was somewhere private we could talk. 'Do you have an office, or a consulting room perhaps?'

My memory goes hazy after that, though in retrospect I can picture nurses and registrars looking worried, looking away embarrassed, looking anywhere but at me. I don't know whether I actually fainted or whether my memory erased the words that were too painful for me to process. Suddenly Clare was there, kneeling next to me, cradling me like I should have cradled my son. Richard was in the same building but was in the middle of a triple heart bypass, there was no question of disturbing him, no sense in putting another life at risk.

It was Clare who shared my grief when the police officer repeated the words that shattered my life. 'I'm very sorry Mrs Spencer but I have to tell you your son James Spencer has been found dead.'

I remember the compassion of the WPC. I have to tell you. I know she didn't want to tell me. As a medical practitioner I know what it feels like to tell someone their loved one has died. I felt so sorry for that woman. I still do. Lucky Richard, he had a further hour of blissful ignorance before his life was torn apart.

I arrive at the hospital a little early. I walked in from home and feel invigorated by the exercise. I have felt nervous about walking anywhere these past few months, not for any reason of confidence or phobia but because walking allows so much time to think. Driving is easier, there is the road to concentrate on, and the radio; but walking, I have recently discovered, offers too much opportunity for self-indulgent, self-destructive thought. Today was different though,

13

knowing I would be meeting Clare, and that I would soon be returning to work. I pause and consider calling into the administration offices. I decide against it though. Any papers I might have to sign will be at home in the buff-coloured envelope and the office staff will probably be at lunch. Instead, I fill in the extra minutes by browsing in the League of Friends shop.

Clare has already staked her claim on a small table when I arrive at the canteen. She is wearing a gorgeous tailored suit in Cambridge blue wool. She stands as I approach the table and I admire her grace, her elegance. I envy her, as I join her in my jeans and fleece top. But then, Clare is dressed for work, whereas, I must not be dressed for going out. Somehow this makes our lunch date more acceptable. Clare is younger than me, she has no children – although, for her, there is still time. She is one of those people who are naturally and effortlessly glamorous. She wears her long dark hair loose, sweeping it casually over her shoulder or twisting it into a corkscrew, yet it always looks as though it has been freshly brushed. Her tights never run, her shoes never scuff, and in the summer she wears crisp white blouses which, by five in the afternoon, are still as pristinely un-creased and unblemished as though she had just taken them from a hanger. If I were to wear anything like that it would be crumpled and stained in less than an hour. Sometimes I tell myself looking good is easy for Clare because she doesn't do a 'hands on' job. But I know it is just an excuse.

She smiles and hugs me, stepping to the side of the table so nothing is in our way, so we can press warmly against one another with the whole length of our bodies. I am sure she has been taught to do this in the course of her training. I am equally sure that, without such learned prompting, she would do it naturally. And, whilst Clare has a gift for communicating with people, I am glad that she is a professional. I do not need to worry that she will patronise me, sit in silence, or pick her way over the broken eggshells that are my emotions.

'How has your week been?' She pushes a long gleaming strand of hair behind her ear.

I smile. I don't need to force myself. Something in Clare's demeanour elicits this response. 'Good,' I reply, thinking of yesterday afternoon. I wonder whether I should tell her about this. But I don't want to seem obsessive. Conveniently I remember my manners, my friendship. I must give as well as take. 'And yours?' I enquire.

She nods. 'Busy as usual. Shall we order?' We are in a small restaurant area of the canteen with table service. There is more space, more privacy for conversation. We sit down and pull our chairs in close, an island in a choppy sea. The menu is predictable but varied. I choose a chicken salad with bread and butter pudding to follow, the healthy and the comforting.

Clare's mobile rings as we wait for our food. I am relieved. It takes away the necessity to talk. Conversation during a meal is easy. You make time, between mouthfuls, or during the careful dissection of a grilled fish, to say the things you want. It is the lull between courses that I have grown to fear. It looms like a void demanding to be filled. Nature abhors vacuum and I have come to hate silence.

'Sorry.' Clare finishes her call and deposits the handset on the table.

I have noted the way she smiled as she spoke to the caller, the way the muscles in her face relaxed, the excitement that is still in her eyes. I raise my eyebrows.

She laughs. 'I'm meeting him for a drink tonight,' she admits.

'And are you going to tell me who?' This is a game I have played with her many times during the ten years we have known one another.

'You might not approve.' She feigns coyness.

'Married then, I assume.' I feign displeasure. Or, rather, I feign an attitude that hides my feelings on the matter. As

much as I am fond of Clare – in many ways I love her dearly
– I cannot understand her behaviour in terms of romantic
relationships. Perhaps I am naïve, innocent even. Having
married, and stayed married to, my only serious boyfriend;
having remained in this constancy, this predictable stability,
for so many years, I cannot understand why others should
not want to do the same.

I try not to be judgmental. Clare has never mentioned –
and I have thought it tactful not to ask – what happened in
her life before she came to Nottingham, before we met.
Perhaps there are things I could not imagine, a husband who
beat her, a father who inflicted abuse. Or maybe, for no
apparent reason, we just want different things. Either way,
one thing I have learned about Clare, during our friendship,
is that she does not 'do' long-term relationships. Instead she
flits this way and that, pursuing a series of flings and flighty
affairs. Sometimes the men are much younger offering nights
of fun and uncomplicated passion. Others are older, buying
her expensive jewellery and taking her for weekends in Paris.
Often they are single, young registrars, new to the area. They
become involved, they part, no-one gets hurt. Or so Clare
assures me. But often they are married. I have come to spot
this early on by the omissions in Clare's descriptions. She
doesn't tell me the details any more. Not since the first time
when I couldn't hide my anger and shock. Perhaps it is
because I am married myself. I think how I would feel if it
were Richard, tempting her into bed with promises he would
(hopefully) never keep. What if she were to break up a
marriage? Perhaps with children involved? If she confided in
me then I would feel complicit, guilty by association of some
crime I could never condone. So I have learned to back away,
to shield myself from the truth.

Luckily the arrival of the first course prevents me from
commenting further. I pop a piece of celery into my mouth
and chew gratefully as I remove the skin from the roast
chicken. I perform this procedure carefully and methodically,

my surgical skills hampered only by the clumsy design of the cutlery. I tell myself it is the need to turn the conversation away from Clare's affair rather than my need to share my secret that makes me decide, suddenly, to tell her about Kimberley Place.

'A strange thing happened to me yesterday,' I begin, casually. I try to keep my tone light as I tell her about the house, the garden and the girl on the swing. I try to appear indifferent, yet even as I speak I feel passion creep into my voice. I'm aware that Clare has stopped eating, propped her knife and fork on her plate; that she is staring at me with a look of professional concern. And instantly I wish I had never mentioned the subject. I feel myself flush red; I couldn't be more self-conscious if I had listened to her describing her sexual liaison with a married man. Suddenly, even that immoral act seems more socially acceptable than the encounter I have just related. I manage a strained laugh. 'I hope you're not going to tell me I'm going mad,' I giggle, nervously.

She smiles but I know it is forced. 'Not mad,' she tries to reassure me, 'but grieving.'

'You're saying I imagined it?' I snap the words out too forcefully.

She takes a deep breath. 'Julia, the mind is a complex organ. If we picture something very vividly, if we think hard about something that we desperately want to happen, then the mind cannot always distinguish between our thoughts and reality.' She takes a mouthful of salad, as though to focus attention on the here and now.

'But I saw it,' I protest. 'It definitely happened.'

'I'm sure you believe it did,' she agrees gently, 'but if I had been with you do you think I would have seen it too?'

I shake my head. 'Probably not,' I concede. 'Because it wasn't your life.'

She sets down her fork again and reaches to take my hand. 'I wouldn't have seen it, Julia,' she explains quietly, 'because it didn't physically happen.'

We eat in silence for a few moments but I cannot disguise my feelings. I am acutely aware that to any observer, never mind a psychologist, I will appear agitated.

'Has it ever happened before?' she asks, eventually.

I am more guarded now. I nod. I tell her about the time I visited the garden before Jamie was born. I don't mention the other times recently, or the other lives.

Now Clare smiles in genuine relief. 'But that's when you were pregnant!' she exclaims, as though she has made a life-changing discovery.

'Does that make a difference?' I ask.

She nods eagerly. 'Pregnancy and grief are two of the most powerful influences on the mind,' she explains. 'The fact that you had these thoughts, visions – call them what you will – at such times indicates what is going on.'

'Which is?'

'At the end of the day we are all driven by chemicals. They are finely balanced, easily knocked out of step by the hormones during pregnancy or the change in endorphins etcetera after emotional trauma. They're a safety valve, if you like – or they were, back in our hunter-gatherer days. What you've experienced is perfectly normal under the circumstances. But it's also a sign you need to look after yourself, busy yourself more.'

I focus on my plate, concentrate on boning the last of my chicken. Inside I feel cheated; insulted that Clare isn't taking me seriously. I could change all that easily. I could tell her about everything else that has happened over the years; risk her deducing that I really have cracked up. Or I could pretend to accept her explanation and keep my true feelings to myself. I am in turmoil. I want to be true to myself, to let her know that I know my mind and who I am. But equally I want to return to work, to do a responsible job, to fulfil my calling. And I won't be able to do that if one of my colleagues certifies me as, what she would jokingly refer to as, a basket case. So, regretfully, I choose to keep quiet.

During the remainder of our meal we stick to safe topics of conversation – the autumn fashions, whether we will have snow this winter. I am secretly relieved when, during dessert, Clare's mobile rings again and she apologises that she is needed back in her department, that she won't be able to stay and chat with me over coffee. We hug our premature good-byes and she goes on her way.

I am surprised to say that I quite enjoy the afternoon. As soon as Clare has left I remind myself that she didn't intend to offend me. In the medical world it isn't always easy to balance a friendship with professional integrity. And as I find myself thinking about my own job I decide to pay a visit to my department. It is the first time I've been there since the week after Jamie's funeral when, knowing I would be taking extended leave, I called into my office, still in shock, still feeling like I was observing a world in which my actions had no consequences, to collect some notebooks and journals to read at home.

This time is different. I feel in control, I know that when I return I will make a difference. It makes me realise how far I have come these past few weeks. I don't stay long; just enough for a brief chat with the nurses and my registrar, to accept hugs and smiles and reassure them that I will be returning the following Monday. Everyone seems pleased. I don't get to speak to my locum as she is busy in theatre but I am told she is keen to return to a study sabbatical.

Afterwards, I feel so good that I catch a bus into town and browse round the shops - something I haven't done for a long time. I choose some clothes to celebrate my return to work. I used to complain about my job; about the tedium of paperwork, the lack of funding, the bureaucracy that prevented me from giving patients the service they deserve. But, after my break, I can accept those things as a way of life. Now I welcome the challenge. I look forward to the nurses' complaints, to being up to my elbows in surgery, even to getting unmentionable stains on my unfashionable clothes. Grief is an unpredictable condition. I know that I am nowhere near over Jamie's death, that in many ways I never will be. But I also know that my healing process will continue while I heal others. Although there is a long way to go, I begin to feel positive about the rest of my life.

Chapter 3

It is late afternoon, when I am checking the contents of the fridge, thinking about what to cook for dinner, that I realise I haven't opened the envelope yet. It's a formality really. I know what it will say. The contents will outline what I agreed with personnel a week ago; that I will resume full time work at nine a.m. the following Monday. There might be something I need to sign and return though. I close the fridge door, stroll over to the notice board and pick it up. Idly, I rip the buff-coloured paper and draw out the sheet inside. I glance at the words, my eyes scanning the page for the agreed confirmation. Then I freeze, because the letter doesn't say that at all. I go back to the beginning now and read it more carefully.

Instead of being welcomed back, I am advised that, since our conversation, a new development has taken place. I am told that, not satisfied with the Board's findings, which exonerated me completely of all blame, the complainant has advised the Board that he will be pursuing action against me in a private prosecution. In view of this, the Board feels it would be inappropriate for me to continue working at the hospital until the case has been heard. They are sure I will agree, they tell me, and, whilst I am not officially suspended, they suggest it might be easiest for all concerned if I extend my compassionate leave.

I am in shock. Work is my life and also my lifeline. And just when I need it most it is gone.

I think back to how it happened. It was a Tuesday in July. It was two days before Jamie died. I was giving an informal presentation to some new junior doctors as they decided whether to request being assigned to our department on their rotation, telling them about the way we worked, how it differed from what they had studied in medical school or from what they might have seen on television. That was

21

when my pager sounded.

I cut the chat short, summing it up in a couple of sentences.

'You can stay and shadow me,' I called over my shoulder to the students as I hurried towards the door. 'Just mind you don't get in the way.'

On reporting to the department's main desk, I was informed that a patient was on the way up having been brought in by ambulance and referred directly by A and E. The information forwarded from paramedics was that it was an advanced labour with possible placental abruption and septicaemia. Before the patient had even arrived in the department I made sure that a theatre was on standby, an anaesthetist and a paediatrician were paged and my registrar was scrubbed up in readiness. We were as prepared as we could possibly be.

It turned out the situation was worse than I had anticipated. The patient, a woman in her early thirties, was already unconscious from shock due to the copious blood loss. I ordered a cross-match of six units before I even began to examine her. Her husband, meanwhile, shouted at us angrily to get on and do something. As one of the nurses ushered him aside I paid little heed to him. I blocked out his torrent of abuse. His words, after all, were uttered in terror. You have to learn, in this job, not to take things personally. People lash out in fear. You have to learn to shut it out and get on with the job in hand.

The woman's oxygen saturation and blood pressure were dropping by the second and there was no sign of a foetal heartbeat.

'Take her directly to theatre!' I ordered the nurses, and to the students, 'I'm sorry but you'll have to leave.'

As the registrar made the initial incision and a nurse squeezed foreign blood into the woman's veins, I scrubbed up. Then we got down to the serious business. After swift cuts through successive layers the baby flopped into my

22

hands, limp and lifeless. When I saw that the uterus had ruptured, I made the radical decision to go straight for a hysterectomy, despite the fact that there was little chance of reviving the baby and this was a first pregnancy. We did everything that was humanly possible but still the blood kept coming. When I pronounced the woman dead, I did so in the certain knowledge that her fate had been sealed long before she reached the hospital.

Birth and death, a death that should have been a birth; they are emotive subjects. I sat in my office with the grieving husband for half an hour. I explained that it was already too late when his wife came in, that there was nothing anyone could have done. What I couldn't tell him was the whole truth, that, if anyone was to blame for his wife and child's death, it was himself. The couple, and in particular, the husband, had insisted on a home delivery against medical advice. I am very wary of home deliveries for a first child. This case had had further contra-indications, both during the pregnancy, which had not been straightforward and didn't bode well for an easy birth, and also because the couple were farmers, living in a comparatively remote and inaccessible location. They had turned down our advice to admit the woman ten days before she was due and placed their faith in the unlikely possibility of an easy birth combined with the availability of a midwife to attend it. In the event, the sudden speedy labour had taken them by surprise. There had been insufficient time to get a midwife to them or to transport them to the hospital. The husband needed someone to blame. I can understand that. That was why he made a complaint to the Trust.

Startling memories of blood and death swirl before my eyes. I stand in the kitchen and read the letter again. And, after that, I read it once more. I read the words and I feel terror. I am terrified because I am being taken to court. And I have no idea what that means. I know what a court is, obviously, but I've never actually been in one. And what sort

23

of court will this be? Will I need a lawyer? Will there be a jury? Because, if there is a jury, I could go to prison, even though I am innocent. I know this happens, and it could happen to me. Secondly, I am terrified because I am no longer returning to work. But the more I think about it, the more this problem is superseded by the implications of court. I am out of my depth. My mind is running out of control with unthinkable possibilities. Three months ago I could, perhaps, have dealt with this: but not now. I need someone to do the thinking for me. I need someone to tell me what to do.

My first instinct is to call Richard. It is well after five and his theatre schedule should have finished. I dial his direct line, punching desperately at the keypad on the phone. I relax a little as I hear the ringing tone, then my insides lurch with disappointment as a momentary pause indicates that the call is being diverted. Stephanie answers. She is a mature and efficient secretary. That is to say, secretary is her official job title; in truth she is a bodyguard and a bouncer, cleverly deflecting the daily onslaught of callers and visitors so that Richard is free to perform his work.

'Ah, Julia!' Stephanie's manner softens as she recognises my voice. 'I was about to ring you. Richard asked me to.' Experience tells me this is not a good sign. Stephanie goes on to explain. 'A donor heart has become available. The likely recipient is due to arrive any time now and the organ is being delivered by helicopter. Richard has gone for a coffee and sandwich.'

Stephanie doesn't have to tell me the rest. Richard will be making the most of these minutes of comparative calm before the action begins. In the department, preparations will follow a well-rehearsed drill. For me at home, the implications are predictable. Richard will be in theatre until late. It is unlikely he will be home before midnight – indeed, it is more probable, under the circumstances, that he will sleep the night at the hospital, so he will be on hand if any post-operative complications arise.

I thank Stephanie and hang up. Now, I don't know where to turn. It is possible, if he isn't on the ward, that I might reach Richard on his mobile. But that is out of the question. He has a life to save. The donor heart will last only a few hours before it must be implanted, whereas my own problems will continue far longer.

I call the administrative office. It is getting late now but there is usually someone available for staff enquiries until six. I feel relieved when Janice answers the phone. She has worked at the hospital as long as I have, though we were both juniors when we first met. Now she sits on the senior boards and I trust her more than anyone to explain to me in simple terms what is going on.

'I'm so sorry Julia,' she says as she recognises my voice. 'The Board, the hospital, we all know that this is not down to you.'

I am aware of my voice shaking. 'Then what's going on?' I quaver.

She explains that, as I already know, the inquiry could attribute no blame either to myself, to the department or to the Trust as a whole. The reason they couldn't do this, she goes to pains to point out, is that we each acted in the most appropriate and correct manner and that I personally did everything humanly possible that could have been done. There was no question of the possibility of a criminal prosecution.

'So how can I be taken to court?' I demand, still shaking with shock and disbelief.

'It's complicated, Julia,' she tries to explain. 'But essentially, anyone dissatisfied with a decision or refusal to prosecute by the Crown can pursue a private prosecution. The complainant's solicitor – if he has one – will have advised him that his case would never hold up against the hospital Trust. That's why he's going for you. And on the matter of your extended leave, I voted that you should return to work if that's any consolation. We all know you're innocent but in today's political climate that doesn't count for much unfortunately.'

'You mean that when it gets reported in the paper I'm on my own.' Bitter tears are forming in my eyes.

Janice tries, she really does. 'I really am very sorry – especially after everything else that's happened.' I know she means it. 'And try not to worry – I know that's easy to say, but you're innocent, and that's what the court will decide.'

I mumble my thanks.

'I haven't helped. I really wish I could.' Janice is upset herself, I can tell. She rings off after instructing me that I must feel free to call her any time.

But I need someone to help me now. In desperation I dial Clare's number – she should be home by now. When I hear her voice my own words tumble over one another.

'Clare! Thank God!'

'Julia? What on earth's the matter?' She is surprised - and no wonder. When we parted, just hours ago, the world seemed a very different place. I tell her what has happened. I tell her garbled words in my panic, I doubt they make much sense. If Clare tells me to calm down I swear I will scream. But she won't do that. She knows better.

'Let's think this through logically,' Clare says. Her voice soothes me.

We talk for half an hour. Clare sympathises with me, assures me that what has happened is very bad luck, but I am innocent. Nothing bad will happen. A lawyer will be able to confirm that. Probably the matter will be settled quickly and easily. Clare is sensible and I believe her. Gradually relief spreads through me. It is like the warmth from a fire when I come in from the cold, like sipping a mug of cocoa on a frosty evening.

'But what about my job?' I moan. I am still upset but I speak more calmly now, more resignedly.

'It will still be there when all this has been sorted.' She pauses. 'And perhaps it isn't a bad thing to take a bit longer off.'

'I need to work. I need to do something.' Right now, I feel that what I need most is to visit Kimberley Place, but I don't tell Clare this.

'Yes, I can see that. Look, perhaps you should consider doing some voluntary work. Just for a few weeks, until you're back in your department.'

I almost laugh. 'I suppose that's what you suggest to your patients.'

'Well yes I do – but only because it's a good idea, for many people it's a stepping-stone. I'm suggesting it to you as a friend. There are probably other things you could do too. What about a research project? There must be aspects of your work you've wished you had more time to pursue.'

I am silent as I think about these new possibilities.

'Julia? Are you still there?'

'Yes,' I acknowledge. 'I understand what you're saying but I'm too upset to think about it properly now.'

'Of course you are, that's only natural. Listen Julia, I have to go now. I'm going out and I need to get ready – unless you'd like me to come round. I can cancel easily enough.'

I desperately want to say yes, to beg her to come over straight away, but I remember Clare's date and how excited she is about it. 'Don't do that,' I say. 'I'll be fine. I'll think about your suggestions.'

Half an hour later I receive a hurried call from Richard. He is about to go into theatre. He tells me that, assuming all goes well, he will sleep in the on call room. He keeps a change of clothes and bag of toiletries at the hospital – just as I used to myself – there is no need for him to return home. He will see me the following evening.

I do all the right things. I steady my voice and wish him luck with the surgery. I don't tell him what has happened. What good would that do? He can do nothing about it today. He has another life to save.

When I finish the call it is dark outside and I haven't yet switched on the lights. I feel trapped, claustrophobic, like I am already confined in a prison cell. Gripped by a panic I cannot explain, I run from room to room. I switch on ceiling lights, table lamps, up-lighters and fluorescent tubes. I click the power buttons on radios, televisions and hi-fis. I do not stop until the whole house is ablaze with light, sound and moving pictures. Until it feels as though it is full of people, bustling with activity, a party here, a market there; until I am surrounded by life.

In the morning I wake early. Perhaps I should say that I rise early – to wake implies that I have slept. I would prefer to leave the house at first light but the thought of the rush hour, where cars are corralled like wild beasts, forced along inadequate drove-ways and held in never-ending queues from which there seems no escape, is too much for my exhausted mind. That, combined with the possibility that Richard may yet call in home before his day's work, keeps me in until after nine. In the meantime I try to swallow toast, dry and painful against my throat, whilst the words and pictures of breakfast television play on the screen before of me.

As I lock the front door it is drizzling. A grey mist hangs over the day, blurring the transition from night into morning. I know from experience that this cheerless haze will probably last all day, clinging onto buildings and trees, until, in the late afternoon, it is gulped down the dark throat of a premature night. I don't know whether it is a phenomenon of Nottingham, the Midlands, or cities in general, whether it is caused by the lie of the land or pollution. Certainly I never saw the like in Somerset. I hurry to the car and, safely inside, switch on the engine and the radio. While popular bands play rousing songs I drive north.

Part of the reason I was reluctant to tell Clare the whole truth about Kimberley Place is that I'm somewhat scared about it myself. Not of the concept of a past life, of my 'gift' if you want to call it that, but of my increased indulgence, my growing reliance on a time and a place that is no longer mine. It is an escape. Each visit is a fix, an injection of happiness as surely as if I were mainlining heroin (God, how I shudder at the thought of that word). I thought, when I returned there after Jamie's death, that I'd just go back a couple of times, to tide me over a bad patch. Then I'd go back to work, I'd be in control of my life again. But everything has gone wrong and now I need it more than ever.

I pull up outside. During the past few weeks I have invented an excuse, a cover story. If anyone stopped me, asked what I was doing I would say I lived here as a child. In a way that is perfectly true. I switch off the engine. Outside, the rain has become torrential and there is no-one about. I listen to the radio as water drums on the roof of the car. I take the A to Z out of the glove compartment and pretend to look at it. At last the rain eases off a little and I get out, pulling the hood of my jacket over my head as I run to the fence. I peer, optimistically, but there is nothing, only the sound of the rain pattering on the gravel and the acrid smell of the wet fir trees. I wait for it to happen, to feel the warm sun on my face and smell the scent of summer flowers. Instead I become increasingly aware of the moisture soaking through my jeans, pasting them in a clammy poultice against my legs.

'Hey you!'

The shout makes me start. I look up, trying to form the words of my prepared speech. 'I'm so sorry,' I begin, as I turn, 'but you see I used to live…'

The man draws level with me. 'Sorry love,' he says as he sees my face. 'But with yer hood I thought ee were one o' them youths.'

I hurry back to the car and climb in, bedraggled. As soon as the man has gone I burst into tears. I have been mistaken for a common criminal 'casing the joint'. But worse than that I have been let down. For the first time nothing happened,

Chapter 4

My hand breaks the surface and pulls down, slowly, steadily. I turn my head, twisting my face above the water, breathe out the last remnants of air from my lungs, breathe in warm, humid, chlorine-scented mist. Then I turn my face back into the water, see the blue tiles of the pool floor through my goggles, watch the bubbles that form from my exhaled breath, rich with carbon dioxide that has travelled in my blood all round my body. I glide forward, enjoying the tingling of my skin as the water rushes past me and imagine the pool as a vast bed, a mattress that supports me as I stretch my body across it. Sally has taught me to do this. Not to flounder indiscriminately or to rush headlong and reach the side, gasping and breathless, but to slow my whole body down, to savour each stroke, enjoy the repetition like a mantra, so the art of swimming becomes a moving meditation.

We spent the weekend picking over the remnants of my career, planning my court case. At least Richard did. Thank God the official letter informing me of the complainant's intention to proceed against me didn't arrive until Saturday. If it had been delivered when I was alone on Friday morning I don't think I'd have coped at all. Richard was very calm about it - at least he seemed so to me. Straight away he telephoned a lawyer friend. Andrew and he were at school together. I believe I met him at our wedding. I have always felt somewhat overawed by Richard's public school background but suddenly I am glad of the old boys' network, of their expertise, their influence. It is like an insurance policy, a safety net into which I can let myself fall knowing that I will come to no harm. Anyway, Richard spoke to Andrew for half an hour and assured me afterwards that I was not to worry. It would be a formality. It would take time, unfortunately; several months – and that was if we were lucky. But it was a process that I would have to go through. Andrew would drive over the following weekend and go through the preliminaries with me.

I change to a slow breast stroke, holding my head up so that my chin skims the surface. My arms and legs know what to do without any conscious thought on my part, I can look about me, let go and let nature take its course. It is the same with the court case. The wheels have been set in motion, the professionals have taken over and I feel relieved that, save supplying information as instructed, I no longer have to think about it. That doesn't mean I'm not worried of course. But I am like a small child being led by the hand, entrusting my safety to a higher power.

And now it is Monday, the day on which I should have returned to work, resumed my career, looked to the future. Yet even the pleasure of my job has been denied me. And, fired up by this thought, I draw my arms round to my sides then clasp my hands together, as though in prayer. My legs kick out, frog-like and I shoot forward. I have grown to love swimming just as Richard loves his music. It is away, far away, from everything else in my life.

I found this place by accident, six years ago. I had been attending a conference in Derbyshire, a long busy but enlightening day on the benefits of caesarean section in premature delivery. Unlike the pregnancies to which they referred, the lectures ran beyond their allotted time and it was after seven by the time I got away. I decided to take the scenic route to Ambergate and then cut down through Ilkeston. When my mobile rang near the centre of the town I pulled into the nearest car park to answer it. It was Richard, telling me he'd been asked to dine with some colleagues and discuss his department's application for further specialist care funding. I told him to take his time and secure that money, that I would see him later in the evening. I replaced the phone in my handbag and went to turn the ignition. Then I stopped. Jamie had flown the nest just a fortnight previously, having left to start his medical training in London. Suddenly I realised that I didn't want to spend the evening alone in that huge empty house.

More cars pulled alongside me and I noticed people walking past carrying sports bags. I looked up and realised that I had parked outside a swimming pool. I'd never been that keen on water unless it was in a bath or shower but right then, compared to pacing the long cold corridors at home, swimming in a pool seemed a good option. Of course, I didn't have the necessary kit with me but I was sure I would be able to buy or hire a towel and costume. I jumped out of the car and followed the people into the building.

'I'm sorry love but tonight's a private club.' The girl on the reception desk shrugged apologetically. 'The pool's booked out by a social club you see, from a local factory. This session's just for them and their families.' Disappointed, I was contemplating whether to buy a coffee and sit for a while in the viewing area, when a voice behind me said, 'Don't worry, sign the lady in as my guest.' I turned round. The woman was around my own age, a little on the plump side perhaps, with short blond slightly greying hair. But more than her appearance I noticed her manner. She had a quality that we look for in midwives. Maternal perhaps? The sort of person whose sheer presence makes one feel safe, protected. I thanked her and accepted immediately. That was how I met Sally.

A whistle sounds. The lifeguard is signalling that our session is over. I swim to the ladder at the shallow end and climb out.

'Staying for a coffee?' Sally asks as we comb our wet hair in the sub-tropical climate of the changing room.

I nod. I relish the time I spend with these people. They are not doctors or nurses, not, in most cases, professionals of any kind. Yet they are like me, like I used to be. I feel more at ease with them than I do with almost all of my work colleagues. We cram soggy towels and costumes into our bags and make our way out to the café. Pete, Sally's husband, is already at the counter. He turns with his tray and smiles at us, nodding towards a table nearby. Pete has anticipated that I will stay. He has bought three mugs of hot chocolate and a selection of biscuits.

We sit at the Formica-topped table and I find myself next to the window looking out onto the dazzle of urban lights. Ilkeston is not a pretty town but rather a gateway to the north, a foretaste of the dark satanic mills to come. Half a century ago it thrived on industry. To the south the hot grating steel works belched acrid smog, leaving a grey sheen on the houses and a metallic taste on the tongue. To the north, men spent their days down the pits, hacking coal in tunnels blacker than night. Those that survived to retirement grew old and gnarled before their time, and spent their last days coughing sooty phlegm. Now the heavy industry has gone yet the town still remains the same. It is as though the streets are kept dirty and the buildings dull in memory of its polluted past. There are parks to relieve the tedium and hopeful footpaths that lead to nowhere along with the disused canal. But it is a place that has lost its purpose; by rights it should be a ghost town. Tonight it mirrors the way I feel.

'So how was your first day back at work then?' Sally asks. This is the first time we have spoken properly this evening – Sally and Pete were both already swimming when I arrived.

'I didn't go,' I tell them. 'I wanted to of course but the hospital advised against it.'

Pete frowns. 'So what's going off then?' He speaks with the soft burr of the local dialect. It is a world where things go off rather than go on, where long vowels are extended to two syllables, Pee-at is how he pronounces his own name. Sally does too, though I have long since ceased to notice. Richard wonders how I can possibly have anything in common with people who speak this way. Yet to me it is familiar, homely, comforting. And, whilst far from the regional accent of my own birthplace, it conveys a warmth that the sterile enunciation of Richard's own speech will always lack.

I tell them about the letter, the court case, how it may all take weeks, months, maybe longer. Even though I feel calmer about it now, I am aware of the squeak of anxiety in my voice. 'In the meantime,' I conclude, 'Richard says I should put it from my mind.'

Pete laughs in exasperation. 'As if you could! I'd like to see how he coped if he was the one being taken to court. If it was me I'd be shitting bricks.'

Sally nudges Pete. She is playful, although her eyebrows are drawn together with worry. 'Julia's a lady don't forget – she's got better control of her bowels than you have!' She turns to me and gently presses her hand over mine. 'We're really sorry about this love. Goodness knows, you've had more than your share of bad luck these last weeks. I don't know that we can do anything useful, but you know where we are, you're always welcome for a cup of tea and a chat.'

I nod and sip gratefully at my drink.

'But you'll be able to work somewhere else in the meantime,' Sally insists. 'I mean – it wouldn't be right wasting all your training. You'll be able to get one of those temporary locum jobs.'

I shake my head. 'No. Not until the trial's over - and only then assuming I'm found innocent.' I pause for a moment, the full implications of my situation have still not completely sunk in. 'If my own hospital won't have me I'm not going to be welcome anywhere else.'

'Whatever happened to innocent until proven guilty?' Pete mutters.

'It will all get sorted out. It's just a nuisance.' I try to sound confident but know that I am not convincing, even to myself. I take a chocolate biscuit – more for comfort than for calories – and nibble at it, squirrel-like. 'What about you?' I ask, aware that I have neglected my friends these past weeks. 'And Debbie – I haven't seen her for ages.'

Their elder daughter is the same age as Jamie. The age he would have been had he lived. Invisibly I correct my thoughts, even though I haven't spoken out loud. I wonder how long it will go on, thinking, speaking about him as though he were still alive. I know that it is a process that everyone must go through yet that does not make it easier. It is as though my brain is a huge filing cabinet, reorganising its records. And every time it comes to a folder marked Jamie – which it does every second, every minute of every day – it removes it from the bright much-used drawer labelled 'present' and puts it instead into a fusty box of half-forgotten memories labelled 'past'. And every time, in some inner battle, I resist. I fight against this heartless relegation of his life. I want him with me forever in the noisy colourful confusion of the here and now. I clear my throat, thankful that I have not made a verbal blunder and plunged those around me into an embarrassed silence.

As I leave Jamie behind and return to the present, I am aware that Pete and Sally are looking at one another. For one horrible moment I fear the worst. Surely nothing bad has happened to their child too.

'Should we?' I hear Pete ask quietly.

Sally nods and smiles. 'Of course we should. She'll be along next week anyway. Julia will see for herself.' She turns to me. 'We didn't like to tell you before – what with Jamie and everything, we were going to tell you this evening, thought it would be fitting with you going back to work. Except now you haven't.' She pauses, watches me carefully. 'You see we're going to be grandparents. Debbie's pregnant.'

There is a moment's silence. It is up to me to fill it. 'I'm thrilled!' I say.

Pete looks relieved. 'We didn't want you getting upset again.'

'Of course not,' I assure him. 'If I were back at work I'd be dealing with pregnancies and new babies every day. As it is I'll have to make the most of this one. When's it due?'

Sally looks guilty. 'Early in February,' she tells me.

'What? But you must have known for months.'

She nods. 'We found out the same time everything started going wrong for you. There just didn't seem a right time to mention it.'

And I know she is right. Sally has not had the opportunities that I have, nor the privileged education, yet she has a wisdom of life that I envy.

Outwardly, I congratulate them. I ask polite questions, smile at their excitement. But inside my thoughts are racing. I cannot help but draw parallels between Debbie and Jamie. Debbie went to Shipley House, the little independent school a mile or two up the road. Although it stands apart from the state system it is neither expensive nor intensive. It is one of a progressive group that concentrates on the wellbeing of the child. It nurtures confidence and kindliness and encourages artistic and creative pursuits. I wanted to send Jamie there, all those years ago. I wanted him to find freedom and happiness in learning and still be close to home. I wanted him to have choices in life; to live the way he wanted, not be restrained by what was expected of him.

But Richard wouldn't hear of it. He insisted that nothing less than public school would suffice, following in his own footsteps and his father's before him. He made his argument convincingly. It was essential, he maintained, both for Jamie's preparation for medical school and for the pursuit of our own careers, that he attend a reputable establishment where he would board, at the very least, on a weekly basis. He made a case that I could not counter, made me see that I would be denying Jamie the fun and camaraderie of living with his friends if I objected. Reminded me that I too had chosen a career that I had an obligation to follow, full time, from Monday till Friday, in a way that left no space for bringing up a healthy young teenage boy. And I did not have the experience, at the time, to understand that it was only Richard's upbringing and schooling that gave him the confidence to speak in this way, the ability to convince me that he was right and I was wrong. I was so intimidated by what I perceived as Richard's superior intellect that I didn't even notice that he had Jamie's career mapped out before he left primary school. With hindsight, I can see that it was decided before our son was even born.

I think about all these things and reduce them to a simple formula. Debbie lived at home and went to Shipley House. Jamie went away to boarding school. Debbie is alive, happy and pregnant. Jamie is dead.

Chapter 5

I sleep late on Tuesday morning. Perhaps the exertion of swimming has brought fatigue even to my over-active mind. Whatever the cause, I am grateful when I look at the clock and see that it is almost nine and Richard has long since gone. I am quietly coming to and savouring the moments of benign neutrality before the familiar dark spectres infiltrate my thoughts when, suddenly, I remember that it is one of Mrs Blackstock's days and I have only an hour to leave the house.

My life has become inverted over the past months. My waking hours have centred round the need to fill empty time. They say that work expands to fill time and perhaps, if meaningful occupation had been available to me, that would have happened. As it is, I have struggled to draw out every activity to its fullest extent in a futile attempt to fill an ever-expanding void. Now, faced with what previously would have been a generous deadline, I find myself thrown into disarray, panicking at the dilemma of whether to shower first or whether to make coffee. I decide on the former and stumble with unproductive haste towards the bathroom, tripping over my slippers on the way.

Ever since we moved into this over-sized abode we have employed a housekeeper. It was the previous owners who suggested it. They had employed Mrs Blackstock for the past decade and it was their hope – though of course they couldn't insist – that we would do the same. Of course, to Richard it all seemed perfectly natural. He had grown up in a household that employed, not only a housekeeper but also a gardener and a live-in nanny. To me, the idea was quaint and not a little intimidating. And the fact that she 'came with the house' made her seem like an ancient retainer in a stately home. I remember the first time I met her. She was older than me and dressed austerely in dark skirt and blouse and sensible lace-up shoes. She was Mrs Danvers to my second Mrs de Winter and I was terrified that she would spot my naivety as I failed clumsily to exert my authority; that she would discover that I was an interloper, of the same 'servant class' as herself.

Of course, I deferred to Richard, and from that first week Mrs Blackstock came to our home on Tuesdays and Thursdays, cleaning and ironing and cooking wholesome casseroles. I have to admit that, as the responsibility and seniority of our jobs increased, Richard and I could not have managed on our own. And to be fair she was invisible, arriving after we had left for work and long since gone when we arrived home. Yet my fear of her persisted and I was always careful to leave the house neat and tidy in readiness for her judgmental eye and to take care what personal items were left around lest she should compare me to her more suitable employers.

But in the months that I have been off work my relationship with Mrs Blackstock has changed. No longer a ghostly figure inhabiting a parallel dimension, suddenly it seems that she is always there, invading my physical space. My first thought, when, having recovered from the initial shock of Jamie's death, I felt able to cope with day-to-day life, was to dismiss her - at least until I returned to work. I felt two things. Firstly that I would like to do her jobs myself, that they would, to some extent, heal me. Secondly I felt that, no longer being at work, those tasks were my duty.

As it was, I quickly revised the idea of giving Mrs Blackstock enforced and indefinite leave. I put the notion of her dismissal down to unclear thinking in time of grief and realised that, even if I didn't need Mrs Blackstock, she needed me – or at least, she needed the money I paid her. It would not be fair to suddenly deprive her of a large part of her income. I considered suggesting that she, like me, should take a period of paid leave. But I knew she wouldn't accept money for work she hadn't done. More than this, in the early days following Jamie's death, I had come to realise what a kind and compassionate woman Mrs Blackstock was, and how I had misjudged her. Looking back, I believe that if it hadn't been for her persistence, tempting me to sip tasty soups, brushing my hair as though I were a child, I would have taken to my bed and withered away. I could not simply forget her kindness as soon as I was able to care for myself.

So I quickly came to the conclusion that the only fair answer was for her employment to continue as normal. However, once I was back on my feet, I soon learned that it did not do for me to be around the house on her days. Not because we didn't get on, indeed I had grown to like – almost to love – her. But, like me, she needed her own space in which to work. During her hours, the house became her domain and I must respect that. I must not jeopardise our relationship by forever getting in her way or appearing to be checking up on her. And anyway the situation was only temporary. I soon found that the simplest solution was for me to be out of the house when Mrs Blackstock was on duty.

Hurriedly, I rinse the conditioner from my hair and turn off the water. I fumble blindly for the towel only to find that, in my haste, I have left both that and my bathrobe behind in the bedroom. I wipe my eyes on my face flannel then run dripping and naked down the landing, praying that Mrs Blackstock does not choose today to arrive early.

I have developed a routine these past months: one of writing lists, checking the calendar, sorting the post; all carefully planned and executed in precise order; an occupation for my hungry mind. This morning there is no time for me to think, only to do. Our housekeeper is due to arrive at ten o'clock precisely. Accordingly, at five minutes to, I put on my jacket and a pair of outdoor shoes and leave the house. I don't go to the car. This time last week I went to Kimberley Place, but not today. I don't want to risk repeating the disappointment of Friday's visit anytime soon. So this morning I set out on foot.

It is at times like this that I wish I had a dog. I would enjoy the routine of taking it out in the morning and the evening, for a constitutional round the recreation ground. And sometimes for longer hikes, in the Peak District perhaps, along the meanders of gentle rivers or trudging up the steep edges of millstone grit. Then, later, it would keep me company in the house. I can picture how it would be: quite a large dog I think, because the house is so big, perhaps a collie or a golden retriever. It would sleep in a basket next to the Aga and bury bones in the garden and doze on the rug before the log fire in the drawing room on winter evenings.

But Richard doesn't like animals. It took months of persistent persuasion on my part before Jamie was grudgingly allowed to keep a pair of guinea pigs when he was younger. There has been no such acquiescence on the matter of a dog. Richard insists that the house would smell – houses with pets always smell, he says, you notice it, an offensive intrusion, as soon as you step inside. Sometimes I suspect, somewhat bitterly, that this remark is directed at my parents' home. And he claimed it wouldn't be fair on Mrs Blackstock, expecting her to clean up all that awful fur and maybe worse. His only argument that I did, reluctantly, agree with was that it wouldn't be fair on the dog. It was true that the animal would be left alone for unreasonably long periods due to our work commitments.

Privately, I suspect that Richard's objection to dogs is caused by the fact that he is secretly afraid of them. I remember Clare telling me once that our attitude to fear is moulded by society. Women are persuaded to confess their fears, admit to them as failings, as weaknesses of character and to seek treatment in the form of counselling or tranquilisers. Men, on the other hand, simply modify their lifestyle and their environment so their fears are accommodated.

I stroll, dogless, out of the estate and down towards town. I don't know where I am heading. It is too soon after breakfast to go into a café and sip coffee, and too chilly to sit on a bench beside a litter bin (and, if I am lucky, a tub of mournful flowers) and read a magazine. I could browse around the shops I suppose, but the clothes I bought last week are already stowed away and will probably not see the light of day until they are as unfashionable as the rest of my attire, I certainly don't need more. So as I walk towards the anonymous noise of the city, I think over Clare's suggestions of the previous week.

The idea of a research sabbatical would be tempting. There have been occasions over the years when I wished I could spare the time to pursue personal interests in my field of medicine. And, to an outsider, it might seem an obvious opportunity to follow these up now. But in the real world it doesn't work like that. Research projects have to be planned carefully in advance. Feasibility studies must be carried out, funding must be applied for, permission must be sought from the relevant trusts, boards and departments. Formal study of this kind is, sadly, not possible. Granted, I can still attempt to broaden my own knowledge. I can visit the library once or twice a week and read through journals and overseas research papers. In an academic sense I can plan my own refresher course, bring myself up to date. That is all well and good, but it is no substitute for treating people in the here and now. It does not make me feel useful.

I am on the outskirts of town, on the edge of the main shopping centre, when I find myself standing outside a place that calls itself 'the drop in shop'. It is not somewhere I have particularly noticed before. Rather shabby and outside the fashionable precincts of the centre, it is the sort of place I would normally hurry past. But there is a board in the window announcing that volunteers are needed for a number of projects and this reminds me of Clare's other suggestion about doing voluntary work. So, before I have chance to change my mind, I go inside.

The establishment is what one might call 'multi-tasking'. It seems to combine the functions of an employment agency, a volunteer bureau, an advice centre and an internet café. I find myself wondering who owns such a place, whether it is administered by the local council or funded by a charity. The first thing I notice is that everyone in the room is sitting in front of a computer terminal. Whether they are young or old, staff or clients (and in this respect it is hard to know which is which) this is what they have in common. Although there are racks of leaflets and piles of magazines and folders, the only thing anyone seems to be looking at is a computer screen. I look around me. Most of the people are young, late teens I'd say, or early twenties. Perhaps they are students planning exciting adventures in overseas places for their gap years. One or two look older than me. Perhaps they, too, have a newly found freedom. I wonder whether they have taken voluntary redundancy or leave, or whether, like me, they were pushed. The other thing everyone has in common is that they all seem to know what they are doing and to be deeply engrossed in doing it. I stand in the middle of the room for a few moments, trying to look casual, like I belong, whilst desperately looking for a sign saying 'reception' or a bell to press.

Eventually a youth gets up from a desk in the corner and walks over to me. He looks to be around Jamie's age – that is to say, in his early or mid twenties. He seems very young to be in charge.

'Can I help you?' he asks politely. Although he is dressed casually in jeans and T-shirt, his voice suggests that he is well educated.

'I'm looking for some voluntary work,' I reply.

'Ah. Good. Come this way and take a seat.' He ushers me over to his desk. 'I thought you might be another university applicant; there are lots of those at this time of year.'

I laugh. 'At my age?'

He grins. 'Makes no difference these days. You'd be surprised how many people take degrees in their forties and fifties. If you time it right you never have to pay off your student loan.'

'Oh, I see.' I have never had reason to consider these things.

Tim (I notice now he wears a name badge with Client Advisor typed on it) taps busily into a keyboard then twists the screen so that I can view it. 'Did you have any idea what sort of thing you'd like to do?'

I hesitate. The truth is I have not thought about this at all. 'What about meals on wheels?' I suggest, remembering that some of my mother's friends from the Women's Institute used to do this. I picture myself delivering hot roast dinners to elderly ladies, serving the food on their Sunday china and arranging it on a tray with carefully placed cutlery and perhaps a miniature posy of flowers that I will have taken with me.

Tim taps another key. Some lines of type, which I can't make out without my reading glasses, come up on the screen. 'Do you mean as a delivery driver?' he asks.

'Pardon?'

'You deliver the meals every week or fortnight and put them in the person's freezer,' he explains.

'Oh, I see,' I answer, not seeing at all. 'I meant serving the meals, then washing up.'

He shakes his head. 'Usually the old folks do that themselves, or a friend or neighbour helps. There aren't any vacancies for that anyway.'

'What do you suggest then?' I ask.

Tim goes through a list of possible activities, none of which appeal to me. We seem to have reached stalemate. 'Well there is one other thing,' he ventures, tentatively.

I look up expectantly.

He continues, almost reluctantly. 'They need visitors up at the prison, people to go and chat to the inmates.' He pauses, looking worried. 'I'm sorry, I probably shouldn't have suggested it – I mean you don't look the sort of lady…well we've been through everything else so I just thought I'd mention it.'

I think about it. This is a whole new world to me, something I'd never thought of, something shocking, forbidden even. I consider the proposition, tumble it around in my mind faster than the speed of light. My answer is instantaneous. 'I'll do it,' I say.

I have to suppress my laughter when I look at Tim's expression. He is too young, too inexperienced to have learned to hide his emotions. I delight in his look of surprise.

'I'll call the liaison officer,' he says at last. 'It's probably best if you speak to her.'

I wait patiently while he makes the call, while he chats amiably to someone he has clearly spoken to many times before. At last he passes the phone to me. 'Have a word with Lizzie,' he says.

Lizzie, whom I picture as an efficient middle-aged lady, not unlike Janice or Stephanie, explains the job and the procedure to me. It is the prison's policy, she tells me, to arrange volunteer visitors for inmates who don't have regular contact with family or friends. There are many reasons for this, she says, including those of travelling long distances or estrangement or simply that the individual has few, if any, living relatives. It is considered particularly important for those serving long sentences to have regular contact with the outside world, not only for their morale but also to aid their rehabilitation process in anticipation of release and to reduce the likelihood of their re-offending. Often, she tells me, such prisoners have been convicted of very serious crimes such as grievous bodily harm or even murder.

I think of the stories you read in magazines about women befriending prisoners on death row and I shudder.

'Bearing all this in mind,' Lizzie says, I have to ask you if you still want to go ahead.'

I reply that, yes, I would still like to apply but stipulate that I can have nothing to do with anyone convicted of a drug-related crime. I don't apologize for my prejudice and she doesn't pursue it further. Normally, she says, the application process takes several weeks of form filling and administration. However, they are in urgent need of volunteers and if I can fill in the form online then Tim will email it to her and she will contact me in due course.

And so it is done. After the call I spend ten minutes entering details about myself into the computer. Then there is nothing more to it – for me anyway. I sign up for another job as well. I volunteer to work every Tuesday in an old peoples' day centre. I don't especially want to do this – although certainly I don't mind the idea. Instead, it is as though I am a man buying a pornographic magazine, who takes it to the till hidden between the acceptable pink pages of the Financial Times. The Tuesday job is my cover.

I arrive home as Mrs Blackstock is leaving.

'It's good to see you looking a bit perkier Doctor,' she says, as we pause on the front doorstep. 'Your return to work obviously agrees with you.'

I tell her that, in fact, I am not working and have extended my leave. But I don't mention the reason. I am sure that she would not gossip, that even if she felt so inclined (which I am certain she wouldn't) she would not risk losing her reputation and her employment through indiscretion. I keep my silence because it has occurred to me that the more people I tell about my court case the more it becomes a reality. And it already looms large enough in my nightmares. Instead, I mention, cheerily, that I will be doing some voluntary work for a while. This seems to satisfy her and she trots off down the drive nodding her approval at what I feel, guiltily, is a false impression of my virtue.

The next day I am going about my usual routine, tending my plants, when my mobile rings. To my surprise it is Lizzie. I gave her my personal number to avoid the horrifying possibility of Richard or Mrs Blackstock answering a call from the prison service. Yet when I did so I thought that I was planting a seed that, like the lemons on the trees, would take months to mature if indeed it ever reached fruition.

'Hello?' I greet Lizzie tentatively, feeling sure that she is calling to tell me that my application has been turned down, that, having discovered my disgrace at the hospital, I am found to be an unsuitable person. But I am wrong.

'We've processed your details already,' she tells me. 'Normally, of course, it would take much longer, but, as I said yesterday, they have an urgent need of volunteers at the moment. I take it you still want to go ahead?'

There is a pause. I realise I am nodding. 'Yes,' I reply.

'Good. There's an inmate whom we have in mind. Tell me, could you visit on a weekly basis? This man is coming towards the end of a long sentence. The regular contact is crucial for his rehabilitation.'

'Yes,' I hear myself say. 'I can do that.'

She tells me the details of his crime and sentence, waits for me to express my shock and disgust. But I don't. And then she surprises me even more.

'In that case,' Lizzie says, 'I know it's short notice but could you come for your first visit tomorrow?'

Chapter 6

The next day I leave the house early and spend the morning in the central library. There I pick through the reference section and read about the history of Britain's penal institutions. By the time I eat lunch in a nearby café I am well briefed on the subject and, armed with my new knowledge, I feel much better than I did yesterday.

It wasn't until a full hour after my conversation with Lizzie that I began to panic. Perhaps it was the thought of the prison itself or the people detained there or simply a reasonable trepidation at doing something new. I was tempted to call back and cancel. But I couldn't do that. It wouldn't be fair on the person I was due to visit, who might already have been told of my acceptance. So at five-thirty I rang Sally. Like an explorer, setting off into the wilderness, I told her the details of my venture into the unknown. And somehow that act, that sharing of information, became an insurance policy, a guarantee of my safe return.

Now, as the time draws near, I feel a morbid sense of excitement. I have decided to travel by the prison bus. I think the authorities prefer it, there is no chance of a visitor smuggling out an inmate in the boot of their car. After lunch I wait at the dedicated bus stop for fifteen minutes. It amuses me the way people look at me – or look away. They probably pity me for being married to a convict, for I suspect that is the most common assumption. Of course, I find it funny because I know my reason for going there, but I can imagine what it must feel like for someone who is visiting a relative.

When the bus arrives I take a seat on my own. It is one of those that face across the vehicle, a vantage point from where I can see my fellow passengers. I try not to think pityingly or judgementally of them, yet I find myself curious about who they are, whom they are visiting, whether they are volunteers like myself. I watch them cautiously during the journey.

Some greet one another and chat like old friends. Maybe they are; maybe they have been making this journey together week after week or month after month for many years. Others stare fixedly ahead or purposefully read magazines like travellers on the tube.

As the bus judders and jolts, I ponder my motives for what I am doing. There is empathy certainly. In the blacker moments of the past week I have considered the possibility that I might, rightly or wrongly, go to prison myself. For the first time in my life I have contemplated what such a fate might be like. Right now I am only paddling in this uncertain underworld. All being well, I will leave it unscathed. But others are thrown into its deep murky waters and I cannot leave them to drown. There is a fascination too. Clare may be the psychologist but I too can wonder what sort of mind can lead a person to commit desperate and criminal acts. And there is a third reason. Perhaps it is of the least importance but still it is there. The fact is that I enjoy the certainty that Richard will disapprove.

I feel a slight buzz, a thrill, as we approach the perimeter of high walls and fencing. I stare at my lap, smoothing imaginary creases from my jeans, trying not to let my feelings show. I have been advised to 'dress down', to remember that I will be in a room full of men, some of whom will have had no intimate contact with a woman for many years. Inwardly I laugh at the idea that my appearance could arouse even the slightest excitement. But nonetheless I have followed the instructions to the letter and chosen baggy and boring clothes. Now I feel positively frumpy compared to the other visitors.

There is something sinister about the way the gates close behind us and I am reminded, suddenly, that this is not a game. I will be leaving in an hour, indeed I could turn round and walk out now if I so desired. But the inmates wait on someone else's approval, some might be in here for the rest of their natural lives. In some ways it could be a monastery

50

or a convent, the sort that belongs to a closed order; but the inhabitants of those have chosen their imprisonment.

The bus pulls up outside a bleak building and, one by one, the passengers alight. Everyone files through a heavy grey door and, while the others head down a corridor towards a reception desk, I meet Lizzie as arranged.

'You must be Julia,' she says as she shakes my hand. Lizzie reminds me of Clare and I warm to her immediately. She is younger than I expected and attractive. I am sure she would look quite glamorous in the right clothes. However, that manner of dress would not be appropriate in this environment. Lizzie wears tailored dark blue trousers with flat shoes and an understated jacket and blouse. She has applied no make-up and her hair is tied back in a simple ponytail. 'I'm afraid we have to search you first,' she apologises and leads me down to the desk my fellow passengers have already passed.

A uniformed female officer checks my pockets and handbag and asks me to sign a record book. Then Lizzie ushers me into a side room. 'There are a few more bits of paperwork for you to sign,' she says, 'then I'll take you to meet Frank.'

I scribble my signature at the bottom of a variety of forms. I don't stop to read them in detail – who does in these situations? I do, however, listen carefully as Lizzie tells me of the person I am about to meet. Already I regard Frank in a similar way that I would if he were one of my patients. In a hospital you don't get to choose whom you treat. When you start out as a junior doctor it is difficult. Human nature makes you judgmental, makes you think, how could this teenager be so irresponsible as to get pregnant, or, why should this woman be given an abortion when she is married and carrying a healthy child? It doesn't stop at the clinical details either. It is too easy to judge people on their private lives or their educational background – how can it be right for someone illiterate, with no job to be having their seventh child by their seventh partner while a couple of intelligent, hard-working university graduates struggle with IVF? Sometimes I think overcoming these prejudices is the hardest part of the job. But if you are to be a good doctor in today's society you have to learn to treat everyone as equals.

And so it is fair to say that I have no expectations about the person I am to visit. I am simply here to do a job, to chat to whomever I am assigned, to provide him with a link to the outside world, an umbilical cord through which he may feed, building sustenance so he may one day walk through that heavy grey door as a full adult member of our society. It is possible that we will not like one another, even that I will feel revolted by who he is and what he has done. But I will do my job in a professional manner. Recently, I have become adept at hiding my feelings, and I will not let them show today.

As we are leaving the office Lizzie turns back and takes a packet of cigarettes from the desk. She hands it to me. 'Give him these,' she says. 'It's always good to get off on the right foot.'

The man sitting opposite me is Francis Michael Sykes. He is serving a life sentence for murder. He is a recovering alcoholic. He was drunk when he killed his wife. He has always claimed that it was an accident; that he never intended to harm her. Everyone thought the charge and the conviction would be one of manslaughter. But you can never tell with a jury, even if you are innocent. He showed remorse from the outset. Early on in his sentence he was confirmed into the Anglican Church and since then he has been a devout practising Christian.

These are the things I have been told. I am in control. I know everything about him, while he knows nothing about me.

'I'm glad you came to see me.' His voice breaks the silence.

I am on my own now. For the first ten minutes, after introducing us, Lizzie sat beside me. It all seemed easy, natural. Now I realise how subtly she was directing the conversation. From now on it is down to me. 'I've nothing better to do,' I reply. And instantly I reprimand myself for saying the wrong thing. I feel awkward, exposed, like a teenager on a first date. I pause for a moment, trying to recall the list of suitable conversation topics I had thought of earlier. They seem trite. I can hardly ask him what he does for a living or whether he has been anywhere interesting recently. I am about to tell him that I live in Nottingham, that I am a doctor, when I think again of the recommendations for the first meeting. Don't give too much of yourself away. For Goodness sake! He isn't Hannibal Lecter.

I smile at Frank and hand him the pack of cigarettes.

'Thanks,' he says. He takes it automatically, as though that is his job, as though the pack is a ticket for a bus or for the theatre.

'So…I suppose strange women like myself have visited you before?'

He nods. 'Last one visited me every fortnight for three years, until she went to live in Canada.' I wonder to myself whether this was simply an excuse to end the friendship but Frank intercepts my thoughts. 'She still writes though.'

I nod and strive to find something else to say. I do not find that conversation comes naturally to me in these circumstances. I don't just mean the fact that Frank is a prisoner but that the environment itself is distracting. It is quite a large room furnished with rows of bare grey-topped tables, a moulded plastic chair on either side of each one. The prisoners, wearing their distinctive uniform, all face the same way. While Lizzie was sitting next to me I found myself looking about, mentally trying to guess what each inmate was in trouble for, matching my fellow visitors with their prisoners. Now I remind myself that to do this is impolite on several counts and make an effort to shut out the bustle of chat going on around me and focus on Frank.

'Tell me about yourself,' I suggest.

Gradually, I relax and we begin to chat. We talk of everything and nothing. What we like to watch on television. What books we read. Reading is encouraged, Frank tells me, the prison even has its own branch of the county library.

For me the recognition does not happen instantaneously. It grows, slowly and methodically, like an embryo in the womb, at first just a cluster of cells with no discernible pattern, later a gradually emerging human form, and then, at birth, a person more familiar to me than my own self. The man sitting opposite me is a stranger. We have never met. I have never seen the tattoos that decorate his bulky forearms, never been touched by the stubby fingers that drum, occasionally, on the cold grey tabletop. But when I look into the clear blue eyes and glimpse beyond, to the soul, I see that he is someone I have known all my life.

As I listen to him talk, my eyes track slowly, cautiously, across his chest, lingering on the regulation blue short-sleeved shirt, dawdling on the open collar and the firm clean-shaven chin. But eventually they meet his gaze and I fancy his pupils dilate and constrict again, momentarily, in a fraction of a second.

But I don't mention any of this. Instead I do my job. I chat to Frank. We talk more about our hobbies – he likes swimming too. We talk and we laugh. We are laughing when the bell rings and I am taken aback. Not just because the time has passed so quickly, but because I find myself laughing.

It is time to leave. I stand up and put on my coat. That is when Frank reaches across the table and takes hold of my hand. He grips it so tightly that I gasp, in the shocked anticipation of pain. Out of the corner of my eye I see a warder looking at me, concerned, his eyebrows raised, ready to intervene if need be. I shake my head that everything is all right. Frank relaxes his grip. Then he leans across, his head close to mine, and he whispers in my ear. 'It's good to see you again,' he says.

I shake my head, 'But this is the first time…'

It isn't though. Somewhere, in another time, another place, another life, we have met before. And both of us know it.

Chapter 7

The following morning I think about Frank as I water the plants in the conservatory. It is the first day of the rest of my life. That is how I feel. Melodramatic. I feel like something important has happened, that something else is yet to happen, though I don't rightly know what. Then I think of Kimberley Place, of the garden and the girl on the swing. But I have no desire to go there. I am like a fickle lover, so easily do I exchange one past life for another. I trickle winter feed granules onto the compost around the lemon trees. When I have finished I go and sit at the wrought-iron table where a cup of coffee is waiting. Outside it is drizzling, the water is almost invisible, as though someone has fitted a fine rose onto a watering can. Beneath the glass canopy I am enveloped in white noise.

What happened yesterday was something new, something I have never experienced before. There have always been other lives. Until now each has been discrete, complete in itself, separate from the here and now. But this time it is different. For the first time I have met someone in this life, someone whom I knew before in a previous existence. And the realisation is thrilling, shocking.

I rang Sally and Pete as soon as I arrived home yesterday. They weren't back from work, of course, but I left a message for them to call me as soon as they got in. I needed to tell someone about what had happened. But when Sally rang at five-thirty I couldn't say that important thing. Even though Richard was not yet home and there was no-one to overhear I couldn't describe the way I'd felt. Of course, Sally was eager to know what the prison was like, how it had gone, what 'my convict' was like. She put the phone onto the speaker setting so that Pete could join in the conversation. I could hear her gasp with excitement as I described all the locked doors, how it had felt like going through an air lock to be decontaminated. They both laughed when I told them how we had to leave our mobile phones at a security desk and how we had to walk through one of those detectors like they have at airports to check we weren't carrying knives. But I couldn't tell them the thing I most wanted to share. I couldn't bring myself to describe that certain feeling I'd had that Frank and I had met before. Perhaps I was scared they would think I had suddenly gone batty. Or maybe – and this worried me more – maybe I was beginning to doubt myself.

Outside the fine rain drifts in flurries, moisture moving through the air. It softens the outline of the trees and shrubs, bends the world into soft focus. There are no longer clear boundaries between one thing and another. Where there was certainty there is doubt.

I feel the need to write things down. If there is no-one I can talk to then that is the next best thing. I take a sip of coffee before rising silently from my chair and going through to the main part of the house and up the stairs.

Richard and I each have a study on the first floor. Richard's is a large room at the front of the house. It has bookcases housing eminently penned leather-bound volumes, an antique solid oak desk and two leather-upholstered chairs. It is the consulting room that never was. The ornamentation is ugly and heavy, a brass-stemmed standard lamp in the corner and a grotesque bronze statuette of a man on horseback (I cannot bring myself to throw blame on the animal but its rider looks cruel and murderous), both inherited from a great-uncle who clearly had plenty of money but no sense of beauty. Apart from the telephone and writing equipment, the desk is clear. Everything is kept securely locked away. Richard says this is to protect patient confidentiality but in truth I don't think he keeps much here that would fall into that category. Rather, it is a symptom of his private, perhaps secretive, nature.

My own room is the opposite of my husband's. It is the only room in the house that is truly mine. The only place not invaded by Richard's family heirlooms. Everywhere else in the building they are there: huge heavy dark-stained chests, fussy picture frames protecting portraits of long dead ancestors, ugly vases presiding over claw-footed sideboards. They are undoubtedly antiques; they are unquestionably valuable; they are certainly monstrous. Sometimes I feel as though these hideous objects are ganging up on me, as though Richard's parents are spying on me through the oil-painted eyes of their forefathers.

But, in my study I am safe. It is my refuge, a sanctuary for the meagre evidence of my ancestry. The walls and surfaces are crammed with photographs from happier times. My parents watch over me protectively from distant Christmases and Jamie grins mischievously from the safety of childhood. It is a small room, yet cosier for this, with a window overlooking the back garden. There is a bookcase with novels as well as medical reference books, and a snug sheepskin rug in front of the small two-seater sofa. We had planned, when we first moved in, to change the rooms around, to swap my study with the bathroom so that we could have an en suite instead of having to walk down the landing. But I quickly realised that I would have to relinquish my view for a window on the cold bare north side of the house and protested the change until Richard gave in. With hindsight, I think it was the fact that he had, by then, taken to using one of the shower rooms attached to a guest bedroom so that we would not get in one another's way, rather than consideration of my wishes, which decided the matter.

Unlike Richard, I do not feel the need to lock things away. I open the second drawer of my desk and take out a brightly covered notebook. Then I return downstairs to the conservatory where the room has warmed to the temperature of early summer.

It was the bereavement counsellor who suggested I keep a journal. Working at the hospital, referral to a counsellor after our tragedy was automatic. Although not compulsory, appointments are recommended in such circumstances, partly, I think, because our employers are concerned for our mental welfare and its obvious impact on our work; and also because it looks better if we ourselves are seen to use the facilities which we recommend to our patients and their relatives. I attended two appointments. Not because I thought anyone could take away my grief – I already knew that was impossible – but because in the early days I could not think for myself, could not make even the simplest decision: quite simply, I needed someone to tell me how to get on with my life, to tell me what to do. Richard, on the other hand, cancelled three appointments in a row because of 'work commitments'. After this they left him alone.

The counselling sessions comprised a variety of exercises for coming to terms with what had happened and for carrying on with one's life. There were activities which I definitely did not feel inclined to pursue, such as writing letters to the deceased or going to a private place and speaking to them as though they were still alive. Then there were others I felt would be useful and still continue now, such as planning my day with a list and writing in my journal. At the counsellor's suggestion, I chose a book with a lively decorated cover. It has a green background sprinkled with bright red field poppies. I think that originally the idea was to record the things I did and felt so that I could read them back and see that not every minute of every day was bad. Indeed, I was instructed to try and find at least one thing that I enjoyed about each day and to acknowledge that it was allowable for me to enjoy myself. And for a few weeks I did this obediently. Now, however, it has simply become a diary, a description of each day, without striving to highlight hidden pleasures. Writing my journal has become a habit that I enjoy for its own sake.

I open the book and read the previous entry, written on Monday night. It tells the honest truth of how I came home from swimming and wept at the realisation that I would never have grandchildren, that I was unashamedly jealous of my friends. That I still am. But I turn the page, as I have been taught, and put aside those feelings as I tell the events that have happened since.

For a while, I am engrossed as I relive the past two days; commit their highs and lows to paper. When I pause and look up, the rain has become heavier; the light plays tricks on the senses, refracting this way and that, until its infinite paths become blurred. I think about the theory of parallel universes, the possibility that millions of worlds inhabit the same time and space, that in other dimensions we are living a palimpsest of subtly different lives, a new one branching off every time we make a decision. I remember reading about this, though in truth I never fully understood it. The proof can be demonstrated with a beam of light, as I recall. It is a phenomenon that has always appealed to me, that goes some way to explaining my own perception of the world. And today it all seems infinitely possible.

I feel cold suddenly. Perhaps it is the effort of sifting through all these thoughts beyond my comprehension. Or, maybe, it is just winter creeping into the conservatory. I pick up my journal and the lukewarm remains of the coffee and step back into the kitchen. Closing the glass door behind me I head for the warmth of the Aga. Too much time to think, that's what my mother would say. And she'd probably be right.

In a little over two hours I am due to meet Clare. I am glad of this, of having a focus to look forward to. In the meantime, as it is hardly suitable weather to go out, I stroll round the ground floor in search of company. It is a habit I have fallen into these past few months. In the kitchen I tune in to Radio Four; in the drawing room, a lively discussion springs from the television and in the morning room I slide a classical CD into the hi-fi. In the dining room, I deliberate for a few moments before choosing a classic rock channel on the digital radio. This last one makes me feel slightly subversive as it is something Richard would neither like nor approve of. I search for jobs that won't offend or disappoint Mrs Blackstock; unnecessary jobs such as reorganising the kitchen cupboards. I arrange the herbs and spices into alphabetical order, deliberating whether black pepper should be placed as a 'b' or a 'p'.

At some point I wander back into the drawing room. The discussion show has finished and been replaced by one of those more leisurely daytime shows where the presenters sit on plump sofas and introduce features on subjects as diverse as how to achieve the perfect home-made pasta and what to do about domestic violence. I am just about to go and check out my teenage favourites in the dining room when something on the television catches my attention. 'After the break,' they say, 'it will be time for this week's journey into past life regression.'

I am startled. How can it be coincidence? Quickly, I take a blank video from the shelf (I have never got to grips with the DVD recorder), I fumble to free it from its cellophane wrapping and push it into the machine. Whatever is said, I don't want to miss a word. I sit on the floor in front of the television and press the record button as the adverts come to an end. And then it starts. A celebrity, in this case a well-known radio presenter, has already been regressed under hypnosis. Clips of video footage show him relaxing, eyes closed, as the therapist guides his subconscious. He chooses a life (it seems there are more than one) and, prompted by the therapist, describes significant events in this previous existence. His voice is different from his everyday radio voice, the words, the grammar, are archaic. It is as though he is reading the lines from a historical play. Eventually, he describes how this person died. The therapist instructs him to let go of any pain or suffering his former self experienced and to wake up refreshed as he is today.

Now they are live, in the studio, the celebrity, the therapist and the presenters. They discuss what happened. The

61

celebrity is amazed at his past life – though he always knew there was 'something', he says. The therapist says that many problems such as illness and fears can be the result of past life experiences. She says that, in acknowledging them, they can be cured. The presenters say how fascinated they are. They go on to name famous people – including some in very respectable jobs – who have, through hypnosis, discovered some of their past lives. There is an opportunity for viewers to ring the show and tell their experiences. I think about it. I even pick up the phone. But I am scared. Even if I give a false name, someone may be watching and recognise my voice. In my job I cannot take the risk. Instead, I listen, enthralled, as other people tell their stories. Only when there have been two minutes of adverts followed by an item on dieting do I switch the television and video off.

I feel dizzy with excitement. It seems my 'gift' is shared by others. True, not many of them have spontaneous flashbacks but they all have memories, buried deep in their subconscious minds, waiting to be tempted out. Suddenly it is acceptable to have lived before. It seems that, not only should I accept my previous existences, I should welcome them, explore them even. How I wish I could talk to Clare about this when we meet later for lunch. She, after all, is the expert on the mind and its workings. But she made her opinion clear a week ago. To broach the subject again would be to invite speculation that I am truly going insane. Neither, dare I tell her about my visit to Frank. I would be scared that I would let down my guard and reveal my true feelings. Instead I must enthuse about my voluntary work with the elderly. I must edit my life until it is acceptable, until there is none of me left.

Chapter 8

On Monday evening at eight o'clock I am already in the pool. I strike out with powerful strokes, feeling the water rush past me. The first of the rest will be getting changed, but for now, apart from the lifeguard, I am alone in this empty echoey space. I've never had a full size pool to myself before and I laugh to myself when I think that, in many ways, it is like being alone in my house. I contemplate doing something anarchic like swimming diagonally across the water, ignoring the roped lanes and striking out, instead, from one corner to another. There is something liberating about being able to twist and turn, to close my eyes without fear of bumping into anyone. I suppose that being in the womb must be something like this; a delicious feeling of being suspended, fearless and innocent, by water. For the next hour I will feel confident, certain of who I am, what I am capable of and where I am going. Unlike the previous weekend.

We had arranged to meet Andrew to discuss my case. Originally the plan had been for him to come to us. That was what I understood was to happen, and, indeed, Mrs Blackstock had faithfully prepared one of the guest bedrooms and left soup and a cheesecake in the fridge to take the pressure off the catering. But at some point and for some unknown reason, Richard had decided to change the plans. It was only at the last minute that he informed me he had arranged for us to go to his parents' house near Lincoln and that Andrew would meet us there. To say I was annoyed was an understatement. Richard's argument was that it would be easier for everyone but seeing as Andrew lives in London, a direct train route from St Pancras or a straightforward drive on the M1 to join us in Nottingham, I failed to see the logic of this. However, as Richard pointed out, all of this was being done for my benefit and I should be grateful for his efforts, certainly I had no grounds for complaint. Truly, I know I am lucky having people fight for me. But the whole business of discussing an inquiry, a prosecution and court hearing is stressful enough without combining it with a visit to Richard's parents.

I cannot say I have ever felt comfortable with my in-laws. Our worlds are so different that it is difficult for us to find common ground. And far from being united in our grief, I fear the tragedy of Jamie has driven us further apart. Richard and I are both doctors, both consultants, but there the similarity ends. Whilst I am a first generation medic, having broken the mould of my upbringing, my husband is maintaining the tradition of the family firm. Richard's ancestors have been physicians since the profession was invented, plying their trade with leeches and fearsome brass instruments, waiting for the modern age to bring them antibiotics and anaesthesia. His father was an eminent cardio-thoracic surgeon prior to his retirement. Now he sits in his country pile, reading 'The Lancet' beneath his fishing umbrella as he waits for the trout to bite and for his achievements to be honoured with a knighthood. Richard's mother, hoping soon to be Lady Spencer, rehearses this role in her daily life. A former matron, she gives orders freely, substituting lowly charity workers for her nursing staff, expecting obedience and dedication from everyone.

I would hesitate to say that Richard's parents don't like me. But certainly I am sure they think he could have done better. Many times I have failed their tests. Despite gaining a place at medical school, I was hampered by my background and the fact that my father did not have a recognised profession. And as for myself, not only did I not ride to hounds – an activity in which I would never have participated on moral grounds even if my parents could have afforded to send me to riding lessons - constantly I displayed signs that I lacked the breeding necessary to be a true member of Richard's family. Only one thing redeemed me in the eyes of Richard's parents, the fact that I produced Jamie, their beloved grandson. And now that he is gone I feel that I serve no further purpose in their eyes. Now I am an encumbrance with nothing to justify my presence.

I feel myself speed up, fuelled by the adrenalin that rushes around my body when I think of all these things.

We arrived in time for Saturday lunch. For me it was a sober affair, a stilted hour, trying to make polite conversation whilst all the while my mind was worrying about the meeting with Andrew later in the afternoon. I say all the while, but in truth, there were moments, as I chewed my salmon steak slowly and deliberately, that I allowed my mind to stray far away from the dinner table and back to Thursday, to Frank, imagining where and when it was that I knew him before. But there was little time for daydreaming. Every spoken word, every thought seemed to bring me rushing back to the cold reality of the court case.

As it turned out, the time that I had dreaded the most, the meeting with Andrew, proved to be the easiest part of the day. He is a kind man, skilled at putting people at their ease. He is also one of the best defence lawyers in the country. As soon as I began to tell him about the incident and the inquiry I felt a burden lifting from my shoulders. In this respect, at least, I feel slightly happier. Andrew has assured me that the case will not go to court. In the coming weeks he will speak to the prosecution lawyer. They will exchange letters, he has told me; perhaps they will meet. And, after the legal niceties, after the 'learned friends' have got the measure of one another, Andrew will point out the pointlessness of the exercise. The complainant will be advised that nothing will be achieved by facing me in court. He will simply incur costs, which, as a farmer, he can surely ill afford; more than this, he will prolong his suffering, defer his grief. Andrew is confident that once Ashby recovers from his shock he will withdraw all the charges.

Now I slow to a steady gentle pace, calm and efficient. I think of Frank. My thoughts have returned to him repeatedly over the weekend. It is not a sexual attraction. I am happily married to Richard and, despite our current difficulties, to be close in that way to someone else would be unthinkable. Neither is it that Frank and I have much in common, in truth I haven't considered whether we even like one another. It is something quite different. I used to be a believer in fate, to feel that certain things were meant to be. Since Jamie died all that has changed. There is no way I could ever reconcile that his death was for the best, was a necessary part of some greater whole. So I cannot say that I was fated to meet Frank. But I do feel that we have met again for a purpose, that he is a guide who will lead me to the next stage of my life. And I wonder whether finding out about our previous life together could tell me what that purpose, that next step, will be.

I hear the splash of someone else diving in and change my course and my stroke and my direction to a more conservative lengthwise crawl. After completing a couple of lengths in this fashion I climb out of the pool and sit on a bench while I catch my breath. At the end of the hall Sally and Debbie walk out from the changing rooms. I note that Debbie is carrying her pregnancy well. Besides the obvious bump she has put on little extra weight, a healthy sign at this stage. I watch as she lowers herself carefully into the water. If Jamie had attended Shipley House he and Debbie would have been in the same class. I've no doubt they would have been friends. He might even have been the father of her child. As it is, they never even met. I struggle to stop the flow of my thoughts, reprimand myself silently, tell myself it is just the chlorine that is stinging my eyes.

By the time we have finished our swim I am feeling better.

'I've been telling Debbie about your convict,' Sally tells me as we sit in the café, stirring our hot chocolate.

I laugh. 'You make him sound like he's about to be transported to Australia! And he's hardly mine.'

'But you will see him again?' she persists.

I nod. 'The prison want me to visit every week if I can. It will help prepare him for the outside world apparently.'

Pete looks surprised. 'You mean he's being released soon?'

I shrug. 'Sometime next year, I think. Does that make a difference?'

He looks worried. 'Well it's all very well you making friends with him while he's safely locked away. But when he gets out...he is a murderer don't forget.'

Sally pats him on the back. 'I'm sure the authorities know what they're doing. They wouldn't put Julia in any danger.'

'In any case,' I say, 'there are hundreds of official prison visitors all over the country. They don't seem to come to any harm.' I sip my drink then ask Debbie how she is getting on with her pregnancy. We chat more easily as the hot drinks warm us. There is a subject that I want to talk about but I am cautious now after Clare's reaction to Kimberley Place. So I steer the conversation around, build up to it carefully, wait for the moment to be right.

'Did you see that feature on past life regression on television on Friday morning?' I mention it casually, having already commented on a recent episode of 'Coronation Street'.

Sally shakes her head. 'I was at work I'm afraid. Debbie saw it though, didn't you?' She turns to her daughter who nods confirmation. 'Rang me up later to tell me how fascinating it was.'

Good, I think to myself, so far, they don't think I'm completely mad.

'I'm surprised you were interested,' Sally continues, 'what with you being a proper doctor and all. I'd have expect you to dismiss it as mumbo jumbo.'

I decide to risk it and come clean. 'Actually, I thought it was amazing how people remembered such detail,' I say. 'Of course no-one could actually prove whether they had lived those lives, most of the time there'd be no written record. But it was very convincing the way they remembered things, emotional things.' I take a deep breath. 'And I think it's happened to me.' There it's done now, for better or worse.

'Really?' Sally is visibly surprised. 'You mean you've been hypnotised?'

I shake my head. 'No. Not that. Just, sometimes I get the feeling I've been somewhere or met someone before.'

'Oh that!' Sally laughs. 'I think we all get that. You know, one time it happened to me and it was really powerful. There was a new girl at work, a few years back now. I had this really strong feeling that we'd met before. And when I plucked up courage to mention it, it turned out she felt the same. But she came from Sussex and I've never been there, there was no way we could have met. To be honest, it was quite spooky, if I hadn't been so busy at the time – what with Nicola discovering boys and Debbie getting engaged – well, I could easily have believed there was something psychic in it. But then, a good two years later, we were chatting about where we were going on holiday and blow me it turned out we'd both stayed at the same hotel on the Isle of Wight. Years ago it was, the girls were tiny.'

I hesitate for a moment. Could Sally's logical explanation, or something like it, apply to me - in the case of Frank anyway? Is it possible that he and I have met before in this life? On Thursday I was certain it was more than that, convinced that we shared a past existence. Since that moment, I have nurtured the thought, encouraged it to grow in my mind, precious as a pearl. Just as I am beginning to flounder in self-doubt Debbie jumps in and saves me.

'There's a woman here in Ilkeston does it,' she says, 'regresses people.'

This time Sally, Pete and I all gasp in amazement.

'You didn't tell me this on Friday,' Sally accuses.

'I didn't know then. We were talking about it at work today. Helen – you know her, she lives over in West Hallam – well apparently she's had some consultations with her.'

'Do you mean Helen's been regressed into past lives?' I

ask excitedly.

Debbie shakes her head. 'No, but she's been hypnotised. She was trying to give up smoking and finding it difficult, then a friend recommended this hypnotist. It worked too. She said this woman – what was her name now?' She pauses and rummages in her handbag, produces a business card. '"Rose Langley",' she reads. 'Helen says this Rose Langley is really good. I thought I might see her myself.' She looks round tentatively, guesses what we will ask next. 'She uses hypnosis for all sorts of things. I thought it might be useful for the birth.'

'For the birth? I expect Julia will have something to say about that,' exclaims Sally. 'I've heard of underwater births but not hypnotised ones. What do you think?' She looks at me to back her up.

'Entonox if it's straightforward and an epidural if it's protracted or there are complications,' I reel off automatically. Then I think of Clare, dismissing my life at Kimberley Place. I soften and smile. 'But there's no harm in using hypnosis to relax you and help control the pain,' I add. 'Providing you have a midwife in attendance and are preferably in a hospital. I've seen it done and it certainly works for some people.'

Debbie hands me the card. It is a reward for supporting her. 'Have this,' she says. 'I can get another. And be sure and tell me about it if you meet her. In fact,' she looks at me slyly, 'if you were to do that you could check her out for me, assure Mum she's capable of helping me with the baby. You'd be doing us all a favour.'

'And in the meantime,' Sally says, 'let's work out some questions for you to ask your convict next time you see him. Let's find out whether you really have met him before.'

I pop the card into my bag. For three months my life has stood still. Now, suddenly, everything is moving much too fast.

Chapter 9

I visit my mother on her birthday. I had thought it would not be possible. I had expected to be caught up in a deluge of jobs, busy with my return to work, tired after the unpractised routine. But, of course, things haven't worked out that way. Apart from the day centre on Tuesdays and the prison visits each Thursday, my days are empty of meaningful activity. I plan to leave early so that I will be in good time to take my mother to lunch. She is of the class and generation that have never enjoyed evening dinner. Instead, her main meal of the day is consumed by one p.m. and she becomes fretful if circumstances cause this habit to be disrupted.

Even though it is a Saturday and barely seven-thirty, Richard has already left the house. I set my overnight bag by the front door before checking that all the lights are turned off and the doors and windows locked. There is food ready to heat up in the fridge but I doubt Richard will touch it. More likely he will eat out with a colleague or perhaps accept an invitation to their house for dinner. Perhaps he will return home early with a take-away and play the piano, undisturbed, into the early hours. I lock the door to the conservatory and close the tiny window in the downstairs cloakroom. This is a good area, we don't have much crime, but the houses feel isolated from one another. There is privacy for the occupants but also for the burglars.

I choose not to take the motorway; it is too monotonous; apart from other vehicles there is nothing to occupy my thoughts. Instead, I take the straight, busy 'A' roads as far as Coventry then branch across to the Fosse Way. I drive through Stow-on-the-Wold and Moreton-in-Marsh, through places whose names echo with the rise and fall of the country hills; through busy market towns and picturesque villages, where golden Cotswold stone glows warm in the sunlight, drawing me south towards my birthplace. When I stop for a coffee in Cirencester the air feels quite balmy despite the time of year.

In the café I pay for my drink and take out Rose Langley's card. I have thought about it – the possibility of consulting her – for the past week. But I have not yet made the call. I tell myself I would rather let nature take its course, bide my time and let the details of this past life gradually reveal themselves to me. But those are just excuses. The truth is that I am scared; scared of what I may discover, about myself, about Frank, about other lives. And scared of the process of hypnosis, the conscious decision to relinquish control of my mind to the will of someone else. How I wish that Clare were more amenable, that she could guide me through this journey.

I had hoped that things would become clearer when I visited Frank in prison for the second time two days ago. But I was disappointed. On this occasion he made no reference to a previous life and neither did I. I had hoped that, when I saw him, when I let him take my hand, scenes would play out in my head and I would begin to understand who I was before, and what he meant to me. But none of that happened. I was aware of the clock counting down the time allowed, like an exam where you struggle to scribble the answers before the bell rings. There was nothing left but to ask him about his life now. I felt like an inquisitor as I demanded answers to all the questions Sally had prepared. Where did he grow up? Had he ever lived in Somerset? Was he living in Nottingham prior to his arrest? Needless to say, all of them drew a blank.

I skirt around the edge of Wiltshire and, sometime before twelve, arrive in the small Somerset town where I grew up. Within minutes I am turning onto the narrow driveway outside my mother's home – my home. My mother is opening the front door before I've even turned off the engine. I suspect that she has been sitting at the front window for the past hour. She is standing, waiting to hug me as I step out of the car.

'It's good to see you,' she says. 'It's been a long time.'

In fact, it has been hardly any time at all. I last saw my mother four weeks ago to the day. Under normal circumstances, if I were working, it would have been much longer. I pause to wonder whether she is disappointed in me. Not for becoming a doctor, obviously, I know she is proud of that, but because I have gone away. If I had attended the local school and gone on to work as a hairdresser or a shop assistant I would still live nearby. I would see her every day, every week at least. I would pop in for a coffee and a chat like Debbie does with Sally. Instead, I, the only child, have moved to a distant city. If my mother is lonely then it is my fault. For a moment I remember how I couldn't wait to get away, to pursue my own life, my own career, far from my dreary hometown. It seemed quite reasonable at the time. Of course I had feared that I might get homesick, that I would miss my parents; it never occurred to me that they would miss me. Now, with a pang, I remember how I felt when it was Jamie's turn to leave, first to boarding school and then to university.

'Are you all right?' my mother asks. 'Tired after the journey I expect.'

I pull myself together and nod. 'Happy birthday Mum!' I say, as we go inside.

My mother fusses over me, wondering what I need after my long trip. Coffee perhaps? Or tea? I give her the card and present and insist I will get my own drink. As she unwraps the silk scarf and perfume, which I hope she will use and not just consign to a drawer 'to keep them nice', I go through to the kitchen. In the narrow extension I open the cupboard where I know I will find the coffee. There is only instant. My mother is not fond of freshly ground coffee. Indeed, she still mourns the day when the blends diluted with chicory disappeared from her local supermarket shelves. During the past thirty years I have come to appreciate what my mother would call the finer things in life. Somewhere in the car I'm sure I packed some ground coffee but for now I decide to drink tea. I make a pot so my mother can have some too, though I know she will only sip at it to be polite, this not being her allotted time for morning coffee or afternoon tea. I carry through the tray and set it on the table in the back room.

'No husband with you?' My mother feigns disappointment but she isn't a good actress. 'I suppose he has to work.'

I nod, though I have no idea whether he is at the hospital or on the golf course. I didn't exactly press Richard to come with me and was secretly quite pleased when he said he thought he'd be busy. It is more relaxed without him. If Richard were here, my mother would worry about using the best china and doing things properly. There is an extra bonus to this arrangement. When Richard next visits his parents, I will not feel obliged to accompany him. As it is, on my own, I will stay the night. I will sleep in the room that has been mine since I was born, then drive back at my leisure tomorrow afternoon.

As I drink my tea my mother frets over which coat and shoes she should wear. I assure her that anything will be fine. People are informal these days, especially at lunchtime, I tell her. Then I add that she could wear her new scarf and try out the perfume.

'You shouldn't have,' she says, by way of a thank you. 'I'm sure they were expensive.'

'Nonsense,' I say. And, thinking of Clare, 'some of my friends wear things like that to work every day.'

My mother shakes her head at the extravagance of it all but obediently dabs a splash of the perfume on her wrists and behind her ears.

We drive into Bath and I park as close as I can to the restaurant I have chosen. My mother is in her early eighties and quite fit for her age but she doesn't like the weekend crowds, especially the youths who wear hooded tops and clatter past at speed on cycles and skateboards. With some difficulty I have managed to find somewhere that specialises in traditional English food. My mother tucks into roast chicken while I pick, with less appetite, at grilled fish. When we have finished I suggest a stroll round the shops, but my mother is keen to get back; I think the single glass of wine she drank with her meal has made her dozy. I drive her home and she immediately settles down 'to rest her eyes for ten minutes' in her favourite easy chair. I smile to myself and collect my overnight bag from the car.

My childhood home is a slice of a stone-built terrace, one of many, built originally for the miners who used to dig for coal. For many years, the history books say, the area was a real community, established long before I was born. The men could walk together to their shifts down the pit and gather in the evenings to smoke their pipes. The women could gossip as they swept the front yards or hung out their laundry on Monday mornings. Beyond each of the standard two up, two down buildings, each home was allocated a long narrow strip of land – much like an allotment – where the occupants grew neat rows of potatoes, onions and runner beans to feed their families.

Since the mining industry closed, all of that has changed. Now, each abode that once housed a family is considered an ideal starter home for an upwardly mobile couple. Internal walls have been removed, porches and double-glazing added, central heating and modern kitchens fitted. Instead of setting out together, already grubby, to the darkness and danger of the mine, the occupants rush out each morning, freshly showered and styled, jump into their tightly parked cars, and drive to their warm dry offices in Bath or Bristol. But my mother was never part of this. She is one of a select club. She is a miner's widow.

I take my things into the house and drop the latch on the door behind me. I creep past my mother, as she snores quietly in a chair beside the wood-burning stove, and climb the steep narrow staircase to the first floor. There are two bedrooms here, the larger occupied by my parents – and now just my mother, while the smaller back room has always been mine. In here I set my bag on the bed and breathe a sigh of familiarity, security, contentment. This is still my space. Indeed, few other people have slept in it. When Richard and I got married my parents replaced my old single bed with a double so the two of us could stay. That didn't work out though. I don't think Richard has slept in this house more than twice – and the second time was only because it was an emergency, when we arrived in the middle of the night five years ago, when my father died. After the first time we stayed here as newly weds, Richard vowed never again; insisting that, thereafter, we would spend the night in a nearby motel. He claimed it was for my parents' sake, the intrusion, the disruption, was not fair on them, he said, especially in such a small space. But really I suspect it was because Richard is used to grander things. I don't mean that he is a snob, simply that he is used to having things a certain way. Spending the night in a tiny room, with a trek down the stairs and through the kitchen to the only bathroom in the house, made him feel uncomfortable, out of control. And Richard is a man who needs to feel in command of every situation.

I sometimes worry about my mother living here. About ten years ago, when my father was still alive, I tried to persuade my parents to move to a bungalow. I had enough money from my doctor's salary to help them buy somewhere spacious, comfortable, and, above all, safe. It would save me worrying, I argued, about whether they might fall down the stairs in the night, or slip in the steep garden in bad weather. But they insisted that they wanted to stay here, in the only house they had lived in since they were married. It was not the money - wherever they lived they would leave the property to me in their will so that made no difference – it was the fact that this was their home. And I am rather selfishly pleased at their decision.

I push open the window – only a couple of inches because Joe, the latest in a long succession of feline companions, has sidled in behind me, hopeful of some attention while my mother is asleep. I run my hand across the ginger fur as he jumps onto the bed and his back arches as he turns tail on me and sniffs at my bag. I wonder how Richard would react if I took a kitten home.

So this is my space, just as it always was. Apart from the bed, the rest of the furniture has not been replaced since I was a child.

It was in this very room that I had my first experience of a past life. It was the summer before I started school and I was in bed. Being July, the sky was still light well past my bedtime. I am certain what happened was not a dream. On the other hand, looking back with the knowledge of an adult, I suspect that neither was I fully awake. I remember opening my eyes to darkness, although some light crept round the slightly open door. I was not aware of the detail of the room, either it was too shadowy or I simply didn't pay it attention. But I do remember that I was thirsty and I was scared. There was noise somewhere beyond the door, somewhere else in the house. There were voices shouting. There was a crash, the sound of splintering wood and shattering glass. Then I began to scream. I screamed again and again until I woke. When I say woke, I mean that I came to from the nightmare, but I still believe that I hadn't actually been sleeping. I opened my eyes and found the room was quite light. Downstairs I could hear voices. But I knew instantly that the sound came from the television.

I shouted to my parents and, within seconds my father appeared at the door. Seeing my distress, he carried me downstairs. I remember sitting in front of the television; the programme showed people dancing, the men in smart evening suits and the women in full flowing skirts. My mother told me to look at the pretty dresses while she fetched me some hot milk. Ten minutes later, as I sipped the drink, my mother asked me to describe what had happened; and when I told her she spoke to me soothingly and assured me that it was just a dream. Everyone had dreams like that, she said, including herself and my father. I wanted to please her so I nodded and nestled into her lap. But I knew it wasn't a dream. I knew, without doubt, that it had really happened. Children understand more than we can imagine. They know things on an intuitive level long before they have the vocabulary to explain them.

It was many years before I understood that what I experienced that night was the memory of a past life. And several more before I realised that this was not a phenomenon that most people shared.

I turn back into the room and unzip my bag. Automatically, I go through the same routine I always do on these visits. I place my nightdress, neatly folded, on the pillow and my slippers on the floor. My sponge bag goes on the dressing table next to a framed picture. It is a photograph of Jamie, Richard and myself, taken when Jamie was twelve, young enough to be seen with his parents, to be seen at all, just before he retreated into adolescent embarrassment. There is nothing like this in my own house outside of my study, nothing carefree, unrehearsed. Of course there are pictures of Jamie but they are all formal, the pose and expression directed by professional photographers. They record prize-giving ceremonies and achievements, rites of passage. The pictures in Nottingham are works of art, technically perfect, but none of them is truly my son.

After I have stowed fresh clothes in a drawer and hung a dress and jacket in the wardrobe in readiness for church tomorrow, I put the bag behind the door and settle myself on the bed. I have brought a couple of books with me: novels. I have always enjoyed reading. Perhaps that comes, in part, from being an only child. It was an activity which I could pursue on my own in the days before all children seemed to be supplied with televisions – and, more recently computers – in their bedrooms. I have always relished the opportunity to escape into a fictitious world. Even before the events of the past few months I would feel vulnerable, uneasy, if I finished a book, left that place of fantasy and escape, without having another, waiting, in which to immerse myself. I prop the novel I am currently reading on my pillow and open it at the marked page but the words blur in front of my eyes. I have left my reading glasses downstairs in my handbag. I should go and get them now, perhaps brew a decent coffee too. I need something to wake me up. But Joe has settled next to me. I love the feel of him, warm and purring, his chin resting contentedly on my arm. It would be a shame to disturb him.

I am standing on the seafront, on the southwest corner where the road meets the sea, where the steep ramshackle streets meet the crumbly cliff. A cold, brisk, sea breeze burns my skin, stings my cheeks with salt. The sunlight is piercing, icy blue, glaring on the water; it lacks the yellow fullness of summer. The salty fishy smell of the harbour penetrates my nostrils. I wrinkle my nose. I am counting. One. Two. Four. Six. It is a game. I count some more as I stare out towards the streak of purple which lines the horizon. Ten. Twelve. Fifteen. Seventeen. Do I not know my numbers or am I deliberately cheating? Mostly the latter, I think. Suddenly and unexpectedly I reach one hundred. I call out. 'Coming! Ready or not!' My voice has a lilt, an accent that surprises me, as though it is not my own.

Now I am off, bounding up the stone steps onto the harbour wall. Down to my left, fishing boats are tethered to iron rings by soggy, sea-green ropes or hauled up like stranded porpoises on the shingle. There are discarded fish-heads with glassy staring eyes caught amongst wrack and kelp, hungry gulls with sharp beaks circling above. On the lower level there is a skinny cat searching for scraps. Further along there is a man with greying hair and leathery storm-beaten skin, sitting mending a net. He hears my footsteps, looks up.

'Morning to ee young Maggie,' he says. His words whistle past occasional teeth that bob up and down in his mouth, yellowed with tobacco, stranded like buoys in the harbour.

'Morning Alf,' I reply.

'Ee out on your own then?'

'I'm with Freddie,' I say.

'You don't want to be out on your own this time of year, a pretty young thing like you. Tisn't safe.'

'I told yer, I'm after Freddie,' I sulk.

'Well, ee'll be looking a long time I reckon, cos he didn't come this way.' He turns back to his mending and the conversation is over.

I carry on anyway. Everyone knows Alf tells lies. The wall narrows. It twists and slopes, slippery with seawater, a protective arm around the boats; and in stormy weather a treacherous walk for those on top. I can feel the breeze more strongly here. It slices through my insufficient clothes – a dress, cotton, billowing, splashed and stained by play, and a cardigan, thin, grubby, the knitted threads unravelling here and there as it runs to holes. I shiver. I've had enough of this. I turn and leave the sea behind, retrace my steps along the wall. Before the road I jump down onto the shingle and run towards the cliff, my feet, in boots too big for them, slipping on wet weed-strewn boulders. I leap, at times onto a firm footing and at others onto precarious stones that rock beneath me. At some point I pause to kick the boots off, leaving them discarded like jetsam, and continue barefoot like a wild animal. I search, scrambling up the debris of rock-falls, peering over huge boulders. But it is his cough that gives him away, dry rasps, several one after the other, like the rattling drum of a woodpecker. And, tucked into a crevice at the cliff base, I find him, a dirty blue-eyed boy, hardly bigger than myself.

Chapter 10

'Look who I bumped into in the foyer on my way home.' Richard is clearly pleased with himself as he ushers Clare through the door. It is Tuesday, just after seven. I have been sitting beside the Aga writing my journal, unwinding after my stint in the day centre.

I hurry down the hall and greet my friend. 'Come in,' I say. 'Let me take your coat.' Clare smiles with an effortless perfection. Her lips gleam with the lightest touch of colour, outlined precisely as though drawn by an artist. There are no smudges where the rose-coloured pigment meets the creamy blush of her foundation. She could have stepped from the glossy pages of a magazine, where all the blemishes, the imperfections of reality have been airbrushed away. 'I hope you don't mind,' she apologises. 'Richard insisted I should come over for dinner. I tried to explain to him that women like to be warned about these things but he wouldn't even let me call you.' She takes off a stylish woollen scarf and shakes her hair loose. I feel instantly dowdy and dishevelled. I would not look like Clare even if I had spent hours perfecting myself for a night out.

'I thought it would be a nice surprise,' Richard says.

'It's a lovely surprise!' I reassure them. I wouldn't be too happy if Richard had suddenly expected me to entertain his work colleagues but Clare is different. She will take me as she finds me. Far from minding, I am touched that Richard has thought of me in inviting Clare. I have always thought that he tolerates her only because she is my friend; I am sure she has never been his first choice of dinner guest. Indeed, he has commented to me in the past that he finds her somewhat frivolous and flighty.

After they have hung up their coats, Clare follows me into the kitchen.

'Let me help,' she offers, 'I am invading after all.'

I glance at Clare's carefully manicured nails and wonder how they survive the rigours of cooking, or indeed, any housework at all. 'Nonsense,' I dismiss her. 'I was planning pasta with a sauce if that's all right. I've already prepared most of it so I'll only have to chop a few extra vegetables. You know me, I'll get it done quicker on my own.'

'That's true,' she laughs. 'We'd just end up chatting and eat all the vegetables raw.' She picks a freshly cut slice of carrot from the wooden board and nibbles it, as though confirming our thoughts.

'Go and get Richard to pour you a drink,' I instruct her. 'And persuade him to play the piano for you. I'll have this ready to eat in half an hour.'

Once alone I get to work. I take a carrot from the rack and a red pepper from the fridge then rummage in the cupboard for a tin of butter beans. And as I slice into the pepper it happens again. Even though I am not preparing seafood, the salty smell of freshly caught fish haunts my nostrils. It has been like this, one way or another since Saturday afternoon. The dream drifts back and forth throughout the day, hazy, like a ghost. I will be walking down the road when, beyond the screech of the traffic, I will hear the rush of water on shingle. As I climb into bed I will feel sharp rock biting into my bare feet as I step onto a bedside rug.

On Monday evening, after swimming, in the bright plastic reality of the leisure centre café, I told Sally and Pete about it. 'It sounds so real,' Sally had said. 'That place you're describing feels familiar but I just can't place it.'

Debbie had taken the opportunity to remind me of her request of the previous week. 'Maybe if you were hypnotised you'd find out where it was,' she'd suggested. Pete had simply shaken his head and said that it was all very rum.

Sally had sat pondering while we drank our hot chocolate. 'I can just picture those two kids, Maggie and Freddie,' she'd said. 'I only wish I could put my finger on the place.'

I was quite surprised at myself telling them about it. There was one thing I didn't say though. I omitted to mention my certainty that the boy, Freddie, was Frank.

I drain the pasta then go into the morning room to tell Richard and Clare that dinner is ready. They are both seated at the piano where Clare is attempting to play something akin to 'Chopsticks'. Richard is leaning over her, guiding her hands. They are both laughing. I pause, an intruder who will surely break the spell. But Clare looks up.

'He started off playing dreary dirges,' she says, 'but I persuaded him to lighten up a bit and give me a lesson!'

Reluctantly, I smile. Clare sparkles. She is succeeding where I fail. But I should not be jealous. I should be pleased that Richard is looking happier than he has for months, grateful that someone is getting through to him even though that someone is not me.

'Dinner's ready,' I announce. 'I thought we could eat in the kitchen. It's warm in there.'

Minutes later, we are tucking into the food.

'How is your voluntary work going?' Clare asks.

I am showering pepper onto my pasta. I set the mill on the table and look up. 'Tiring,' I admit, 'but it's good to be doing something useful again,' I grin. 'I don't think I'll be asking to transfer departments when I get back to work though.' I laugh. Richard and Clare laugh with me. We are seated around one end of the overly-long kitchen table. I feel warm, secure, proud of the meal I have prepared which, although simple, is tasty. It is flavoured with fresh basil which I have grown myself, defying the season, on the windowsill beside the Aga. Perhaps because of these things, because Clare is with us, because I feel that neither of them will criticize me in front of the other, I decide to tell them about the prison visiting. It is a perfectly respectable form of voluntary work, after all. Something I should be proud of, not keeping a secret.

'I thought I'd do something else as well.' I say this casually, as though I am taking on new challenges every day.

'I've been accepted as an official prison visitor.'

For a few moments there is silence. I am self-conscious suddenly, aware of the food as I swallow, as it warms my stomach. Richard is the first to respond. 'Do you think that's wise?' he asks. He doesn't react with surprise, doesn't stop eating, merely glances up at me briefly between forkfuls of pasta.

'Wise?'

He chews, swallows, then looks at me more intently. 'I don't want to worry you about this Julia, and I know Andrew is hopeful it will come to nothing, but remember you have a possible court case coming up. Do you really think it's a good idea to fraternize with convicted criminals right now?'

I feel flustered, judged. And I haven't even mentioned Frank. I won't now either. I am fumbling for the right answer when Clare states her opinion.

'I think it's a very good idea,' she says. 'The fact that Julia has been accepted indicates that she is a respected member of society. They're very careful whom they approve, as I understand. They don't just take anyone. If it came to it – which of course it won't – but if Julia did have to vouch for her character in court then I'd say this would count in her favour.'

I smile at her gratefully.

Richard looks up at Clare. 'Perhaps you're right,' he concedes.

I feel my face flush. I am glad that he approves but disappointed that it is Clare who convinces him.

'You seem to know a lot about it' I say.

'Ah yes.' Clare pauses to dab the corner of her mouth with a napkin. 'Well, I worked for the prison service myself, years ago, when I first qualified.'

I pause; surprised. 'Oh? I never knew that.' But then, there is a lot about Clare that I don't know, especially concerning the time before she came to work at the hospital.

'I think you'll find it very rewarding,' she tells me. 'Once they allocate someone for you to visit and you begin to get to know them.'

I don't correct her. Don't tell her that this process has already begun.

After dinner, Richard announces that he has some paperwork he wants to do in his study. Clare and I settle ourselves in the drawing room with a pot of coffee and a box of chocolates. It is almost like old times.

'Have you been back to Kimberley Place recently?' Clare asks me, when we are alone.

I shake my head. 'No,' I answer, honestly. I am about to continue, to say that I have had other things on my mind. But when I think about what those things are I check myself. I have never been good at telling lies, never needed to, never wanted to.

'Good,' Clare nods. 'It's easy and not uncommon,' she continues, 'at times of stress and trauma, to become reliant on things outside of ourselves.' She speaks slowly and precisely, selecting each word carefully, as though she is dispensing a medication. 'For some people it is alcohol or prescribed drugs, or simply to regularly seek the company or ask the opinion of another person.'

I listen attentively, somewhat nervously, under her gaze. I love Clare dearly, yet, because of her job, because of the talent she has for reading people so intuitively, I sometimes feel as though I am laid bare in front of her, as though she can read my innermost thoughts.

She selects a chocolate, picks it up delicately with her fingertips and bites into it cleanly, sensuously. 'But ultimately,' she says, 'any one of those things is an emotional crutch. It is a sign that we have not yet fully healed.'

I nod agreement, hoping she will not diagnose me with such a disability.

'The danger...' She pauses here to sip her coffee, the

timing, the effect, is dramatic. 'The danger,' she continues, 'occurs when such a crutch becomes incorporated into our daily lives. When it becomes, not a choice, but a necessity.'

I feel my insides tense, as though I am being found out. I hope my face gives nothing away.

'Obviously, if this has physical implications, it can become a serious problem. It can lead to someone becoming alcoholic, say. But even an innocent habit can become an obsession, a compulsion.' She looks at me searchingly. 'And I have to say, Julia, that for a while I was quite worried about you. I didn't tell you at the time obviously – it could have made matters worse.'

I hold my breath, a naughty child with a guilty secret.

'But you're clearly getting better now.' She smiles and settles back into her chair. 'I'm glad you're working through it at last.'

I smile back, releasing my breath slowly in relief, and take another chocolate.

'Enough of analysing me,' I joke, as the tension is released. 'What about you?' I quiz her as I kick off my mules and tuck my feet on the sofa. 'Are you still seeing that man?'

'You mean the one you don't approve of?' She smiles now. I nod.

She shakes her head. 'You'll be pleased to hear that's over.'

'Ah.' I watch her carefully, look for the glint of excitement in her eye. 'But there's someone else,' I conclude.

Clare laughs. 'God, don't say I'm that transparent. Perhaps we should swap jobs, maybe you should be the psychotherapist.'

'I'm right then!' I push the chocolates towards her across the table triumphantly. One good thing I've noticed – if there is any good to be found in the course of my life recently – is that, in taking a step back from the hustle and bustle of my working life, I have become more observant, more in tune with the people around me. I suppose, quite simply, I have had time to pay attention to the details. 'Come on,' I say. 'Tell me all.'

Clare looks at me doubtfully. 'I came round to see how you are, not to sit here talking about myself.'

'You've just pronounced me to be on the mend,' I grin. 'Anyway, a bit of gossip will cheer me up. And goodness knows, it must drive you mad listening to other people talking about their lives all day and never being able to mention anything about yourself. I mean, counselling and therapy are talking but they're hardly conversation.' We both laugh. It is good to be laughing again. 'So,' I am persistent. 'Who's this one?'

Clare tells me about her latest boyfriend or rather her lover, as she prefers to call him. She describes how she bumped into him – literally – in the hospital canteen as an excuse to speak to him. He is a newly appointed registrar.

I do the maths. 'So doesn't that make him ten years younger than you?'

She nods. 'At least.'

'Gosh!' I try, unsuccessfully, not to sound shocked.

'Anyway, after I'd apologised for bumping into him, I asked if he was new to the area – which he is – so I offered to show him some of the nightlife. We went to Yates's and The Trip, I didn't know which would be his kind of thing.'

'Then I suppose you went back to your place.'

'You guessed.'

'Actually, I was joking.' In some ways I admire Clare for being so forthright and upfront. But part of me can't get used to her permissiveness. I remind myself that she is ten years or so younger than me and probably had a more relaxed upbringing in that regard. 'So did you – you know?'

'Did we have sex do you mean?' she laughs. 'Honestly Julia, you're such a prude. I don't know how you do your job, you must have to ask your patients intimate questions all the time.'

'That's different,' I protest. 'Those are medical details.'

'It's like "Trust me, I'm a doctor",' Clare says. We both

laugh. 'And yes,' she continues, 'in answer to the question you couldn't quite bring yourself to ask, yes, we did have sex.'

'On your first date!' I find myself gasping in wonderment. Sometimes I think Clare must despair of my reacting like a nun.

'When else?' Clare says. 'After all, there might not be a second one.' She reaches for the box and helps herself to a truffle. 'Unlike chocolates.'

'So will there?' I press. 'Will you see him again do you think?'

She ponders for a moment. 'I'm not sure. I mean, he's ever so sweet and all that, and he's got lovely eyes and a pert bottom.' She pauses, grinning mischievously. It is a game she plays, trying to provoke me into expressing my disapproval. I am learning the rules. I do not rise to her challenge but simply nod and wait for her to continue. 'He's a bit young for me though. Anyway, what about you? When did you and Richard last have sex?'

Her question takes me by surprise. It is so unexpected and I am so drunk with laughing that I answer without even thinking about it. 'Not since Jamie died, obviously.'

Suddenly, Clare is serious. The game is over. 'You're kidding!'

I shrug. 'It isn't important. Have some more coffee.' I lean forward and reach for the coffee pot, dither as I lift the lid and check the contents before holding it, poised, over Clare's cup, my eyebrows raised. This is what Clare would call a displacement activity (I have learned some of her jargon over the years) or more simply a diversion. It is meant to distract her from the subject in hand. It doesn't work.

'No more coffee thanks.' She dismisses my feeble attempt to outwit her and continues undeterred. 'Not important? Julia, are you serious?'

I squirm uncomfortably. I do not like answering this kind of question. I do not believe it achieves anything. 'It wouldn't seem right,' I say. 'It wouldn't be appropriate.'

'Of course it's appropriate,' she challenges. 'More so now than ever before, I'd say.' Clare goes on to tell me about the importance of physical love. The different functions it fulfils. I resent her intrusion. I feel that it is not her business. Perhaps I am prudish as she suggested earlier but surely that is no worse than being permissive. At last I can bear it no longer.

'I'd rather not talk about it any more if you don't mind,' I say.

Clare stands up, walks round to me, rests her hand on my shoulder. 'I didn't mean to upset you. But I wish you'd reconsider having some counselling.'

By now I am so edgy that I recoil from her touch. 'Would that be for grief or for marriage guidance?' I ask, a little too sharply.

'Very well.' She gives in reluctantly and backs away, sinks back onto the sofa. 'But remember, Julia, men have needs. And Richard is still a very attractive man.'

It takes all my willpower not to shout at Clare. How dare she instruct me on my private life? Suggest that Richard could be unfaithful. I struggle to contain my feelings. 'I'm sorry,' I say, 'but I've had a hard day. Thank goodness I don't work on geriatrics.' I make a futile attempt at a joke. It is like a replay of earlier but this time neither of us laughs. 'It's been good seeing you but now if you don't mind I'd really like an early night.'

'Of course.' She stands up.

I follow her warily into the hall, keeping my distance as she puts on her coat.

It is fully dark as Clare leaves. There is not even a sliver of moon to soften the intensity of the night. I see her out to her car where she pauses to hug me, whispers apologies into my ear. I wave as she drives off, then I dawdle at the end of the driveway, breathing in the spicy winter scent of myrtle. Somewhere in the distance a cat meows. I don't see it though, for between us there is a blackness that would challenge even Dylan Thomas. I pause for a moment looking around me, allowing my thoughts, my emotions to settle. Our road is lit by Victorian gas lamps – that is to say, I'm sure they are powered by electricity these days, but the posts at least are original and the effect they create is reminiscent of the past. Their light is not forced out in a harsh unnatural beam, but rather it trickles and billows, soft as a cloud, and drifts stealthily to the ground like a fall of snow. Indeed, in the fog, hardly any light escapes at all and figures loom like spectres out of the darkness.

In happier times, when my mood was bright and colourful, the dimly lit night-time of our street seemed quite beautiful. Tranquil and atmospheric, the dark would blend hazily, gently, soothing the eyes after a busy day. But these days it is quite different. The intense shadows frighten me, as though they will suck me into their dark centres, never to return. In the mists of autumn, I imagine that I am in some dank corner of Dickensian London, with cut-throats lurking in black doorways. The night is filled with murderous intent, trapping me in my home until the grey dawn wakes me up and releases me from my prison. I no longer walk after dark but take my car on even the shortest journeys. The lingering exhaust from Clare's car swirls silently about me like a lethal London fog and I turn and walk back towards the welcoming beacon that glows from the open front door.

Chapter 11

On Thursday, I go for my third visit to the prison, to Frank. I am beginning to feel more relaxed about the whole process.

On the bus I casually read a magazine. It is one of those modern weeklies with articles on how to lose a stone in a fortnight and photographs of celebrity makeovers. I flip the pages with little interest. I picked it at random from the newsagent's near the bus stop, feeling that it would somehow bestow me with anonymity. Yet, once settled in my seat, I find I am no longer so self-conscious about who might be looking at me or what they might be thinking. Of course, for my own part, I am still curious about the other visitors, but I must respect their privacy just as I would have them respect mine. I can begin to understand how, even in this strange context, friendships grow. Today a woman visitor, already on the bus before my stop, smiled at me as I climbed aboard. Another said 'morning' in greeting as I sat down. Already I am becoming trusted, accepted into this inner circle. I wonder what the 'rules' are, how I should acknowledge these people if I were to see them somewhere unconnected with the prison, in a shop say, or a café, even in my own department in the hospital. I imagine there is a whole system of social mores that I have yet to learn.

As we enter the enclosure I look up at the fence. Perhaps I feel more positive because it is a sunny day but really it doesn't look that different from those I have seen on the television footage of popular music festivals. And the CCTV is much like the surveillance devices in every high street. Even the buildings no longer feel so doom-laden. I suppose the difference is that now I am drawing my information from my own experience rather than from television dramas. I can see how unreal they are. They portray a world where sadistic prisoners savagely maim or even kill one another on a daily basis. In truth, from the little I have seen so far, I suspect the inmates are far more likely to die of boredom.

Yet, even if I no longer find the prison intimidating, it is still a stark environment. Of course, I've only seen the public areas, but I imagine that, if anything, they are more homely, more inviting, than the world beyond. Everything is so functional, I think to myself. There are only necessities, none of the touches of humanity, the niceties we have in our homes or even in a place of work. How different it would feel with a rug here or a vase of flowers there.

I think about what Clare said. About how she worked in a prison when she first qualified as a psychologist. Somehow I cannot picture her in this environment. I cannot imagine her dressing down to suit the severity of the surroundings. Neither can I see her behaving with the restraint that would be needed. I cannot see her suppressing her sensuality or sympathising with convicted criminals. It occurs to me then that I assumed her work was of a counselling nature. But now I think back she never actually said that. It could be that she specialised in psychological profiling, that her recommendations helped decide whether a prisoner was released early or banished to solitary confinement. Perhaps she is an expert on the criminal mind, able to predict who will re-offend, who will be a danger to society. I shiver at the thought. I could never take responsibility for someone else's life in that way. Performing surgery is so different. You do it because it needs to be done, because the physical evidence of scans, X-rays and blood tests deem it advisable. You can see the problem before you and decide best how to solve it. Yet in Clare's world everything is hidden. Her own mind takes the place of any physical test.

I step off the bus and follow the other visitors as they file through the steel grey door. I feel like an old hand as I check in my possessions at reception and offer the things I will take 'inside' with me, the gifts I have brought for Frank, to be approved. This time I pay less heed to the surroundings and the other prisoners.

Frank is glad to see me. You never know, he tells me, when you meet a prison visitor for the first time, whether they will actually come back. However polite and friendly they are at that first meeting, some are just too overwhelmed by the whole prison scenario to return. Some wrestle with uncertainty and come a second time just to make sure. It is the third visit that qualifies a visitor as a regular. And I am promoted to that dizzy height today. Frank tells me about the 'one-timers' and the 'two-timers', as he calls them. He leans across the table to whisper conspiratorially, 'I just hope none of them ever find themselves banged up for real,' he laughs. 'Because really I can't see how they'd survive it!'

I find myself momentarily thinking about my own situation and wonder how I would cope. The thought scares me so much that I shudder. I force it to the back of my mind and focus on Frank. I give him the chocolate and cigarettes for which he is grateful – he doesn't smoke himself but it seems that tobacco is a sort of currency in here and can be exchanged for other commodities.

We exchange the polite enquiries and replies regarding one another's health and general wellbeing that could be part of any conversation, anywhere. I comment on the weather, though it occurs to me afterwards that it may have little relevance in here. And all the time I feel that same familiarity that happened on the previous meetings, an invisible bond linking Frank and myself. If anything it is more intense than before. At first I am aware that I am watching, listening for a sign, an indication that he feels the same. But after a while, when he makes no such acknowledgement, I begin to relax. I adopt an attitude of acceptance. Just because I am sensitive to these things there is no reason that Frank should be too. The thing he said about seeing me again on the first visit may have been a misunderstanding on my part.

I chat to him more openly now. I have already told him more about myself on the previous visit. I have told him that

I am married – happily so, I qualified this to signify that I am a friend; that my feelings will go no further. I have told him that Richard and I are both doctors, that we each love our jobs and one other. I have told him that I am currently taking some time off work. A sabbatical is how I describe it. I have not yet told him about Jamie. I must talk to Lizzie sometime to ask whether this would be appropriate. I am not comfortable censoring my conversations; I seem to do that so much recently. Equally, Frank has not told me about his life before prison. He has not mentioned his wife or the circumstances of her death. And really, I don't think I want him to.

I focus on him, shutting out the other conversations going on around us. On previous occasions I have felt distracted by the environment. I have found that, when I think about it later at home, I cannot recall precisely the manner of Frank's speech or the details of the way he looks. Today, as we chat, I listen to the faint accent that surely originates from somewhere further north. I try to memorise his rather round face, his balding head with the last remnants of greying hair, the way his brow wrinkles when he laughs or frowns. I notice his muscular limbs and hands. They are a workingman's hands, I think to myself. I wonder what jobs men do in prison these days. Presumably they no longer sew mailbags or pound rocks into aggregate. I've heard that some inmates even study for university degrees. It begins to feel natural, like two friends idling over coffee in a café. I talk about what books I am reading and about where I like to walk in the Peak District. Frank tells me he also likes the countryside. 'I like that too Maggie,' he says.

My heart misses a beat. Maggie. He says it so easily, so naturally that for a moment I barely notice. My mind does a double take and replays the words. I like it. I like the way it feels to be called by that name. It seems right, like that is how it is meant to be, how it has always been. 'What did you call me?' I whisper.

'Julia, I mean.' He corrects himself instantly. If there is any emotion then he hides it well. 'Sorry.' He smiles now. 'You'll be thinking I've got another lady friend,' he jokes.

I laugh nervously, wondering how to ask him whom he knows called Maggie. But then the bell rings to mark the end of visiting time and the moment is lost.

I travel home in a daze. All the time I am thinking about what Frank said. 'Maggie'. I replay it in my mind, over and over. Then I picture him talking to me and have him call me by my own name. 'Julia'. But that is just everyday, that is normal. It is the name 'Maggie' that stirs me, as though it reawakens some part of me that has been waiting, dormant, all these years, for this moment. It quivers inside me, like a child waiting to be born. It is something I am powerless to control, a separate being, gathering its own energy. It will grow and punch and kick until it is free.

Normally, I would browse around the town centre, take afternoon tea in a café, time my arrival home so that it coincides with Mrs Blackstock leaving. But today I am languishing so deep in my thoughts that I alight the bus and walk automatically and directly home.

'Doctor!'

'Mrs Blackstock!'

We are each so engrossed in our own worlds that as I step into the kitchen we jump simultaneously, startling one another into the present.

'I didn't hear you come in.' She resumes stirring the contents of the pan that bubbles optimistically on the Aga.

'I'm sorry,' I say, 'I'll go up to my study and leave you in peace.'

'There's no need to do that. Let me put the kettle on, you look like you could do with a cup of tea and I was about to have one myself. I've nearly finished here anyway.'

So I sit obediently at the table while Mrs Blackstock bustles around me, setting cups and saucers – she doesn't hold with mugs, she's told me on several occasions – and a plate of biscuits in readiness.

As we sip our tea I think again about Frank calling me Maggie. How I wish I could talk to someone about it. It occurs to me how easy it would be to tell Mrs Blackstock about this afternoon, about everything. It would be an unburdening, a confessional, knowing my words would go no further. But it wouldn't be right.

Really, I wish that I could talk to Richard, about my past lives, about Frank, about Jamie, about everything. We have not always been so far apart. We met in our second year of medical school, that is to say, that was when we first became friends. Of course we saw one another before that, in lectures and in the common room, but the first year was a jumble of new experiences – for me at least – it wasn't the right time to settle down with one particular friend. When Richard and I met we shared the most important thing in our lives, the desire to heal others. And, from the start, that superseded everything else in our relationship.

Richard was traditionally handsome – tall, dark hair, slightly rugged looks – the way Hollywood says a leading man should be. I felt flattered that he chose to spend his time with me when there were so many beautiful, intelligent students to choose from. Of course, when we talked about our backgrounds, our homes, it was evident that our experiences of growing up were different. Yet, if anything, these discrepancies heightened our attraction, they gave us something to converse about, comparing our childhoods. And even though our material worlds were different, we shared an important emotional bond in that we were both only children; we understood one another in a deep and profound way.

Richard was more widely experienced than me, both socially and geographically. I had only been to London two or three times before, to see the Tower and Buckingham Palace and to look in the shops in Oxford Street. But to

Richard it was a playground. At the weekends he took me to the museums, to see the skeleton of 'Lucy' the little australopithecine from millions of years ago, and Lindow Man, young by comparison, preserved in a peat bog. How strange they seemed, after our anatomy classes. I wondered what they had looked like in life. Then, in the evenings, we might go to the ballet or the opera. Richard knew to book tickets in the front row of the Dress Circle, the best view in the house. And so, within the privileged and protected world of the university and the medical school, our relationship matured and flourished.

Richard and I married when we had just finished our training and were embarking on our journey into the professional world. But just as we were taking our first steps down differing paths of medical specialties, Jamie came along. And he united us more firmly, more completely than anything else. In one world we travelled in different directions. And in another a tiny baby steered us along a common course.

I am not sure that Richard has ever been a communicative man though, in the past, his feelings were always clear. When he chose me from the dozens of young hopefuls and asked me to marry him there was nothing else he needed to say. But I suspect – though I am surmising here, for I've never seen him in action - that in his work he is happier in the anonymity of the operating theatre, working deftly and precisely, with music by Handel playing in the background, than he is in consultation, talking to patients and relatives. I suspect that he is more comfortable with his patients when they are asleep. I, on the other hand, relish the interaction; which is just as well, considering an increasing number of surgical procedures in my department are carried out with the patient at least partially, and often fully, awake.

Since Jamie died Richard and I have hardly spoken. Grief has robbed us of our conversation, left us with a meagre vocabulary. There are so many words that must not be said, lest they take on a truth, a finality that neither of us is yet ready to accept. There is so much that cannot be spoken that there is little left to say. I could blame Richard, say that it is he who hides from the truth, who goes upstairs, shuts the door of his study, shuts me out. But I am equally responsible. Instead of turning to one another for solace we have each retreated into our past, Richard to his parents, to his ancestral home, and me to my previous lives.

'Well I'll just put these in the dishwasher then I must be going,' Mrs Blackstock announces as she drinks the last of her second cup of tea. I pull myself back to the present and offer her a lift home but she insists that she will enjoy the walk, especially on such a fine afternoon.

When Richard arrives home I do something unheard of. I suggest that we might go out for dinner. Unfortunately, it turns out that he has a patient he is concerned about. He has promised he will stay in, be unofficially on call. Indeed, he will call the hospital himself before going to bed. He is worried that he has let me down but I assure him, no, I am more than happy to stay in. We agree that we will eat the meal Mrs Blackstock prepared earlier so I do not have to cook. Afterwards we relax in the drawing room and listen to some CDs which Richard bought recently. There is a fiery performance of Berlioz' Symphonie Fantastique and a moving rendition of Elgar's Cello Concerto. Richard limits himself to one glass of wine in case he has to return to the hospital but he urges me to have a second. It occurs to me later, as I undress, that the evening is almost normal.

Eventually we go to bed. Richard has called his registrar and been assured that all is well. It seems he can relax once more. We are each propped up on our pillows, each reading a book. Richard's is something technical, something work related, mine is a novel, the same one I took with me to Somerset. My eyes scan the words, perhaps some part of my brain reads them, but my conscious mind does not process what they say. Instead, it is roaming around the events of the past few days, the past few hours. The comparatively small amount of wine has loosened my mind. My thoughts spin round in circles like a dog chasing its tail, the resolution always just out of reach. I think of Frank and my visit earlier today. That leads me to Clare, when she worked in a prison, and this in turn brings me to the uncomfortable conversation I had with her on Tuesday; the one about Richard. I think again about what Clare said and why it upset me so much. Perhaps it is because she is right. She is an expert on these things after all. Yet, what can she know that I don't when she has never even been married? I dismiss the subject from my mind and reread the paragraph I've been looking at for ten minutes. Then I think again about visiting Frank; and about how I deliberately avoided mentioning this to Richard and Clare on Tuesday. I feel as though I am being unfaithful. Which brings me back again to Clare, and what she said.

I take a deep breath. 'Clare says we should make love.' There. I have said it. Strange that the suggestion should be so remarkable, as though we are teenagers who have never touched, rather than a middle-aged married couple who have shared the same bed for more than twenty-five years and long since produced a child. But my voice is foreign to me. It is without emotion. I know, after they are spoken, that the words are more a challenge than an invitation.

Richard puts down his book, marking the page before setting it neatly on the bedside cabinet beside the clock and his pager. It is something technical involving the intricacies of medical physics. It describes microscopic, mechanical ways of keeping the heart pumping.

He stares at me, betrayed. 'So now you're discussing our sex life with your friends.'

'Of course not!' I protest. Well, I hadn't intended to, I reason with myself. But Clare caught me off guard, asking me outright whether Richard and I were still having sex, in the same way that we doctors inquire whether a patient has been taking their medication. I try to reassure him. 'Clare was just speaking generally about couples who've had a...' I pause, searching for a word that is not emotive, not forbidden. '...a trauma. She said that often they don't make love any more because they would feel guilty about anything that gave them pleasure. But she said that we – they – should. She said it would be a comfort.'

Richard does not reply, just lies there silently looking at me. I wish I'd never spoken. It isn't as though I want this, I'm thinking of him. His needs. His fidelity. I am about to turn out the light when suddenly he grabs my shoulder and draws me to him. He doesn't caress me, doesn't kiss me even, just reaches between my legs as he rolls on top of me. He is as mechanical as one of his false hearts.

'Sorry,' he mumbles, minutes later, 'I've had a long day at work, maybe another time.'

I want to hold his hand, reassure him, whisper that it doesn't matter, that sometime in the future things will be right. But instead I turn my back to him and clasp the duvet to my breastbone. Secretly, I am relieved.

I wake when Richard wakes. I feel the movement of the mattress as he gets up. I hear his footsteps as he pads into the bathroom, water splashing as he showers, the hum of his razor as he shaves. But I pretend to sleep. Only when I have heard the definitive click of the front door do I contemplate getting up. I sit up in bed and listen to the whirr as the car engine starts and to the gentle rise of its pitch as it accelerates down the road.

How I wish I'd had the confidence to trust my instinct rather than listen to Clare. For practical advice on overcoming a phobia or dealing with lifestyle changes she is brilliant. But what can she possibly know about married love? How can a woman whose longest relationship has lasted barely six months be qualified to advise a long-term married couple? When did we last have sex? What a

100

question. How often does she think middle-aged couples have sex – even in ideal circumstances? I suspect most people exaggerate these things in any case. If she's basing her idea of what is normal on what her patients tell her then I doubt she has a realistic picture. For Richard and me, the physical side of our relationship reached a crescendo during the first few years of our marriage. Of course, Jamie's arrival created something of a hiatus. It is not just the practical aspect before and after the birth, or the fatigue in the following months. It is now widely believed that the act of nurturing a young child can provide a woman with more gratification, of a profound sexual nature, than the attentions of any man. For me too, it was not just the birth itself from which I had to heal but also the accompanying surgery. Of course I did eventually recover and Jamie grew and flourished and became self-sufficient enough to sleep in his own room. At that point there occurred what might be termed a second honeymoon period. After that, it was not so much that our lovemaking dwindled, but rather that it was superseded by other gestures and emotions. By the time we reached our forties it had all but been replaced by the affectionate touches that characterise adolescence. If I tried to tell Clare this she would regard it as a loss. How can someone addicted to the thrill of sex with a new partner appreciate the emotional richness that the mere touching of hands can bring in a mature relationship? But I cannot blame her for what happened. It was my choice after all.

I am glad that this is not one of Mrs Blackstock's days. After I have made a pot of coffee I take a bath rather than a shower. I feel the need to immerse myself completely, to fully wash away the failure of the night before. Not any physical inadequacy on Richard's part but my own inability to read the situation, to communicate. I lie there for a full half hour, until I find myself shivering in the tepid water, until the bubbles from the bath foam have reduced to oily patches on the surface.

Chapter 12

I feel nervous as I pull over by the side of the road. I look at my watch then I take my reading glasses out of my bag and check the address for the third time. It is quite an ordinary house, semi-detached, bricks stained dark with the by-products of coal and steelworking. There is no plaque to announce that the occupant practices anything more than housewifely drudgery. Although the street name and house number match what is written on the card, I am still not convinced. Nonetheless I park the car and walk the few yards to the front door.

I ring the bell and wait. After a few moments I am worrying that I have got it wrong, that perhaps I should have gone round the back, that maybe I have the wrong house entirely when, all at once, the door opens. A striking woman stands on the threshold of a very different world.

'I'm Rose,' she says. 'And you must be Julia. Come in.'

I hesitate. She is ethereal, Titania, welcoming me into her fairy kingdom. I am a mere mortal, out of place. But it would be rude to turn away now. So I step tentatively into the hallway, scared that I will break the magic spell.

'Come through to the lounge.' Rose ushers the way.

I creep past bronze-framed mirrors and pictures of strange fantastical lands. On glass shelves, tiny figurines seem to float on the air. There are cross-legged Buddhas and angels with gleaming wings. There are unicorns spun out of coloured glass and a figure with the body of a man and the head of an elephant that I already know, from an Asian work colleague, is the Hindu god, Ganesha. Wind chimes and tiny cup-like bells ring as I go by. A black cat rubs against my legs and, although I adore pets and would dearly love to have a cat myself, I would willingly believe, in this instance, that Rose is a witch, a high priestess, and this seemingly innocent pet is her familiar.

I stoop to stroke the cat while Rose glides in front of me, leading the way. She is serene. A sense of calm radiates from her and I feel safe and protected in her presence, like a child does with its mother. Even her footsteps are soft. She moves gracefully, noiselessly down the hallway and I feel clumsy in her wake.

The room into which she leads me is gentle yet exciting. It bathes my senses. Soft drapes in semi-opaque fabrics soften the windows. On the chairs and sofas there are throws made of patchwork, shapes of silk and velvet in purple and green and bright pink, the colour of fuchsias. Here and there, cloths are woven with sparkling golden threads and decorated with fringes and huge sequins that glow like moons in the night sky.

Rose sees me looking and laughs. 'I love colour and texture,' she explains. Then she smiles mischievously, 'And I don't want my clients to feel like they are visiting a psychiatrist or a dentist!'

I laugh too. It breaks the ice. Rose continues to giggle. Her laugh is light and refreshing, it reminds me of springtime. She shakes her head and her hair sparkles as it catches the light. Rose has a cascade of golden hair. It trails down her back in an explosion of corkscrew curls and makes her look like an artist, or an artist's model. I could imagine her immortalised by Titian or Klimt. She wears a dress of cornflower blue and its colour resonates where it meets the gold of her hair. The neckline plunges in a deep 'V' with a blue polished stone, on a silver chain, resting between her breasts. There is something about her presence that is charismatic. She will always stand out in a crowd.

I explore the details of the room. Tea lights burn in saucers, glittering crystals of semi-precious stones sparkle on silken mats. Rose gives me some to hold and tells me their names: aventurine, sodalite, lapis lazuli. Each has a special property. Each vibrates at a precise frequency, which, in turn, corresponds to a different part of the body. Many people used to find this hard to comprehend, yet now quantum physics tells us that, at some almost infinitesimally small level, so tiny that even the most powerful microscope cannot reveal it, all matter is energy. Science may one day substantiate what healers have known for centuries. I am fascinated by this interpretation. The words 'quantum physics' ring a bell of familiarity. Inwardly, I promise myself that I will try harder to understand these elusive subjects. As a doctor I have been more concerned with chemistry, with cause and effect and remedy. She places a pink semi-opaque stone in my palm. 'This is rose quartz,' she tells me. 'As you hold it, it absorbs your negative emotions. After a while, when it is full of negativity, the surface goes cloudy.'

'That's a shame,' I say, 'it's so pretty.' But Rose assures me that one has only to bathe the crystal in salty water and its brilliance is restored. This seems a little far-fetched to me. My scientific mind is already calculating how one's sweat may coat the surface, perhaps even initiate a chemical reaction with the outer layer. Rose senses my doubt. I don't want to appear a sceptic before we have even started. I strive to change the subject.

'What is the perfume?' I ask. It is an exotic spicy smell, sweet and penetrating, noticeable as soon as I entered the house. I sniff the air thinking that it is familiar. It reminds me of a wedding Richard and I went to once, university friends, a Roman Catholic couple. I remember smelling this, or something like it, in the church.

'It's frankincense,' Rose says, as I twitch my nostrils involuntarily. 'It's long been used as a spiritual purifier. It will cleanse the room of anything that has gone before and ensure that your experience is pure.' She looks at me searchingly. 'Did you tell me your profession?'

'I work in a hospital,' I tell her, almost apologetically. 'As a doctor.'

'Ah!' It is Rose's turn to nod, to breathe out laughter that ripples and sparkles like flowing water. 'You must find some of this difficult to understand. It goes against everything you have been taught.'

'No, no!' I say. I don't want Rose to think I have come here to test her, to catch her out. I shrug. 'I'd already formed my own opinions on many things before I went to medical school,' I say, and to back this up, 'I already knew I'd lived before.'

Rose seems satisfied with this. She waits silently for a few more moments while I look around me, then, when I have taken in my fill of the surroundings, she gestures to me to sit down. I choose the sofa, lowering myself carefully onto the soft upholstery and setting my bag on the floor beside me.

'I usually spend some time getting to know my clients,' Rose begins. 'It helps if you tell me a bit about yourself, what you do now, things you've done in the past, what you would like to try in the future; and most of all what you're hoping to achieve by coming here. After that, if you feel comfortable with it, we could make a start and do a short regression.' I notice that Rose speaks with barely a trace of the local accent. There is the familiar lilt to her voice but none of the vernacular. She is well educated, I suspect, perhaps she has travelled widely or attended college or university outside the area.

At Rose's invitation I make myself comfortable, kicking my shoes off and tucking my feet up beside me on the sofa. Rose sits in a more upright chair a few feet away. She holds a pen and a note pad, the top sheet of which I can see is already covered with small flowing handwriting. I begin to chat, to talk about myself. I find myself readily smiling too. The room is a sanctuary where I am allowed, if not to be happy, at least to feel some contentment.

'And what about the other people you meet?' I ask, as Rose fills the paper with elegant notes. 'Do many people talk to you about their past lives? Do they have similar experiences to me?'

Her clients have different beliefs, different reasons for

consulting her, Rose tells me. Some believe they are recalling the lives of others, some feel they have lived each life themselves and some buy fully into the whole concept of karma and reincarnation.

Rose explains that we may have many memories of the past. There are different theories about where they come from. Cynics would have us believe that they all originate in this life, she tells me. That they are an accumulation of information we have witnessed and seemingly forgotten, perhaps not consciously experienced at all. This might happen when we are very young or when we doze in front of the television. Certainly this rational explanation accounts for some memories perceived as past lives, but definitely not all. Then there is the possibility of inherited memories from ancestors, the suggestion that, for example, the girl I see at Kimberley Place might be a great-great-grandparent, that elements of her life may have been passed on to me in my DNA. This started out as a controversial idea, apparently, but with increasing research in genetic inheritance, the idea of receiving information in this way seems ever more likely. Again, Rose tells me, this might account for some but not all memories. Yet another theory is that of a cosmic consciousness, a shared system of thoughts existing between all people, alive or dead, telepathy without the limitations of time. In this way, Rose tells me, by hearing the thoughts of others, we may bear witness to their lives, their experiences, perhaps help right the wrongs of the past.

I nod and take in the information. It is overwhelming. There is so much more than the simple acceptance I have hitherto employed.

Rose continues. 'But the definition of a true past life is much more specific,' she says. 'In this case you inherit – or share, if you like – the same soul. This is the basis for concepts of karma, of a continued existence of which our present life is only a small part. Your behaviour in each incarnation – whether you live a good life – affects the situation, the fortune you are born with in the next. Our existence, here and now, is merely a stepping stone between our previous lives and those to come.'

I pause for a moment, thinking about what Rose is saying. Suddenly I feel small, insignificant.

Rose smiles. 'Try not to feel too daunted by it all,' she reassures me. 'You may live other lives as other people but you only live this life once. That's what you should remember. That's what you should concentrate on now. The memories you may have of a past life should not be seen as ghosts, haunting you with past mistakes, rather you should use them as an insight, allow the knowledge you gained then to help you now. Look around you,' she continues, 'concentrate on the colours, the textures, the sounds and the smells. Think about how the fabric of your clothes feels against your skin. This is called grounding. It brings you back to where you are now.'

I do as she says. I smell the sweetness of the frankincense and stroke the silky surface of a cushion with my fingertip. She is right. It makes me feel secure. 'So why do most people consult you?' I ask.

Rose runs her fingers through her hair, shakes it into life. It shimmers like a waterfall in the sunlight. 'About past lives you mean? Some have a block in this life, a phobia maybe, or an undiagnosed chronic pain. If we can trace that to a memory, be it a past life or some psychic connection, then usually we can resolve the cause and heal the problem now. Some have a specific question, something in a recurring dream perhaps or just a feeling connected to a place or a person. And others are simply curious. They come here to experience a regression in much the same way they might watch a film, a very personal film of course.'

'And what do you believe?' I ask.

'I believe in healing,' she says.

I have a feeling of empathy. 'So do I,' I agree. 'So do I.'

Then Rose asks me to tell her of my own expectations and

experiences. I find that I am describing easily the things I have kept secret until now. It is a release to talk of Maggie and Freddie and of the girl on the swing and all the others I have encountered. I even speak about the nightmares in my childhood. But I do not tell her about Frank. I feel like I am setting a test, trying to catch her out. I feel bad about this. Yet I need to be certain that Rose will not inadvertently, innocently influence me. I need to know that anything I might experience on this subject comes entirely from my own mind. I almost give myself away though. 'Do you believe we can meet the same person in several lives?' I ask.

Rose looks at me intently. For a moment I think she will press me with questions but she does not. Instead she answers readily. 'Oh yes,' she says. 'It's generally thought that we meet the same people again and again in successive lives. We will have different relationships with them. In one life they might be a lover, in another a parent or a friend. There is also a theory – and don't worry if you find this concept a little confusing – that a soul may split into two halves, that two people in this life may inherit the soul of one person from a previous existence.'

I express surprise.

'It's such a huge subject to explore,' she says. 'I could recommend you some books if you're interested. Now, if you feel ready we could try a short regression.'

I find myself tingling with trepidation. Rose briefs me. She tells me the process she will use to regress me and to bring me back to the here and now. She reassures me that, whilst relaxed, I will retain my control and my free will. There is no danger, she says, that I will partake in a life or recount experiences unwillingly. She does warn me, though, that the memories retrieved are often traumatic. Therefore I may experience extremes of emotion as I revisit or witness events. But nothing can actually hurt me, she points out, and if she senses that I am distressed at any point she will bring me straight back to the present.

And so we begin. To my surprise Rose sets a small digital recorder on the table beside us. It feels somehow incongruous to incorporate modern technology into the secret world of the past. But Rose assures me that I will be glad of this record later. 'Sometimes,' she explains, 'we don't remember the details that happen under hypnosis. We are aware of them at the time but don't necessarily commit them to memory.'

'Like a dream?' I ask.

'Just like that,' she confirms. 'And in any case,' she tells me, 'many people like to have a physical reminder of what happened. They can play it back later in the privacy of their own homes; find that it does, indeed, have meaning for them.'

Rose tells me to lie back, to make myself comfortable. She drapes a light blanket over me because, she says, the body temperature may drop slightly, like it does during sleep or deep meditation.

I do as I am bid but I am scared that I will not be a good subject. I am fearful that I will embarrass myself by resisting the invitation to enter an altered state, another world; that I will remain fully conscious throughout the process. Yet, as I listen to Rose's voice, I find that I quite readily follow where she leads. I find myself gratefully closing my eyes, walking down a corridor into my past, travelling beyond the point where I was born. I peek behind several of the doors that line the route, see people who I do not recognise physically, yet on an intuitive level, know intimately. One day, perhaps, I will visit again and meet them properly. But this time, there is one particular door I am searching for. And when I reach it I know instinctively that it is the one, even before I push it fully open.

Freddie and I are strolling down the shopping street. It's full of noise. Not the screech of gulls or the crashing of waves but human noise, the hustle and bustle of carts, people's voices

110

calling greetings, bartering prices. Freddie is bigger than me now, stronger too I don't doubt. I look at him, with his bare arms, sleeves rolled up, braces cutting across his back, making him appear broader. There's the beginnings of the muscles he'll need when he's hauling nets full of silver wriggling fish into his boat. I'm changing too, in a way that rather pleases me. Freddie is a few steps ahead of me. I watch him out of the corner of my eye as he slides an apple into his pocket when the shopkeeper isn't looking. I dawdle where I am so as not to attract attention. Another apple disappears and Freddie shoves his hands in his pockets so you can't tell. In the meantime I catch sight of my reflection in a shop window. I pause, standing this way and that, admiring myself. My hair spills in tousled ringlets. I imagine, if my mother were to twist it in rags overnight and then tie a ribbon in it after it was brushed, I could look quite fine, quite a lady. I pull the neckline of my dress so that it exposes a shoulder, pretend it is a ball gown, then I stoop down so the hem brushes the ground, stand straight again to show my ankles. Really, I tell myself, I am getting quite grown up. In another year or two I might be old enough to have a gentleman friend. I wonder whether this friend will be Freddie.

'C'mon Maggie!' His shout pulls me out of my daydreaming. I wrinkle my nose, stick my tongue out at my reflection and run off after him towards the beach.

We scamper down to the seafront, Freddie in front, me always a few steps behind. We both call 'Mornin'' to Benji, who's lifting a crate of fish off a boat down at the harbour. Benji's a couple of years older than the Freddie. He already goes out with the boats and earns enough for a tankard of ale at the end of the day.

All of this time, all the while that I am preening myself, skipping along, I am aware of a voice. It's in my head. I know that. It isn't like it's a real person or anything, and not like I'm imagining things either. It's a soft voice, gentle, a girl's voice. It's like I'm having a conversation with myself, like I'm thinking out loud.

'Where do you live, Maggie?' she asks.

'Why, in the town of course,' I say. 'An' you should know that if you're me,' I feel like adding – but don't.

'And how old are you?'

''Bout thirteen I reckon.'

It's like when you're thinking ahead. Planning what you'll say and do before it happens. I could tell her to go away if I wanted. But it feels quite nice really, like she's a friend. And as I jump down onto the shingle I almost forget that she's there.

Freddie climbs onto a huge boulder, takes out the apples, juggles with them like he's in a circus. 'Come on then!' he shouts.

I climb up after him, picking my way over strange white spirals that decorate the rock.

'What's keepin' yer?' he asks.

'I don't want to tread on the fossers,' I reply.

He laughs. 'There's plenty more of 'em.'

'Maybe,' I say. 'But the vicar says that they're amnites an' they're special.'

'What? Yer mean like angels or something?' He catches the apples, looking puzzled.

'Dunno,' I admit. 'Give us an apple then.'

The tide is way out, almost on the turn. I look out to sea as I bite into my apple – a sweet dewy one today, last time Freddie grabbed cookers by mistake and they made our mouths hurt and our eyes water; we still ate them though. Today the sea looks innocent, like you could swim right out and come to no harm. I know it's pretending though. That's what it does when it's hungry, my Grandma says; acts like it wants to be your friend when really, underneath, it's treacherous. People can be like that too, she says. I look at Freddie, pitching his apple core away into the shingle and tugging down his shirt sleeve to wipe his mouth. I wonder if he could be treacherous. Somehow I don't think so.

There's that voice in my head again, counting. The beach is growing hazy, rushing away from me, like it's being blown by a ferocious wind.

'Wide awake!'

I blink.

'Wide awake,' Rose is saying.

I rub my eyes. I stretch out on the sofa and wriggle life into sleepy limbs. I feel heavy. As though I have fallen asleep in front of the television after a long hike, as though I have not slept enough.

'How do you feel?' Rose asks.

'Exhausted,' I reply.

She laughs. 'That's perfectly normal,' she assures me.

I thought that I would feel refreshed, relieved, light. But Rose tells me that it is hard work, all that thinking, that my subconscious mind has been very busy. She checks that I feel all right to be left alone then goes off to make us both a pot of tea.

Chapter 13

The next day I decide to drive out into the Peak District, to go walking. It has occurred to me, since I mentioned it to Frank two days ago - and indeed, my thoughts keep drifting back to that moment because that was when he called me 'Maggie' - that although I described to him how much I enjoyed it, getting out into the countryside is something I have not done for some time. Not since Jamie died, in fact. The truth is that, until now, I have been scared of the space, the isolation, the danger that, when on my own, I may drift into those desolate and forbidden areas of my mind in which I fear I could be lost forever. But despite the fiasco of Thursday night I feel happier with myself, no longer so scared to be alone with my thoughts. Whether this is due to the healing that I am promised time will bring or whether I simply have more things to occupy my mind I am not sure. What I do know is that I feel claustrophobic in the house, the city. I need to get out into the greenness of the outdoors. In the cloakroom I stow a waterproof and thick woollen hat, scarf and gloves into a small backpack. Then I put on a snug fleece jacket and rummage on the shoe rack for my walking boots.

In the car I switch the radio on and head north out of the city. Although I drive within a mile of Kimberley Place, I don't feel tempted to take a detour. Instead, I turn onto the A610 and then north onto the motorway. I feel exhilarated by the movement of the car. I would like to go faster, to feel the rush of freedom, but I don't need any more problems right now so I travel at a steady seventy. In half an hour I reach the Chesterfield junction. I turn off, past the crippled spire of the church and head out towards the national park. Luckily, it is a fine day. I have learned, since I moved to Nottingham, that good weather must be taken advantage of rather than taken for granted. Autumn and winter come sooner here than they do in Somerset. They sneak up, reaching with chilly fingers through the grey polluted air, and steal away the last days of summer.

I park near Grindleford station, where, occasionally, trains still pause on their way from Sheffield to Manchester. I pull on my woolly accessories and exchange my shoes for bulky socks and boots. I don't take a map. I have walked here many times before. Although there are several dozen cars there are few people about. It is possible that one or two locals have taken the train into Sheffield to browse around the modern Americanised shopping centres. Rock climbers will be uncoiling their ropes and grappling their way up Millstone Edge. Walkers, like myself, have already dispersed onto the numerous pathways and camouflaged themselves into the landscape. The sun struggles to warm the air as I set off at a brisk pace and think about my first venture into hypnosis.

When I left Rose yesterday afternoon, part of me wanted to share my experience right away. I pondered the possibility of idling away the time in the library or a café until Sally arrived home from work, of waiting on her doorstep to greet her. But, besides that time being a full two hours away, I knew it would not be fair to impose, unannounced, when she was tired after a long day. I knew too that Richard was likely to be home at the same time, to wonder where I was. Yet I do not think it was either of these considerations that make me go directly home. It was the fact that, for the greater part, the lingering memory of my life – Maggie's life – gleaned from the regression, was something I wanted to keep secretly to myself, for the time being anyway. It was like the first sign of a pregnancy, something to be treasured and nurtured until it has grown strong enough, secure enough, to withstand the scrutiny, the judgment of others.

I wanted to relive Maggie's life, to indulge in it, to reach back into her thoughts while they still hovered in my mind. So, when I arrived home, I went directly to my study. I switched on the halogen heater to supplement the efforts of the central heating then I popped the CD Rose had given me

– the one she'd recorded while I was under hypnosis - into the player, lay back on the sofa and closed my eyes.

I listened to my voice – Maggie's voice – as she described herself, as she described Freddie. I pictured the beach, the cliffs and the town where she lived. I played with the scene, as though I were adjusting the picture on the television. I tried to make the colours brighter, the objects more defined. I tried to get a closer more detailed look at Freddie – at Frank. Yet, the harder I tried, the more that life seemed to slip hazily out of reach. It was as though someone, something else (Maggie perhaps?) was in control of the process and I was merely a passive observer.

At some point, when I returned to the here and now and went down to the kitchen to make coffee, I noticed that there was a phone message from Richard, left earlier that afternoon. He informed me that he would be dining with a colleague, that they had work matters to discuss, that he would be home late. I would already be asleep, he suspected. I was relieved not to have to make conversation with him that evening and also glad of the space to myself. This morning he announced that he would be visiting his parents. It was not up for discussion. Together with his late night out, it was his way of avoiding me after the embarrassment of Thursday night, his way of avoiding the issue. When I said that I would like some time at home after travelling the previous weekend he didn't attempt to change my mind. He could just go for the day, he said. He could get back tonight. But I knew that, even if he were not trying to stay away from me, he would want to relax, to share a few glasses of port with his father, discuss the latest technological advances in cardiothoracic medicine. Maybe smoke a cigar or two – for some reason, in Richard's family, cigars have always been considered exempt from the evils of other forms of tobacco. So I assured him that I would be fine, encouraged him to stay the night, to make the most of his break.

I'm warming up now. I have always loved the act of

walking. I love the way you can settle into a rhythm, just like swimming. I love the way, with each footstep, you can decide whether to go fast or slow, whether to take this path or that one. A thousand parallel worlds could be born as the result of just a short stroll. As a child, I used to walk with my father, in the days when he could breathe easily, before the coal dust tightened his lungs. Together we would explore Somerset and the Mendip hills. He would tell me tales of witches in the caves of Cheddar Gorge, and of the circle at Stanton Drew where people had been turned to stone for dancing on the Sabbath.

But today I walk alone. I cross the railway bridge and go through the gate into Padley Gorge. It is an enchanted forest, a world of perpetual twilight, with paths twisting between gnarled trees, climbing over sinewy roots, dipping into trickling streams. I've read history books about it. They say this is what the whole country would have been like, thousands of years ago when people first came here to farm. Down to the left the river hurries by, cutting a ravine through the valley. In the summer, children in bathing costumes splash through the white water, pretending they are explorers, forging a route through a treacherous canyon. Now, as autumn turns to winter, here and there the light sneaks in, a silent intruder. It trickles, golden, past sunburned leaves, sketching speckled shadows beneath the canopy.

I hesitate for a moment. I'm leaving the car behind now, the café, the people. Despite my confidence of earlier, I question whether I am ready to do this. I could compromise maybe, give myself half an hour then go back to the café for coffee and a sandwich, set out again in another direction, perhaps explore the ruined masonry of Padley Manor before returning again to my base, never venturing far each time, always safely near to habitation.

Earlier, when I was getting ready to leave, I feared that, when it came to it, I might feel this way. I asked Sally if she wanted to come with me when I spoke to her on the phone this morning. It was the first time we'd talked since my appointment with Rose. Sally was really excited when I told her about the hypnosis. 'You must come over and tell us all about it,' she said. 'Are you free this evening? Come to tea, I'll invite Debbie, she'll want to hear about it too.' Having agreed that I'd go round later, I tentatively asked if she wanted to come out for a walk first. But she was apologetic. 'We've got some family business we need to sort out,' she said. I didn't press her. After all, if Richard and I had paid more attention to our family, things might have turned out differently.

I harden myself. I have to learn to control my thoughts. Clare says that, to a large extent, our thoughts are determined by habit. That we think in a certain way simply because we have become accustomed to doing so. That we can relearn the words we speak inside our heads, the ones that encourage us on or instil fear. We cannot always prevent bad things from happening but we can change the way we interpret the world, the way we perceive it. I tell myself, determinedly, that I will enjoy the freedom of this adventure. And in any case, to turn back now would be to fail. I decide to make my way down towards a point on the river where I know there is a wooden footbridge. The ground is slippery underfoot with a mulch of fallen leaves. I must concentrate and pick my way carefully.

I first came here with Richard. Jamie was just a baby and Richard carried him on his back in one of those child carriers. We had plans, in those days, to get out each weekend, to explore different areas of the national park. It worked quite well when Jamie was small and not too heavy for Richard to carry. Then there was a lull where we favoured flat grassy picnic spots with gravelled or tarmac paths suitable for a pushchair. As Jamie grew enough to walk a reasonable distance unaided there always seemed to be other activities competing for our time. Jamie had a party to go to or Richard had to work or was invited to play golf. Increasingly, when

Jamie did come out with us he did so under protest. It was all right if one of his friends came along. On those occasions the two of them would play together all day, climbing onto rocky outcrops - this always scared me - or building dams across streams. But, on his own, Jamie would soon grow bored with the countryside and clamour to be taken to places that sold ice creams and had 'rides'.

There is one certainty about having children. Nothing turns out as you imagine.

For a moment I fight back the tears. I stumble blindly through the gloom. I remind myself to have faith, to have belief. Suddenly the trees end and there is bright sky ahead.

I cross the sunny open grassland of Lawrence Field and head towards the rocky outcrop of Mother Cap. But I do not climb up to it. Instead, I bear right as I cross the road and pick my way through a marshy patch where I am glad of my boots. Above me the flat-topped fort of Carl Wark ignites in fiery orange as the withered bracken catches the sunlight. I climb the path that leads up through the curved stone entrance into the fort itself. I don't pause but continue up the steep rocky path onto Higger Tor. This is where I stop and sit on a rock, overlooking the walled fort below and the valley beyond.

From here I can see for a long way. I can see the whole picture. I can see the desolate, high, peat-soaked plateaux, which were once covered in lush vegetation; where hunter-gatherers fired flint-headed arrows at unwary deer. I can see the uplands, with their the stony platforms where prehistoric houses stood, where there are Roman walls and Iron Age hill forts and millstones carved out of the rock then left discarded on the hillside as they were superseded by Sheffield steel. This is a land of stone. There are stones in circles, stones that form burial chambers, stones carved with mysterious symbols. They have survived all these millennia yet, after just a few years in our acidic, chemical-laden twenty-first century atmosphere, they begin to erode. The patterns disappear as they dissolve into the air. And now the stone is put to a different purpose as, somewhere in the distance, today's adventurers are hauling their way up the rocky wall of Stanage Edge.

From here I can see it all, everything existing together. Just as I can see all these times in our history overlapping in a complex palimpsest, I can see my own lives – all of them – dotted about the landscape, blending together, affecting one another, impacting on me now.

The wind grows chill and shots of cold penetrate my fleece and taunt my skin. I stand and pause for one last look. Then I anticipate the lure of the café that occupies the former railway station back near my car. I set off at a brisk pace. I'll need to get a move on if I'm to get there before it closes.

It is dark as I drive into Ilkeston. The dirt and neglect that masquerade as progress disappear into the night. As I pull up outside Pete and Sally's house I could be in any suburb of any town.

'Come in!' Sally smiles as she holds the door open. 'Sit down,' she instructs me, in a motherly way. 'I'll put the kettle on.' She shuts the back door behind me as I step into the kitchen. Pete and Sally always use their back door rather than the front. They tell me everyone does around here, even if it means going down a dark tunnel between the houses – which they call an entry – and through several neighbouring back gardens to get there.

'That's better,' she declares, five minutes later, as we warm our hands around our mugs of tea.

In the kitchen the two of us sit on opposite sides of a rather old and battered pine table. Next to my mug, Debbie's name is scratched into the wood in crude angular writing, Sally tells me her daughter did this when she was ten and received a severe telling off for it. In our house this would be viewed as unacceptable damage and Richard would have the furniture replaced. But here I love the way the wear and tear tells the story of their lives. I love the chip on the windowsill where Nicola once leant her bicycle. I love the lines drawn alongside the doorframe, measuring the two girls' growth over the years. I regret that there is no such evidence of Jamie in my home. Of course there are formal posed photographs and a couple of trophies and certificates that he won for sport. But there is nothing to show that we once had a young boy who played and laughed and enjoyed life.

I take a long gulp of tea. I only accepted it to be polite, having consumed a large mug-full at the café an hour previously along with a generous slab of fruit cake, but I find that I am surprisingly thirsty, hungry too come to that.

I ask whether they have sorted out their family crisis.

Sally laughs. 'Ah, that. Would you believe Nicola had some silly notion about dropping out of college? Said she couldn't afford it. I think it's the fact that some of her school friends are earning quite a bit now, with full time jobs. She goes out with them and they're wearing all the latest fashions and driving their own cars and everything.'

Sally goes on to talk about Nicola. She is their younger daughter. She is studying for a degree at the university in Derby. But I don't hear it. I'm thinking about Jamie.

It wasn't until he died that we found out. He'd been doing so well, or so we thought. He had graduated from medical school – we knew that because we went to the degree ceremony - and started his rotations. It must have been soon after that things started to go wrong. Training as a doctor doesn't end when you finish university. It carries on for several years - many years, if you study surgery. Not only do junior doctors have to work long hours, not only do they have to do most of the on-call shifts, getting constantly woken in the night, they also have to study for regular exams. Everyone knows it is like this. You have to have tremendous stamina and commitment to what you are doing. You have to really want it.

For the first six months we had regular reports because

Richard had a friend who was a consultant at the hospital where Jamie was based. After that Jamie told us he was doing rotations at other hospitals, spending time in each of a variety of departments or specialties. We thought he was enjoying it, that he was continuing to do well. We didn't know that he was unhappy, that he'd failed some exams, that he'd dropped out of his placement a month or two afterwards. It wasn't as though we had the excuse of not knowing how tough it was. We'd been through all that ourselves. He still came home occasionally. We should have realised. But we didn't see the signs. Not for that or anything else.

'So I told her,' Sally is saying, 'I told her. Just one more year – less than that – and it's done.'

I pull myself back to the present and take another long gulp of tea, hoping I haven't missed anything important.

'Anyway,' Sally continues, 'Pete's promised to teach her to drive and to buy her a car when she's passed her test. I think that's what clinched it. Mind you, I don't think she realises what sort of car he has in mind!' She laughs and so do I.

I ask where Nicola is this evening.

'Gone round to a girl friend's,' Sally tells me, 'a university friend. There's a group of them going to get a pizza and watch DVDs. We could do that,' she suggests. 'Get a pizza that is. DVDs too if you like. Are you hungry?'

I admit that I am.

Suddenly there is a flurry of excited barking as Pete comes in with the dogs, having taken them on their constitutional walk round the block. Ben, a Jack Russell, and Polly, a spaniel, rush into the room. They flit backwards and forwards between Sally and myself, trying to jump up and lick our faces when we are not looking and slapping our legs with wagging tails. They are rescue dogs, lovingly nurtured by Sally and Pete, transformed from the terrified quivering animals they were when they arrived in this home to the happy confident pets they are today. I should offer to take them with me next time I go walking, I think to myself.

In the midst of the chaos the phone rings. Sally answers it while I make a fuss of the dogs and Pete takes his coat off.

'That was Debbie,' Sally explains after a few minutes conversation. 'She's tired after a busy day so she and Steve have decided to stay in.' She looks up, sees my concerned look. 'It's just work that's doing it,' she reassures me. 'She goes on maternity leave in a couple of weeks. She'll be better then.' She smiles at me and laughs. 'She says I'm to ask you everything about this Rose woman and being hypnotised. Perhaps we should order dinner first though. It's Saturday, it's bound to take a while. What do you think Pete? Julia and I fancy a pizza.'

Pete nods agreement and, with the phone still in her hand, Sally rings through with the order.

'Now,' Sally says, as she replaces the phone on the table, 'what about you and this hypnosis? Tell me all!'

'If this is women's talk I'm off to watch telly,' Pete says.

We laugh. So, with Ben falling asleep on my lap and the sound of talking and laughter drifting in from the television in the front room, I begin to describe my appointment with Rose. I tell Sally about the house, the smell of essential oils and the brightly coloured ornaments. I tell her what being hypnotised feels like, how I didn't even realise it was happening, yet, suddenly, I was aware of being in another time, another place, and readily telling Rose all about it. Suddenly I chastise myself. 'I should have brought the CD,' I say. And I tell Sally how I have a recording of the conversation, how I could not possibly have imagined it.

At this point she asks me to remind her of what happened in the dream I had down in Somerset. I reiterate this although the details are already fading into the distance. Then I tell her what I saw in the hypnosis. I can speak about this much more clearly having listened to it through several times.

When I finish, Sally is transfixed, excited almost. She looks at me searchingly. 'Tell me again,' she instructs me. 'Everything you can remember. Every detail about the seafront, the beach.'

I rake into my mind now. I describe the cliffs, the boulders with spiral patterns on and the harbour wall curving like a protective arm around the fishing boats.

'Was it like in The French Lieutenant's Woman?' she asks, when I stop.

'The what?'

'That film with Jeremy Irons and Meryl Streep, don't tell me you've never seen it?'

I shake my head. 'I don't think so. The title rings a bell, perhaps I've read the book, if there is one.'

'You need to see the film,' Sally insists. 'Come on, we've got it on video.'

In the lounge Sally searches for the video while Pete is banished to finish watching his game show on the portable in the bedroom.

'I feel awful disturbing Pete,' I protest. 'And we can't watch a whole film now surely.'

'Well we could,' Sally takes the video out of its box and slides it into the player. 'But we only need to see the opening sequence.' She presses 'play' and we sit back and watch.

It is ghostly to see my dream, my previous life coming back to haunt me. I sit entranced as I watch the images. Sure enough, there is the Cobb, hugging the fishing boats against the safety of the bay. There are the terraces of shingle huddled beneath the cliff. Although the filming is misty and moody, I know it is definitely the same place.

'Well?' Sally is impatient. 'Is that it? Is that the place in your dream?'

I nod, silently.

'Well I'll be blowed!' Sally is impressed. 'That's downright spooky! And you're sure you've never been there?'

'Quite sure,' I answer. 'Where is it?'

'Lyme Regis. It's in Dorset. Gosh! I thought everyone had

been there. Pete and I used to rent a caravan in the next bay several years running when the kids were little. They used to love hunting for fossils – that'd be the spirals on the rocks that you described, ammonites. I can't believe you've never been.'

'We used to holiday overseas,' I explain, 'Or on the Norfolk Broads.'

'Well!' Sally exclaims. She shakes her head in disbelief. I don't know whether she is more astonished that I have apparently recalled a past life or that I have never visited Lyme Regis.

We pause for a moment while I marvel at having seen my dream on film and Sally congratulates herself on solving a mystery.

The moment is interrupted by a knock at the back door. 'That'll be dinner,' Sally says, as she stands up. 'You call Pete while I pay for the pizza.'

We don't sit at the kitchen table but 'picnic' in the lounge with a television talent show for entertainment. And I love the decadence of it. Of course, I've had TV dinners on my own, especially during the past few months, but not with Richard – not since we were students anyway - and certainly never with guests. I like the fact that we have, not only pizza but garlic bread and even chips. 'Death by carbohydrate!' Sally says jokingly, as she assures me that they do eat healthily most of the time. There is something forbidden about our feast, as though we are naughty children, raiding the kitchen while our parents are out. We will probably have ice cream later. Pete drinks beer while Sally and I open a bottle of white wine. It is quite cheap, I suspect, not the sort of thing Richard would buy from his wine club by the case. But it is cold and refreshing. We do not stop to swirl it around the glass or inhale the bouquet. We do not even consider whether it is the right accompaniment to pizza and chips. But I enjoy it all the more for this. We plough, gluttonously, through most of the food before we come up for air and make an attempt at conversation.

I shake my head as Sally offers me another glass of wine, but she insists. 'Stay here the night,' she offers casually. 'The spare bed's made up. And after all, there's no point in driving back to an empty house.' So I agree. My welcome here helps to compensate for my lack of popularity at my in-laws'. I like the way my friends are easy-going, the way they don't stand on ceremony. I like the way that I feel part of their family.

At last, the television programme draws to an end. Pete presses the mute button as he vociferously disagrees with one of the television judges who has all but reduced a rather out-of-tune singer to tears. After expressing his solidarity with the poor woman he turns to Sally and me. 'What was all that stuff with the video earlier?' he asks.

'It's the place in Julia's dream,' Sally tells him. 'And she's been hypnotised now as well, she's seen it all again. I thought it sounded familiar the other day. Then, when she was describing it earlier, I just knew where it was.'

He looks up, eyebrows raised.

'It's Lyme Regis,' Sally announces triumphantly. 'I wanted to make sure before I said anything so I showed her that film – that French Lieutenant one with Meryl Streep - just to check.'

Pete laughs, he turns to me. 'You probably saw a clip of the film once – or someone sent you a postcard.'

'It's a bit more than that,' I say. Carefully I explain. This time I tell them everything. I tell them how things like this have happened before. I tell them about Kimberley Place and the girl on the swing. And, when they do not challenge me or say I am imagining it, I tell them the most important part of all. I explain how I feel certain that the boy Freddie, in my dream, is one and the same as Frank, the prisoner whom I visit.

They are silent for a few moments.

'Now you've really got me spooked,' Sally admits.

126

Pete is unconcerned. 'It isn't that I don't believe you,' he says, 'but I'm sure there's a logical explanation. And dreams are funny things, you can see the face of one person but know they're someone else, get your wires crossed, like. And, when you think about it, it isn't surprising that Frank bloke popped up – I mean, meeting him in prison is a pretty weird thing for you to do compared with the rest of your life isn't it?'

'Well, I think it's fascinating,' Sally defends me. 'Maybe there's something in it. Maybe we've all lived lives before and just can't remember.'

'But how many of those stories add up?' Pete is still unconvinced. 'From what you say, no-one ever proves any of this. It all seems a bit convenient to me. I mean, Debbie's scared of spiders, I bet you if she got hypnotised she'd come out with some story about a previous life where she was bitten by one of those poisonous ones they have abroad. Mind you,' he looks at me more seriously now, 'I'd be careful with that Frank chap. Are you sure he didn't start all this? Maybe he said something that got you thinking.'

'I'm perfectly safe,' I say. 'He's locked in prison after all. What motive could he possibly have for trying to make me think we've met before? And anyway, he didn't; I'd have remembered.'

'Well just take care, that's all I'm saying,' Pete pleads. 'He was locked up for a good reason. Don't forget that. Now, does anyone want the last slice of garlic bread?'

Chapter 14

The next morning I sleep in late. I can hardly believe it when Sally sets a mug of coffee and a biscuit on the bedside cabinet and tells me it is ten o'clock.

'I'm so sorry,' I begin. 'I'm usually up long before this.'

But Sally laughs. 'There's no hurry,' she says. 'It's Sunday after all. And Pete's still asleep.'

I blink the sleep from my eyes and see that Sally is wearing a dressing gown. I wriggle to a sitting position. I feel rather grubby having slept the night in yesterday's T-shirt. Luckily I have a comb and toothbrush in my bag.

'I'm going to have a shower,' Sally says. 'I'd get in there straight after me if I were you – Pete always stays in ages and uses all the hot water!'

It feels strange to wake up in a different bed. It is as though I am on holiday. Of course I stay with my mother often enough but that is home from home. And there are occasional nights at Richard's parents'; but those are definitely not a holiday at all. This morning I feel free. I don't have to adhere to any routine or worry about pleasing anyone. I look around the room, which I suspect was Debbie's before she got married. It reminds me, in it's cosiness, of my room in Somerset. I sip my coffee and conclude that, all in all, this is a good weekend.

Despite being pressed by Sally and Pete to spend the day with them and go out for a pub lunch, I decline, feeling that I have intruded enough. I arrive home late morning, knowing that Richard will not leave his parents' home until after a traditional roast. Indeed, he will be lucky to be back before dark.

As I hang my coat and go to set the kettle on the Aga, I think about yesterday evening. I am amazed that I talked so freely with my friends, and that they are still my friends. My worst fears – that I might be declared over-imaginative, batty or even unstable – have proved unfounded. Any negative feelings I may have had towards my beliefs have been dissipated, if not dissolved. I am officially sane. If I wanted to I could go to Kimberley Place right now without feeling that I am indulging in some clandestine activity. I could, but I won't. I do not feel the need. Instead I feel a sense of freedom, as though I have been pronounced cured of a life-threatening illness.

When I have had a coffee and glanced, perfunctorily at the Sunday newspaper, I potter about the house looking for any jobs that need doing. I am aware that my mood is almost carefree. I am no longer feverishly seeking occupation, as I would have been a few weeks ago. This is just as well because, as usual, it is difficult to find tasks that would not invade Mrs Blackstock's stoically defended territory.

I go through the conservatory and out onto the patio. Our garden is large for a city plot. We are lucky to have space for a sizeable lawn as well as fruit trees and flower borders and even a small pond.

When we first moved here, just before Jamie went away to school, I made my first and only attempt at growing vegetables. Inspired by childhood memories of my father planting neat rows of peas and potatoes, banking up the soil against the celery to ensure crisp white stems and interspersing the cabbages with onions and leeks to keep the slugs away, I decided I would try this too. I dutifully bought a new spade and fork and set about preparing the soil. Obediently, I followed the television gardeners' instructions on composting and double digging. I marked out precisely measured rows, with lengths of string, scooped out seed drills and constructed complex frameworks of bamboo canes. I had notions of harvesting bright abundant crops, all organically grown and collected and displayed in traditional baskets.

The experiment began well and soon green seedlings

appeared, reaching optimistically above the newly enriched soil. Runner beans spiralled their way up the canes and even began to produce bright orange flowers. But then the rain came. At first there were gentle showers. I welcomed the light droplets as they softened the ground and saved me from having to go out with the hose each evening after work. All that the garden needed now was a few weeks of sun. But instead the rain grew heavier. As the plants attempted to grow upwards it seemed that they were constantly being forced back. Eventually, on the solstice, a day that should have celebrated the summer, a pounding deluge broke the backs of the last survivors, and in the following few short hours of darkness, as the remains of the vegetables lay strewn across the battlefield, slugs and snails appeared as if from nowhere. It was as though they had been secretly summoned to the banquet. They skated effortlessly across the moist ground at a speed that belied all that is said about them. Even the valiant sentinels of garlic, still standing guard against all the odds, could do nothing to deter them. I remember how I stood in the garden in the darkness, after Jamie had gone to bed, and I swear I heard the crunching of tender young leaves as my feast was devoured.

I have not tried to grow vegetables since, although I am told that what happened that year was simply bad luck. Instead I cheat and, since they have become available, I have boxes of organic produce delivered each week.

I zip up my jacket. Although the light is fierce, the temperature is already chilling down in readiness for the night. I look about me, assessing what jobs need to be done. There is a scattering of crisp dry leaves on the lawn. Right now they look pretty but in a week or so they will wilt into a slippery brown mulch on the grass. I ponder whether to leave them for a while – to let nature take its course. First the worms will smell them and wriggle their way to the surface then the blackbirds will appear, cramming their bright beaks with fat juicy prey. I decide in favour of the blackbirds and compromise by clearing the leaves that have fallen into the pond, scooping them out with an old shrimping net before they sink beneath the surface and turn the water to acid. When I have done this I step carefully onto the flower borders and gather up spent stems of sidalcea and verbascum. I pile them in a corner, hoping they might provide a shelter for any hedgehogs late in taking to their winter beds.

After lunch, I settle to cleaning my walking boots, which have been in the back of the car since yesterday afternoon. Today they are clammy with trapped moisture. I take them out of the carrier bag, releasing the smell of mouldering leaves, and go outside the kitchen porch to clean the worst of the mud off with a brush. Back in the utility area, between the kitchen and the side door, I set to with a damp cloth, carefully wiping clean the areas around the eyelets and the stitching and the join between the upper and the sole. Without this attention, I have found, any remaining mud will draw the natural moisture out of the leather, leaving it to dry and crack like an ancient manuscript. When all this is done I will set them to dry on a sheet of newspaper on the kitchen floor. Already, I look forward to the last stage in the process when, this evening or perhaps tomorrow, I will rub wax into the leather, feeding it, softening it, and all the while breathing in its nurturing smell.

I am glad, as I stand in the utility area, methodically working on the left boot, that we do not use our back door for visitors. The dark, forbidding area outside the porch is hardly welcoming, I think to myself. And I would always feel worried, if someone should arrive unexpectedly, that there might be dirty dishes not yet stacked in the washer, or hand-washed clothes hanging on the rack, that the kitchen might not be presentable for receiving guests.

I reach into the cupboard beneath the sink for a clean cloth. Behind the laundry products are the steel grill and cooking utensils for the barbecue, the main body of which, is consigned to one of the brick outbuildings. I think we last had a barbecue about eighteen months ago. In fact, that is the only time Pete and Sally have been here. I remember they thought it rather comical but pleasant that our fare consisted of steaks or fish cooked in foil, that Richard and myself, as hosts, provided all the food and that our guests did not turn up clutching packs of partially defrosted burgers and sausages. That is the only time that Richard met Pete and Sally. He didn't talk to them much and, at the time, I thought this was rather rude. I was afraid that he would appear snobbish and they would be offended. I suspect, in truth, that Richard did not feel comfortable with my friends because he did not see any common ground on which to base conversation. It wasn't that he considered his fellow surgeons and medics to be better in any way, simply that he was in his comfort zone chatting with them about the benefits of keyhole surgery and local anaesthesia. Luckily, Pete and Sally seemed unperturbed. They chatted amiably with all the guests in a manner that suggested they were totally comfortable with themselves. That ease, that confidence, is something I envy.

It is mid afternoon when the phone rings. I am relaxed as I click the button to answer.

'Julia? This is Andrew. Look, I have some news. Is Richard there by any chance?'

I remember there was a message from Andrew when I got in. It was left yesterday and simply stated that he had called. I assumed that he wanted to speak to Richard rather than to me and therefore did not deem it necessary or appropriate to call back. 'He's at his parents' house,' I reply. 'You could try him there.'

'Well, it's you I want to speak to, strictly speaking.' I hear him falter at the other end of the phone, imagine that he is tapping his pen on his desk or scratching his chin. 'Look Julia, I wanted to speak to you directly but I'd have been happier knowing Richard was with you that's all.'

I go hot and cold. The last time anyone said words like that was when they told me Jamie had died. I grit my teeth. Those words back then were the worst I could ever hear. Nothing, now or in the future, will ever be as bad again.

'I'm sorry,' he continues, 'it's about Ashby. I've spoken to his brief and we're both in agreement. But he's insistent and there's nothing we can do. It's absolutely ridiculous but I'm afraid the chap's determined to take you to court.'

I stop as though caught in a freeze frame of a movie. I've never been to court. It is something new, something frightening. The possibility gapes before me like a black hole. Like the depression of the past few months, it is some dark place that I might step into and never come out.

When I say I've never been in a court, I suppose that isn't strictly true. I attended the coroner's court, the inquest, after Jamie died. I didn't have to go, legally speaking. I was a witness only in the sense that I watched and listened to the evidence. I hadn't wanted to go; indeed, I had dreaded it. But I felt I had to be there as a mark of respect, that, not attending would be like casting Jamie aside as though he had never mattered, as though I only wanted to know the good things about him and deny the rest. As his mother I had to love him unconditionally, even after his death. I had stupidly hoped the inquest would be comforting, that it would answer questions, encourage acceptance. But it did none of those things. At best, it was a cold clinical disposal of Jamie's life. By contrast, I remember that, though I struggled through the funeral in a state of shock, I can look back on that now with some sort of affection. Although the tear-stained pictures are hazy, I can remember the warmth of the mourners, I am touched when I realise that so many people loved Jamie so much. But the memory of the inquest is one I would gladly erase.

'Are you all right?' Andrew asks. I can feel the warmth in his voice as though it were a woollen wrap, soft about my

133

shoulders. Andrew has a nice voice, clear and gentle, like a warm day. He doesn't have a snooty accent that shouts 'public school' at you. He doesn't sound like he is defending his ancestral territory or trying to impress. He speaks simply, with clear and precise diction. I am sure that he treats everyone he meets with the same care and respect, whatever their background or situation. My mother would warm to him easily, as would Pete and Sally.

'But surely,' I protest, 'surely, there will be an inquest.'

I am talking about the patient now. Not about Jamie. When you work in a hospital, inquests are routine. They are about other people. They are not about the death of your son. They are about filling in forms, administration, the last rites for those you cannot save. For Richard, in a department that routinely performs high-risk procedures on patients who would die anyway without this last chance, they are a fact of life, a fact of death. In obstetrics and gynaecology it is different. It is rare, these days, for a woman to die in childbirth, certainly it is far less likely than TV dramas imply. There are stillbirths and neonatal deaths however. Often they are expected. Either in the very premature or in cases where it is already known that a woman is carrying a child with severe congenital abnormalities such that it stands little chance of life. In such cases, many women would rather go through childbirth than opt for a late termination. In all of these cases we are legally obliged to notify the coroner. But that's where the matter ends for us. The coroner reads the reports and signs them off. Cases of malpractice or negligence are very uncommon. And nurses afflicted by Munchausen's syndrome, systematically killing off their patients, rarely stray beyond the world of fiction.

'Surely,' I reason more to myself than to Andrew, 'surely, if the coroner gives a verdict of natural causes then there is no case to answer.' I am grasping at straws, I know. Andrew is the expert. If there were such a simple way out he would have found it.

134

I am aware of Andrew sighing at the other end of the phone. It is out of sympathy for my situation. The fact that sometimes the law does not work in a way he considers fair. He attempts to explain a potted version to me. 'The purpose of the coroner's court is to explain the manner in which someone has died,' he tells me. 'Most cases referred from a hospital will be deemed natural causes.'

I nod, forgetting that he is over a hundred miles away, that he cannot see me.

'Occasionally, one might be judged as neglect or unlawful killing – very rarely suicide.'

'Yes.'

'But more importantly for you is what they don't do,' he continues. 'It is not for a coroner's court to decide who is responsible for a death – that would be handed over to a criminal court. And to an extent, your reasoning is right Julia. If the coroner's court found death by natural causes – as they eventually will in this case – then neither you nor anyone else could be held responsible. Normally, in these circumstances, an inquest would take place first. There would be no action taken by the crown prosecution service unless the inquest gave a verdict of unlawful killing. The problem here is that Ashby is pursuing a private prosecution. And the law states that, in the event of any criminal prosecution, the inquest must be postponed.'

'But that's silly,' I say.

'In this situation I have to agree with you. But you see, that law wasn't established for cases such as yours. It was designed to speed up justice in the case of intentional and cold-blooded murder. Inappropriate or not, the law stands.'

I am becoming distraught, trying to make sense of what Andrew is saying. I attempt to reiterate his words. 'So, because Ashby has intervened, the inquest is postponed.' I pause, thinking it out. 'If – when I am found innocent, the inquest will be resumed. Natural causes will be found. My court appearance, your work, my time off, all the costs will

Chapter 15

On Monday, holding Andrew's words of encouragement in my mind, I go into town. Despite my fear of the situation, I am doing my best to take Andrew's advice, to get on with my life and leave the legal team to worry about the technicalities of going to court. Around Richard this is easy. When I told him, late on Sunday afternoon, about the developments, he was, unsurprisingly, annoyed. Yet, after this initial reaction he appeared to find the whole business a nuisance rather than something that he, or more particularly I, might be worried about. Thank goodness my disappointment at Richard's lack of sympathy has been offset by the support of my friends. I rang Clare and told her about it soon after Andrew's phone call, before even Richard knew. She assured me straight away, without my having to ask, that, if it might help, if it were allowed, she would speak on my behalf in court. I decided to wait and tell Pete and Sally after swimming. They were always so amenable, so ready to absorb my problems that I didn't want to add to their burden. I decided to wait until I saw them and then to drop it casually into the conversation, as if it didn't matter.

In the sanctuary of a bookshop, I buy the DVD of The French Lieutenant's Woman. I also buy a paperback copy of the book. There is an offer on so I choose another called The Magus by the same author. As soon as I arrive home I settle myself in my study and begin reading The French Lieutenant's Woman. I immediately feel an affinity with the heroine, Sarah, despite the fact that she seems rather delusional. I can identify with her sense of loss and empathise with the way she holds on to such a tentative thread of hope. I am also intrigued by the way the book is set in the past, at the way the author writes so convincingly that one might imagine he himself journeyed back to that time. Although it is set longer ago than my life as Maggie, I feel that perhaps the buildings, the roads, the ambience of the place did not change much in those intervening years. But most of all I enjoy reading the details about Lyme Regis, about the beach and the Cobb and the fossils. I can almost imagine Maggie describing it this way. For me, it does not simply conjure images, it triggers memories of that former life. I don't just see the huge ammonites on the boulders and the slippery stones on the Cobb wall. I remember standing on them, touching them, feeling them, cold and clammy against my skin.

On Thursday, it is my day to visit Frank in prison. It should be easy. I've done it before, several times. Perhaps I have become complacent. But this time I am caught unawares. As we approach the outer perimeter, a seed of foreboding plants itself deep in my stomach. Suddenly, in some part of mind, over which I seemingly have no control, I am entering this forbidden place, not as a volunteer, a visitor, but as an inmate, a convicted criminal. I cringe at the finality of each door and gate locking shut behind me, find my breaths coming short and shallow as a feeling of claustrophobia engulfs me. The seed inside me has quickly grown and, as I walk through the cold grey door, it becomes a flourishing plant whose leaves and blossoms scratch and press on my insides until I am sure that I will vomit.

I take deep breaths as I sign in and go through the search. This is not about me, I remind myself. It is about Frank, about boosting his morale, preparing him for his release. But I cannot convince myself. As I sit at the table opposite him, it is as though our positions are reversed: that I am the one 'doing time' and Frank, freshly released, is my official visitor. My sight blurs and my head buzzes. I push my chair back with a clatter and rush to the safety of the ladies' lavatory.

I am not physically sick, as I feared. Instead, I grasp the washbasin and bend forward, taking deep breaths. I remind myself of the things Clare has taught me about thoughts.

This is not real, I tell myself determinedly. It is only my mind playing tricks, hoping to catch me out. But I won't let it. I am stronger. All in all, I have coped so well this week; I will not give in now. The door creaks open behind me and, in the mirror, Lizzie's reflection appears alongside mine.

'Are you all right?' she asks.

I remember then that she was in the visiting room escorting a newcomer to their inmate.

'I don't know what came over me,' I say, apologetically. I describe how the feelings swept over me from the moment I arrived.

She smiles sympathetically. 'Don't worry,' she reassures me. 'It happens to all of us – even the staff.' She pauses and takes a pack of mints from her pocket, offers them to me. 'Have a couple of these,' she says, 'they'll stop you feeling sick. The first time you come here,' she continues, 'you expect it. But it doesn't happen. You're so curious, taking in the surroundings, watching the prisoners, wondering what they've done, chatting to your friend or relative or whomever you've been allocated to. It's nearly always a few visits down the line – just when you think it'll be all right – that the place gets to you.'

I smile gratefully. I like Lizzie. I want to tell her that it is more than that, that it is the fact of being on trial myself that worries me. It is the imminent possibility, however slight, that soon I will be a prisoner myself. But I am afraid that if the authorities know about this, I will no longer be eligible as a volunteer, that I will no longer be allowed to visit Frank. So I say nothing.

'Thank you,' I reply, accepting a mint. 'I'm feeling much better now.'

'Good,' Lizzie smiles. 'I'll be over at the desk. If you feel queasy again just come over.'

I expect everyone to stare at me as I return to the room but no-one seems concerned. Either they are too engrossed in their own conversations or a similar thing has happened to them.

'I thought you were sick at the sight of me already,' Frank jokes, as I sit down.

'Just a queasy tummy,' I lie. 'Probably the prawn cocktail last night.'

We chat for the remainder of the allowed time. I skirt around the subjects I most want answers to. I talk about holidays, about how I used to go to Norfolk. I don't mention our trips abroad. I don't want to taunt Frank, gloating about my vacations in exotic locations, and anyway it isn't relevant to what I really want to know. Casually, I tell him that my friends used to go to Lyme Regis, that it sounds very interesting, that I would like to see it for myself some day. 'Have you been there?' I ask. But he shakes his head and tells me he is more familiar with places in the north, Scarborough, for instance, and the Lake District. Disappointed, I take his lead and we laughingly compare notes on the times we each attempted to climb Scafell Pike.

On Friday, I go for my second regression. This time I have no feelings of doubt about Rose or the process of hypnosis, instead I eagerly anticipate my journey into the past. I look forward to the escape that is offered to me, the chance, if only for a few hours, to swap my life for another.

'How have you been this week?' Rose asks as I settle myself on her sofa.

'It hasn't been the easiest time,' I admit, more because I suspect that Rose will pick up on my mood, will know instinctively if I am not telling the truth, than any feeling of negativity or plea for sympathy on my part. 'But I've found out where Maggie lived,' I say. And I tell Rose about the film and how I recognised Maggie's hometown as Lyme Regis.

'Will you try to track her down?' she asks.

'How do you mean?'

'Some people try to find evidence,' Rose tells me. 'They want proof of the reality of a previous life. They go hunting

140

for birth certificates and gravestones. And so often they are disappointed,' she says, 'when they don't find what they are looking for.'

I am confused. 'Do you mean you think Maggie isn't real?' I ask. I want Rose to believe in this, indeed, I need her to if she is to lead me on this journey.

She picks up an amethyst from the bowl of glassy stones on the coffee table. 'It isn't for me to judge,' she says, as she rolls the purple crystal around in her palm. 'When you go back in time you go to a place where records are not kept as fastidiously as they are today, a place where you could change your identity simply by moving to a different part of the country and calling yourself by a different name. A lack of evidence is not proof that someone didn't exist. If it were that easy then we could all instantly trace our ancestors for many generations. And then again, we do not always tell the truth, we have secrets. Perhaps this girl's name wasn't Maggie at all, perhaps that's what she wishes she had been called, perhaps it is Freddie's pet name for her. I think it is too easy to become obsessed with looking for proof and forget the reason you are interested in this person in the first place. Do you understand what I mean?' She replaces the stone in the bowl.

I nod. 'She's real in my mind,' I say. 'I don't need any other kind of proof.' I sniff the frankincense, pondering whether perhaps I could induce a hypnotic state at home just by breathing in that scent. I wonder, before we start, whether I should tell Rose about the court case, about our silly legal practices that never seem to favour the innocent. But I feel it would somehow contaminate this sanctuary. This is a place I want to reserve for Maggie and Freddie, for the girl on the swing, maybe even, in some way, when the time is right, for Jamie.

As Rose sets up the recorder and takes her notepad I think about Frank and my visit to him yesterday. How, having recovered from my embarrassing spectacle, I was looking for

141

clues again, how, disappointingly, there were none. Seek and ye shall find. That's what it says in the Bible. But it isn't as simple as that. It is like an enigma, whereby, if you seek something you will be sure not to find it, where, only when your mind and your heart are completely open, will the truth be revealed.

Invited by Rose's soft comforting voice, I drift back in time. I open the door. I know where it is this time. I can go directly there.

Once more I am playing on the beach. I'm busy, concentrating, bending over, grubbing my fingers between the huge sloping slabs with their sketchy white patterns, fishing out the debris, the lucky dip of rotting kelp and cuttlefish bones and sharp, freshly-broken rock. I'm searching for fossils, small ones that I can take home or hide away in some secret place, to take out and hold covetously in my palm when I have the mind. Although it's warm today, there was a storm two nights ago. And that's the best time, when the soft muddy layers of the cliff have been loosened and slid down to shatter on the boulders below; when the rock's been cracked open and you can see what's inside. That's when you'll find the best pickings.

But something pulls me back. A voice. I feel as though I have been here before, as though I am a spectator. Like my life has been lived before and I'm watching as it is replayed. Gently, the voice tells me to move forward in time. I'm not sure that I want to. I'm enjoying myself where I am. Being a child is fun, comfortable, safe. I don't know that I want to grow up, not yet anyway. But the voice is insistent, pleading with me. She's my friend, this invisible girl, and I don't want to disappoint her. There's a flurry of wind gusting past me. I'm no longer watching. I am living this life here and now.

It's warm, hot even, more than you'd expect for the time of year. As we climb up the hillside I think how good it feels to have grass under my feet instead of rocks and shingle.

I lift my skirt a little so I don't trip. It's a heavy winter one, too thick for today as it turns out. I'm getting puffed so I call to Freddie, who's walking ahead, and sit down on the ground, looking back the way we've come.

It's a different character here from the beach. More calm, more constant. By the shore the sea is moody, sometimes gentle, sometimes angry, sometimes playing tricks to catch you out. But the meadows don't know any of that. They just get on with their being and don't seem to mind if you come and go.

Freddie settles himself down a few feet away and unlaces his boots, pulls them off and wriggles his toes in his much-darned socks. I'd like to do that too but don't know if I should. Up above, there are skylarks twittering and hovering. It hurts my eyes to look at them in all that brightness and I hold up my hand to shield my face from the sun. Ah the sun. There's so much more of it without the sea breeze to carry it away. I'm not wearing a coat but my dress has long sleeves and a front that buttons all the way up to my throat. I undo a couple of the buttons and roll up the sleeves. I take my boots off as well, whether I should or not, and stretch my stockinged feet. Really I'd like to go barefoot but I know it wouldn't be seemly. I sigh to myself as I think of how much easier it was being a young girl. I make to lie back on the ground. Freddie has already taken off his jacket and spreads it out between us, offering for me to lie on it. I'm tempted because I know the sun hasn't been up long enough to dry all the dew on the grass. But I decide I'd best not and stay where I am.

Freddie chews on a piece of grass. I look at the sky for a moment then close my eyes. There's lots to hear but the sounds are small compared to those of the sea. There are insects buzzing and grasses quivering in the breeze.

'Yer gonna wake up or what?' Freddie is asking.

I stretch and open my eyes. But it's too much trouble and I close them again.

Something is tickling my nose. This time I come to with a start. Freddie is dangling a head of grass seed over my face. I roll over and grab it from him laughing. He laughs too and rolls back right on top of me. He has hold of my wrists. It's just a game, like we used to play often. But this time he kisses me. And I expect I quite like it really but I'm not going to let him think I'm that easy. I wriggle to get free. It should be easy enough, I could pitch him over without any trouble before. But he's heavy on me and my legs are trapped. I try to push him off with my arms but his grip on my wrists is too tight. I get panicky then, knowing that I can't get away.

'Gerroff!' I shout, resorting to unladylike language. 'Gerroff me Freddie yer bugger!'

He lets go then, shocked I think.

'Sorry Maggie,' he says. 'I thought yer was likin' it.'

I scowl at him and pull away. Not because I'm cross at him or anything. But because I'm beginning to realise why some women give in to their husbands; get beaten by them; get scared of them. I used to think they must be a bit pathetic, women like that. I wondered why they didn't just fight back. But now I'm beginning to understand some of the things that being grown up is all about. And I'm not sure I'm liking it.

I can feel the damp beginning to seep through my dress. I stand up, cross that I've let it go in creases. People will think the worst. Quickly I pull on my boots and stumble half across the field before I stop to lace them up. It's time to go.

Chapter 16

On Saturday morning it is raining. I am almost tempted to go walking despite the weather. I have always been intrigued by the different effect rain has, depending on where it falls. In the countryside it makes everything sparkling and clean. It sharpens the smell of aromatic plants and leaves the world refreshed. Yet, in town, it seems to do the opposite. Roads and pavements look dirtier, grass verges turn to mud and puddles are grimy with spent oil. After deliberating for a while, I decide that, whilst I would still enjoy an outing in warmer weather, walking in the clammy cold at this time of year is not so appealing. As it is, I have the house to myself. As usual these days, Richard is out, catching up with some paperwork in his office at the hospital.

I sit by the cosiness of the Aga and write in my journal. It occurs to me, as I describe my experience under hypnosis, that I write as though I am Maggie. I remember the details much more clearly this time. Perhaps I was 'under' more lightly. Perhaps there are different levels of hypnotic state just like there are variable levels of anaesthesia during surgery.

So, as Maggie, I tell of how I am growing up, of how my relationship with Freddie is changing. And then, from my own point of view, I write about my conversation with Rose, about the possibility of looking for physical evidence of someone from a previous life. I am not sure that I would want to do this. I picture the reality of standing before Maggie's grave. Somehow, the thought of this makes me shiver. It makes her real in a different way, a way that is separate from myself. Whereas, to contain her life within my head, within my thoughts, keeps everything in my control.

By eleven, I have finished my account of the previous day. I fill the heavy Aga kettle and lift the lid on the fast hotplate, releasing a blaze of heat into the room. I return the journal to my study and exchange it for the DVD – still wrapped and in its bag – of the French Lieutenant's Woman. Perhaps I will watch it now, part of it at least. I am already half way through the book and feel I can safely see the first hour of the film without spoiling the story.

As I return down the stairs, I pause to pick up a newspaper from the front doormat. It is one of those free local papers that contain mostly advertisements. When I was working I never even used to open them but these days I tend to flick through the pages, turning past trivial stories of city life and lingering wistfully over the descriptions of pets waiting to be re-homed from the local rescue centre. I take the paper, together with the DVD, through to the kitchen where I deposit both on the table and set about the important task of making coffee.

Minutes later, I settle myself at the table – it is too hot near the Aga since the hotplate has been open – and take that first luxurious sip of my drink. Idly, I spread the paper on the table in front of me. I scan the pages leisurely, vaguely taking in the words.

And then I stop. And I freeze.

The words are written in front of me in big bold letters.

'DR DEATH IN CHILDBIRTH TRAGEDY', they say.

I read on, horrified. 'Nottinghamshire farmer, Mr Jack Ashby, is taking action against a local doctor following the tragic death of his wife and daughter at Nottingham General Hospital last July. 'My life has been destroyed,' Ashby said, 'and someone should be held accountable.'

I don't take in the rest of the words. My eyes are blurred with fear and anger. After a moment I force myself to look again. There isn't much more. It is only a short piece. There is a photograph of me though, albeit an old and rather indistinct one.

I rip the page and throw it on the floor. When that does nothing to make me feel better I cry. And yet, moments later, when the initial shock has passed, I take a deep breath and steel myself. This is terrible, it is distressing, but it is nothing compared to losing Jamie.

The practical side of me takes over, the controlled doctor who copes in a crisis. I fetch the phone ready to call Andrew. Just as I am looking up his number, which is pinned on a card to the notice board, the phone rings in my hand.

I click the button. 'Hello?'

'Is that Dr Julia Spencer?' It is a man's voice. I don't recognise it. The fact that they address me as Doctor makes me suspicious. As a consultant surgeon I do not use that title. I suspect it is probably someone trying to sell us a new kitchen or double-glazing. I would prefer a new house, I think to myself.

'Sorry but we don't accept sales calls,' I say firmly.

'I'm not trying to sell you anything Dr Spencer, I'm calling from the Nottingham Echo. I wondered if you'd like to comment on the story in the Advertiser. What do you have to say about the allegations made by Mr Ashby?'

I am taken aback. Moments later I will remonstrate for not having said something assertive such as 'You'll have to speak to my solicitor,' or, 'I'm sorry, Dr Spencer is not available to comment.' But I am caught off guard and instead I simply press the button to end the call.

Quickly, before anyone else has chance to ring, I dial Andrew's number. When he answers I realise that I am shaking. 'Andrew, thank God,' I say. And I tell him what has happened.

I sit down at the table. My legs feel too weak to stand. Andrew soothes me. 'It's partly my fault,' he says, 'I should have warned you something like this might happen. I'm so sorry Julia.' He talks to me softly, words of encouragement, reassurance. 'It's a pity Richard isn't there to support you,' he continues. Then he says something that I don't quite take in; don't quite understand. He makes some comment about a man's first duty being to his wife rather than his parents.

'Sorry?' I say.

'Please forget it,' he mumbles. 'I shouldn't have spoken out of turn. Look, Julia, we'll have to meet up soon and make a start on putting your case together. In the meantime, don't answer any phone calls or letters from anyone you don't know, don't answer the door even. Do you understand? It might not be the press next time. It could be someone trying to gain material for the prosecution. It shouldn't happen of course but not everyone behaves fairly or according to the rules.'

'I'll be careful,' I say.

'How are you now?' he asks, when I have had a few moments to calm myself. His voice is gentle, kind. I know that he cares. Not just because he is my lawyer or Richard's friend, but because he is now my friend too.

'A bit shaky,' I admit.

'I wish I could do something,' Andrew continues, 'but, unfortunately, I have to meet a client. Do you have a friend who could come round? I'd come up myself if I could, I'm only sorry that isn't possible.'

'I could ring Clare,' I say, half to myself. 'Or Sally and Pete.'

'Do that,' he says. 'I want you to turn your phone onto voice mail now. Don't answer any more calls today unless you recognise the number calling. I'm going to try and get through to Richard myself. He should be at home with you now.'

'There's no need,' I say, thinking that I would rather be with one of my friends, someone who will talk to me, than with Richard who will not.

'Look Julia, I have to go. Do as I say now. And if you can't find anyone to come round then get out of the house, get out of Nottingham for a few hours.'

'I'll do that,' I reply, obediently.

Half an hour later I am drinking coffee with Clare. We sit in the kitchen because it is cosier. Clare had tried to persuade me to go back to her house, to get right away from everything. But that would have felt like giving in.

'But why don't you?' she insists.

I look up at her, raise my eyebrows.

'I know we all think it's somehow admirable to stick it out and face things, but sometimes it isn't. You're a sitting target here for the press – or anyone else come to that. The Echo shouldn't have been able to get hold of your number – you're ex-directory. But they did. I expect they have your address too. Why don't you go away for a weekend, a week, even. Surely Richard could get some time off. It might be good for the two of you.'

I think about telling Clare what happened with Richard but it would be too much of a betrayal. And she would think it was her fault – which it wasn't of course. It was entirely my own choice. But even I can see that spending time with Richard right now will not help anyone. 'He's very busy,' I say. 'It would be different if it were an emergency. But this isn't really. They'd have to get a locum. And anyway, Richard's patients trust him, they want him to perform their surgery.'

Clare nods. 'But you could go away on your own. To your mother's for instance.'

I shake my head. 'I won't be driven away,' I say. 'And in any case I'd have to be careful. My mother doesn't know about any of this and I don't want her to, she's had enough to cope with over Jamie. She isn't young and she isn't strong. If she found out about this I think it could push her over the edge.'

Clare picks up the paper and turns to the offending article. 'Well, it isn't as if it's on the front page,' she says, 'and the picture doesn't look much like you. And in any case,' she continues, 'does anyone actually read this rag?'

'I did,' I point out. 'And so did the reporter from the Echo.'

'Oh Julia!' She looks at me sternly. 'You only noticed it because it was about you. And the news hack read it because that's his job. Most people either aren't interested or they don't have time.' She gulps the last of her coffee. 'Honestly. You've heard the saying 'yesterday's news'. By tomorrow – next week at the latest – there'll be more exciting things to gossip about. People will have forgotten. The pages of the Advertiser will be lining cat litter trays all over Nottingham.'

'But the Echo might run a story,' I point out. 'People pay for that paper so they'll read it.'

Clare is practical. 'If it is in the Echo it'll be sometime this week. If you can get away or lie low for the next few days it will all blow over.'

'I suppose I could go and visit my mother,' I concede. 'Maybe next weekend.' I pause, something occurs to me. 'You never talk about your family,' I say.

Clare shrugs. 'There isn't much to say really.'

I raise my eyebrows.

'I'm an only child like you,' she says. 'My father died when I was twelve. My mother and I aren't close.' She clips the sentences in a way that says this is her final answer. The subject is not open for discussion.

I think about it as I finish my coffee. About Clare losing her father. I can't help wondering if that loss, especially at such a sensitive age, has any bearing on her attitude to men and relationships now. Perhaps it is the reason she flits from one man to another without ever making a commitment. Perhaps, in the past, I have judged her too harshly, ignorant of all the facts. I have always thought that, considering Clare's job, you'd expect her domestic life to be a bit more settled. In order to understand other people's relationships, their lives, I'd expect her to be an expert on her own. But who am I to say? Me, an obstetrician who only ever managed to produce one child, and couldn't even keep that one alive.

Chapter 17

I end up taking Clare's advice, about getting away, that is. But if she knew the real reason for my trip I'm sure she wouldn't approve at all.

It was Sally who suggested it, on Monday, after the swimming club. I'd told her and Pete about the article in the paper. When I told them about the reporter ringing, Sally was horrified; she gave me a hug and insisted I have the last chocolate biscuit. 'Why don't we go away for the weekend,' she said, 'the three of us. Why don't we go to Lyme Regis?' I had hesitated. It was so long since I'd done anything spontaneous. The idea seemed somewhat anarchic. 'Let's do it,' Sally persisted. 'You need a break. The best thing you can do about that thing in the paper is get away. No-one in Lyme will have read it after all.' I began to come round to the idea. 'And you can explore the town and the beach, see if it triggers any memories. I tell you, I feel so spooked about this Frank chap – and I haven't even met him – it's like I'm reading a book. I can't wait to find out the rest of the story.'

I thought about it, a weekend by the sea, waking up to the call of gulls, exploring the beach, visiting the place where Maggie lived. I realised I could be persuaded to do this.

'And it'll be fun this time of year,' Sally continued, 'with everyone getting ready for Christmas.' Christmas. I hadn't even begun to think about that, the first one without Jamie. It wouldn't seem right to celebrate it. Not anywhere. But I would still have to buy gifts, for my mother and for Richard at least. It would be less painful to do that somewhere other than Nottingham. Somewhere that wouldn't remind me of previous years. 'What do you think Pete?' Sally had pressed.

To my surprise, he genuinely seemed to like the idea. 'We like to get away for a break in the winter,' he told me, 'and we probably won't get chance after Christmas because of Debbie's baby. It would be nice to go back to Lyme as well.'

He grinned. 'And I can always find a nice pub to sit in while you women go off sleuthing the past.' We all laughed. And suddenly it was settled. We agreed to go the next weekend and Sally rang me the following evening to say they'd booked a bed and breakfast.

And now we are half way there, I am half way there. That is how it feels. At the motorway services we eat surprisingly good lasagne and perfectly cut chips, we all drink coffee to keep us awake, although I am not doing the driving. We are travelling in Sally's car. She and Pete are taking turns at the wheel. For me it feels strange to be a passenger with anyone except Richard.

The car is hot and despite the coffee I doze. When Pete finally turns off the engine I feel like I am in another world. As I get out of the car the cold air wakes me. It is fresh, salty, stained with fish and kelp. I recognise it instantly.

The next half hour is taken up installing ourselves in the guest house. I don't know how long it is since I have stayed in such a place. Richard will not use them; he prefers the anonymity of large hotels. I have childhood memories of boarding houses with stern proprietors and strict rules: out by nine in the morning, in by ten at night; long midnight walks down dark corridors to find the lavatory, and complicated coin meters and permissions to take a bath. Although Pete and Sally assure me all this has changed, my expectations are not good. So I am pleasantly surprised when I am shown to a tastefully furnished room with a television and an en suite bathroom. Although there is a tray with a kettle and a selection of drinks in each of our rooms, the landlady insists on serving us hot chocolate and sandwiches in the lounge. We must need it, she says, after our long journey.

'Well this is nice,' Sally says, helping herself to a cheese and tomato sandwich. 'What's your room like Julia?'

'It seems very comfortable,' I concede.

'Not looked out of the window then?' she asks.

I shake my head. 'The curtains were already drawn.'

'Give her a chance,' Pete says. 'It's night don't forget. It's dark!'

Sally laughs. 'Only we asked for you to have a room with a sea view. Thought it might help you have one of your dreams!'

I laugh too. 'I think if I do dream tonight I'll be too tired to remember it,' I say.

The next morning I wake to the sound of seagulls. Immediately I get out of bed and pad over to the window. I draw back the curtains and undo the latch, pushing the window open slightly so that the sounds and smells fill the room. We are on a steep hill. Down, over the rooftops is the sea, wide and exciting. As I expected, I slept soundly. I look at my watch. It is half past eight. I panic for a moment that I have overslept, indeed, apart from a couple of occasions, it is months since I have slept this late, I never thought to set the alarm on my mobile. Then I remember we agreed to have breakfast at nine. I relax again and fill the kettle; there will be time for a cup of tea before I shower.

At ten, when we have lingered over what Pete described as a good hearty breakfast, we set off. We wind our way downhill, through steep narrow streets, in the direction of the sea. Although I have never been here before, I find myself leading the way. Soon we reach a road lined with shops. I am eager to get past all of this to get to the beach, I do not even realise that I am speeding up.

'Hang on!' Pete calls out. 'I'm getting puffed already and if you're not careful you'll be knocking over someone's granny.'

Sally laughs. 'Watch it!' she tells him. 'I'm going to be a granny myself soon, remember.'

'Sorry,' I say as I slow to a more respectable pace.

Soon we reach the seafront; we are at the east side of the

bay, where water trickles under a stone bridge and a walled fort-like structure reaches out over the rocks.

'We need to go this way,' I say, as I turn right and head towards the west.

Although it is winter, the temperature is noticeably warmer than Nottingham – or even than Somerset. I undo my jacket, which I had automatically zipped up before we left the guest house. We veer down a slope to a lower level away from the road. The tide is on the way out (Pete checked the times on the internet before we left Ilkeston) and although waves break onto the shingle they seem benign, pulling gradually back, secretly hiding the treacherous undertow. Indeed the sound of the sea is calm compared to the screeching of the gulls. I know exactly where I am going. As we approach the harbour, I feel like I am coming home.

I hurry up the stone steps leading onto the harbour wall, the Cobb. Sally follows close behind me. But Pete doesn't like the upper level; he says it gives him vertigo. Instead, he walks along a lower path, down by the boats. That's where Alf and Benji used to mend their nets, I think to myself. I shiver suddenly.

'Someone walk over your grave?' Sally asks.

I shake my head and zip up my jacket again. 'Probably just the sea breeze,' I say.

The walkway narrows slightly so, even though we stay in the middle, we are closer to the edge, more exposed. It curves to the left but, contrary to what you would expect, it slopes downwards to the right, towards the open sea.

Sally sees me looking. 'You'd go right off it on a skateboard!' she jokes. I think to myself that if it were built today there would be regulations about railings and things. I hope they never add anything like that. It would spoil it entirely. Right at the end, where Sarah used to gaze out to sea yearning for her French captain in the film, we pause. The huge concrete blocks at sea level, that have seemed out of place all along the outside of the wall, continue to the tip of the promontory. They shouldn't be here, I think to myself. We stare out to sea for a while, trying to make out boats on the horizon, wishing we had thought to bring binoculars.

Pete climbs a flight of stone steps, shiny with thousands of footsteps, to join us. 'It's not so bad up here after all,' he says.

After we have walked back to the land, I want to turn left immediately onto the beach. I feel drawn there, as though I have unfinished business to settle. But Pete stops me.

'Wait till after lunch,' he says. 'The tide'll be right out then.

Sally agrees. 'Let's do some shopping first,' she says.

We stroll along a street that runs parallel to the seafront. I get a vague recollection here of my second regression, of the shop where Freddie stole apples. Soon we arrive back in the shopping centre where we browse for gifts. I choose a tie and some after-shave for Richard and a brooch for my mother, along with a linen tea towel depicting the town. For Clare I buy a pair of earrings that I hope will be to her taste.

For lunch we are unanimous in our vote for fish and chips and we decide, in view of the mild weather, to get a takeaway and eat it out on a seafront bench rather than in a café. No sooner have we sat down, with our hot parcels oozing vinegar, than we are visited by several gulls. I throw them bits of fish but Sally tells me that I mustn't, that people don't like it because the birds are becoming pests. I feel rather sad that the world has come to this but do as she says anyway. I eat hungrily. I have noticed that, since getting involved in this past life, my appetite has returned. I see this as a good sign, an indication that I am dealing with the things that I need to face, that I am no longer 'in denial'.

Eventually, when we have crammed the last of the chips into our mouths and stuffed the greasy wrappings into a bin, we set off to the fossil beach. Pete tells me that there are fossils the other way too; that, at low tide, you can walk over them all the way to Charmouth. But my memories lie past the Cobb, to the stretch of rock and shingle that, the sign announces, is called Monmouth Beach.

Again I lead the way. We walk through car parks, past a boat-building school where keen youngsters are hard at work constructing wooden craft, past a boat club, past a row of mobile homes set just above the shingle, until at last we step out onto the beach. For the first hundred yards there are other people about, people walking dogs mostly, and a group of youngsters drinking canned beer. As we get farther from the town and the terrain gets rougher underfoot, so we leave the others behind.

'So, what do you think?' Sally asks. 'Is this where you were? Does it feel like you're that girl Maggie now?'

It feels somehow familiar, that is certain; like I am revisiting my home. But if I had expected to feel a rush of lost memories flooding into my conscious mind then I am disappointed. I think it is because the walk takes a fair amount of concentration. Some of the boulders are slippery and others move unexpectedly when I step on them such that I have to pick my way carefully. Indeed, Pete has already had to reach for my arm to prevent me from falling over. For the moment, my mind is fixed very firmly on the present. It is only when I chance upon a huge ammonite, fully twelve inches across, that I come to a stop.

'I recognise this one,' I say. We stop and look at it: a white spiral on a grey rock. Just an imprint now of the sea creature that lived millions of years ago.

'That one's certainly a beauty,' Pete agrees. He takes out his camera and Sally and I pose in the shot, either side of the giant fossil.

It seems like we walk for miles although, in reality, when we turn back, the Cobb is not so very far away. The time is absorbed in stopping and starting, clambering over fossil-speckled rocks, marvelling at the way the past is trapped, turned to stone by an act of nature. Most of the remains are ammonites: snail-like creatures that lived in the deep seas, perhaps bobbing up and down like the nautilus of today. Sometimes one animal is vast, occupying its own huge lump of rock, sometimes dozens of tiny creatures cluster together in a complex pattern. I am fascinated by the science, by the timescale that is so long that it is almost impossible to comprehend. But there is also a past that I do not see, that I wish I could release into the open.

Strangely, I am the one who suggests turning back. Sally and Pete agree. They know that, on this short winter day, by the time we are back in the town it will already be close to dusk.

We spend the rest of the afternoon completing what Sally and Pete refer to as their regular round. That includes a pot of Earl Grey and toasted teacakes in a café, followed by a browse round a place that seems to be a cross between a shop and a museum. Here there are fossils - some found locally and others imported from abroad - skeletons of dinosaurs in glass display cases and imprints of fish and leaves in carefully polished stone. I buy a paperback book describing fossils that may be found in Britain.

I could spend hours, gazing at the remains of all these creatures from the past. But it is getting late. The shop is preparing to close. Outside it is already night but the town is bright with Christmas lights. I have not really thought about Christmas yet; of the day, itself, that is; of how I will get through that time without Jamie. I choose not to think about it now.

As we persuade our aching legs up the steep hill I realise that I am really quite tired. The gradient makes the journey back to the guest house seem much further than it did this morning. Once there we are all agreed that we don't want to walk all the way down, and more importantly up, that hill again tonight. As we sit in Pete and Sally's room drinking tea, Pete suggests that we drive to an inland pub for dinner, somewhere in a village he says, somewhere we can park nearby.

Perhaps it is the sea air, but it is as much as we can all do to eat our dinner before the three of us are dozing. Luckily it

157

is only a short drive back to the guest house and, while youngster's in neighbouring buildings are setting out for a night on the town, Sally, Pete and I retire to our respective rooms to sleep.

It's a ferocious day. I've only come out because my mother sent me to buy bread. And I've only stayed out in the hope of meeting Freddie. Last night a fearful storm coincided with the spring tide. Luckily it was brewing before the fishing boats were due to put out. If it had happened just an hour later there'd be a lot more bodies besides the broken gulls and cormorants battered against the wall of the Cobb. I pull my coat around me as the wind makes a joke of my hair.

Raucous voices spill out from the Cobb Arms where the fishermen are sitting out the weather. I don't doubt that they went in there last night instead of to their boats and that they've not been home since. As I draw near I hear singing. 'What shall we do with the drunken sailor?' The voices waver on the wind. There is laughter and the crash of breaking glass, then shouting that I fear will make the building explode. As I watch, Benji stumbles out of the door, closely followed by Alf. Benji goes round the side and pees against the wall. Alf makes to follow but instead he looks and sees me. 'Not i' front o' the lady,' he drawls. Then he swaggers and falls to the ground.

I turn the other way, towards the town, but out of the corner of my eye I fancy I see Freddie back along the seafront. I call out and try to run after him but the wind is buffeting against my face. It makes my eyes stream and blows the words back into my mouth. I duck down for a moment in the shelter of the Cobb. Behind me, the waves stop, startled, as they reach the wall, then, having nowhere else to go, they surge upwards. They seem to pause for a second in mid-air, as though surveying the town in readiness for their attack, then they plummet down onto the walkway like buckets being emptied. Before me the fishing boats bob about restlessly. They strain at their ropes, anxious to get away, creaking ominously as they jostle together. The rigging clanks and clatters, begging to be set free, for the boats to set sail, to throw themselves into the wind.

When I venture to stand, Freddie has gone. I need to see him, to talk to him, about what happened last week, about what nearly happened.

The wind gusts, delivering a fishy spray with every blow. It's getting towards high tide again and the sky darkens as if it might send more rain to go with it. I clutch the bag with the loaf against my chest and scamper off towards home.

I wake quite suddenly. Quietly I lever myself out of bed and walk over to the window. I open it cautiously, fully expecting to find that a storm has crept up overnight. But outside everything is calm. Across the town, lights flicker in the darkness. There are occasional sounds, a car struggling to accelerate up the hill, a cat patrolling its territory. I fancy that, somewhere in the distance, I hear the gentle swish of the sea. But all of these are everyday comforting things, highlighted by the stillness of the weather.

I pull the window to, leaving it open just a fraction then I return to bed. I wonder, if I go straight back to sleep, whether my dream will resume where it left off. Certainly that has happened to me in the past, usually with terrifying nightmares that I would prefer not to revisit. But this time I lie awake, listening to the night-time sounds, much too alert to venture near the altered states of sleeping or dreaming. Eventually, I switch the bedside light on and look at my watch. It is still only four o'clock; there are four more hours of darkness. I get up again and rummage in my case for my book. Then I return to bed and resign myself, if necessary, to reading until morning.

As I stand on the Cobb and half close my eyes against the brisk sea breeze, it feels a different world from yesterday. We

159

are not in a hurry exactly, we are not planning to leave for a couple of hours. Yet the fact that the car is packed and waiting in the nearby car park, the knowledge that we are not returning to the guest house, signifies that we are already on our way home. It gives an edge, an urgency to the remainder of our time here.

Over breakfast I told Pete and Sally about my dream. Sally was not surprised. If I could dream about the place before I'd even been here, she reasoned, then how much more likely that was to happen when I'd explored it only hours before. It was spooky, nonetheless, she conceded. I smiled. She was growing so accustomed to my visions of a past life that she was beginning, not only to accept them, but to expect these occurrences as the norm.

I brace myself against the wind as it blows tangles into my hair and the taste of salt onto my lips. Although more lively than yesterday, the weather is certainly not stormy. The concrete blocks below the wall catch the waves and quell their power. Yet, even so, there is a more sinister quality to the sea. Water splashes up unexpectedly and showers my legs with a light spray. It catches me unawares, makes me feel suddenly vulnerable, reminds me that, in a fight between man and nature, there can only ever be one winner.

'Do you want to go on the beach?' Sally's words break the spell. 'Pete says the tide's on the turn so there's no danger of us getting cut off.'

Almost reluctantly I leave the harbour behind. I notice, as we descend the steps near the road, that the pub is silent, swapping Saturday night revelry for Sunday morning reverence. I try to imagine rousing choruses of 'Drunken Sailor' and 'Bound for South Australia' but somehow it doesn't work. When the pub opens at lunchtime these echoes of the past will be lost beneath the chatter of modern families eating roast dinners.

Yet, as I step down onto the beach, I once more step back in time. I am surprised at how noisy the sea is, how the

160

incoming breeze takes the sound of the waves as they shatter, like breaking glass, over the rocks, and hurls it at the cliff; how each clattering gust bounces this way and that, fighting with the next, engulfing us in confusion. We walk slowly, caught in the crossfire. We become isolated, each corralled by the sea and the wind. Each trapped in our own world.

Sally calls something to me but I don't hear, only see her lips move. She points at a crab the sea has left behind. I nod, smile, give a thumbs up. Pete has seen it too and takes out his camera to take a picture. I walk on, drawn by the wildness that exists today. There is no-one else in sight. Nobody has walked on the beach since it lay beneath the sea. And as the water retreats and the rocks with their fossils are revealed, it is like they exist for the first time.

At some point I turn and look behind me. I have left Pete and Sally behind. They are like children, playing chase with the waves at the water's edge. As I watch they reach out their hands to one another, like teenagers on a first date. I look away and walk further into the unknown.

As always, it happens when I least expect it. I am climbing over a rocky outcrop, looking forward to that moment when, as I step down onto lower ground beside the cliff, I will, for a short time be sheltered. It will be as though some invisible machine is switched off and the wind suddenly stops. Except it doesn't. As I enter the rocky cleft that should be safe and still as a harbour, suddenly the wind knocks my legs from under me, growls about my ears, the sea becomes a tidal wave, rushing to pin me against the cliff; above me gulls howl in sympathy. The wind screams; the sea screams; the gulls scream. Something terrible is about to happen.

'Julia?'

The voice seems to come from a different time.

'Julia! Are you all right?' It is Sally. She is standing over me. Now she is kneeling beside me. 'Over here Pete!' I hear her call. 'I think she's slipped.'

I am lying on the ground, on a scatter of broken rock

where someone has hammered into the stone in search of fossils. I struggle to sit up against the force of the wind. Except there is none. It is calm. It is as it should be.

'Are you hurt?' Sally asks.

I wriggle my body, testing my arms and legs. My right arm is sore and I rub it carefully. I expect I will have a bruise tomorrow.

'I'm fine,' I reassure her.

Pete has joined us now, he holds out his hand to help me up.

'Wait!' Sally stops him. She frowns at me. 'Are you sure you didn't hit your head?'

Cautiously I examine my scalp. 'Honestly I'm OK,' I insist. I smile, as though this will prove the point. I accept Pete's hand and stand up.

'What happened?' Sally asks. 'I thought I heard you scream then suddenly you disappeared.'

'You probably slipped,' Pete says. 'Look, there's weed and algae on the rock here. The tide wouldn't have reached this far but it's still got damp in the spray. I expect that was the culprit.'

I nod. 'I'm sure that's what happened,' I say. If I tell them the truth they will worry that I am concussed and we will spend the next few hours in A and E. I will tell them what really happened later.

'Come on,' Sally says. 'I think we all need a good strong cup of tea before we set off home.

Chapter 18

It seems an obvious thing to do to call on my mother on our way home. We plan it carefully, stopping for lunch beforehand, timing our arrival for around three o'clock. Hopefully, my mother will have finished dinner and had her customary nap.

'This is nice,' Sally says, as we drive into the town where I grew up. She says it contentedly, just as she commented on the guest house in Lyme. I look at her, wondering if she is just being polite, trying to make pleasant conversation. The surroundings are familiar. To me they are comforting, secure, full of childhood memories. But they are not attractive or pleasing to the senses. They are not what most people would call nice.

'Well it's home,' I say.

'No,' Sally insists. 'It's more than that. Look at the people.'

I follow her gaze. There are quite a few people about. They are the people I left behind. The shops and the businesses are staffed by people I went to school with – or by their children. I was the only girl in my year to go out of town to school let alone to university. I passed the eleven-plus and was awarded a place at a direct grant academy, a school where there was compulsory Latin for everyone and optional elocution so the girls from poorer backgrounds could learn to speak like their more privileged class mates. While the girls I had played with as a child grew up and wore make-up and short skirts, I caught the bus each day in my pleated checked skirts and drab shapeless jumpers that were compulsory at my school. Only years later did I realised that these clothes were designed to make me unattractive to boys, they were a primitive form of contraception, simple yet effective. While I hurried past, embarrassed, with my childish satchel and straw hat, my old friends became women. They smoked cigarettes, met boys, got married and got pregnant (not necessarily in that order). While I read books and took exams, they left school and trained as hairdressers and secretaries. While they became adults, I was still a child. While they staggered onto the council house waiting list, draped in nappies and bulging with unborn children, I went to university to train as a doctor.

Although winter, it is a mild dry day and these people are walking about. They are stopping in the street to chat to one another and tending to sleepy front gardens. Perhaps Sally sees something I don't. 'Yes?' I say.

'Well you can see they belong. The town's small enough that people know one another, watch out for one another,' Sally explains.

'It is changing though,' I say, thinking of the loss of industry, the commuters, the four by fours and the 'his and hers' runabouts.

'Everywhere changes,' Sally admits, with a hint of regret. 'Even so, I bet if your mother was ill, say, someone would notice straight away. They'd see that her washing was still on the line when it started to rain, or if she hadn't taken the milk in, in the morning.'

'Well I hope so,' I say, not liking to think of the possibility of my mother being ill, falling perhaps, being unable to get to the front door even.

'Even though things change,' Sally continues, 'even if people aren't in and out of each other's kitchen doors, drinking tea like they used to, they're still aware of one another. I mean, I bet where you live – and don't get me wrong, I know it's a nice area with big gardens and everything – but I bet half the people don't even know who their neighbours are.'

I think about my own neighbours and maintain a somewhat shamed silence. Sally is absolutely right of course. On one side of us the house is divided into flats. I do not know whether each is privately owned or whether they are rented out but either way they seem to change hands regularly. Occasionally someone will say 'Hello' to me, if we happen to go to or from our homes at the same time, but I will probably only see that person once or twice again before they move on to a bigger home or a new town. The building is a stepping stone, a transitory camp for the upwardly mobile. I do not think I have even been to the door since Jamie was in his teens and accidentally kicked a football into their garden. On the other side, an old lady – the only occupant as far as I know – seems to be reclusive, or keeps herself to herself, as people used to say. I tell myself that, by keeping my distance, I am respecting her privacy. But perhaps that is a convenient excuse for my not caring.

I give Pete directions and we are soon pulling into the drive.

'Its good to see you under happier circumstances,' Sally says to my mother. I remember then that they have only met once before and that was at Jamie's funeral.

My mother makes a pot of tea and we drink it at the table in the back room. Pete finishes his quickly and says, in his familiar way, that as he's outnumbered he'll leave us to our 'girl's talk'. He suggests that he'll have a look out the back, if that's all right, and see if there are any odd jobs need doing.

My mother is grateful. 'If you're sure you don't mind,' she says. 'The apple tree could do with cutting back a bit and it's the right time of year for it.'

Pete grins, rather comically tugs his forelock and disappears out of the kitchen door. I run after him with the key to the garden shed and show him where the basic selection of tools are kept.

When I get back in the house, Sally and my mother are chatting as though they have known each other all their lives.

'So where was it you say you've been?' my mother asks.

'Lyme Regis.' Sally mouths the words clearly, guessing correctly that my mother is a little deaf.

'Isn't it a strange time of year for a holiday? It's a bit cold for sitting on the beach. You don't want to be making yourselves ill.'

'Oh, Pete and I often have a little break in the winter,' Sally reassures her. 'There're plenty of other things to do and it's fun to buy Christmas presents somewhere new.'

My mother shakes her head, amazed at this idea.

'We walked on the beach and along the seafront,' Sally continues. 'Here, I've got some pictures in my camera. They're a bit difficult to see on this screen I'm afraid.' She pulls the camera out of her bag and my mother takes her spectacles from the sideboard. Out of the window I can see that Pete has leant a rather old and wobbly wooden ladder against the tree. He climbs up so that his head and arms disappear amongst the branches.

'Look at these,' Sally is saying, as she holds the camera so my mother can see the display. 'They're fossils. Ammonites. There are hundreds of them. And here's the harbour wall – it's called the Cobb.' She pauses. 'Really, I'm surprised you've never been there. It isn't that far.'

My mother shivers suddenly. She takes her spectacles off. 'I'm sorry dear,' she tells Sally, 'but I'm afraid my eyes are too tired for this.'

I look up, suddenly alert, wondering if she is all right.

'No, I'm sorry,' Sally insists. 'It's my fault - expecting you to look at pictures on this little thing. Tell you what, I'll print off the ones with Julia in and she can post them to you with your Christmas card.' She switches the camera off and replaces it in her bag. 'Now how about I make you another cup of tea – we've got some chocolate biscuits in the car too.' My mother brightens up considerably at this suggestion and I relax and go to put the kettle on.

We have to call Pete in when it is time to leave. In addition to pruning the tree, he has trimmed the hedges, adjusted the shed door so that it now shuts properly and generally tidied the paved area around the washing line. I think he has done more for my mother in the space of an hour than Richard has managed in all the years of our marriage.

166

'Come again,' my mother says to Sally and Pete as we get into the car. 'Come and stay with Julia one weekend. There's plenty of room.'

'That would be nice,' Sally agrees. 'We'll have to see about it next spring.'

As we drive away I think about what my mother said. There's plenty of room. By Pete and Sally's standards there is. When Jamie was five, my parents had the loft of their cottage converted into a third bedroom. From then on Jamie spent much of his school holidays there. I'm sure Richard would rather Jamie had spent this time with his own parents, where he could have been trained for his role as the family heir. But, like Richard and myself, they were both working and any such arrangement was out of the question. As a result, Jamie was always close to my parents. I'm sure my mother felt his death almost as keenly as Richard and I did.

When I arrive home, Richard is playing the piano. Instantly I feel that I have neglected him, failed in my wifely duties. In the past, the only times I went away without him were either to attend conferences, to visit my parents or to accompany Jamie somewhere. This is the first time I have taken time away for myself and it feels suddenly indulgent, an indulgence that must surely be a sin. I leave my bag at the bottom of the stairs and go straight through to the kitchen. Overwhelmed by the heat, I take off my jacket and hang it over the back of a chair then I check the fridge and the cupboards. Only when I am confident of the recompense I can offer in terms of a meal do I venture into the morning room.

I am conscious, as I walk across the room, that I am still wearing my outdoor shoes. That they clump intrusively on the floorboards. For this reason I pause, over by the fireplace, and wait for Richard to finish his piece. It is something by a Russian composer, I think: fiery, climactic, demanding intense concentration. The score is illuminated by a standard lamp beside the piano. It is the only light in the room, highlighting Richard as though he is performing on a stage. As I wait in the wings, in the shadows, I ponder that it is a long time since he has played this sort of music.

When he finishes I emerge from the gloom.

'You're back,' Richard says. He does not ask if I enjoyed my weekend away, whether I had a good journey.

'Have you eaten?' I ask. It is an academic question; Richard would never have dinner this early. When Jamie was young I wanted us to have family meals, to sit round the kitchen table together or even eat in the dining room (a much cosier and less formal prospect in our previous house). I had thought that Richard would welcome that extra time with his son. But, instead, he insisted that I give Jamie high tea on his own then put him to bed before the two of us settled down to our main meal of the day. I can see now that Richard was simply echoing his own childhood. Perpetuating what had been instilled in him as the right and proper way to behave. But to me it was archaic, a relic of the Victorian ethos where children were seen and not heard.

Richard shakes his head. I suspect that he has been engulfed in his music for hours. That he has been oblivious to the passing of time. The fact that the standard lamp was the only light on in the whole house when I arrived back suggests that he has been in this room since dusk.

'We'll eat at eight,' I tell him, assertively. I ask whether he would like a tea or coffee but he declines. I suspect he will pour himself a glass of sherry from the decanter in the drawing room. 'In that case I'll get on,' I say. 'I won't disturb you.'

Back in the kitchen, I kick off my shoes and push them under the table. I have become more relaxed about these things since I have not been working. Partly it is necessity – or rather the recent lack of it. Although, theoretically, my job has regular hours, there always lurks the possibility that I may be called, needed, at any time. And that when that happens everything must be ready, predictable, in its proper place so that I can be suitably dressed, dosed with caffeine, in the car and in the hospital in the minimum of time. And partly it is that I am learning to be rebellious, to assert myself by defying the rules to which I have adhered for so long. It is an act of defiance, of taking control of my life in whatever way I can.

I lay the chopping board on the work surface and take an onion from the trug. One or two of the vegetables show signs of wilting and I make a mental note to keep them somewhere other than in the heat of the kitchen in future. With my being at home most days the heating is on more than it used to be. There is a small lobby before the side door into the porch. This area houses the washing machine and dryer and would be suitably cool, I decide, for the purpose. I take a knife out of the sharpening rack and cut through the onion. I am the sort of person who doesn't like having sharp knives about, I would far rather have just a peeler and a small simple vegetable knife like my mother has and keep them safely stowed out of sight in a drawer. This is despite – or even perhaps because of – the fact that, in my work, I regularly use scalpels to cut through living human flesh. But the kitchen knife set was a wedding present, added to the list at Richard's request and given to us by one of his cousins. I can hardly hide it away in a cupboard.

As I settle into the repetitive task of chopping vegetables, I begin to think about the newspaper article and the forthcoming trial. Within less than half an hour of returning home I have left the weekend behind and am engulfed once more in the ongoing dramas that have befallen my life.

Whilst I feel his actions are unreasonable, I feel desperately sorry for Jack Ashby. I can, to some extent, understand what he is going through. I can feel it deep inside, where it brings back memories of my own experience.

When I was expecting Jamie, I remember how Richard and I felt in the weeks leading up to the birth. With each day our anticipation grew, swelling constantly like the bump in front of me. Just as the growing child vied for space and obliterated my feet from my view, so the emotional focus of what was to come pushed thoughts of anything else from our minds. By the time the due date arrived there was room for nothing else in our lives. As I went overdue, the trepidation, the emotional burden, reached unbearable proportions. There formed a feeling of tension that only the birth of our child could release.

Of course, already working in that field, I had high hopes for the birth. I had made detailed plans for the environment during the early stages of labour, the furnishings I wanted around me, the music I wanted playing in the background. I had also discussed the options of medication with the midwives and agreed the drugs I would be happy to use, should they prove necessary, and those I wished to avoid at all costs. For the delivery itself I wanted a water birth. They were not so common back then but research suggested that they helped the mother by supporting her bodyweight and the child by easing its transition into the world. I hoped that I would pioneer their use in our hospital.

I am not sure at exactly what point things started to go wrong, whether it was during the birth itself or whether our fate was already sealed much earlier due to the relative sizes and positions of Jamie and myself. I don't know whether, had someone spotted the problems sooner, it would have made any difference. Certainly the outcome would have been avoided had I planned to have an elective caesarean but that can bring its own problems and in any case I would never have agreed to it.

For me, the experience that had started out as an idyllic dream turned into a nightmare. I remember the early stages, gasping Entonox and doing the breathing exercises I had learned at antenatal classes and practiced faithfully every day. But gradually, these methods of pain control ceased to be effective. Even the warm gentle water in which I was immersed failed to sooth me. Then the midwife said that 'baby' was becoming distressed and that she was calling for an obstetrician. Immediately, I was dragged from what I perceived as the safety of the pool. People started to tell me that I should push or that I should pant or that I shouldn't do either of those things. After that I began to feel that I was no longer in control of the situation and my memory of what happened next becomes vague. Even in retrospect I don't know whether I passed out due to pain or loss of blood or whether, simply, I succumbed to the swift administration of a general anaesthetic.

The next thing I knew, things were very hazy. As the mist cleared, I remembered that there should be a baby and a moment later Richard appeared holding Jamie. I held out my arms, which I discovered were sore and connected to drips, and Richard pressed Jamie to me. I remember being scared that I would drop him and begging Richard not to let go. It wasn't until I had slept and woke to what I thought was a new day that they told me what had happened. My uterus had ruptured, they said. They had performed an emergency hysterectomy. There would be no more babies.

I remember, during the following weeks, as I slowly recovered from the physical aspect of the ordeal, I felt cheated, not only that there would be no further additions to our family but also that I had been robbed of experiencing the birth of the only child I would ever have.

Of course, with hindsight, I realise how lucky I was, how lucky I still am. Not only did I survive the ordeal but Jamie did as well. And in the face of this current crisis I try to imagine how Richard would have felt if, as so easily could have happened, he had lost both Jamie and myself. Already fired up for the imminent birth, how would that energy have dissipated without Jamie, without me, to restore the balance? Who can say how he would have lashed out, in ways totally out of character to his usual mild manner?

I set the vegetables ready in the steamer and prepare a

171

bowl of seasoned flour to coat the chicken pieces. Then I set the dining room table. We will eat in style I decide. I will make an effort.

It is some time later, when I am clearing away the dinner things, that I get round to taking my jacket and shoes to the cloakroom. That is when I find the scarf. It is hanging on one of the pegs on the right hand side, the ones we generally leave free for guests. After I have deposited my own clothes I pick the scarf up. It is a stylish Paisley design made by Liberty. I know whose it is straight away. I take it through to the drawing room where Richard is doing a crossword in the Sunday paper.

'You didn't tell me Clare called,' I say, holding the scarf up.

He clears his throat. 'Ah yes. She called round on Friday night. She was hoping to catch you before you left.'

I laugh. 'Well I hardly thought she'd be calling to see you,' I say. 'I wish you'd told me earlier though. I'd have given her a call. It's a bit late now.'

'Sorry,' Richard mumbles as he scribbles letters into boxes. 'I expect if it was urgent she'd have called you on your mobile.'

'Yes,' I say. 'I expect she would.'

I take my bag upstairs to unpack. My mind is full of Lyme Regis, of Maggie and Freddie. I do not really pay much attention to matters at home.

Chapter 19

Andrew says that we must meet as soon as possible to discuss my case. He tells me, regretfully, that he has little free time in December but that he can see me on Thursday afternoon if I can come to his chambers in London. I am hesitant. Thursday is not the best time. For one thing I will have to cancel my visit to Frank. I am also apprehensive about going back to London. I have only been there once since Jamie died, since we went to his flat to collect his belongings. Previously to that, the last trip was to his university graduation. Of course, I wanted to go in the intervening time, to visit him, to make sure he was all right. But he always made excuses that it was not convenient, that he was studying or on call. It was only after he died that we realised that all that was a lie. Only when we finally saw his home, learned the circumstances of his death, did we understand why he didn't want us to go there.

'Richard has to work,' I protest. 'He won't be able to come.'

'It is you going to court, not Richard,' Andrew says simply. 'My business is with you.'

So at ten-thirty I catch the train to St Pancras. I do not want to arrive too early, to have spare time to fill. But on the other hand the train might be delayed and I cannot risk being late and missing my appointment.

But the train, at least, departs on time. Once settled, I open my bag and take out the book I have brought to read on the journey. It is The Magus, the second one I bought ten days ago. At first, I was disappointed that this one did not feature Lyme Regis. Instead, it is set on a Greek Island. But after persevering with what, to me, is an unknown location, I have become absorbed in the story. It is about a man who controls people's lives, playing with them as though they are characters he is directing in a play, letting them believe they have free will but, in reality, taking all their choice, all their power, away. It makes me realise how, since Jamie's death, other people have attempted to control my life. Richard, Clare, staff at the hospital. I know that they have done it out of a sense of love, an act of caring. Yet, despite this, rather than making me feel protected, their intervention has taken away my confidence, left me feeling powerless. I have become very aware that there is a different way. That friends such as Sally and Pete – and now Andrew – have supported me yet still let me live my own life.

It is a long time since I have travelled anywhere by train. Although I am interested in the book, I get distracted looking at the countryside through which we pass. I am excited to see a fox slinking across a field and feel voyeuristic as I peek into the back gardens that back onto the railway.

Clare came round for a coffee yesterday evening. She had tried to persuade me to meet her for lunch but, whilst I was happy going to Lyme and am reasonably confident going to London today, I didn't feel able to go into the centre of Nottingham and certainly not to the hospital. Last week, my fears were confirmed and the Echo printed the story about the prosecution. In fairness, it was more about the tragedy of Jack Ashby than making allegations about myself. Andrew told me, when the story ran in the Advertiser, that I should copy that and any other pieces that might be published about me and fax them to him immediately. Firstly, he said he needed a record of them but also, if they actually made any accusations in writing about me then that would be libel and he would demand an immediate retraction and threaten them with prosecution themselves. He assured me that most editors were very aware of the law and that anything they printed would, in all probability, be worded very carefully.

So, worried that I might still be recognised from the paper, I turned down Clare's invitation to lunch but asked if she would like to come round after work instead. I would hold her scarf hostage, I joked, until she came to see me. Richard had already said that he would be working late and Clare suggested she come round at five and leave before he returned home. I teased that she must be determined to avoid him.

'So,' I said, as we sat at the kitchen table drinking tea. 'I hope that Richard invited you in and made you coffee.'

She shook her head. 'Oh no. As soon as he said you'd already gone I made my excuses and left. For some reason I'd thought you were leaving in the morning.'

I took a chocolate biscuit. They have become my regular comfort food these days. 'It's unlike you to forget details like that,' I said. 'Unless your mind is on a new man of course.' I looked at her closely, trying to work out if she was blushing under her make up.

'You haven't told me about your weekend,' she said quickly, changing the subject much too obviously. 'Did you have a good time with your friends in Lyme Regis? Do you have any photos.' I smiled and went to get my camera. I was sure my hunch was right. Clare had found herself yet another boyfriend.

Eventually, we arrive in London and I take the underground to Sloane Square, which is the nearest stop to Andrew's office. I arrive there with time to spare and find a café where I order a toasted sandwich and a pot of tea. I feel glad that I decided to wear a suit. People in London dress more formally than in Nottingham and I am pleased that I seem to fit in with the city dwellers. It feels like many lifetimes ago that I used to live here myself.

At precisely ten minutes before the agreed time, I arrive at Andrew's chambers. The receptionist shows me to a waiting area with sleek black leather sofas, and rings to let Andrew know I am here. The building is Georgian, with tall rectangular windows draped with velvet curtains and expensive-looking highly polished furniture. Men and women, wearing dark tailored suits, and with immaculately styled hair, come and go across the main foyer. I feel quite over-awed.

'Julia! What a pleasure to see you again.'

Andrew is standing beside me. I stand too and reach out to shake the hand that he offers. He clasps my hand reassuringly between his palms and holds it lingeringly for a few seconds. Then he leads me through to his office where we sit, not at the main desk (too much like being called in to see the headmaster, he jokes), but in armchairs on either side of a coffee table. He picks up the phone and asks the receptionist for a pot of coffee. 'Or would you prefer tea?' he asks me. I answer that coffee would be lovely. We exchange pleasantries while we wait for the drinks to arrive. Andrew asks after Richard, and I comment on this luxurious workplace, joking that it is rather more upmarket than that provided by an NHS trust. 'The downside is that I have to pay for this!' Andrew reminds me. There is a discreet tap on the door and the receptionist brings in a tray of coffee and a comprehensive selection of biscuits.

When we are alone, Andrew pours the coffee. 'And now I'm afraid we have to get down to business,' he says.

I sigh. I had been enjoying myself so much I had almost forgotten my reason for being there.

For almost two hours we go through the details which Andrew says will help him prepare the case for court. First we talk about the event itself. I find it distressing reliving an occasion on which someone – two people – died. Although these situations happen and, at the time, you have to deal with them professionally, you never really get used to it. Or, at least, you never feel happier about it. If you did it would be a sign that you should consider giving up medicine. Andrew wants to know everything that happened from the time I first examined Mrs Ashby until the time I recorded her death. He also notes down the names of everyone else involved including the paramedics who brought her in and the porters who transported her to the department. He will cross check with the Board's inquiry, he tells me, but, painful as it is, he needs to hear everything afresh, directly from me.

In the second stage of his preparation, Andrew asks me to think of anyone, professional or personal who can provide character references and vouch for my professionalism generally. I know that Clare will speak on my behalf – she has already promised this – and also my clinical director. In addition, Andrew plans to track down previous supervisors from the time before I became a consultant.

When it is almost time to go Andrew says there is one more thing he needs to speak to me about.

'How are things with Richard?' he asks me.

I am taken aback. It seems rather a personal question; especially coming from a man, from someone I really don't know that well. I hesitate. 'He's still very shocked by everything,' I say.

Andrew looks at me intently. 'Richard has always been a good friend to me,' he says, 'but his upbringing is a little old-fashioned, a little stiff upper lip.'

I nod. I know these things.

'But the thing is,' Andrew continues, 'just because he comes from a family with money, just because his folks have their own way of doing things, that doesn't mean he is always right.'

I feel uncomfortable. I stand ready to leave. Andrew stands too.

'I remember at your wedding,' he says, 'I could see exactly why Richard would want to marry you.' He pauses, bites his lip. 'But I wasn't quite so sure what you saw in him, or whether you really knew what you were letting yourself in for. I remember you back then, how spirited you were. And I know you've had a difficult time but I can see the change in you. Equally, I can see the old you again when you begin to relax.'

He takes both of my hands in his. 'Don't let Richard undermine your confidence,' he tells me. 'Don't forget who you are.' He draws me to him and kisses me lightly on the cheek. He pauses and I feel his breath, warm, close. For a moment I think he is going to kiss me properly, on the lips. I pray that he will not. I am answered. Andrew kisses me briefly on the other cheek then relaxes his hold letting me draw back, though he still holds my hands. 'I'll see you after Christmas,' he says. 'I won't tell you not to worry, that would be insulting. But, in the meantime, if there's anything I can help you with – anything at all – then don't hesitate to call me.' He smiles at me, a warm gentle smile. It reminds me of the way Richard used to look at me. And then we are done. He walks me through the reception foyer to the front door and we say our formal good-byes. Then I go. Dizzy with something I cannot explain.

Friday is a fine day and I potter in the garden, sweeping up leaves that have fallen from the fruit trees and pulling yellowed lily pads from the pond. I have learned, in my years up here, to make the most of the short murky daylight hours at this time of year.

I also make the most of a more positive state of mind. I feel encouraged, having spent the previous afternoon with Andrew. His words and his presence continue to reassure me that everything will be all right. The feeling will not last. I know this. The strength, the certainty, will fade over the course of the coming days. But in the meantime, like the sunlight, I will savour every moment of it.

Eventually, I replace rake and gloves in the shed. The old brick building is at the north side of the house close to the kitchen door. I had hopes, when we first moved in, of making this a patio area with a wisteria-covered pergola and wrought-iron benches. I didn't realise then how dark and dank this corner was, how plants would wither, cheated, or just give up and die within their first year; how the sun would struggle to find a way in even in the height of summer. A hedged path leads up here directly from the road.

178

It is used occasionally to transport garden supplies in and, more regularly, to take rubbish out (and Mrs Blackstock does this job). To me it is a dark void, a black hole that would suck me into its heartless centre. It gives me the creeps, makes me feel chilled and depressed. Generally, I circumvent the problem by accessing the garden either via the conservatory or occasionally through the French doors in the morning room.

But today, I stop to sweep up the leaves before they have chance to moulder. I am defying nature, I tell myself, confronting my fears. The foliage that survives here is dark and dense. Beyond the hedge, I can see the spiky finial and steeply-pitched semi-circular roof of a porch tower. The neighbouring house – or at least what you can see of it from our garden and from the road – is more Gothic than ours. The roof looms from amongst the dark overgrown garden in a complex pattern of pinnacles and eaves. It has an air of foreboding, as though it belongs to the strange world of Gormenghast.

This house is where Mrs Perriman lives. I have only spoken to her on a handful of occasions since we came to live here, and those were mostly in the early years. Certainly, I have never been inside her home. I accept that she is reclusive, that she chooses to keep her privacy in her own world. At first, I used to worry about her. What if she fell ill? Died even? Nobody would know for months. But I have observed that supplies are regularly delivered to her door. During the time I have been off work I have noticed that her back door creaks open followed by a rustling sound and then a creaking shut and a click of the lock as, presumably, she takes the milk in, at precisely seven-thirty every morning. I have grown accustomed to listening out for this event each day, as though it signifies that the world still continues.

Sometimes, when I am in this part of the garden, when I am in fact only yards from her back door, I find myself imagining what her life within those walls is like. I picture wild fantastical images of my neighbour as Miss Havisham, sitting in her bonnets and petticoats of ancient yellowed lace, amidst vast rooms of crumbling furniture, draped in sheets heavy with dust, with rats gnawing at the upholstery beneath. On blacker days, when the sky is overcast or the air murky with fog, I picture even more sinister scenes of long-dead grandparents, decomposing amidst swarming flies attracted by the dreadful stench, in long abandoned attics.

The thought of this now makes me shudder. I hurriedly discard my boots in the porch and make for the reassuring comfort of the Aga. But when I am safely installed with my coffee and my book I stop to think about what Sally said when we were in Somerset, about neighbours watching out for one another. And I make a mental note, as it is almost Christmas, to buy a small gift for Mrs Perriman.

Chapter 20

The following Wednesday, I go to Rose for another regression. I am beginning to look forward to my appointments with Rose, not just as an opportunity to find out more about my past life but simply for the pleasure of spending time in her company. I remember, one of my patients a few years ago telling me that she sometimes consulted a complementary therapist. She said that, whether or not the particular therapy was effective, she felt instantly uplifted by being with the practitioner, by talking to them. Now I am beginning to understand what she meant. I wonder whether all alternative healers have this effect and what it is they have that we medically and surgically trained professionals do not. So it is that I arrive at Rose's house in the sure knowledge that, however I feel now, whatever is revealed by the hypnosis, I will feel better than this after the visit.

We relax in the soft scented world. Rose brushes her hand softly on my arm as she ushers me to sit down. This is a little part of it, I think to myself. Now I consider it there is always some physical contact, however casual, however fleeting. Physical touch has been overlooked in our society for so long. We are only just recognising the importance of skin-to-skin contact between mothers and premature babies, how nestling against the mother's skin can provide some hidden healing that the safe constant world of the incubator cannot.

First, Rose and I discuss the previous regression and my feelings in the days that followed. Then I tell her about my visit to Lyme Regis, about my dream and what happened on the beach.

'There is something you need to resolve,' she tells me. 'It isn't necessarily anything terrible. Maggie is clearly becoming more educated than Freddie. Perhaps she is simply more intelligent, but I suspect there is something else, a fundamental difference.'

I think about it. 'I haven't seen her home life,' I admit.

'Exactly,' Rose nods. 'It may be that her parents consider Freddie is no longer good enough for her. They may have bettered themselves somehow. Perhaps they have in mind for her to marry a rich merchant. If this were the case Maggie might feel that she let Freddie down.' She pauses. 'I shouldn't really be surmising like this. I don't want to influence what you experience in your regression. But on the other hand, I don't want you to be scared when perhaps there is no need.' She takes my hand. 'Sometimes,' she tells me, 'our past lives are a learning process. They show us the mistakes we have made previously so that we may live better in this life. They may become apparent at a time when their lesson can help us. And you must also remember,' Rose continues, 'that you usually only ever see a snapshot of these lives, one or two incidents, out of context. It would be a mistake to dwell too much on any of this or try to equate it with your life now. Think instead about how the experience can help you.'

I nod and settle myself on the sofa. Maggie is waiting for me. I can sense it already.

I'm skipping down the hill. It's steep and I go fast, bouncing, like a pebble, down to the jetty. On the seafront it's quiet. The fishing boats are out with the tide. Freddie's gone with them too so I'm on my own.

First, I run down the Cobb. With Alf away at sea there's no-one to tease me. I go all the way to the end and call out to the seagulls. I wonder if they like flying or if they only do it to get food. I'd like it, I reckon. But I wonder, if they do enjoy it, why they always sound so sad. I bound back up to the beach and jump with all my might onto the shingle. I'm trying to make a really big crunching sound even though it scuffs my shoes. I know really that I'm getting too grown up for all this lark but there's no-one about to see me so what does it matter?

I don't expect there to be anyone on the beach but it turns out there is. The first I know is a clinking sound that rings and echoes, like there's a whole line of boats with their rigging going in the wind. It's only when I'm right up next to him that I see him. He's up close to the cliff, hidden behind a spike of rock. He's got a hammer and he's picking out stones from the bottom of the cliff and hitting them so the rock splinters and shatters. I've never seen the like. I stand back and watch, amazed. He's well dressed, like a gentleman. Not the sort you'd expect to see doing this sort of work.

Suddenly he looks up. I move back because I'm not sure I should be there. Perhaps I've caught him up to no good.

'Good morning,' he says to me, and raises his hat briefly.

I don't answer cos I'm not sure I ought.'I'm the new curate in Uplyme,' the stranger tells me. And I notice then that he's wearing the right sort of clothes for it, I reckon he's probably telling the truth.

'I'm Maggie, sir,' I say, 'and morning to you too.' I'm aware that, though it isn't polite, I'm staring at the hammer.

'I'm looking for fossils,' he tells me.

'What? In there?' I ask, nodding at the piece of rock he's holding.

He nods. 'Sometimes you can tell by the size and the shape of the rock, which ones will have a fossil inside.' He offers me the hammer and the stone in his hand. 'Here,' he says, 'you have a go.'

And he seems friendly and safe and with him being clergy and all I'm sure it'll be all right. At first I give it a little hit and nothing happens. Then I get more confident and hit harder. The hammer swings and hits the rock with a searing crack. I'm amazed as it splits right in half.

'There,' the curate says. 'It's just like cracking an egg. But lets see if there's a yolk.' He bends down and turns the two halves so I can see them. Sure enough, there's a perfect spiral nestled inside, like the creature's gone to sleep in a safe place.

He picks it up and offers it to me. 'Here,' he says, 'you found it.'

I'd like to stay and find some more fossils. I feel safe here. Nothing bad's going to happen to me. But my friend's calling. She's telling me I have to go. I don't want to, that's for sure. But she's pleading with me again. I wish, as I stow the fossil, heavy in my pocket, that I could just live days like today over and over.

The beach is changing. It's warmer but I don't like it so much. I don't want to be here. Please don't make me.

There's been a storm again. There's lots of storms. It'd be a good time to go hunting for fossils but I'm not interested in them just now. I'd rather be at home. I'll go back there soon but I have to find Freddie first. I know he's down here somewhere.

'Freddie! Freddie, where are you?'

The wind's getting really strong, the sea too. I can hardly hear anything, it's so noisy. Can't see properly either with the salt spray in my eyes.

I've had enough now. Please don't make me go any further.

Thank God, Freddie's here.

I want to go home now. I can't go on. If I do then something terrible will happen. Let me go back. I hurt. I can't breathe.

Help me!

'Wide awake, Julia!' Rose says.

I'm coughing, my hand is cradling my throat.

'It's all right,' Rose assures me. 'It's all right. You're Julia. You're perfectly safe.'

And although, at first, I feel scared, disoriented, I know that Rose will look after me, that for today at least, I will be all right.

On Thursday, as I wake, the events of yesterday's hypnosis

return to haunt me. Rose has explained how the hypnogogic phase, the transition between waking and sleeping, is now becoming recognised as a previously overlooked altered state of consciousness. It is a time when our minds are open to new ideas, she has told me, when creative people have their most powerful insights. It is also a time when the real and the unreal, the physical and the imagined, become confused. She has suggested that I make a note of the ideas, the thoughts that I have at this time, but also that I rise immediately, take a shower, have a coffee; that I do not interpret the unreal as a portent of the future. I wish I could see it all more clearly. I remember every detail of the curate and finding the fossil. But after that it's a jumble. The recording that Rose made gives no further clues. Whatever happened to Maggie, she didn't want to tell us about it; didn't want to relive it.

I will do as Rose advised and get out of bed, get on with my day. But this morning, I know that however much coffee I drink, however long I spend in the shower, I will still maintain the belief that, many years ago, Freddie killed Maggie on the beach at Lyme Regis. It is beginning to scare me. I wish I knew what Maggie was trying to tell me. I almost wish I had never started this. But there is no going back now. Maggie's life is becoming so entwined with my own that sometimes I feel I cannot separate the two.

I think about the fact that I am due to visit Frank today. It is two weeks since I last saw him and I am feeling increasingly apprehensive. Because, despite what Rose said, about Freddie being part of a different lifetime, Frank is a killer in this life. That is the truth of the matter. That is the fact I have somehow excused, put to the back of my mind. Until now.

Whether or not Rose is right about learning from previous lives, I take her advice on banishing this dream-like musing. I pull on my dressing gown and go down to the kitchen to make coffee. Whilst I am waiting for the kettle to boil, I hear the clink of the letterbox and pad down the hall to collect the post. There are several letters and a subscription magazine folded in half in its wrapping. The bundle has not fallen onto the mat but stays wedged in the letterbox, allowing an icy draft to cut down the hall. I shiver and pull the handful of post through quickly.

There are the usual circulars and sales pitches. The magazine is an American journal on vascular surgery; it is for Richard. There is only one letter addressed to me. The envelope is written in a hand I do not recognise. I cannot make out the postmark. Carefully, I open it and unfold the single sheet.

Dear Mrs Spencer,

You do not know me but I would very much like to meet you and talk to you. It is too complicated to explain further in a letter. Please could you call me on the above number and perhaps we could arrange to meet.

Yours sincerely,

Sarah Jacobs

I read it through again. There is no address, just a phone number which looks to be on a mobile network. Immediately, I pick up my phone and begin to dial the number. Then I stop. I remember what Andrew said about not answering phone calls or letters, not speaking to anyone I do not know. Given recent events, it is quite possible that this Sarah is a reporter, gathering scandalous information for a newspaper article. Perhaps she is someone from the national press. I shudder in horror. Worse still, she could be someone working for the prosecution, somebody hoping to wheedle her way into my trust, to entice me into saying things I do not mean, to trap me.

186

My first instinct is to throw the letter into the bin. But then I consider that it might be evidence and I retrieve it and put it aside. When I next see Andrew I can show it to him to follow up if he deems this necessary.

Throughout the day, I do my best to focus on the here and now. But as I arrive at the prison, I am thinking again of what I saw, what I felt under hypnosis. It replays in my mind on a never-ending loop, overlaying the world around me. It paints spirals and fishing boats on the blank walls, transforms the clanking of the steel grey doors into the crashing of waves.

When Lizzie intercepts me, as I sign in at reception, I wonder at first if something is wrong. That Frank is ill perhaps, or that the authorities have read about me in the paper and will no longer allow me to be a visitor.

'He's fine,' she reassures me as we sit in her office. 'It's just that I felt I should prepare you. He has a favour to ask.'

I am curious. 'Is it about Christmas?' I ask. 'Obviously, I'll buy him a gift and I'll try to visit during Christmas week.'

Lizzie shakes her head. 'It's something entirely different. I don't want to say any more because Frank wants to ask you himself. All I would say is that it's all been approved. But I don't want you to feel pressured. When he asks you it will probably be best not to give an immediate answer but to say that you will have to think about it. That you will need to speak to me first.'

I am even more intrigued but Lizzie refuses to say any more. 'Go and talk to Frank now,' she says. 'He missed you last week.'

My curiosity about what Lizzie said – what she would not say – helps to banish the ghosts that haunt me. As usual we go through the niceties of polite conversation. Frank tells me that he missed our conversation last week. I explain that I had an appointment in London. I wish I could tell him more, explain that I am not ill, nor was I seeking to avoid him. He is the one person I know who would truly understand how I feel about the prospect of going to court. But I remind myself that I am here for Frank, not the other way round. Whilst I have decided to tell him about Jamie, about how I have recently lost my son, I decide that this other matter would not be appropriate.

We have been chatting idly for a while but suddenly Frank is serious. He looks at me longingly, wistfully. Then he speaks. 'I've been approved home leave,' he says, 'my first chance in years to get out of here for a couple of days. But you see, I don't have a home.' He pauses, looks at me intently. 'So I was wondering if I could spend it at your house.'

I am shocked. This is not at all what I was expecting.

'I'll have to think about it,' I reply, glad that Lizzie has told me the words I should say. 'I'll have to discuss it with Lizzie and with my husband. Find out if it is possible.'

'But you will consider it?' he presses me.

'I promise I will,' I say. And then I leave.

On the way out I stop again to talk to Lizzie. It is more formal this time. She explains the need for prisoners to become accustomed to the outside world; the fact that a good record of home leave will go in their favour when they are considered for release.

'But I thought Frank was coming to the end of his sentence next year anyway,' I say.

Lizzie explains that, these days, it is highly unusual for prisoners to actually complete their sentences. There are a number of reasons, she tells me, including their record of behaviour in prison, whether they are considered to be a danger to the public and the simple fact that prisons are overcrowded and sentences are being reduced to create more space. She explains how, after serving perhaps two thirds of their time, prisoners are released on parole, or on license as it is now more commonly called. Since Frank was sent to prison, the rules have changed.

'And doesn't Frank have any family with whom he could

spend this leave?' I ask.

'No. His mother died five years ago – he was allowed out to attend the funeral accompanied by our officers. There is a daughter but they are estranged. I believe she lives in Australia.' Lizzie pauses. 'Discuss it with your husband,' she tells me. 'We are looking at a weekend in mid January. It would only involve one night.'

By the time we are finished I have missed the prison bus but I don't mind the walk. I have plenty to think about as I make my way home.

Chapter 21

The following day dawns very cold. It rained during the night and by morning the puddles are glazed over. I go outside to chip away at the ice on the pond. It is almost the solstice now. Midwinter is the worst time here. In the morning it is not fully light before nine and in the afternoon the sky begins to dull soon after three.

Today, Clare has persuaded me to have lunch with her at the hospital. She says that I should face my demons. I am sure that in some ways she is right. Certainly, I know that, absent of blame, I should stand my ground. But that knowledge does not make me feel any less nervous. Apart from the prison visits, I have avoided going into Nottingham since the article in the paper. Certainly, I have avoided my place of work. Although the charges against me are ridiculous; although, deep down, I know that I acted in a completely professional way; somewhere inside me, doubt is growing like a virus. During the weeks of the Board's inquiry it was incubating, biding its time. Now it has exploded into my system, day by day it is silently eating away my confidence. For the first time in my career, I am losing my self-belief. I question my ability to do the job I have performed for over twenty years. Whilst, in the weeks after Jamie's death, I welcomed seeing familiar faces in the canteen, now I feel like a disobedient child, expelled from school. I am a trespasser. I imagine I hear people whispering behind my back, 'There goes Dr Death,' or, 'She killed a woman you know.' Perhaps people really are saying these things. Most of us enjoy a scandal after all.

But Clare says this is not the case. People will support me, she insists. This allegation, which has fallen at my door, could have happened to anyone. People will see it as a landmark case, she tells me. They will be watching, not out of a morbid fascination, an opportunity to gossip, but rather to see how the legal system deals with it, because ultimately, the outcome has implications for everyone in the medical profession.

Knowing my fears, Clare has suggested that we meet in her office; that we walk into the canteen together. In this way, should there be any spiteful remarks, any thinly disguised disapproving glances, I will not have to face them alone. Moreover, in accompanying me, Clare will be making a public statement, declaring that she supports me, that she does not believe the rumours and the gossip put about by the press.

I am glad of the cold weather. It gives me an excuse to wear a hat and scarf pulled well down over my face. With my hair tucked into my collar, it is possible to hide almost every recognisable feature. I keep these outdoor clothes on as I walk through the foyer and into the lift. On the second floor, I knock on Clare's door and when, after a few moments, there is no answer, I push it gently open.

I am always a little guarded when I go to Clare's office, aware that she might be with a client, perhaps in a traumatic counselling session or in the middle of some procedure of behavioural therapy. Although she uses a 'do not disturb' sign on her door when she is consulting, I always prefer to err on the side of caution. On this occasion, the room is empty and I go inside and, already sweltering in the hospital's overly hot ambient temperature, I take off my outdoor clothes. It is still five minutes before our agreed meeting time so I sit down on one of the low informal consulting chairs.

I have only been there a few moments when the phone rings. My instinct is to answer it and take a message. Yet as I reach the desk I change my mind and realise that it would be better, as this is not my department, to let it switch onto the answering machine. Clare favours the type of machine where you can listen to the message as it is left and choose whether to intercept it. On this occasion she has clearly left it on the speaker setting because I hear her voice warmly and calmly greeting the caller, reassuring them that she will definitely ring them back at the earliest opportunity. I wander away from the desk, trying not to listen to what might be a confidential message. It is only when I hear Richard's voice that I come to with a start. 'Clare,' he says, 'I need to see you soon. Please could you call me.'

I am about to pick up the phone and say 'Hi', but he rings off abruptly and before I have time to think of calling him back Clare appears.

'Ready?' she calls from the doorway. I stand up to hug her. I would have casually mentioned Richard's call but suddenly I am caught up thinking about more pressing matters, of running the gauntlet of a very public lunch. Clare chats to me, seemingly of everyday things, but really I know she is boosting my morale ready for the test to come. She links her arm through mine and we walk together down the corridor.

As usual, Christmas approaches in a flurry. Not a shower of snow, but rather a hectic rush of things that need to be done, people who need to be paid attention. Even though, without Jamie, there is no question of actually celebrating the festival, it is still going on around me; there are duties to be honoured.

I knew from the start that I would not decorate the house. There would be no tree, natural or artificial, no glittering streamers trailing from one corner of a room to another, no brightly-coloured lights arranged around the front windows. I did feel, however, that it would be appropriate to send cards and to display the ones we received. The first ones trickled through the letterbox even before I went to Lyme. The rest increased exponentially, reaching a peak now, a week before the event, hereafter they will dwindle in ones and twos until the New Year.

If I do not know how to cope with this season of merriment, neither, it seems, do my friends. As I read each card, I sense how the sender has struggled with what to say. Where, previously, they would have bade us a merry time or festive greetings, people wish us peace and comfort and goodwill. There are more religious cards than usual with tasteful nativity scenes in dark or muted colours. Of course, some people send the same general greeting, a standard card and letter, to all their recipients. And in some ways, I welcome the normality of this; the fact that Richard and I have not been singled out for special treatment. Sadly, one or two are also addressed to Jamie. They are from distant friends with whom we maintain minimal contact. And while we tried our best to let everyone know what had happened, it was inevitable that some would slip through the net. When I have got over the shock and blinked back the tears, I display these cards in a group together, as though they form a shrine.

I am glad that I have already bought some gifts in Lyme. Feeling I cannot cope with the reminders that lurk, like mantraps, around the city centre of Nottingham, I decide to do the rest of my shopping in Derby. Although the shops are decorated with glitter and tinsel and although the same repetitive round of Christmas carols is relayed relentlessly and unconvincingly, filling every space, this does not bother me unduly. This is not my Christmas but someone else's.

I buy a selection of luxury chocolates to accompany other gifts. I choose a couple of books and a CD for Frank and some DVDs for Pete and Sally. I cannot imagine what Mrs Perriman would like. I rule out the usual 'elderly' options of a tea cosy or lavender-scented eau de Cologne and eventually settle for chocolates along with a recently published novel.

Back at home a parcel arrives from Andrew. When I remove the outer cushioned wrapping, I find that, in addition to the card and the gift addressed to both Richard and myself (almost certainly a tasteful calendar and a classical CD), there is also a soft parcel wrapped in tissue paper addressed only to me. I feel touched. For some reason, I do not wait to show this to Richard but take it upstairs where I stow it out of sight in my study. I have not sent anything individually to Andrew although I assume that Richard will have sent a gift from both of us as he usually does. I wonder if I should have bought something. It is too late now, in any case. I can choose a gift in the New Year, by way of a thank you for all his help.

Almost everything is done now. I just have to see Sally and Pete to give them their gifts - and Clare, of course.

It is on the Wednesday evening, the day before my Christmas visit to Frank, that I finally pluck up courage to talk to Richard, to mention the request of the previous week.

'The prison authorities have asked if we could entertain someone for the day.' I say it casually, do not use the word prisoner or inmate, do not mention that it would be, not only for the day, but also the night. I am hoping that Richard will agree automatically, will not listen carefully to what I am saying. But I am disappointed.

'Are you mad?' he demands. 'Invite a convicted criminal into the house when you are about to go to court? How do you think that will look?'

'It wasn't my suggestion,' I defend myself, 'the liaison officer asked me.'

'Saw you coming more like,' Richard mumbles as he pours himself a whisky. 'Apart from the fact that he'd probably make off with our valuables as soon as our backs were turned, how do you think it would make me look?' He takes a long gulp.

'I don't understand?'

'For goodness sake. Here I am, my wife about to go on trial for murder or whatever they decide to call it, and then, as if I haven't been humiliated enough already, she invites a convict round for dinner. Really Julia, this is all very difficult for me. I have a reputation to uphold, had you thought of that?'

I feel my eyes burning. Difficult for you? I feel like saying. How do you think it is for me? But I do not want a row. I mutter something about seeing to dinner and leave the room. Part of me is angry at him for refusing so vehemently, for not even discussing the matter with me. But, in view of my misgivings over Maggie and Freddie, I am secretly relieved that the matter is taken out of my hands. That it is a decision I do not have to make.

I speak to Lizzie the following day, before I go in to see Frank.

'I'm so sorry,' I say, 'but my husband won't agree to it.'

'Please don't tell Frank for definite until after Christmas,' she says. 'There's a possibility your husband will come round when he gets used to the idea. Perhaps he would consider it if we change the date. If nothing else, it will give us chance to make other arrangements. But I'd be happier if we didn't have to disappoint Frank right now. It's a difficult time for him.'

It is a difficult time for me too, I think to myself.

I feel guilty about it minutes later when I hand him his present, reminding him not to open it till the day. To my surprise he has something for me too, a beautifully carved and polished picture frame, which, he tells me, he made himself in the woodwork group. Suddenly, my gift to him seems inadequate.

'Have you thought about what I asked?' he says, later, as I prepare to leave.

And I feel guilty, knowing that, really, there is only one present he wants for Christmas and it is down to me whether he receives it.

Chapter 22

It is the first Christmas that Richard and I have spent apart since we were married. It is the first Christmas without Jamie. These things are foremost in my mind as I drive down to Somerset on Christmas Eve. It occurs to me that the day that should be the greatest time of celebration in the Christian calendar is all too often the day of most sadness and difficulty. Once I have got through tomorrow, I tell myself, surely things will begin to get better.

This time I take the M1, branching off onto the M69 to Coventry. From hereon, I follow the same route as last time, stopping at Stow-on-the-Wold for lunch. It is a grey drizzly day such that people rush from cars to shops and shops to bus stops; all the time with their heads bent towards the ground. The weather prevents them from talking to one another or exchanging festive greetings.

When I suggested to Richard, a few days ago, that the two of us might go to my mother's for Christmas he told me immediately that he had volunteered to work. Even though I pointed out that there would probably still be time to book a motel, he would not budge, saying that there were things he wanted to catch up with. With the extra hours he had put in during the past five months, I knew this was almost certainly untrue. I said that in that case I would not go away, I would invite my mother to Nottingham for a few days instead. It was, after all, one thing for him to be working but quite another for him to be alone in the house for the duration. Fitting around hospital schedules has always been a way of life for Richard and myself. There were plenty of Christmases, especially when we were junior doctors, when one or both of us had to work. But we always managed. Even if we sat down to turkey and all the trimmings at two in the morning with a delighted Jamie doubly excited at being allowed up for a midnight feast, we always somehow celebrated Christmas together. But Richard was so insistent that I go to Somerset that I truly believe he is looking forward to spending some time on his own. Although, I suspect, when it comes to it, he will drive to Lincolnshire for dinner, at least.

I drive into the centre of Cirencester rather than taking the fast route round the ring road. In addition to enjoying the hustle and bustle, the security of having people around me, I also want to stop for a last minute errand. I pull over in the market place where others, like myself, make the most of the last few shopping hours to purchase those odds and ends they have overlooked. I go into a general store and buy a box of chocolates for each of the neighbours who live on either side of my mother. It is a small gesture by way of saying thank you to them for keeping an eye on her in my absence. Earlier this morning, I took round the gift for my own neighbour, Mrs Perriman. I was faced with the dilemma of not wanting to disturb her, uninvited, but equally not wanting to leave her present undiscovered, becoming spoiled in the cold and rain. In the end, I decided that the best thing would be to take it round a little before seven-thirty and put it beside her carton of milk. That way, I would know she had received it when I heard the click of the door. I was even able to confirm, half an hour later, by bending down on my hands and knees and peering discreetly past the thick stems of the hedge, that this had been successfully accomplished.

Despite the seasonal traffic, I make good time and arrive at my mother's house by mid afternoon. As usual, she comes outside to greet me and to welcome me back home. I have received this welcome three times now in the past few weeks, far more often than usual. As I step inside, I see she has decorated an artificial Christmas tree in the front room. The lights are already switched on, reflecting bright metallic colours in the tinsel. She sees me looking.

'I wasn't sure whether I should,' she says. But I assure her that it is the right thing to do. I have to resume a semblance of normality. Whether I like it or not, the world is carrying on without Jamie. When I have drunk the customary cup of tea, I say I will go for a short walk to stretch my legs after the drive. I check whether my mother needs anything from the shops before they close. But, as always, I know she will have stocked the fridge and cupboards with enough food for at least a fortnight.

When I return, my mother asks how Sally is, such a nice girl, she says, so homely. And it occurs to me then, why my mother and Sally get on so well, why I get on with her so well. Sally is me. She is the person I would have been had I stayed in Somerset, had I not gone away to university. Pete is the sort of man I would have married. Do I envy them? I ask myself. Would I rather have Sally's life than my own? It is hypothetical, I know. Sally has an acceptance of life, of herself, an inner contentment. Certainly, I envy her that quality, that gift. But I am sure it is due to her inherent personality rather than her circumstances. If I did not have my job, my opportunities, perhaps I would simply be bored and frustrated. One thing I do envy, though, is that she will be celebrating Christmas with all her family, her husband, parents, children. They will all be together in various combinations over the forthcoming days. Sally does not have to choose between them.

But, for better or worse, I have made my choice. I take my bag upstairs and settle in. Compared with the house in Nottingham, at this time of year, my room is cosily snug. When I grew up, it was cold and draughty. There was no heating in the house apart from the wood burning stove and a coal fire downstairs. When Jamie was young, I insisted on paying to have electric storage heaters installed for fear of him freezing in the attic. Although, at first my parents protested, I think they were really quite pleased. Certainly they were glad of the extra heating as they grew older. When I have consigned my clothes to the wardrobe and drawers, I take the presents downstairs to put under the tree. As well as my gifts for my mother there is a separate one from Richard and another from Sally and Pete (I know that this is a framed photograph of Lyme Regis). I also take the presents from Richard, Clare, and Sally and Pete, which are addressed to me. I deliberate about whether to leave the gift from Andrew to open in the privacy of my room but eventually decide to put it with the others.

On Christmas morning, we prepare the vegetables and set the chicken roasting in the oven before we go to church. I exchange smiles and nods with the people I know. I expect they are wondering where Richard is, why my husband is not with me. Perhaps some of them will ask later. I am glad to have the excuse of his work. The church is full to capacity, with extra chairs arranged by the sidesmen to supplement the pews. It takes longer than usual to administer bread and wine to all the communicants.

Richard rings at midday and dutifully wishes my mother and me a good Christmas. He says that he will stay at the hospital until six, at which point a registrar will be on site and another consultant will be at home nearby, on call. He'll drive to Lincoln then, he says; he can be with his parents in time for dinner. Obviously he'll stay over that night and probably the next one too. He asks when I am planning to return and I say that I'll be back in a couple of days.

My mother and I sit down to our roast dinner, not because we are celebrating but because it is the tradition. Afterwards we open our presents for the same reason.

She is surprised to receive a gift from Sally and Pete. 'I wish they hadn't bothered,' she tuts, clearly very glad that they have. 'I haven't got anything for them.'

'They won't mind,' I reassure her. 'I think it's just a little gesture.'

My mother unwraps the photograph. It shows Sally, Pete and myself standing at the shore end of the Cobb. I remember Pete asking a passer-by if they'd mind taking it.

'It's lovely,' my mother says, propping it on the table. But I can see she looks troubled. 'What made you think of going there?' She asks.

I remind her that Pete and Sally used to go there on holiday, that they suggested it. But I don't like keeping secrets from my mother. It is bad enough having to lie about the court case, pretending that I am taking extra time off work by choice. And so I think why not? I described plenty of my dreams to her when I was a child after all. I don't mention Frank. That would worry her too much. But I tell her about the recent dreams and the hypnosis. Once I have begun, it is the most natural thing in the world. I tell her everything I know about Maggie and Freddie. I enjoy describing all the details, reliving the sounds and the smells and the way I felt. I almost wish I had brought the CDs with me (along with a player as my mother doesn't own one) so that she could hear the accounts first hand, but I remember that I have left them with Sally so she can play them to Debbie who, apparently, is still very keen on the idea of hypnosis for the birth.

When I have finished, I expect my mother to laugh, to reassure me that it is all in my imagination, just like she used to. But when I look up she is looking serious, sad even. For a moment I fear that she is going to cry.

She opens her mouth to speak, then pauses, as though she is carefully selecting the words that she will say. The silence is ominous. It scares me.

At last she speaks. 'I think there are some things I need to tell you, Julia.'

I wait, wondering what could be so terrible.

She takes a deep breath. 'You see, I think the reason that you know so much about Lyme is that you were born there.'

I am confused. 'But you said we never went,' I say.

'We didn't – not as a family anyway. But you lived there until you were three years old. Then you were brought to Somerset. That was when you came to live with your father and me, when we adopted you.'

I stare at her speechless. An invisible hand grabs my stomach. The story of my life is about to be rewritten.

Chapter 23

My mother begins to tell me things. Her words spill out in a jumble. She is clearly distressed.

'Stop!' I say. 'Take your time.' I stand. 'I'll make a pot of tea.' But I think better of it and instead I pour us each a glass of the sherry I have brought. It is dark and sweet, the way my mother likes it. Not the pale dry Fino that Richard drinks. Only when she has drunk half of the small glass, when I have finished and replenished mine, do I let her continue.

She can only tell me the things she knows herself, the things the adoption agency told her. My mother worries about this. She frets that what she has to say will not be enough. But what can I do? The story of my life has been passed around from person to person. It is like DNA replicating itself, with details getting changed or lost forever with every repetition.

I listen carefully. This is the ultimate tale a mother can tell her daughter. It is the story of who I am.

'Your natural mother was in her teens when you were born,' she begins. 'She wasn't married and you weren't intended, I suspect - but that doesn't mean you weren't wanted or loved.' My mother tells me this emphatically. She continues and I clutch anxiously onto every word. As though I am very small and she is reading from my favourite book. There was a boyfriend, it seems, though no-one seemed to know whether he was my father. There had been others before him. And they didn't do tests in those days. It wasn't easy back then if you weren't married; it wasn't accepted. It must have been very difficult for my mother, for all of us. From early on, she used to drink too much. But, irresponsible or not, who are we to judge, when she was little more than a child herself and no sign of any parents to look after her?

As she describes all this, my mother is careful not to apportion blame. Whether this reflects her true feelings, or whether it is for my benefit, I cannot be sure. I listen carefully as she tells me more about my natural mother. It is a brief life history; the story of someone too young, too inexperienced to cope with motherhood. Drink seemed to feature regularly. At some point she started using drugs. Heroin. My mother pauses after she says this. She is watching me, fearful of my reaction. But I take a deep breath and say nothing so she carries on. She didn't seem to be taking it when I was born or surely the hospital would have noticed. Retrospectively, everyone said it was obvious. But at the time no-one knew – or at least they said they didn't. Social services were not so bothered back then, so long as children looked well fed at health checks. Twenty years later, they were fired up, constantly taking children away from their parents amidst spurious suggestions of satanic abuse. But not back then.

After it happened, they found me by chance. A neighbour thought she could smell gas and the police came and broke the door down. At that point; I hadn't eaten for two days. That was how long my natural mother had lain dead on the floor. It was an overdose; an accident probably. No-one thought she would have intentionally left me there to starve. There was no sign of the boyfriend. In fact, come to think, no-one had seen him for a week or two. Maybe he'd left. Maybe that was why my mother had taken too much, to take away the pain.

The person I have always called 'mother' looks up to see how I am taking all this.

I am overwhelmed. It is more than I can digest in one go. I pour another glass of sherry to assist the process. Despite her protests, I pour a top up for my mother too. I urge her to continue. I am filled to bursting with unbelievable information but I need to know more, to know it all, whatever the cost.

It was obvious, from the outset, that I would be adopted. There was no-one else, no relative who could care for me. It was decided that it would be better if I were moved out of the area. Lyme was a small enough place that everyone would know. How could I settle into a new family with people pointing and staring? Speed was of the essence. I was just three years old. Everyone wanted to adopt babies in those days. And there were plenty around because the contraceptive pill was not yet readily available. It was tremendously good fortune that a couple in Somerset were keen to take me.

At this point, my mother says she has some things the adoption agency gave her. She will find them now, she says. I try to stop her. She is all I have left. I do not want to put her through so much all at once. I can find these things for myself later, I reason. But she insists. So this time I make the long-deferred pot of tea while she rummages for sealed boxes at the back of her wardrobe.

As my mother sips tea, I pick through the contents of a shoebox. The cardboard box that once held a pair of Clark's ladies' brown lace-ups now contains the entire history of my life. It is a Christmas stocking, full of surprises, little things of no economic worth. Yet each time I put my hand inside, I tingle with anticipation. I hold up a photograph of the girl who must be my mother. The picture is not good. It is black and white and hazy, presumably taken on a cheap home camera, long before they made them easy to use. I peer, trying to make out the features, trying to decide whether I look like her. It is difficult to tell. She is little more than a girl. I unfold a crisp yellowed sheet of paper. It is my original birth certificate. I read the names. My natural mother is Mary Elizabeth Corby. My father is not named. I do a double take when I see that the name I was given is Margaret. Margaret, I whisper to myself. Maggie.

Perhaps it is because I had been thinking about other things, about my biological parents, wondering what they were like, what their hobbies were, whether my father was still alive, even. Maybe it is because my mind is diverted by all these things that it is fully two hours later, when the lights are lit on the artificial Christmas tree and we are eating the traditional dark fruit cake, heavy with royal icing, that I realise something doesn't add up. It is my birth certificate. I have a copy of course. I needed to show it when I took up my place at medical school and when I began my job. It gives my name as Julia Rosemary, it lists both of my parents – and although it is filed away in Nottingham, although I have not looked at it in a long time, I know exactly what is written on it. I remember feeling embarrassed, when I married Richard, that my father's occupation was specified as a miner. I wipe my hands on a paper napkin and take the original from the box. There is something that I missed. The date of birth is listed as two weeks later than my own. For a few moments I am baffled. Maybe there is a mistake and this is not me after all. Maybe there was some confusion with the adoption. Like those instances when babies got mixed up in the hospital and two families unwittingly took home another person's child to bring up as their own.

My mother is watching me. 'There are more things you don't know she says.'

I look up, eyebrows raised.

'Let me top the pot up,' she says, 'then I'll tell you about your father and me.'

And so my mother begins to tell me about another secret life. Not mine, this time, but hers. This time I have no part in it – the beginning anyway – this time I listen in a different way.

She tells me a story of a young couple who fall in love, marry, want a family. Their friends have children but it seems they are not similarly blessed. Eventually, when they have almost given up hope of it happening for them, they have a daughter. They call her Julia – I feel the hairs on the back of my neck prickle at this. For two years everything is perfect. Then, suddenly, tragedy intervenes. Julia falls acutely ill. Before the doctors even know what is wrong she develops a fever. There are fits and lapses of consciousness and then no more. Almost certainly, it was meningitis, my mother tells me, but no-one really knew much about it then, it was one of those awful things that happens. For almost a year they are grief stricken. Then, out of the blue, they hear that the authorities are seeking parents for a little girl. It is purely by chance, my mother has a friend of a friend who works in the adoption service. My parents are worried about the idea at first, worried that they will not be able to love another child as much as the one they have lost. But the authorities persuade them that I am difficult to place, that the alternative would certainly be a children's home.

'So we said yes,' my mother tells me. 'And I have to tell you, we never regretted it.'

'But what about my name?' I ask. 'And the birth certificate?'

'It happened by accident really,' she continues. 'The first thing that happened was we were told that you needed a fresh start, that there were things that had happened to you that were best forgotten. That was what the experts told us, that we should give you a new life, maybe even a new name. It seemed a bit odd but ideas have changed a lot since then – and it wasn't like anyone was going to come looking for you. We knew other couples who'd adopted and often their children came from Ireland – because of them being Catholic there and the strict rules they had. They chose their own names for them. Mind you, they were mostly babies. Well we were thinking about a name for you and we went on holiday. We went down to Cornwall, just like we had in the past and like we continued to after you came along. And of course, staying in the same place year after year, not just the bed and breakfast but the village where we stayed, people knew us there. Well, the first time someone commented on you, it scared me. Isn't Julia growing up, they said. Because of course they didn't know what had happened.'

She pauses to compose herself, to pour another cup of tea.

'We couldn't explain it all, not in front of you. At first it bothered me, people calling you Julia, confusing the two of you, it was like she'd never existed, like you'd replaced her. But by the time we got home, it had stuck. It seemed the most natural thing in the world to call you that. We went to Julia's grave, your Dad and I, we asked her if she minded. And, you know, we felt that she didn't. Some people donate their vital organs after they die. Well, Julia gave you her name and, to some extent, her identity. It was a gift. She gave you the fresh start you needed, that was how it seemed. And there came a point when we felt that at least one good thing came from her passing.'

I marvel at how brave my parents were. I cannot foresee that anything good will ever emerge from losing Jamie.

'We meant to tell you the truth,' my mother continues. 'Not the whole truth perhaps but we always meant to explain to you that you were adopted. But things seemed to get complicated.' She pauses. 'Always remember, Julia, you can never tell one lie. You always end up having to tell more and more, each time a bigger one to cover up the last.' I think about this, I think about Frank. My mother continues. 'Well, you'd been with us almost a year and it was two weeks off your fourth birthday. Out of the blue a couple of cards arrived from the people in Cornwall. Because of course, that was our Julia's birthday. You were bright for your age. You could already read. You'd picked up these envelopes off the mat, seen they were addressed to you and opened them before we knew what was happening. 'It's my birthday!' you shouted. And you went skipping round the house. We had to think of something quickly – and maybe it wasn't the best decision – but you were so excited we didn't want to disappoint you. So I distracted you by baking a cake while your Dad went out to buy you a present.'

I nod. I can understand how all this could happen.

'And we still intended to tell you about being adopted, when you were ten or so, maybe. But something always seemed to crop up. Don't get me wrong, if you'd had natural parents still alive who might have wanted to get in touch then we wouldn't have wanted to stand in their way – or yours. But as things were, it just seemed simpler to leave things like they were.' She looks up at me. 'We never meant it to turn out like this.'

I put my arms round her and hug her close. 'You did everything right,' I reassure her. 'You did everything that was best for me.'

'Does it make a difference?' she asks. 'Your Dad and me not being your proper parents?'

'Of course it doesn't. You have always been my parents. I've had the best anyone could wish for.'

'But what about all those dreams and things? Does it make a difference to them?'

'I don't know,' I admit. 'I'll have to think about that.' Over the next few days, I realise I will have several new things to think about. Yet, right now, I cannot imagine how many.

That night, when my mother has gone to bed, I wish that I had brought my journal. I need to write it all down right now. As though the act of forming the words on paper will somehow help me make sense of it.

My natural mother doesn't seem to have had a happy life – not after I was born, anyway. I wonder to what extent that was my fault. Did I scream all night until she could no longer cope, until she reached for a bottle of whisky to help her sleep? Or was she of an addictive personality that would have gone that way anyway? There are so many questions to which I will never know the answers, will never find resolution. There are tears in my eyes when I think of the drug addiction and the fatal overdose. Please, not that, I think to myself; anything but that.

And where does this leave Maggie and Freddie, Frank and myself? The foundation on which I have built my identity has been rocked. Those dreams I had as a child really were memories of a previous life; the life I had before I was adopted. What if the others are too, in some strange way, by some trick of the mind?

On Boxing Day, I tell my mother that I will return home after lunch. Of course she is worried that I am deserting her, that I am horrified by the things she has told me. Luckily, I have the excuse that snow is forecast for the Midlands during the next few days. I do not want to risk being caught in drifts on the way back. I feel bad about leaving my mother now and try to persuade her to accompany me for a few days. But she refuses. 'I don't like to leave Joe in the winter,' she says. And, as if to reinforce her words, he appears as if from nowhere and jumps, purring, onto her lap.

I leave at two after we have eaten a meal of cold chicken and vegetables. Richard is not expecting me home till tomorrow and I suspect that he will stay an extra night with his parents. I am looking forward to spending the evening on my own, to thinking through everything I have learned, to writing it in my journal and coming to terms with it. When I stop for a coffee and a Danish pastry at the motorway services, I think about texting Richard to tell him I am on my way back. But if I do he will only feel he has to rush home himself, to join me.

As I continue my journey, I think about the past twenty-four hours. Although my mother turned down my invitation to return to Nottingham with me, she did agree to accompany me on a short outing before I set off. I had asked to see where my sister was buried. I felt that I needed to pay my respects, however briefly, before I returned to take her name. And as we stood in the churchyard it was strange to think that my parents had been going there secretly all these years. It was positively eerie seeing the name and date of birth that I thought were mine, carved on the memorial stone. I will have lots to write about when I get in.

North of Warwick, it begins to rain. I turn on the windscreen wipers and increase the volume on the radio a little, to counteract the soporific effect of the combination of the weather and the motorway. By the time I pull into our road, it is a steady downpour. It is the sort of weather that masks sounds, that homogenises the night into a constant dripping world. I am not surprised by the glow of light from the drawing room window. We have lamps on time switches both in there and on the first floor landing, which we use when we are away. We fool ourselves that they might deter burglars. This is probably a false sense of security but at least it is more welcoming than returning to a dark house. I am pleased, yet surprised, that Richard has remembered to switch them on, and persuade myself that he has made an effort for my return. As I get out of the car into the cold and the wet, I decide that, for now, my small suitcase can stay in the boot. I don't stop to look around me. I pull the hood of my jacket over my head and, already holding the keys, I run to the front door.

It is not until I get inside and hear the music coming from the hi-fi that I realise Richard is home. Undoing my jacket I push open the drawing room door. I open my mouth ready to say hello.

And then I stop.

Richard and Clare are sitting together on the smaller of the two sofas. They are deep in conversation, so engrossed in one another that they have not even heard me come in.

It is only when I step fully into the room that they notice me. Clare looks up first. She doesn't say anything, simply looks down at her lap, uncomfortably, as though she has been caught out. It is Richard who eventually speaks. 'Ah, Julia,' he says. 'We weren't expecting you back tonight.'

'Clearly,' I reply, trying to sound stern, hoping my voice doesn't falter.

He looks unsure of himself, clears his throat. 'But since you are, I think we need to talk, the three of us. You'd better sit down.'

Oh please! I think to myself. How corny can you get? We need to talk! What about saying things like, hello, good to see you, I hope you had a good journey, I hope you enjoyed Christmas. But really, I am angry with myself, for not seeing the signs. Clare's scarf left in this house - why was it hanging in the cloakroom if she didn't even come in? The message from Richard in her office - there have been no transplants recently, no patients for Richard to refer.

I have had enough surprises over the last two days that nothing they can say will shock me. So, hoping that I appear calm, dignified, I sit in an armchair several feet away from their cosy twosome and wait for them to tell me that they are having an affair.

Chapter 24

'I'm not sure where to begin,' Richard says.

I sit, silently, watching him. I am certainly not going to make this easy for him.

'I suppose I began to realise something was going on back in November,' he continues. 'And it turned out that Clare felt it too.'

I stare at them blankly. At least, that is the expression I hope to achieve. Clare shows signs of recovering from my unexpected entrance. She is returning to her calm, self-assured self. She is preparing to speak. 'I was surprised the first time Richard called me,' she says. 'But I agreed to see him. Of course I was worried about upsetting you.'

I sit there, speechless with disbelief. How can she say these things so calmly, as though this tryst with my husband is just another of her casual flings? I think that nothing will shock me now. But I am wrong.

'We've been deliberating what to do about it,' Richard says. 'Thinking about what would be best for you.'

He pauses.

I wait.

He continues. 'And Clare and I have decided you should see a psychiatrist.'

'What?' I ask. 'A psychiatrist? What are you talking about?'

For a few moments we sit, the three of us, in what should be silence. Instead the music, which has been playing softly in the background, reaches some sort of strained crescendo. There is no sign of the remote control. I stand up decisively, march across the room and turn it off. As I walk past Clare, I notice that she wasn't just staring at her lap when I came in. My journal lies open across her knees. The handwritten pages of my most private and personal thoughts are revealed for her stark approval. I feel the anger growing inside me, spinning, swirling, gaining momentum. I take a deep breath. I mustn't show it. An outburst now would only confirm their belief that I truly am a mad woman.

I return to my chair. In the space of a few minutes I have come to terms with the fact that the two of them are having an affair. Now I digest the information that this is not the case after all, but that their true betrayal is far worse than if they were coupled together in our marital bed.

'You had no right,' I say. 'That book is something I began at the suggestion of the bereavement counsellor. It is personal, not for you or anyone else to read.'

'Then why did you leave it lying about?' Richard asks.

'Perhaps, deep down you wanted us to find it,' Clare adds, 'because you know that you need treatment.'

I fail to hide my feelings. 'You are both unbelievable,' I say. 'I didn't lock the thing away because, in the privacy of my own home, I shouldn't need to.' I glare at them openly now. 'I trust the people around me to respect my personal space,' I tell them. 'Though apparently that trust turns out to be misplaced.'

Clare fidgets. She is uncomfortable about this, I know. Eventually she stands up, closes the journal, places it on the coffee table. She walks round to me and perches on the arm of my chair, places her hand on my arm. I realise that I am still wearing my outdoor coat, that it is still damp with rain. It is an excuse to brush Clare aside as I wriggle out of the garment and set it on the floor beside me. It buys us all a moment's breathing space.

Clare turns to me. She is controlled now; she has reverted to her professional manner. 'I'm sorry about the journal,' she tells me. 'It was wrong of Richard to read it. Wrong of me to read it too, without your permission.' She speaks softly, carefully, edging her way into my confidence, as though I am one of her patients. 'But that's irrelevant now. What matters is that you need help. And it's down to Richard and me to make sure you get it.'

I take a deep breath. 'Exactly what do you think I need help with?' I ask.

Richard bursts into the conversation now. He is not good at this sort of thing like Clare is. He charges, fully armed, with no thought for the consequences. 'What do you need help with?' he demands sarcastically. 'How about your obsession with a convicted criminal? A criminal whom you are convinced was your lover in some previous existence – and whom you are now suggesting we welcome into our home!' His voice has risen so that he is shouting. It is high-pitched, like a yelping dog. 'I'd say that was enough for starters.'

Clare holds her hand up to him, shakes her head quietly, in a gesture that I am not supposed to see.

'We're only doing this because we're concerned for you,' she says. 'You're in a vulnerable state. A state where perhaps someone who is not too scrupulous, shall we say, might take advantage of you.'

You and Richard are the only people taking advantage of me, I want to say, but don't.

Clare continues. 'Take this Rose woman,' she says. 'Here you are, trusting her to put you into a very suggestible state, and yet you know nothing about her. I do. I've checked her out. She has no qualifications or membership of societies recognised by the medical profession.'

'Are you saying she's a charlatan?' I ask.

Richard tries to speak but Clare shakes her head at him firmly. Then she turns to me. 'I'm sure this woman means well,' she assures me. 'I'm sure she truly believes that she is helping you. And others. But the fact is, she is dabbling in an area that none of us fully understand. And in this case a little knowledge really can be dangerous.'

'She's just planting ideas in your head,' Richard shouts. 'Telling you what you want to hear. And she'll go on telling you too, as long as you pay her!'

'Richard!' Clare is more abrupt than I have ever heard her.

'I don't think you're helping. Perhaps you should let me deal with this.' She softens her voice before she turns back to me. 'Like I say,' she continues, 'hypnosis, certainly in terms, of unlocking the past, can be very controversial. There are plenty of cases involving very reputable therapists, that seemed to be ground-breaking at the time; but, years on, with more knowledge and the benefit of hindsight, we think they were inadvertently planting false memories. The mind is very complex, very open to manipulation. Even when such a consequence is completely unintended.'

She pauses. I sit quietly and wait for her to finish.

'I can arrange for you to see someone,' she says. 'It can be very discreet; no-one else need know. It is nothing to feel embarrassed about, or ashamed. Richard and I have discussed it. Believe me, it's for the best.'

I stand up. I take a deep breath. 'Thank you for your concern,' I say. 'But I am not mad, I am not embarrassed and I am certainly not ashamed. Yes, I have been grieving and, yes, I am probably vulnerable but I am perfectly capable of making my own decisions. If, at some point, I feel the need to consult a psychiatrist then that will be my choice. Do you understand? Both of you?' I pause to pick my coat up from the floor. 'And now, if you don't mind, I've had a long journey and I'm tired. Clare, I think it would be best if you leave.'

Clare looks worried but she hides it quickly. 'You're probably right,' she says. 'About my leaving, that is. I should probably leave the two of you to discuss this alone.'

I see her out; shut the door directly behind her. I do not accompany her out to her car. I pause only long enough to see that the rain has turned to sleet.

Back inside, Richard is angry. 'The thought of it,' he says. 'You actually planned to invite a convicted murderer into our home just because you think the two of you have some imagined psychic connection. And you expect me to believe you haven't taken leave of your senses.'

'It was the prison service who suggested it,' I argue in defence. 'And you don't know the circumstances. You're too quick to judge.' I pause, ready to play my trump card. 'I might be convicted of murder myself in a few months. Had you thought of that? What would you do if that happened, divorce me and run back to your parents, try to pretend we never knew one another?'

'Now you're being melodramatic,' he scoffs.

'Am I? Well at least I face up to things. All you've done since Jamie died is bury yourself in your work. No matter how many lives you save you couldn't save him.'

'But I am saving lives Julia, that's the point. All you're doing is trying to pretend that we're all immortal. This rubbish about being hypnotised, convincing yourself that reincarnation exists. You think that if you can prove you've lived before then it must follow that you will live again, that so will Jamie.' He waves his hands in the air, grasping for something to say. 'That maybe the two of you will come back as dolphins and swim around together in the sea.' He laughs scornfully. 'Why don't you go the whole hog?' he says. 'Let's call in a medium, hold a seance! Are you there Jamie? One knock for yes, two for no!' He grasps my wrist and holds it so tightly that it hurts. 'Come on,' he challenges. 'Face up to reality!'

I wrench myself free, burning the skin on my wrist in the process. 'You've become a monster,' I say.

'And another thing!' Richard shouts after me. 'I forbid you to see that murderer again!'

I rush away from him in terror. Not for fear of physical violence, I know Richard would never resort to that, but because I cannot face any more of the hurtful things he has to say. He forbids me! How dare he! Still holding my coat I make for the front door. I run out to the car and lift my case from out of the boot. For a minute or two I stand there in the sleet, the damp white flakes resting briefly on my shoulders before they melt and soak into my clothes. I could just get

216

back into the car and go, I think to myself. I have everything here that I need. I don't even need to go back into the house. It isn't late. I could go to Sally and Pete's or to a hotel or even back to Somerset. But why should I? I will not give in to this. I have done nothing wrong. I am not the one who goes snooping round in other people's private business. I will not be driven out of my home. I lock the car then march resolutely back inside and close the front door loudly and definitively behind me.

This time there is no sign of Richard. He has probably already retreated to the safety of his study. I deposit my coat and shoes in the cloakroom and realise that I am quite wet. I shiver into the kitchen and heat up a bowl of soup, leaning against the warmth of the Aga until it is ready. When I have finished, I carry my bag upstairs and leave it, still unpacked, an insurance policy, beside my bed. I contemplate sleeping upstairs in Jamie's room and decide to defer this decision until after my bath.

As I walk down the corridor I can hear music seeping from beyond the heavy oak door of Richard's study. I soak in the bath for a long time. I have locked the bathroom door – something I only ever do when we have visitors – and I hold my breath, submersing myself completely for several seconds at a time, as though I am swimming. Too much has happened in the last forty-eight hours. I think about it all as I lie here. I wish I could take a rest from it, stop thinking and simply be.

Richard scared me in a way he never has before. His readiness to take charge of my life, to make decisions on my behalf, but not necessarily in my best interest, is a side of him I have not seen. I wonder what he would do if we still lived in a time when a man could have his wife certified insane. I smile ruefully to myself. I suspect I would already be locked up in the asylum.

Chapter 25

I wake early but lie quietly in bed, listening to the sound of the shower as Richard prepares for work.

I spent the night alone in our bed. When I emerged from the bathroom I saw, through the half-open door, that Richard had already laid his pyjamas and his clothes for morning on the bed in the guest room. I did not go to the extent of locking the door, although our room is the only one in the house that has a lock; that would have been ridiculous in the extreme and in any case Richard may have overlooked something he needed for morning. I was, however, relieved that he stayed away from me. The water stops and I lie very still as Richard pads about, dressing, shaving, combing his hair. I fear he will come in here. But he does not. I pray that he will go directly into work and breakfast there. The front door clicks and I know that my prayers are answered.

I couldn't sleep last night; instead I lay awake reading my book. Oh Richard, what a Magus you have become. I slip silently out of bed and creep downstairs, somehow unable to adjust to the fact that I can make as much noise as I like now. I make a mug of coffee and take it back upstairs to drink in bed. Outside it is snowing and the world is silent. I snuggle back under the duvet and sip my drink. When I have finished it, I think about getting up, but decide, instead, to read my book (which I have almost finished) for half an hour first.

I suppose I must have been tired after two nights with virtually no sleep. The next thing I know, it is almost two in the afternoon. I leap out of bed, horrified, as though I am late for some vital appointment. In reality, of course, nobody is even expecting me back in Nottingham yet. I pull on my clothes without showering and hurry down the stairs. There are three messages on the answer machine. The first is from my mother. She has never got the hang of these voice mails and speaks as though she thinks I am there listening at the time. She asks if I have arrived home safely. I reprimand myself for not having rung her last night, as I normally would. The second message is from Clare, saying how sorry she is about what happened, promising she will try to call me again later. The third is from Richard. He makes no reference to the night before but simply informs me, in a business-like way, that, in view of the worsening weather, he will be sleeping at the hospital, in case he is needed during the night. I ring my mother back immediately, apologising for not calling earlier, and tell her a white lie that I was so tired when I arrived back I fell asleep immediately.

Then I think about food and drink. It is far too late for a meal called breakfast. Instead I make a much-needed pot of coffee and fry a late lunch of eggs, bacon and tomatoes. When I have eaten, I take a second mug of coffee through to the conservatory. The room is dazzling to the eyes; the glass panels magnifying the whiteness that spills in from outside, where an unbroken expanse of snow covers the garden. Somewhere underneath it, there are paths, lawns, flower borders and a pond, yet the trees are the only discernible features, even shrubs and bushes are reduced to amorphous lumps. The only signs of life are the tracks left by birds and some larger deeper prints which I attribute to a neighbour's cat or even a fox.

I shiver and scatter a few handfuls of feed around the citrus trees. Then I return to the kitchen and close and lock the door behind me. On the work surface, below the notice board, Richard has left the opened cards addressed to both of us, and the unopened mail addressed to me. There are only three items in the latter. One is a card and letter from an old university friend now living in Australia. The second is a hand-written note from Mrs Perriman, thanking me for the Christmas present. The third is another handwritten envelope. It is a handwriting that I recognise, the same as the note that arrived a couple of weeks ago - the one that I presume refers to the court case. I have no wish to think about that right now so I take the envelope to my study where I leave it on my desk unopened.

When I have also stowed away my journal - although there hardly seems any point in that small act of privacy now - I contemplate going out for a walk. Although mid afternoon, I hope the snow may hold onto the daylight for an extra half an hour. But I quickly talk myself out of the idea, reasoning that there still wouldn't be time to get anywhere interesting. Really, I would like to get out to the countryside but, even if it weren't nearly dusk it would be foolhardy to try and take the car anywhere. So, instead, I sit at my desk and drum a biro on the surface. I want to write in my journal, to record everything that has happened, both here and in Somerset. But the book feels tainted, contaminated, as though anything I add in the future will be scrutinised, dissected and subjected to ridicule. I am only grateful that my hypnosis CDs are at Sally's; left there so that Debbie could listen to them over Christmas. It is good chance that neither Richard nor Clare have intruded that far. For I'm sure, if they'd heard them previously, that they would have mentioned it. In the end, I take a sheet of the plain paper I use in my computer printer and I begin to write. But it doesn't feel the same and I push it aside after a few sentences.

Later, there is a call from Clare. I see her name spelt in angular letters on the caller display and choose not to answer it. Maybe, in the future, there will be a time for forgiveness but right now I do not want to discuss anything with her, do not want an argument. I do, however, take the call that comes, minutes later, from Sally and Pete. As we thank one another for our presents, I wish that I could go over there, tell them about the things my mother told me. But it would be silly to try and drive as the weather freezes over for the night. And I would prefer to wait and talk with them face to face rather than on the phone. We promise to catch up properly as soon as the weather clears. There is no further word from Richard and I am thankful when he does not return.

By next morning, there has been more snow. As I look out from the milder climate of the conservatory, I see that it has frozen, unblemished, covering all the mistakes of the previous days. The television news shows pictures of roads, impassable despite the rock salt; of people, arrogantly attempting to defy nature in their four by fours, only to find themselves stuck behind ageing saloons whose wheels will not turn. I smile to myself. In the end we are all equal.

I pick up the one item of post and open it automatically. It contains the itinerary and booking confirmation of a conference to be held in two weekends time. It is to be held in Edinburgh. It is residential. I look at it puzzled, then I realise it is for Richard. The envelope was mistakenly addressed to Mrs Spencer. I take a biro and write Richard's name on the envelope then take it to his study.

I clear away the breakfast things and wonder what I will do with my day. I rather wish I had a young child to look after then I could build a snowman or go tobogganing. As it is, I would feel rather stupid doing those things on my own. I wish I could get over to Sally and Pete's but it would be ridiculous to try and take the car out, even if I could get it to start. I am already rather regretting ignoring Clare's phone call the previous day. The act of not answering seems childish in retrospect. But then, I tell myself, it is better to say nothing at all than to say something one will later regret. I also ponder as to whether, in view of the weather, I should check that Mrs Perriman is all right, but, having heard her back door click open and shut earlier, I talk myself out of this task.

It is later, as I potter about the house that it occurs to me. The weekend that Richard will be away at the conference is the one suggested by the prison for Frank's home leave. I could agree to it anyway. Richard need never know. I am buzzing. Suddenly, I feel like a naughty child, planning a forbidden prank. I feel excited and scared at the same time. I am not sure what I need. Advice? Inspiration? I need to talk to someone who will not judge, someone who thinks like I think. I am too confused, too caught up in other peoples' worlds to reason properly on my own.

I dress in fleeces and a breathable waterproof. I pull on thick socks and walking boots with gaiters zipped over the top to keep out the snow. I have no idea how long it will take on foot, whether the roads will be cleared, or the footpaths. I feel ridiculous walking through the suburban sprawl looking as though I am dressed for the arctic. I cut through Wollaton Park, trudging across grassland where the snow has drifted so that in some places it is more than a foot deep. The first time it finds its way into my boots and melts around my feet I exclaim in annoyance. But once my feet are wet I don't care any more about where I walk. I stride casually into the white mass, challenging it to creep higher around my ankles. The discomfort is nothing compared to the fun of crossing the snow-covered terrain. It reinforces my purpose, transforms my journey into a pilgrimage.

At the northwest end of the park, I step back onto pavement and stamp the snow from my boots. I walk another mile, maybe two. I pass shops, pubs, children's play parks with white-capped climbing frames rising out of the cloud-like floor. I am surprised at how many details I miss when I am driving. Soon I see roads, buildings that I recognise. Eventually I arrive at Kimberley Place.

The street is silent. There is nobody in sight. Cars lie abandoned below white mounds. Trying to look casual, I trudge up to the fence.

At first I wonder whether it will happen. I wonder whether my state of mind will prevent me from seeing, whether I am too negative, too needy. It seems to take a long time. Perhaps it is too much to ask, for the temperature to

222

rise from a chilly zero to the heat of summer. No wonder it doesn't happen instantly. But gradually, I feel myself warming, the snow melting. Summer arrives at my bidding. This time, I am content to watch the girl on the swing. It is not my time to take part. I press my face to the fence until the wood dissolves and I am standing in the garden. 'What should I do?' I ask. 'You know how to be happy. What do you know that I have forgotten? What does Maggie know that I have yet to learn?' I watch her as she swings to and fro. And then I ask the most pressing question of all. 'What should I do about Frank?'

The girl does not look up. If she sees or hears me then she gives no indication. If I had been hoping for her to walk up to me, to speak the answers to my questions then I would have been disappointed. The girl and the garden fade before my visit feels complete. Perhaps it is too difficult to sustain in this icy weather. Yet as I turn to walk away I think of the replies, the words that I wanted her to say, that I wanted to hear. And I realise that, in some strange way, my questions have been answered.

When I arrive home, I ring Rose. We agree a time for me to see her the following week, after New Year. To me it seems too far away, too long to wait. But wait I must.

At five, I receive a call from Stephanie. She informs me that Richard is to perform a transplant that evening; that, assuming it is successful, he will be staying at the hospital. At first, I feel relieved that I will not have to face him tonight. Then I think about the transplant process, the balance of nature that insists that for one person to have the chance to live, another must die. Suddenly, I feel an overwhelming sadness for the family who have lost a loved one, for whom Christmas will never be the same again.

I replace the phone and think about what to cook for myself. After the long walk, I am already hungry. I decide that this is the time for one of Mrs Blackstock's casseroles. I select a beef dumpling stew from the freezer and set it in the microwave to defrost before putting it to heat in the fast oven of the Aga. I shut the door between the kitchen and the hall so the room feels more cosy, then I switch on the radio, choosing a station that plays sixties and seventies pop music. It is nostalgic, reminding me of the days when we used to smuggle forbidden transistors into school to hear the new top twenty on Tuesday lunchtimes. They play 'Ride a White Swan' by T Rex and 'Starman' by David Bowie. I turn it up louder.

As I mouth the words to the songs, I dance around the kitchen, not timidly like I used to at teenage discos but more freely, without inhibition. Suddenly there is a louder, more insistent beat than that coming from the radio, someone is knocking on the porch door. I start, taken by surprise. Nobody ever uses the side door. I turn the radio down automatically as though I have been caught disobeying rules and switch on the outside light. Clare is standing beyond the half-glazed door. She looks so fragile, huddled beneath layers of coats and scarves, that I forget our recent troubles and welcome her in.

'I was ringing the front bell for ages,' she says as she tumbles through the door. 'I was beginning to think you weren't in. I thought it would be easy getting round the back.'

'I'm sorry,' I say. 'I didn't hear it over the music.' I notice that she is looking somewhat dishevelled compared to her usual standard of dress and she is rubbing her leg below the knee. 'I say – are you all right?'

She attempts to grin but winces in pain. 'Sorry, I fell over a flowerpot or something out there. I hope I haven't broken it. Gosh it's dark round here isn't it?'

'Let's check that you're not hurt,' I say. 'That's all that matters.'

I pull up a chair for her in front of the Aga and get her to roll up her trousers. Unusually for her she is wearing thick corduroys, now damp from the snow where she fell over. 'Just a bruise coming up,' I pronounce. 'Your trousers took the worst of it. It's a good thing you weren't wearing a skirt.'

'Even I'm not that stupid in this weather,' she tells me. 'I left my formal gear at work.'

'Take your boots off and make yourself comfortable,' I say. 'I've got some trousers you could borrow – those are soaked through.'

She hesitates. 'I wasn't planning to stop. I didn't know if you'd want to see me. I just came to say sorry really, for the other night. I didn't feel happy about it – going behind your back – from the start. But Richard was worried about you; he asked me to help. I wish I'd just spoken to you about it weeks ago but Richard insisted I wait, just keep a watch on you for a bit. It was the wrong thing to do, completely unprofessional apart from anything else. I never meant for us to confront you like that.'

'It's done now,' I say. 'You put the kettle on while I go and find you some dry clothes.'

Half an hour later we sit at the kitchen table eating Mrs Blackstock's beef stew. Only when we have satisfied our initial hunger do we speak.

'Richard told me what happened,' Clare begins, 'what he said to you after I left.'

I bite my lip. It is a bitter memory. It takes the sweet flavours of marjoram and bay and turns them into something sour.

Clare continues. 'What he said to you…about Jamie, about how you were trying to prove your past lives, trying, somehow, to make Jamie immortal…it was very wrong of him to do that.'

I hesitate. 'But is it true?' I ask, at length. 'Is that what you believe I am doing? Inventing some fantasy in the hope of resurrecting the past?'

Clare pauses to cut a slice of bread. 'Sometimes,' she feels her way cautiously, 'sometimes we adopt ways of thinking, ways of coping – even when we know they are not real – and when they have served their purpose we have to withdraw from them slowly so that we do not inflict further damage.'

She does agree with Richard, I think to myself. I wait for her to continue.

'What we must never do – and I'm afraid this was Richard's biggest mistake – what we must never do is take away someone's hope.' She takes her bread and crumbles it into her bowl.

I take the ladle and scoop us both second helpings of the casserole. 'You know,' Clare muses, 'I know that Richard is your husband and I can see he has many good qualities.'

I wait for the 'but'.

'But in many ways he is a very harsh man.'

I stare at her. 'Do you realise that when I arrived home on Boxing Day I thought the two of you were having an affair?'

It is Clare's turn to stare. Her expression is one of disbelief. 'I'm sorry,' she says. 'It never occurred to me that was how it looked – though I can see it now, of course. I'm sorry you could think that of me. But, like I say, Richard contacted me a few times when he thought you were acting strangely, decided to keep a close watch, tried to involve me – I wasn't happy about it but I just thought better me than someone you didn't know. Then at Christmas he read your journal and called me over. The rest you know. But as for anything else… even if he weren't your husband…I'm sorry Julia, but sometimes I'm not sure I even like him.' She pauses to eat a spoonful of carrot and swede, tilting her spoon delicately away from her, chewing the vegetables slowly and thoughtfully, before she elaborates. 'I thought he was unnecessarily cruel about the idea of prison visiting, for instance. And his reaction to your suggestion of offering a prisoner home leave – yes he told me about that, I didn't just read it in your journal – well that was nothing short of bullish. It hurt me quite personally in fact.'

226

I look at her, raise my eyebrows.

'There's something you don't know,' she tells me. 'No-one knows apart from my mother - and we don't talk about it.'

I don't probe, don't question her, I simply wait for her to speak. I wait as long as it takes. It is something Clare does herself, one of the first things they teach you in counselling, she has told me.

'You remember I told you my father died when I was young?'

I nod.

'It wasn't an illness or anything.' She pauses. 'He was in prison. He hanged himself.'

I am shocked, in a way that I cannot hide. This is something that does not fit into Clare's neat, controlled word.

'It was drink-driving,' she tells me. 'I don't think he was really drunk or anything but he was over the limit. He hit a pedestrian. They were crossing the road. Dad was probably going a bit too fast and didn't respond in time. The pedestrian was killed outright. Dad was convicted of manslaughter. He'd served eighteen months of his sentence. I suppose he just couldn't live with what he'd done, couldn't live with the consequences.'

She waits a moment while we both take time to come up for air, to digest what she has said.

'I know what he did was wrong and I'm not condoning it but it could have happened to any of us. We've all driven when we've had an extra glass of wine. At any rate, we've all broken the law in some way. But for most of us there were no consequences. No-one died. We didn't get caught. But we might have done. There but for the grace of God...what I mean is, he didn't deserve to die for it. My mother hadn't been to visit him for six months – she wouldn't let me go either – I suppose, in a way, I partly blame her for what happened. I've never really felt close to her since.'

There is nothing useful I can think of to say, so I sit in silence. At last I cannot bear the tension any longer. 'Is that why you worked in a prison?' I ask.

She nods. 'I didn't want that to happen to anyone else, to anyone else's father. I thought I could make a difference.'

'And did you?'

'For a while I thought I was helping. Then one of the prisoners in my care took his own life. It brought it all back. I couldn't go on after that. I realised that whatever I did it didn't help the overcrowding, didn't compensate for families who'd turned their backs on them, wives who'd run off with their best friends. What you're doing, volunteering to visit someone, that really means a lot to the prisoners concerned. It can make the difference to them surviving their sentence. And giving this chap, Frank, a chance of home leave – well I just wish someone could have been there like that for my father. To be honest Julia, if it wasn't for this past life thing, the way you feel a connection to him that perhaps isn't healthy, I'd be urging you to go ahead with the home visit.'

'I'm sorry,' I say, 'about your father. I'm sorry all this business with me has stirred it up.

I sit in silence for a few minutes. I wonder whether I should tell her. I need to tell someone. I decide that I will. 'You're not the only one with secrets,' I say. 'Something happened at Christmas. I found out some things about myself, things I should have known years ago.' And then I tell Clare everything my mother told me, about how I was born in Lyme and how I was adopted. It is a long and complicated story. I am surprised at how long it takes to tell it.

'How do you feel about it?' Clare asks when, at last, I have finished.

'Well it's certainly a surprise,' I admit. 'But it doesn't make any difference to my family – I mean my mother is the best anyone could wish for and my Dad was the only Dad I'd ever want. I wouldn't even consider trying to trace my natural father, even if it were possible. I just feel sorry for them, feeling they had to keep it a secret all these years.'

228

'Views on adoption have changed,' Clare agrees. 'I can see how, back in the fifties and sixties, your parents were probably encouraged to help you forget your past. Especially in your case when any memories you did have would probably have been distressing.'

I nod. 'It explains all those nightmares when I was very young, and also why I felt so at home in Lyme, why it seems so familiar to me.'

Clare nods eagerly. 'Now you know why you grew up thinking you'd lived before. Those were real memories you had, of this life. No wonder you thought you'd been this child Maggie in Lyme Regis – you actually were, that was your name even. It will take a while for you to fully come to terms with it all but when you do you can put all this past life business behind you and move on.'

Clare beams triumphantly. She is thrilled to discover that I am in fact completely sane and have no need of a psychiatrist. And, although I feel guilty about it, I have no wish to disappoint her. True, many of my childhood memories were real, true, I have good reason to feel at home in Lyme Regis. But apart from that nothing has changed. Kimberley Place still exists, as do Maggie and Freddie, as do many other past lives with which I have had brief encounters. But for now it is easier to leave Clare in blissful ignorance.

Chapter 26

When I eventually get to see Rose, I want answers. I know that I should go into her hypnosis with an open mind: that I am more likely to get results that way. But I cannot help it. There are things, about Maggie and Freddie, about Frank and myself that I need to know. And I need to know them now.

I have no fear of the process any more and readily follow Rose where her words lead. Indeed, I feel almost as though I have memorised the route and could find my way unaided.

The breeze is strong, blowing through my hair, tangling it into knots. I lean back onto the cliff, listen to the waves. There isn't much beach, just a thin strip of rock and shingle. Then there's water. Freddie is standing in front of me, blocking my way. He is angry.

'Yer shouldn't lead me on so,' he says. 'Not if yer don't mean it.' The wind grabs his words and throws them at my face. They hit me with a slap.

'But I do,' I say. 'I do mean it Freddie.' I take a deep breath. 'I want us to get married.'

'Married?' he shouts. 'How can we get married when I'm not even earning yet?' The sea is angry too. It surges up behind him and the surf crashes in agreement.

'We'll have to wait,' I say. 'People do.'

'Monks, maybe,' he says. 'An' saints.'

I sigh. How much simpler it was when we were children. But the incoming tide has covered over the fossils. There's no past now, only the future. The future, a voice says, go to the future. The voice is gentle and alluring. I want to follow it, I really do. But I can't move, not forward nor back. I'm trying to get my breath but I can't. The voice is telling me to go forward but I don't want to. There's nothing there. And I'm scared. I'm panicking now. I want to go back to when I was a girl. I was all right then. It wasn't great but it was all right and I know what happens there. Whereas I don't know what happens in the future – except that it's bad. Go forward, the voice insists. But it doesn't understand. I try once more because I like her, this girl, this friend, and I want to please her. So I stretch as far as I can. And I'm trying to say the name Freddie. But the word is choked back down my throat.

I have been struggling, gasping for breath. But Rose is there. She leads me slowly and surely back to safety, back to now. When I open my eyes the terror dissipates. I blink a few times, make sure of where I am, who I am.

'You'll be all right in a minute,' Rose soothes. 'It's a long-forgotten memory. It's happened. It's over. It can't hurt you any more.'

'But what happens to Maggie?' I ask. The ending is unresolved though I cannot imagine a good outcome. This not knowing causes me more distress than the event itself. 'It was Freddie wasn't it?' I demand. 'It was Frank.' It is a statement this time, one of uneasy acceptance.

'I'll make you a cup of tea,' Rose insists. 'And we'll talk over what happened.'

'Is there no way I can find out for sure?' I ask. I sip my tea and think more calmly now. If it were only about Maggie and Freddie then I could wait. Wait for Maggie to tell me in her own good time. But the implications for Frank and myself pull this life out of the past, where it rightfully belongs, and into the present, the future, even.

'I think you just have to be patient,' Rose says. 'Trust that Maggie knows the right time for what she's got to say. Perhaps she feels you aren't ready to cope with the truth yet.'

I deliberate it for a while. In the end, I decide I must tell Rose everything, about Frank, about the home leave. 'I think there's something else I should tell you,' I say.

Rose listens quietly while I describe what has been happening. I tell her everything. About Frank, about Richard and Clare, about being adopted. At last I finish the story.

Perhaps I had expected Rose to be worried for me. To warn me off, like a gypsy fortune-teller with tales of doom and destruction if you don't cross their palm with enough silver. Instead, she is unperturbed. She smiles. 'What do you feel about Frank?' she asks. 'Listen to your instinct, your inner voice. Do you believe he would harm you?'

I shake my head. 'I don't think he would intend to,' I say, 'but he maintains he didn't mean to kill his wife – yet it still happened.' I put my cup and saucer down. 'Could we try once more?' I suggest. 'Go back to the beach. Maybe you could explain to Maggie what's happening now. Maybe then she'd tell me.'

Rose pauses to think for a moment. 'I don't feel it would be fair on Maggie to do that,' she says. 'Clearly something very traumatic happened to her. We can ask her if she wants to tell us but we mustn't put the responsibility of your life onto her.' She finishes her tea. 'And I think you're missing the point,' she tells me gently. 'Lives don't replay themselves over and over in the same way. If they did we would never learn from them. I agree, sadly it does seem likely that Maggie died at that point, that Freddie murdered her, even. But that happened in their lives. Even if you and Frank have inherited their souls you are different people. Perhaps Freddie feels remorse, needs to say sorry. It is very unlikely you would meet again simply to re-enact what you lived before. And the fact Frank has already killed someone in this life – it wouldn't make sense. Do you understand what I'm trying to say? If history were going to repeat itself then you would have been born as Frank's wife, you would already be dead. I feel that if Maggie needed to warn you of danger with Frank then she would be doing so with graphic descriptions, with no ambiguity.'

I sigh.

'I'm sorry,' Rose says. 'I know it isn't the reassurance you're looking for.' Then she brightens up. 'I have an idea. I don't like leaving you with just a traumatic memory. If you let me hypnotise you again then we can move forward in time, to a future life, where there is something good. Whatever happened to Maggie, you – and she - will see there are better times to come.'

I need no persuasion. It will not give me the answers I want but I am happy to go along with this idea. I do, however, have an alternative suggestion. 'What about the girl on the swing?' I suggest, 'the one at Kimberley Place. She's always happy. Perhaps I could see more of that life.'

But Rose disagrees. She looks sad. 'You only ever see her during that one summer don't you?'

'What do you mean?' But I know what she is saying. The memory that survives does so for a reason. It may be the only happy interlude in an otherwise sad and perhaps tragically short life.

'Sometimes,' Rose explains, 'it is better simply to accept what we are given. To go seeking more can so often lead to disappointment.'

'Very well then,' I say as I sit back on the sofa. 'The future it is.'

I step into the other world, into the corridor. This time Rose tells me to turn the other way. I will know the door when I see it, she says. And I do. It is golden yellow, glowing with promise. It is already ajar just a crack and a comforting warmth spills out, curling around me. When I push the door fully open, the room beyond is filled with love, with contentment. I feel the sensation a young child might feel, warm and fed and cuddling up to the safety of its mother. And there is a child. It is there in front of me. And I am there, me, as I am now. I am holding this tiny baby. It looks up at me and blinks its eyes open. It is a girl, I am sure. I stay there for a while, savouring the feeling. I am aware of Rose speaking softly to me, inviting me to take my time, to return when I am ready.

When I eventually open my eyes the images are gone but the feeling of contentment remains.

'How do you feel now?' Rose asks.

'More optimistic,' I say, and I tell her about what I saw, what I felt.

'You've seen a child you will have in a future life,' she tells me. 'That's a great privilege.'

'But it was this life,' I insist. 'I'm sure of it.'

'Well, perhaps you will have another baby,' Rose suggests.

I shake my head sadly. 'Even with the wonders of modern medicine and older women giving birth that wouldn't be possible,' I say, and I tell her how I had to have a hysterectomy when Jamie was born.

'Well maybe it's indicating your return to work, that this trial you told me about is resolved and you are back working as an obstetrician. That would be a positive step into the future.'

I think about this possibility but it still doesn't feel right. Then, suddenly, I understand what it is about. 'It's my friends, nearby,' I say. 'The girl who gave me your number is due to have her first baby next month. That was what I saw.' And with that I do begin to feel more positive. I rise above the tide of envy and wonder if Debbie might ask me to be a Godparent.

I am reluctant to leave Rose. I feel safe in her presence, as though, when I am near her, I will always make the right decisions. But she has a life too. She has a husband to cook dinner for and children to meet from school. I thank her and pull on my jacket and scarf. Yet, as I turn towards the door she calls me back.

'Wait!' she says. She presses something into my hand.

I look down at the orange stone. It feels familiar. It brings back a memory of a holiday in Norfolk almost twenty years ago. The weather was too rough to take a boat out, even on the comparative calm of the Broads, so we had walked on the beach. Jamie had picked up a stone much like this, plucked with his tiny fingers from amongst the pebbles. He had placed it proudly in my hand. It was much smaller than this one of course but it was smooth and glassy, polished by the sea. I don't know what happened to it, whether he kept it or threw it into the hungry waves.

'It's amber,' Rose tells me. 'For protection.'

'Thank you,' I say, as I stroke the smooth surface with my fingertip.

'It's millions of years old,' she tells me, 'like your fossils on the beach. Carry it with you, in your bag or your pocket. It will shield you from anything evil – be it psychic or physical.'

The stormy beach and Maggie's feelings of terror haunt me over the next few days. During the daytime I can block them out; but when I lie alone in bed, in that time before sleep takes over, that is when they return. It is as though she will not let me forget. When I go to visit Frank on Thursday the feeling overwhelms me. All the while he is talking, his words drift past me, carried away on the salt breeze of the beach. I find myself looking at his hands, his fingers, etched with tattoos. I imagine them squeezing tightly around Maggie's throat, my throat.

'Are you all right?' Frank asks. I realise that I am gasping, that I am trying to breathe in but my throat constricts and the air cannot reach my lungs. 'I'll get some help,' Frank says. And he stands, calls to one of the guards. I can tell that he is worried. Yet when they reach me I am perfectly well. I clear my throat. 'Sorry,' I say, 'just a bit of a tickle.' The guard offers me a honey and lemon lozenge. I don't need it but I accept it anyway just to stop anyone worrying.

'So have you decided?' Frank asks.

How can I? How can I let him down because of something I think happened in another lifetime? It is this life that matters. And in this life his hands are those of a murderer. There is no getting away from that. I play for time, say that I

235

Chapter 27

We had provisionally arranged the date before Christmas. It was Andrew's suggestion that, when we next met to prepare for my court appearance, Richard and I would both travel to London and spend the weekend with him. When we had dispensed with the business, he said, we would go to a West End show then have dinner out. It would be a break, a sociable occasion for all three of us, and a chance for me to take my mind off everything that was going on. But now the weekend has arrived Richard says he will not be participating. He maintains that he confused the dates, that he has promised to spend the time in Lincoln with his parents, that there is, in any case, no point in his being present since, as my husband, he will not be allowed to speak for me in court. Andrew thinks that he is shirking his responsibilities; that he is siding with his parents, dissociating himself from the scandal I may yet bring on his family. And, indeed, he is guilty of those things. But of course, I know it is more complicated than that. Since I arrived home after Christmas, Richard has slept either at the hospital or in the guest room. Although I have prepared meals for him, we have not actually eaten together. He has either taken his to eat in his study or put them aside to reheat later.

But when I suggested to Andrew that we would have to cancel our original plans and settle for a brief meeting, he wouldn't hear of it. He insisted that, just because Richard was being difficult, there was no need for me to miss out.

And so, on a chilly Saturday in January, I find myself on the London train once more. I have a small suitcase with me this time, with a choice of formal clothes for tonight, as well as my overnight things and more casual wear for tomorrow. Andrew has said he will pick me up from the station and drive me to his flat in Knightsbridge. In deference to my weekend in the city I am wearing a calf length woollen coat and court shoes. I have also experimented wearing the scarf that Andrew gave me outside my coat the way Clare does.

Although I have brought a book to read, I find that I cannot concentrate, cannot get beyond the first chapter. There are too many things spinning around my mind. For one thing, I am still coming to terms with the revelation of my adoption. Clare suggested that I consider having counselling – not a formal therapy but simply an opportunity to converse with someone trained in these matters, who would ask the right questions, allow me to form my own answers. And for many people, I can see why this would be helpful. It is a shock to discover that the people you have called mother and father for as long as you can remember are not your biological parents. For children, I suspect it is easier. The young seem to have a tendency towards acceptance. They are more open to change, and, with the idea of stepfamilies being commonplace, as a result of divorce and remarriage, they have a more fluid concept of the family unit. I can understand, also, the desire of many people to trace their natural parents, the need to understand how and where they began their lives. Add to that the dilemma of feeling disloyal to their adoptive parents if they take this path and I can see how counselling would be very useful.

But for me, the situation is different. I already know the circumstances of my birth and the fact that my natural mother is long dead. I will always regard the couple who brought me up as being my sole parents. For me, it is other implications of the adoption that will churn around forever as unanswered questions.

I pause from my thoughts to show my ticket to the guard. While my bag is open I check my mobile but there are no messages. I resume my gaze through the window, seeing into the void far beyond the ever-changing world. As a doctor, it is obvious to me that a potential problem for those adopted is their lack of medical history. Whilst we have apparently

238

mapped the human genome, it will be many years before we can test a person's DNA and fully understand their medical potential. Diagnosis is a two way process. It is about checking for imbalances in the body, but equally it is about knowing what to test for. And the most obvious questions in any situation involve asking what diseases, what tendencies to medical conditions, a person's family have experienced. Forewarned is, indeed, forearmed and many conditions are avoidable or preventable if we are aware they are likely to happen.

For my own part, I am not overly concerned to know whether I am at a higher risk of developing heart disease or breast cancer. There is something far more sinister that worries me. I am trying to remember something Richard's mother said when we visited just after the inquest. I cannot recall the exact words but it referred to Jamie's death and the fact that such circumstances were unheard of in Richard's family. Her remark carried the implication that it was me, my inheritance, that was, in some way, to blame. At the time I was still stunned by everything that had happened. I did not fully take in what was being said. And even if I had, I would simply have interpreted it as some spiteful dig on her part, some denial of responsibility by the ruling classes, to conveniently blame anything they found distasteful onto one of humble background.

The manner of Jamie's death was uncertain enough to warrant a police investigation and an autopsy. They found him in his flat. Not the cheerful, cosy place we had imagined, but a sordid squalid dump; a slum that was piled high with unwashed dishes and laundry; that reeked of vomit and urine. They found him in the bathroom, a partitioned room with no window, mould on the paint-peeling walls, rips in the linoleum, sewer-smelling water leaking from the cracked toilet bowl. That was where my son died; his body slumped against the bath, his cheek cold against the floor, a pool of vomit beside his mouth, an empty syringe by his side.

And now, a terrible thought occurs to me. What if it is my fault? Surely it cannot be a coincidence that my own mother – his grandmother – died in a similar way. I must have inherited the tendency from her, and unwittingly passed it on to Jamie. New information is coming to light all the time. The most unlikely traits, one's preference for certain foods, even the political party one votes for, are proving to correlate with genetic inheritance. What if Jamie's fate was sealed at the moment of his conception? What if I have passed on the addiction that killed him? What if I am responsible for dealing Jamie the hand that ultimately led to his death? Richard's parents were right when they said nothing like that could ever happen in their family. It was down to me all along.

I cannot bear these thoughts. I buy a coffee from the buffet, open my book and force myself to read it, like it or not.

To my surprise, Andrew is waiting for me on the platform. He greets me, kissing me on both cheeks, and takes my bag. He has brought his own car rather than taking a taxi and soon we drive south through the city. Andrew knows all the short cuts and ways of avoiding traffic jams and we are soon pulling into his allocated parking space. I follow him through the grand doorway and up the stairs to the first floor. The flat is stylish yet simple. It is not the harsh grey bachelor pad I was expecting but is softened with rugs and plants. The sitting room opens onto a balcony, which overlooks a mews garden.

'We'll have a late lunch while we work,' Andrew says, as he pulls tasty plates of canapés out of the fridge. 'I'm afraid I don't get round to much cooking. I cheated with most of this and bought it from delicatessens.' There are various cheeses, rye breads and oat breads and rolls baked with oil and seeds. There are bowls of olives and tomatoes and exotic fruits that I don't recognise. I note from the packaging that most of the food comes from Harrods or Fortnum and Mason.

We picnic while Andrew takes me through the preparations he has made for court. There are two different lines of defence, he tells me. The first will focus on the actual events of that day back in July. It will comprise evidence in the form of written records detailing the times of the request for an ambulance, the arrival of paramedics at the patient's home, admission to hospital etcetera. It will also detail medication and other treatment given at every stage. He will need to speak to as many of the staff who were on duty as possible. The evidence will also include information about previous consultations and my advice regarding a home birth. The second part of the defence will be a more general overview of myself. This is where Clare's testimony will come in, along with others including the now retired consultant for whom I worked as a registrar and who Andrew has somehow tracked down to her bungalow in Suffolk. Andrew has long since given up trying to tell me that it will not go to court. I think we are both resigned, now, to this, but at least seeing all his meticulous plans helps me to accept the second best option.

As it gets dark outside, we are finishing our legal business. After Andrew has cleared it away into his study, he says that we will have tea and cakes. I must be sure to eat plenty now, he says, because we won't be having dinner until much later. When we have finished, Andrew shows me to the guest room so I can get changed ready for the evening. I have brought two dresses, partly because I wasn't sure what the weather would be like. It is remarkably mild compared to the recent chill in Nottingham and I choose a blue sleeveless dress with a hemline just above the knee, together with a silky pashmina. For the first time in months I apply a little make-up.

A little before seven, we take a taxi to the theatre. Although it is past twelfth night and the Christmas decorations have been taken down, there is still a festive feel to the city.

241

'I've booked seats for the ballet,' Andrew says. 'I hope that's all right. It's a modern piece, has very good reviews. If Richard had come I expect he'd have preferred the opera – Wagner or something – but I feel under the circumstances we could do with something a little more light-hearted.'

'I totally agree,' I say. 'The ballet sounds wonderful. It's a long time since I've been to anything like that.' And I realise that my social life dwindled long before Jamie's death pushed me into self-enforced mourning.

Andrew gets us glasses of white wine and orders the interval drinks to save queuing later. He looks very at home in the theatre. He is of a slighter build than Richard with dark blonde hair. Whilst not effeminate, he has a delicate quality that seems to imply an appreciation of the arts. Several friends or colleagues come and say hello to him and I like the way he introduces me as 'my very good friend, Julia'.

I enjoy the ballet immensely. When it has finished, we walk to the restaurant, which is really just round the corner. It is French and, like Andrew's flat, it is simple and stylish. The menu is entirely in French and Andrew translates it for me. I feel lacking in social graces now that I have been away from the city for so long and am glad of Andrew taking charge as he talks to the waiter in what I suspect is an impeccable French accent. Again we drink white wine and I am aware that I am drinking rather more than I am used to. I find myself telling Andrew about the fact that I am adopted. He listens attentively as I tell him the strange story that is my past.

When we leave, Andrew hails a cab – something I always used to hate doing and not be very successful at – but the taxi pulls over immediately and we are soon back at the flat.

Andrew graciously takes my coat and offers me a nightcap. I say that I shouldn't, but accept a glass of wine anyway. We sit on a soft cream sofa and Andrew puts on a CD. It is not anything I recognise and I suspect it is something modern.

242

'So are you going to tell me what's wrong?' he asks.

I hesitate. 'Nothing,' I say. 'I'm having a lovely weekend.'

'I don't mean here, now,' he says. 'I'm talking about Richard, or whatever else is bothering you. I know something is and, whilst I know you will be grieving over Jamie for a very long time, I don't think that's the problem.'

I wonder whether to say anything, whether it would be disloyal. But the wine has gone to my head slightly and I find the words pouring out. 'Richard thinks I'm going mad,' I say. 'He wants me to see a psychiatrist.'

Andrew laughs. 'I don't normally spend the evening with mad women. I've always prided myself on being rather more discerning.' Then he is more serious. 'Why does he think this?'

I pause. 'If I tell you, you'll probably think I'm mad too.'

'Try me,' he challenges.

I take a deep breath. 'It's because I believe I have lived before. Sometimes I remember things from past lives.'

Andrew shrugs. 'I don't see anything wrong with that.'

I am surprised. 'You don't?'

'Well I'm a Buddhist and we believe in reincarnation.'

'A Buddhist?' I gasp in disbelief. 'But you can't be – you're a lawyer!'

He laughs, naturally, playfully, like he has drunk too much wine as well. 'The two aren't mutually exclusive,' he tells me.

'A Buddhist,' I repeat to myself. 'Is that why you aren't married?'

Andrew laughs again. 'Well I haven't taken a vow of celibacy, if that's what you mean. I'm not a monk. I don't shave my head or wear robes as you can see! But I have been on retreats to India and Tibet and I am ordained into the Buddhist order. It certainly doesn't prohibit me from getting married but I suppose my philosophy, my belief helps me feel self-sufficient. I don't actually feel the need to be with someone else. If I ever do it will be out of choice, because I want to be with that person, not because I'm lonely or unhappy on my own.'

Suddenly, I envy Andrew his conviction. 'So, can you live how you want to?' I ask, intrigued.

'More or less,' he tells me. 'Of course there are guidelines. I like to meditate each day, I try not to create an impact on the world, not to leave physical or emotional damage behind me. And I try, apart from when it would be impolite or impose on peoples' hospitality, to be vegetarian.'

I remember then that Andrew had a cheese and onion tartlet at the restaurant, that there was no meat or fish in our meal earlier.

'But back to your earlier fear,' he says. 'I really don't think you're mad. If anyone is suffering from that affliction it is Richard.'

'I'm glad,' I say.

Andrew takes the glass out of my hand and sets it on the table. He takes both of my hands and draws me close to him. I have that same feeling that I had before, that he is going to kiss me. This time I pray that he does. And I am not disappointed.

Chapter 28

On Monday night, I go swimming. It is the first club night since the Christmas break and I am anxious for my fix. Again I am first in the pool. Tonight, I plough clumsily through the water. I am heavy with guilt.

The first matter on my mind is my trip to London. Andrew. If I were feeling guilty about my actions, the deception, the disloyalty, other words which I cannot bring myself to say or even to form in my mind, then that would be expected. It would be the price I have to pay; the punishment for my actions. But in fact, what I feel is quite the opposite. My guilt is not in feeling shame or remorse but rather in the knowledge that I enjoyed every minute of the experience, and, were it possible to turn back time, would do it all again. I only wish I knew how Andrew felt. Worse than me I suspect, for he has cheated on an old school friend, deliberately and actively cheated. I wonder how he will resolve this, how he will reconcile it in his Buddhist philosophy of taking responsibility. For me, it is more complicated. It was not simply a personal stand of breaking away from Richard but more an act of desperation, a break for freedom from his whole family.

What really brought it home was a visit from Clare a couple of hours ago. She had popped in on her way home from work, to drink coffee and tell me about her latest conquest. 'I don't expect you to approve or understand,' she'd told me, after describing her illicit meetings with a married man. 'But, sometimes, I just feel so attracted to someone that I know it's meant to happen, that, one way or another, it will happen. There's simply no point in fighting it.' I had nodded agreement as I usually did. Because I still do not understand or condone such actions based solely on physical attraction. I do not see them as comparable with my own indiscretion, which was a response to kindness and compassion. Then Clare said something that shocked me – or rather my reaction did. 'You're like a nun, Julia,' she'd told me, as though being a nun was necessarily a bad thing. 'Your marriage to Richard was like a vow of chastity before you even had chance to find out what you were missing. But you know, in some ways I really admire you for your morals and your principles. I almost envy the way you can be faithful to one man forever.' That had done it. I could feel myself blushing and had immediately made an excuse to walk over to the Aga, so that, if commented on, I could claim my face was red from the heat. It is curious that, despite the way she behaves herself, the person I feel I have let down the most is Clare.

I return to the lanes as other people arrive. I choose the slow-paced track where I can relax.

Despite the events of the weekend, I am aware that most of my guilt is directed in an entirely different direction. It is my failure to offer a weekend retreat for Frank. My feelings on this matter ricochet backwards and forwards. After the episode of Richard reading my journal, I had all but decided to go ahead with the visit. I know that my decision was an act of defiance, that it was made for the wrong reasons but nonetheless that was how I felt. When Clare told me about her father that had reinforced my resolve. It had given me an altruistic cause to hide behind. The matter of Frank was no longer about Richard or myself: it was a gesture on behalf of a friend. But now, with the memories Maggie has shared with me regarding Freddie, I am changing my mind again. What is more, I am doing this for no good rational reason but rather to satisfy what others would call a whim, an irrational fear, an obsession even. I am letting my brief visions, of what I believe to be a past life, affect the course of Frank's life in the present. Surely that cannot be right.

After I have climbed, tired but refreshed, out of the pool, when we are sitting under the harsh fluorescent lights of the café, I tell Pete and Sally about the possibility of Frank staying with me on home leave.

'Do you think you should?' Sally asks. 'After whatever happened with Freddie and Maggie.'

'Hang on a minute!' Pete laughs in disbelief. 'You're talking as if all that stuff really happened.'

Sally glares at him. 'Well I believe it,' she says. 'So does Debbie.'

'Seriously though,' Pete looks at me, 'it's who this chap is now that matters. Not something that may or may not have happened a hundred years ago.'

I nod. I know deep down that he is right.

'And to be honest,' he continues, 'I'd be really worried about you. And I'm sure Sally would be too.'

'Perhaps you're right,' I shrug, 'I haven't decided yet anyway.'

On Tuesday morning, I am getting ready to go to the day centre. It is nine-thirty. Half an hour before Mrs Blackstock is due to arrive. Half an hour before I am due to leave. That is when the phone rings.

'Hello?'

'Julia? It's Andrew.' My heart misses a beat. I had half expected him to call yesterday but he didn't. Suddenly I am excited, embarrassed and guilty all at once. I wonder what he will say. That he misses me? That he wants to see me? As it turns out, I am not prepared for what he has to tell me.

'Julia, it's over – the court case – it isn't going to happen. You're free!'

I am shocked into silence.

'There was a possibility yesterday but I didn't want to say anything until I was sure. But now it's official.'

At last, as the words sink in, I am able to speak. 'Andrew, that's wonderful, I'm so relieved I can't think properly. What happened? Did Ashby back down?'

'No. He's furious about the outcome, apparently. But that's

his problem. No. The Crown Prosecution Service took the case over and closed it down.'

'I don't understand.'

Andrew explains that the Crown Prosecution Service – the legal organisation that handles criminal cases referred by the police – have the power to take over a private prosecution, and, if they see fit, to close the case. They do this, he tells me, when there is clearly not enough evidence, when a private prosecutor would needlessly take up court time or make a mockery of the legal system. I am listening though I don't really take in all the technical details and jargon. In my head, I simply replay his words, 'it's over' and 'you're free'.

'I hoped this would happen,' Andrew is saying. 'I always knew it was a possibility but I didn't want to raise your hopes until it was signed and sealed.'

'I don't know what to say,' I mumble. 'But thank you.'

'I can't take any credit for it I'm afraid. But I'm very pleased for you, Julia.'

My head is spinning. It will take some time for me to truly believe it. 'Could you do me a favour?' I ask. 'Please will you tell Richard? You'll explain it better than I would.'

'Of course – providing I can get hold of him this morning.' There are a few moments silence before he continues. 'Look Julia, I'm going to be in court all week,' he hesitates, 'what I mean is, you probably won't be able to get hold of me.'

What is he saying? That he wants to talk to me but cannot? That he doesn't want to and has a convenient excuse? That he is backing off at the mention of Richard? I ask myself these questions but right now the answers are unimportant. All that matters is that I do not have to appear in court.

'Thank you again,' I say. And then I ring off.

I am on a high. I leave voicemail messages for Clare and for Sally and Pete. I ring my mother too. Of course, she never knew anything about the charges but I cannot leave her out of my celebration. So I tell her the first things that come into my head, that the weather has cleared, that I am planning to return to work soon. I cannot believe that, at last, I am assured of my freedom. I want to share it with the world. And I remember that there is one person for whom just a few hours of freedom would mean everything. So I make one more important call. I ring Lizzie and tell her that it will be all right after all, that Frank can come to our house the following weekend.

'I'm so pleased,' she says. 'I thought your husband might come round to the idea when he'd had time to think about it. For many people it is an initial reaction, to say no. But when we explain the details to them they realise it isn't what they feared. I'll go and tell Frank now. Then I'll email you the paperwork. There are some forms you'll need to fill in and sign.'

I tell her that, in view of the home leave, I won't visit on Thursday. We agree that I will print off and sign the forms - Richard has to sign them too - and bring them with me when I come to collect Frank on Saturday. I don't tell her that Richard has not agreed to this at all, that he will be away, ignorant of our visitor's stay.

I am so lost in my own world that I am taken by surprise when Mrs Blackstock walks through the door.

'I'm so sorry Doctor,' she says, 'I didn't realise you were in or I'd have rung the bell.'

Suddenly, I remember I should be at the day centre. I don't want to go. I want to celebrate instead. I am tempted to play truant, to ring and say I am unwell. I have a bizarre fantasy of staying at home with Mrs Blackstock, of the two of us getting hopelessly drunk on cooking sherry and playing charades and hide and seek. But I don't want to let the day centre down and I know that Mrs Blackstock has never accepted more than a small port once a year at Christmas.

'I'm running a little late,' I tell her apologetically. 'I'll get my coat on and be out of your way.'

That evening, knowing that Richard will be working late, I

go round to Sally and Pete's for a celebratory drink.

'We're that pleased for you,' Sally says, as we clink together glasses of sparkling wine. 'Let's hope everything will start to get better now.'

'Thank you,' I reply. 'Actually I've got some more news.' And I tell them how I rang Lizzie earlier. How I agreed to Frank's visit this coming weekend.

'Are you sure about this?' Sally asks. 'You'd be in the house alone with him all night. This is the person you think murdered you in a previous life.'

'I've talked it over with Rose,' I say, 'and with the prison authorities. I'm certain that he's perfectly safe.' I know that it is myself I am trying to convince here.

'Even so,' Sally says. 'They think Richard's going to be there, right? Honestly, Julia, even if the chap's a saint, he's been locked up for years. It just wouldn't be fair being alone in the house with him – never mind irresponsible.'

I know they are right. I was so overwhelmed by Andrew's news earlier that I hadn't really thought it through. 'Well there's nothing I can do about it now,' I say. 'I can't say I've changed my mind. It wouldn't be fair.'

'I think I've got a solution,' Pete suggests. 'We can't let you stay with him on your own so it's obvious – Sally and I will come over and spend the weekend with you. That way everything will be above board and we'll know you're safe.'

I think about it. It would solve all the problems. With Pete and Sally in the house I won't have anything to worry about. 'Well if you're sure you don't mind,' I say, gratefully.

So it is settled. I will collect Frank on Saturday morning and take him out for lunch. Pete and Sally will arrive later in the afternoon. Suddenly I feel much more comfortable about everything.

On Wednesday, I wander round the house, planning where we will all sleep. In addition to the first floor, with its bedrooms and studies, there is also a second floor, an attic.

250

This houses Jamie's bedroom and another room that was generally devoted to him and his friends with a shared bathroom between them. There is also a further guest bedroom with its own en suite.

I walk into Jamie's room. I have not really touched this room since he died. It is not some morbid way of clinging to the past. His room is not a shrine. Simply, during the past three or four years, he has rarely been here. Most of his possessions, anything of consequence, he had long since taken with him to London. And he was never sentimental about childhood toys the way I was with mine. He simply cast things aside as he outgrew them. He probably thought they had long since been thrown away. In fact, I had been quietly picking things out of the bin, the charity bags and hording them away, squirrel-like, in the cupboard under the eaves. I have kept them safe with the thought – the hope – that one day they would be used, loved, again; by my grandchildren. I allow myself a moment of wistful fantasy. Now that I know that will never happen, I'm not sure what I will do with Jamie's things. Give some to Debbie for her baby probably, and perhaps donate some to a children's charity, maybe in a third world country or a hospice. I sigh. I don't need to think about that yet.

I decide to put Frank in the guest room on the top floor and Pete and Sally on the first floor, close to my own bedroom. I put freshly aired linen on the upstairs bed but I can't prepare Pete and Sally's room yet. Richard has been sleeping in there since Christmas and it will have to wait until after he has left for his conference on Friday night.

Chapter 29

At ten o'clock on Saturday morning I collect Frank from the prison. I had imagined how it would be, the sun shining, spreading unexpected warmth, or perhaps a storm, even snow like we had after Christmas, something dramatic anyway. But instead, it is one of those grey misty days that engulf the city in apathetic gloom. I do not want to go directly home. I feel it important for Frank to make the most of his temporary freedom – and in any case, Pete and Sally are not due to arrive until four. So instead, I drive us down into Leicestershire, across the Vale of Belvoir. As we drive we chat. I tell Frank that Richard will not be at home this weekend but that my friends will be joining us. I explain that Richard was keen to meet him and sent his apologies but I do not think Frank is convinced.

I made the last minute preparations yesterday evening after Richard had left. Remembering Frank was alcoholic, I removed the drinks tray with its decanters and bottles of whisky, port and sherry, from the sideboard in the dining room and hid them carefully in the cupboard behind a little-used dinner service. It reminded me of the time Jamie had asked to have a party on his seventeenth birthday when, after lengthy persuasion to secure Richard's agreement, I had removed all traces of drinks or breakable ornaments in advance of the gathering. As it turned out, Jamie and his friends spent almost the whole time in the attic rooms playing CDs and computer games, occasionally venturing into the kitchen in search of food.

When I finished downstairs, I went up to the first floor and changed the linen in the guest room ready for Sally and Pete. Then I went into my study and logged onto my computer. I printed off the forms that Lizzie had sent me and filled in the details of my address – the address where Frank would be staying. There were other details to supply too, declaring that neither Richard nor I had been convicted of a criminal offence. When I had done this, I signed my name at the bottom. Richard's signature was required too. At first I was unsure what to do about this. I didn't think anyone would actually check it, apart from anything else there surely wouldn't be time before Frank was released into my charge. All the same, I didn't want to risk anything going wrong at the last minute. Then I remembered something I'd seen on a detective drama. The person faking the signature copied the real one but turned it upside down so that they transcribed the shapes and were not tempted to write their own version of each letter. I found a copy of a hospital circular that Richard had signed, practised copying it several times, then printed it on the prison form. I was rather proud of the result.

And now this is it, the culmination of all that preparation. All the time that we are travelling, I am hopeful that the weather will clear, that, once we are away from the pollution of the city, the air will freshen and the visibility will improve so that Frank can enjoy the countryside. I am disappointed, yet Frank seems more than happy. He tells me that he is glad simply to be in the outdoors.

Lunchtime is something of a problem. Normally, when out with in a rural area, I would go to a country pub. But with Frank, I know that this would be more than unfair; it would be tempting fate. Eventually, I turn back to the southwest. I park in the centre of Melton Mowbray where we find a bustling café that serves acceptable coffee and toasted sandwiches. And then we browse around the shops until we are chilled and the rain begins to set in.

As we drive back into Nottingham, the overcast sky is already heralding a premature dusk. We will just have time to get in, to make a pot of tea and for me to show Frank around the house then it will be time for Sally and Pete to join us. They have promised to bring some DVDs and I will cook a roast dinner. I have already warned them not to bring wine. I pull up outside the house and turn off the headlights. It is nearly dark already and light drifts cautiously down from the nearby street lamp before being washed away in the drizzle. I am glad that I turned the hall light on before I left, despite the extravagance.

Frank is impressed with the house. He marvels at the stained glass in the front door, the carved balustrades, the tall windows draped in velvet curtains. And although it is indeed a large and complex building, I suspect that he would have been equally delighted with a simple terrace. Even before we take off our coats, I cannot resist showing him the conservatory, with the lemon trees patiently waiting for spring, and the rain now drumming and slithering on the roof. Somehow, I know he will love these things the way I do.

Back in the kitchen, I make a pot of tea and cut into a homemade chocolate cake. Frank is particularly appreciative of this and it is with a sense of guilt and regret that I admit that it was the result of Mrs Blackstock's efforts rather than my own. I also feel rather guilty, as I bite into the cake, that on Thursday I had told Mrs Blackstock of Sally and Pete's imminent visit but carefully omitted any mention of Frank.

I am about to show Frank to his room when the phone rings. He is already poised on the stairs with his bag so I tell him to go on up, that he'll find the room on the top floor. Then I go back to the kitchen to answer the call. It is my mother. I tell her that I have friends visiting and check that nothing is amiss with her before promising to call her back the following evening. Then I go up to the second floor guest bedroom but am surprised to find it empty. I assume that Frank must be in the bathroom but as I go to knock on the door, to check that he has found the towels and has everything he needs, he appears on the landing.

He grins at me casually. 'I'm in the room next door,' he says, 'that's right isn't it?'

That is when I realise he has inadvertently gone into

254

Jamie's room. As I follow him in I am shocked to see that he has already set his bag on the chair and turned back the corner of the duvet.

He looks at me. 'Is something wrong?' He asks.

For a moment I panic. I half close my eyes and picture him sleeping in Jamie's bed. I expect to feel horrified, violated. But instead I am surprised that actually the thought is quite comforting. 'It's fine,' I smile. 'Most people prefer the other room because it has the en suite but I don't mind at all.'

'I'll stay here then if that's all right,' he says, 'it's more homely, more lived in.'

And again I am surprised that those words, which I'm sure a few weeks ago would have depressed me, make me feel warm inside. They reassure me that there was at least one thing I got right for Jamie.

It is five o'clock and I am wondering where my friends are. Eventually I think to check the answering machine. I have one message. Sally's voice is rushed, excited. 'Julia, I'm sorry about this but the baby's decided to arrive early. Debbie's already rung to say she's going into hospital so Pete and I are off there now. Anyway, hopefully it'll all go smoothly and we'll see you this evening to wet the baby's head – with fruit juice obviously. We'll see you later.'

I click the button. They'll see me later? For a first baby, even one that's two or three weeks early I suspect they are being over-optimistic. I check the time of the recording before I delete it. The message was left only five minutes before I arrived back. Suddenly, I feel less confident, less secure. It is not that I don't trust Frank, more a general uneasy feeling, a portent of bad things to come. I take a deep breath and try to reason with myself. It is probably just the weather, the heavy, ominous barometric pressure. A good shower of rain and the world will seem right again.

'My friends will be a bit late,' I tell Frank, by way of explanation. 'Their first grandchild is about to be born. We'll have to have dinner without them.'

I prepared the evening meal earlier, having woken at six and been unable to return to sleep. The vegetables are ready to steam and the chicken and potatoes are poised ready to go into the oven.

I feel somewhat self-conscious as Frank and I sit alone at the dining table. I had debated whether to serve the meal in the kitchen, now that there were just the two of us. Somehow that would feel more casual. But it would not be fair on Frank, I told myself. After all, this weekend is for him. I serve one of those sparkling drinks made with herbs and fruit juices and follow the roast with an orange sorbet that I made the previous day. When we have finished, Frank insists on clearing away the dishes. I protest but he goes ahead anyway, carefully scraping the food scraps into the compost bin and stacking the plates in the dishwasher. While he is doing this I pick up the phone and dial Pete and Sally's number. Predictably there is no answer. Then I try Clare. She would be a good person to have here, after all. If it weren't for the danger of her telling Richard, and putting a stop to the proceedings, I would probably have invited her before. The phone goes to the answering machine and I remember that she is abroad skiing.

I can feel a panic beginning to build. It is only because I had expected friends to be here and now they are not. If I had planned the weekend alone with Frank all along then I am sure I would not worry. Now I am clutching at straws. I have Lizzie's number. She said I might call her if I had any problems. I could ring and tell her that Richard has been called away to an emergency. I am sure the home visit was only approved on the understanding there would be another man in the house. It would be a perfectly reasonable thing to do. But what could Lizzie do? Probably instruct me to return Frank to the prison tonight. I couldn't do that to him. In the end, I realise that all I can do is hold on to the slim hope that Pete and Sally will arrive tonight, however late.

Frank browses through my CD collection and picks out a couple of classical recordings. He says he would like to listen to them while he reads his book if that is all right. I tell him to go ahead and say that I need to check Pete and Sally have everything they need in their room. I imply that they will come here directly from the hospital after their grandchild is born. I let him think that they have a key and will let themselves in during the night even though I know this is not the case. Saying these things somehow makes me feel safer.

At ten-thirty, Frank says he is tired and will go to bed. I check that he has everything he needs and that he knows where the tea and coffee are in case he wakes early and wants to make a drink. It feels strange, as he disappears up the stairs, knowing that he will be sleeping in Jamie's room. I am sleepy myself after my early start and, facing the fact that it is unlikely that Pete and Sally will be round tonight, decide to read my book in bed. It is only as I feel myself dozing that I remember something I have not done. I pull myself awake, pad across to the door and turn the key in the lock.

I wake at seven. The house is silent and I assume Frank is making the most of the opportunity to lie in. Nonetheless, I pull on a sweatshirt and trousers before unlocking the door and making my way along to the bathroom, to shower. It would not seem appropriate to risk Frank seeing me in a dressing gown. I do not linger under the water. Frank could wake at any time and I know that I will feel more at ease, more in control of the situation if I am already primed to start the day. So it is only ten minutes later that, fully dressed and hair combed, I walk into the kitchen.

'Frank!' I am surprised that I did not hear him, uneasy that he can creep about the house stealthily without my knowledge. Now here he is, standing at the Aga, pan in hand, frying eggs.

'I woke early,' he tells me. 'Force of habit I suppose. I tried to be quiet and keep the door shut so as not to wake anyone. There's bacon and sausages in the slow oven.'

I wonder how he knows about these things; perhaps he has cooked on an Aga before. I notice, then, that the kitchen table is set for four. 'I wasn't sure if your friends had arrived,' he says.

'I'm afraid not,' I apologize. 'I'll give them a call later and see if the baby's arrived, if everything's all right.'

'That's your job isn't it?' Frank asks. 'Babies and all that.'

I nod. 'I haven't been working for a while though, as you know.' I have told Frank, over the past few weeks, the two of us sitting either side of that grey table, that my son had died, that I'd taken time off work, but I hadn't told him anything else, about the inquiry or the prosecution.

'But you'll go back soon?' he asks.

I smile. I hadn't really thought that through. I hadn't really thought beyond this weekend. But now I can see the possibilities stretching out before me. 'Yes,' I say. 'Yes I will.'

'The eggs are done,' Frank informs me. 'I hope you're hungry because I've cooked enough for four.'

I laugh and take a seat at the table.

Frank has requested that we go to church. It is important to him, he tells me, to get to a service, preferably a mass, at least once a week. It is one of the things he's been looking forward to this weekend, going to a proper church instead of the prison chapel. The last time he went to a real church, apparently, was when he was granted a few hours compassionate leave, escorted by a prison officer, to attend his mother's funeral. Since then he has been looking forward to taking part in a proper service on a happier occasion.

I do not want to go to the local church with Frank. It is not as though I go there often. I am not a regular member of the congregation. But even so, Richard and I are known because of our jobs. There is a chance that someone will notice, will ask questions, that someone might, however innocently, however well-meaning, mention it to Richard. I know that Frank would like to get out into the countryside so I suggest that we spend the day in the Peak District, making an early start and stopping at a church somewhere on the way. Frank thinks this is a marvellous idea. I calculate that most services don't start until around nine-thirty, if we can be off an hour before that we will find somewhere en route that fits Frank's requirements. I wait until the last minute before ringing Pete and Sally. Their phone is switched onto the answering machine. I have no way of knowing if they are back, sleeping off a long night of stuffy waiting rooms and bland vending machine coffee, or whether they are still pacing the corridors at the hospital. I leave a message telling them my plans for the day and suggest they text my mobile when they get back.

Today, we are lucky with the weather and bright sun beckons as we drive up the A6. We stop in Matlock Bath and find a church that meets with Frank's approval and where the service starts at ten, giving us time, first, for a stroll along the river. The service is more formal than I am used to. The priest's words are interspersed with the ringing of a high-pitched bell and I recognise the smell of frankincense, drifting, now and then, on the cold air. It reminds me of Rose and the hypnosis and I find myself thinking about Maggie and Freddie as the rest of the congregation kneel in prayer. A wave of unease sweeps over me but I tell myself it is just the stone chill of the church and form my own private prayer requesting protection from harm. I close my hand around the piece of amber in my pocket, hoping that this action is not in any way anti-Christian or even satanic.

When we are back on the road, I drive up through Bakewell and park near the bottom of the Iron Age fort of Fin Cop. We put on our warm hats and scarves – I have loaned Frank some old ones of Richard's – and stroll along the meadows in the river valley. There are plenty of people out enjoying the good weather and I am glad that, for once, I am

259

not on my own; glad, also, that I am not alone with Frank. Gradually, we leave behind the families with young children and pushchairs, and climb up the steep path that hugs the hillside all the way up to Monsal Head.

'It's pretty spectacular isn't it?' Frank comments, as we stand near the edge of the precipitous drop. 'But you wouldn't want to slip down there.'

I look down and shudder. That familiar feeling of uncertainty returns and I step back from the edge. 'Let's get a cup of tea and some lunch,' I say.

As we walk in the afternoon, I tell Frank about the whole ghastly business of the inquiry and the private prosecution.

'You should have told me before,' he says. 'Blimey, you must have found it difficult coming into a prison with that hanging over you.'

'The last few months haven't been easy,' I agree. 'But that's all behind me now, thankfully. And so is your own ordeal, almost,' I add, as an afterthought.

We arrive back just as dusk is settling. In another hour or two I will have to return Frank to the confines of his everyday life. For now, I must allow him to make the most of his break. He is on borrowed time. I suggest a stir-fry for dinner, not needing to remind Frank of the reason for cooking something quick or the need to eat early.

'Would you mind if I cook again?' he asks. 'I like the opportunity.

Of course I agree. 'There are vegetables here.' I show him the rack I have installed in the porch as well as the selection, mostly of fruit, in the trug basket and the salad items in the fridge. He selects mushrooms and bean sprouts as a base, placing them to rinse in the colander and pushing the wrappings into the already full stainless steel bin.

'I'll put the bin outside,' Frank offers. He ties up the black plastic bag and takes the key off the hook in the porch. I point to the brick outbuildings where the bins and recycling boxes are kept.

I linger by the table, listening to the click of the shed door and let the night-time sounds drift in around me. Outside it is fully dark. There is not even a moon. I marvel at Frank being able to see in that blackness. Perhaps he is used to it from the strict rules regarding lights in prison. As he reappears at the door I kick myself for not having thought to switch on the outside lamp.

I take my jacket off the back of the chair and go to hang it in the cloakroom, then I check the phone to see if there is a message from Sally and Pete. There is nothing. When I return, Frank is chopping vegetables. I see he has chosen a large knife – one that I never use myself – from the rack. His hands move expertly, delicately and he wields the knife very quickly in a whirring motion. He tucks back the fingers of his left hand so there is no danger of cutting himself. Surely those are not the hands of a killer, I think to myself, not any more anyway. Even so, I feel uneasy at the sight of him brandishing, what I consider to be a deadly weapon.

Frank sees me looking and laughs. 'I do a lot of shifts in the kitchens,' he tells me.

'I'm worried you'll cut yourself,' I say.

'There's a knack to it,' he says, 'same as any job. How many times have you cut yourself when you're operating on someone?'

'Never,' I admit.

'There you are then,' he laughs. 'I enjoy cooking,' he continues. 'I might even try and get work as a chef when I get out properly.'

I nod. His reference to getting out reminds me that I have to return him to custody soon. I ask if he would like to listen to some music or watch a video but he assures me it is a luxury simply to be in an ordinary house, an ordinary kitchen. He pauses to examine the contents of my spice rack before resuming the mundane yet sweet task of preparing food.

When it happens, I know that it does so very quickly. Yet my brain seems to process it in slow motion.

There is no warning, no noise outside. I do not even hear the door open. Yet, when I turn, he is standing in the porch doorway. He is holding a shotgun, the barrel pointing straight at my chest. I do not say anything; just very slowly raise my empty hands in surrender. For me, time stands still.

The intruder is like a tiger, ready to pounce. He is so focused on me that I do not think he has even seen Frank, standing over to the side, with his back to him, methodically chopping courgettes.

I stare at the gunman. I am so overwhelmed, so taken aback, that I do not really consider why he should be here. Frank must have left the door unlocked. Perhaps that is reason enough. Perhaps the world is full of opportunist burglars watching for their chance. I wonder whether I should tell him where the money is, in what rooms he may find the best of the family silver. To me he is a stranger who has chosen to break into my home.

Then, to my surprise he speaks. 'You're a murderer!' he says.

I am confused. Surely intruders tell you to turn round, or lie on the floor, or order you into a cellar where they can hold you prisoner while they make off with your possessions.

'If the law won't give me justice I'll make my own,' he continues.

Then I realise who he is. It is Jack Ashby, the bereaved husband and father, come to claim what he considers a fair exchange for his dead wife and child. Now I experience complete terror. Not a fear of the unknown, but a considered and reasoned conclusion. The man is deranged. Of that I am sure. And that certainty is more frightening than anything else.

There is silence where previously there was noise. It takes me a moment to work out that Frank has stopped chopping. I can see him out of the corner of my eye, slowly turning to face Ashby. He has stopped chopping but he still holds the knife.

I don't think Ashby is aware of Frank, even now. Perhaps his mind is so intent on handing out justice – as he sees it - to me that he simply does not consider anyone, anything else.

'There's only one punishment for murder,' Ashby says. And in an instant I realise what he is going to do. He will shoot me then turn the gun on himself. For him there can be no other resolution. I am resigned. I am calm. How difficult can dying be? After all, Jamie has done it.

And then Ashby lifts the shotgun to his shoulder and peers along the length of the barrel.

'Stop messing about Freddie,' I say. I clamber over ancient rocks, step on a thousand long-dead sea creatures. I peer into crevices. But the beach is deserted – or so it seems.

He appears suddenly, creeping up behind. The first thing I feel is the warm breath on the back of my neck. I feel it even before I hear the crunch of a boot on shingle. At first, it is welcome after the sting of the cold breeze. Then I smell it, acrid with ale and stale tobacco. 'You've been drinking again Freddie,' I say. 'Gerroff!'

I try to turn but a big bony hand grabs hold of my waist, forces me against the cliff. Another hand sneaks under the hem of my skirt, it creeps up my leg like a fat poisonous spider. I wriggle, trying to get myself free but he leans against me with his body, squashing me into the sharp unyielding rock-face. 'I've had enough now, Freddie. It ain't funny any more,' I say, before the last of my breath is squeezed out of me.

I can hear the waves crashing closer. I'm praying they'll sneak up, like he did on me, and gobble him up. I try to scream but my voice is lost in the sea and the wind and, as I struggle for breath, a hand clamps over my mouth.

'Yer've been asking for this for a long time. You with yer

airs and graces, flaunting yerself around. Tain't right ter tease a man. Don't pretend yer doesn't want it.'

It isn't Freddie's voice at all.

I let myself go limp. It isn't difficult. The hand is squashing my nose as well and I'm finding it hard to breathe, I'm getting dizzy. As I stop struggling he relaxes his grip; just a bit, enough for me to lift my right leg, to kick back, hard and sudden with my boot. He howls, like I've caught him somewhere delicate. I push back and twist round in one desperate movement. But it isn't enough. There's rocks on either side of me and he's in the way, a big hulk; I can't push past him. For an instant Alf and I look each other in the eye. Then he's on me again, more determined than before. I shout really loud; to the sea, to Freddie - wherever he is. The hand comes back, slapping into my mouth like dried up leather. The other hand is back under my skirt, pushing, ripping, it's like he has more hands than he should. I get my teeth apart, just a bit, and I bite the hand that's over my mouth. I feel my teeth pierce through the tough hide and sink into the flesh beneath. He squeals in pain and pulls his hand away. I manage one yell before it's back again, pushing against my throat this time.

The waves grow louder and higher. I can feel their spray on my face. Alf is leaning full against me now, he's pulling at his breeches. I close my eyes and try to imagine I'm in the sea. I'm trying not to think about what's happening, what he's doing to me. In my mind, I'm battling with the breakers, I'm shouting for help.

'Shut up!' Alf yells. 'I said shut up!'

I'm getting caught in the current. I shout again.

'I told yer ter keep quiet!' The grip tightens around my throat.

I'm going under now. Getting sucked down under the surface then bobbing back up. I try to take a breath but my throat hurts and the air won't go in. I sink again. This time I feel light, calm even. Perhaps I'm drowning.

The image of Frank rushes before my eyes. There is a bang, deafening, all-engulfing. I am thrown off my feet by the impact.

I'm not struggling anymore. I'm floating up, to the surface maybe? But there is no surface; just a beach – or what bit of rock and shingle the tide has left behind. I can see myself, crumpled and discarded on the ground. Alf is backing away, muttering something, buttoning up his breeches. And as I float higher, as the beach, the cliff, the sea, pan out beneath me, I see a figure huddled, scared and shaking behind a rocky outcrop. It is Freddie.

I am stretched out on the floor. A few feet away, Ashby lies still. I presume he is dead. Frank is between us. There is blood everywhere.

'Frank?' I sob. 'Hold on. I'm going to get help.'

I am leaning against him, my body stemming the flow of blood from his chest, from the bullet that was meant for me. My arm is cradling his head. For a moment I think it might be possible, that there might be a way.

But Frank shakes his head. 'I didn't let you down this time, Maggie,' he says.

Then the blood surges up his throat, froths around his lips. And it is over.

Chapter 30

'Mrs Spencer? Julia?'

I do not know how long I have been lying there, probably only seconds. When I open my eyes to the confusion, I am curled across Frank, my head on his chest, my ear listening for a heartbeat that isn't there. Suddenly, I feel a hand on my arm. I raise my head. 'Frank?' I mumble, desperately.

'It's me, dear. Mrs Perriman. Thank goodness you're alive, are you all right?'

I struggle to sit upright, feel dazed. What is happening cannot be real.

'What are you...?'

'I heard the gunshot,' she tells me. 'Have you been hit?'

'I'm all right,' I say. 'I mean, I think I am.' I look down at myself then. I am covered in blood. It is soaked, dark and doom-laden, into my jumper and my jeans. It is sticky on my hands. No doubt it is smeared across my face and hair as well. I stifle a scream. I try to remember what happened but it was all so fast, so confused. Then I look down at Frank. He is staring, blindly, at the ceiling. I feel tears forming, gathering ready to flood my eyes. 'He's dead,' I say.

'I know dear, but the other one's still alive.'

I look properly at Mrs Perriman now. She is dressed, like me, in trousers and a warm top. There is a large streak of crimson across her jumper. At first, I think she is covered in blood too, then I see there are other colours, green and violet, and I realise that it is paint. As I sit, blinking the mist from my eyes, she takes a towel from the Aga rail and folds it into a wad. She presses it onto the abdomen of the other body, covering the dark stain that is spreading upwards towards his chest.

'You know what to do?' I manage to say.

'Don't worry,' she tells me. 'I was a nurse in the war. Believe me, I've seen far worse.'

266

I nod.

Mrs Perriman reaches for a second towel, folds it with one hand, and replaces the blood-soaked cloth on Ashby. 'Now,' she says to me. 'Do you think you can hold this here while I call for an ambulance?'

I do as I am told. 'I should be doing that,' I try to protest.

'Nonsense. You're in shock. Now where's your phone – ah, here it is. Let's get some help.'

I sit on the floor, surrounded by blood and death. In the background, I hear Mrs Perriman instructing the emergency services. 'That's right,' she confirms, when she has given the telephone number and address, 'knife wound to the abdomen, looks like arterial bleeding.' When she finishes the call she comes back over to me. 'They're on their way,' she tells me. She leans across me then, to Frank, and gently closes his eyes. 'That's better,' she says, 'more dignified. Now, will you be all right for a few more moments while I call the police?' Again she is matter of fact. 'One fatality,' I hear her telling them, 'a gunshot. No. Nobody is armed. We're not in any danger. Thank you.' She replaces the phone on the table and sits beside me. 'Best to be clear with them,' she tells me. 'We don't want them storming the place like the SAS.'

I am feeble, me, the trained doctor, the one who should be making the decisions, allowing myself to be led. I feel weak. Mrs Perriman has resumed her supervision of the casualty. I see her looking up at me. 'You need a cup of hot sweet tea,' she tells me. But I don't get it. Instead, things begin to happen in a flurry.

The paramedics arrive first. I sit on a chair beside the Aga and look on, helplessly, as they move Frank's body to one side so they can work on Ashby. I watch as they set up an intravenous drip and an oxygen mask with Mrs Perriman assisting. I am little use, having only the presence of mind to switch on the outside lights in the side passage as, having pronounced Ashby as stable as they can hope for, one of them goes back to the ambulance to fetch a stretcher.

267

It is during this brief lull of comparative inactivity that Sally and Pete arrive.

Between the two of them they seem to fill up the porch. Sally is standing in front, she sees me first. 'Julia! Thank God you're all right. We saw the ambulance and we thought – well we knew you were here with Frank and – oh my God!' She sees the carnage. She looks beyond the huddle formed by Ashby, Mrs Perriman and the paramedic and she sees Frank. Since the paramedics moved the two men, the gun and the blood-coated knife are now also strewn amidst the chaos.

'What's happened?' Pete asks, struggling to see. Sally makes to step forward but Mrs Perriman lifts her hand up.

'You'd probably better not,' she says. 'The police will be here any minute – they'll be wanting to examine everything no doubt – and, in the meantime, we've got to get this chap out to the ambulance.'

The other paramedic arrives with the stretcher and Sally and Pete manage to skirt round the top end of the kitchen and join me beside the Aga. Sally puts her arm round me and we watch the proceedings in silence. Just as Ashby is being hoisted onto the trolley, there is the sound of a siren followed by heavy footsteps outside as the police arrive. There are two officers, one male and one female. They edge their way in carefully. The paramedics mutter something about 'emergency' and 'no time to lose'. The male police officer speaks to them. The female officer walks over to me. She is just asking if I am all right when, beyond the devastation on the floor, the internal door to the hall opens.

'Julia! Whatever is...?' He stops as he processes the sight before him. It is Richard.

The action seems to go into reverse. The paramedics wheel Ashby out through the porch while the male officer speaks on the radio and asks for a constable to meet them at the hospital. Then he requests for a scene of crime team and a police surgeon to come out. Meanwhile, the female officer is shouting to Richard; telling him not to walk across the kitchen, that it is a crime scene and he must not contaminate it.

'But this is my house,' he shouts back. 'And that's my wife. Who are all these other people?' he demands. 'What are they doing here?'

I take a deep breath, then I speak. 'The man who just left on the stretcher is Ashby,' I say. 'The one who tried to take me to court.' I gesture to my side. 'These are my good friends Pete and Sally. You have met them though I wouldn't expect you to remember them seeing as they're not doctors. This is Mrs Perriman, she's been our next door neighbour as long as we've lived in this house.' Then I point to the floor. 'And that is Frank.' I struggle not to sob. 'He just saved my life.'

For several moments, there is silence. Then everyone speaks at once. The male police officer, whom I hear introducing himself as Sergeant Grant, is asking Pete what happened. Sally is trying to explain that, actually neither of them witnessed the incident because they were in the maternity unit. The female officer is insisting that she will arrest Richard if he walks across the room. Mrs Perriman is the only one who says anything sensible.

'Perhaps it would be easier if you all come next door to my house.' Her voice is shrill and authoritative, like a headmistress. Instantly everyone stops talking. 'It occurs to me, we can't sort this out here,' she says, 'and my house is only a few yards away.'

'Well, if you don't mind,' Sergeant Grant looks relieved. 'Constable Clark could wait here until SOCO and the doc turn up.'

So Mrs Perriman leads the way. Sally and Pete file after her, followed by Sergeant Grant. Richard retreats the way he has come. Moments later there are just three of us left in the room; myself, the constable and Frank. I shiver. The door has been open so long that, even near the Aga, the room is cold. I look at Frank. Then I look down at myself, I am covered in his blood, probably some of Ashby's too.

'I can't go round to Mrs Perriman's like this,' I say.

Constable Clark looks at me sympathetically. 'We'll need to bag up the clothes you're wearing anyway, I'm afraid,' she says.

Take them away, I think to myself, burn them, I never want to see them again.

The rest of the police team arrive then, and the constable takes me upstairs to wash and change. She apologises for having to accompany me in this way but, actually, I am glad not to be alone. I glance back once more at Frank before we leave. 'Thank you,' I whisper.

When the constable (who has said I may call her Angela) and I arrive at Mrs Perriman's everyone else is comfortably settled. If it were not for the events earlier, the gathering would seem like a party, it occurs to me that there have probably never been this many people in the house for several decades. We enter via the side porch and the kitchen. There is a welcoming smell of coffee and freshly baked bread, and a piercing background scent, which I identify as white spirit. I confirm this when I see a bundle of artist's brushes in a jam jar on the draining board. The kitchen is bohemian, crammed with ancient dressers stacked with willow pattern crockery. There is a huge old fireplace where I can imagine some cousin of Mrs Blackstock's black-leading the grate.

Mrs Perriman ushers us through to the drawing room. 'Get Mrs Spencer a chair,' she commands. I find myself guided into a low armchair. Mrs Perriman addresses Angela and Sergeant Grant. 'She won't be answering any of your questions until she's had a drink,' she tells them. 'She's had a terrible shock.'

Moments later, a willow patterned cup and saucer are thrust into my hands. I take a sip. The tea is strong and full of sugar. The taste is horrible, I haven't taken sugar in my drinks since I was a small child, but I force myself to drink it anyway.

'This too.' Mrs Perriman holds a glass to my lips.

I drink and the liquid burns my throat.

'It's whisky,' she tells me. 'It will help you with the shock.'

'I'll talk to everyone else first and give you chance to recover,' Sergeant Grant says.

I almost giggle with nerves. It is like the culmination of an Agatha Christie story where everyone is gathered together waiting for the detective or the amateur sleuth to pronounce who is the murderer.

'Do we have to do this now?' Richard asks. 'I don't know how it happened but it seems my wife has narrowly escaped with her life. Did the paramedics check you over?' he asks me.

'I'll be all right,' I insist, as the whisky and the sweet tea revive me. I look round the room properly for the first time then. Everyone, apart from myself, is seated on a low sofa or bench. The decoration is minimalist with a pale coloured carpet and similar curtains. But the walls are a shock. They are hung with huge canvases, not the delicate watercolours or heavy classical oils that I usually associate with old people but striking abstracts with bold forms and fiery interplay of colours.

Mrs Perriman sees me looking. 'I trained at the Royal Academy,' she says, by way of explanation. 'My studio is upstairs where the light's better. I'm working on some pieces for the Summer Exhibition right now. I'll show you later if you like. I wouldn't usually, of course, but maybe it will help take your mind off everything. You could have a go yourself – wonderful how therapeutic it can be.'

I am certain that I must be in a very strange dream.

'Perhaps I could take some statements now,' Sergeant Grant suggests.

Half an hour later, Sergeant Grant and Angela have established that the only real witness to what happened was myself, although Mrs Perriman's testimony is also important because she was first on the scene.

'We'll have to wait for forensics to get the full picture,' Angela tells me. 'And you may find you remember some more details as you get over the shock. There's Ashby too of course – if he regains consciousness, that is.'

It is only as we are all leaving that I realise why Pete and Sally came round. I look at them enquiringly.

'A girl,' Sally tells me, 'six pounds and ten ounces. Mother and baby are doing fine.'

'Congratulations,' I manage to say. Thank goodness something good has happened today.

Chapter 31

Richard and I spend the night in a hotel. I couldn't stay at the house, not after what has happened. We are not allowed to anyway. It has been sealed off by the police. It is a crime scene.

We check in. We have little luggage, only the small overnight bags which we packed, hurriedly, under the watchful gaze of Angela. It occurs to me, as Richard signs the register at the reception desk, that I do not even have a book with me. This fact alone makes me feel lost, vulnerable.

Richard takes both of our bags and silently leads the way. When he pushes open the door of our allocated room I pause in the doorway and stare. The curtains, the bedspread, they are the same design, the same fabric as Andrew's. It is like stepping into his bedroom. Richard sees me staring. He thinks I am bothered by the double bed, by the thought of sleeping next to him.

'I'm sorry,' he begins, 'I could ask for another room.'

'No,' I say, quickly. 'The room is fine. I'm just tired. The day is catching up with me.'

'It's probably delayed shock,' he tells me. 'Come and sit on the bed and I'll make you a drink.' He sets the bags down and takes the kettle from the tray, goes into the en suite to fill it. 'Would you prefer Ovaltine or hot chocolate?'

'Chocolate please,' I whisper.

He turns to look at me as the kettle boils. 'When did you last eat? Properly, I mean, not the biscuits at Mrs Perriman's.'

I shrug. I notice that I am shivering too.

'I'm calling room service,' he insists. 'I'm sure they can rustle up something, even though it's late. Now, I wonder if this bed has an electric blanket. If not I'll ask for a hot water bottle.'

I sit in silence while Richard calls reception. I wait like a child for him to finish the call, to pour boiling water into the mugs of chocolate powder, to bring mine over to me, gently bend my fingers around the handle, help me raise it to my lips. I look up at him after I have taken a few sips. He is frowning, like a stern headmaster.

'Are you angry?' I ask. 'About me letting Frank stay?'

'How can I be,' he says, 'when that is the only reason you are still alive?'

Before I finish the drink, there is a knock on the door. I let Richard answer it. I do not even look up. I am spent.

'I hope soup and sandwiches will be all right,' a female voice says. 'The main kitchen is shut until morning.'

Richard thanks her and assures her that it will be fine. The door shuts and he sets a tray down beside me on the bedside cabinet. There are steaming bowls of leek and potato soup and a plate of neatly cut sandwiches. Suddenly, I realise how hungry I am. I hope it is not inappropriate to feel like this. To eat when someone has just died seems, somehow, disrespectful. I bite into a grated cheese and tomato sandwich while the soup cools. Frank died to save my life. I owe it to him to look after myself now, I reason, to make the most of this second chance.

When we have finished eating, Richard pours himself a whisky from the mini bar. He suggests I should have one too, if only to help me sleep. I accept a glass of port.

'Get into bed,' Richard suggests. 'Before you get cold again. I switched the blanket on over half an hour ago; it's nice and snug now.'

'I was going to have a shower,' I protest. 'My hair…' I have just looked in the mirror and noticed that it is matted, with blood, I suspect, Frank's blood. I do not want to think about it.

'It's late,' Richard says. 'You'll wake people up if you use the hairdryer. Anyway, it doesn't matter.'

'If you're sure you don't mind,' I say, knowing that I mind a great deal myself.

'Why should I mind?' he sounds surprised. 'I'm your

274

husband. I married you for better or worse.'

'I kept thinking this last year couldn't get any worse,' I say, as I take off my jumper and blouse, and pull my nightdress over my head. 'But somehow it kept proving me wrong.' I wriggle out of my shoes and jeans and slide gratefully into the comfort of the bed.

'It could have been a lot worse for me,' Richard says. 'I realised that tonight.' He climbs into bed beside me. It is comforting and familiar to feel his body next to mine.

I am propped up on my pillow, sipping the last of my port, wondering whether to switch off the bedside light when Richard does something I have never seen him do before. He cries; a great wave of tears that has been building up, secure behind a dam of respectability, all of his life.

It is so unexpected that I do not know what to do. He is my husband of more than twenty-five years and I do not know how to soothe his hurt. I set down my glass and then I fold my arms around him and I hold him close while he sobs. I hold him for a long time. Everything is wrong. Outside, where there should be blackness there extends the brightness of the city, where there should be rain, cascading down in sympathy, there is only the hum of traffic. Everywhere, instead of sleeping there is wakefulness.

Eventually he quietens, becomes still.

'I never meant to leave you on your own,' he says. 'I never wanted to hurt you.'

'Sshh,' I soothe. 'It doesn't matter.' But we both know that it does.

'The things I said, about you trying to find Jamie, about trying to prove there are other lives…'

'Perhaps you were right,' I say. 'Perhaps I was trying to do that.'

'I should have understood that you were just coping in your own way.'

We are silent for a few moments. I stroke Richard's brow.

'Perhaps it was all imagination,' I say at last.

'But it wasn't, was it?' he asks. 'This thing with you and Frank, I don't understand it but it's why you met, why he saved your life.'

I think about my adoption, about growing up in Lyme. I have not told Richard about this yet. 'There may be a rational explanation,' I say. 'It's too complicated to explain now. But I'll tell you all about it soon. And as for Jamie, I know he's gone forever, I've always known that. If there is such a thing as reincarnation, if we were to meet again in another life, then we would be different people. There was only ever one Jamie and we were fortunate to have him in our lives.'

'I should have trusted you,' Richard continues. 'But I was worried. I was so scared I would lose you too. And I just couldn't bear that.' He squeezes me tightly, like he will never let go. 'And tonight I nearly did.' He begins to cry again. Softly, this time, gently. I rock him like a baby.

And as the city night hums and flickers around us, we make love. For the first time in many months, years even, we exchange pure selfless love. Slowly, cautiously, we embark on a journey of healing, of rediscovery. It will be a very long road, we both know that, but, exhausted and overwhelmed, we take the first tentative steps.

The following day, I am in shock, and in limbo. Richard does not want to leave me alone but at seven-thirty he receives a call from the hospital. He has urgent surgery to perform, another life to save. I should take it easy and try and sleep it off, he tells me as he hurriedly pulls on his clothes. He could prescribe me a mild sedative, he suggests, allow me to get some proper rest. But I shake my head, insisting that I would rather be up and about. After he has left, I order breakfast in my room. I should have asked for a newspaper or magazine with it but my mind is exhausted and I do not think. So I force myself to tuck into the coffee and scrambled eggs, which I hope will help me to feel human again and, in the absence of anything to read, I switch on the television.

276

It is a mistake of course. If I had been thinking sensibly, I would have known what would happen, but my brain is still numb from the day before. And suddenly, there I am, on the screen before me. True, there is only a minimum of information on the national news but it is still there for all the nation to see and hear. The local coverage is worse of course. On this, I am the main story. The events of the previous twenty-four hours of my life are, apparently, the most important things to have happened in the county. There are pictures too, an inanimate photograph of Frank, presumably taken when he entered prison and – goodness knows where they found this – a short video clip of me at the hospital. I switch the television off quickly and push my food aside.

At eight-thirty, Andrew calls me on my mobile. He is on his way into court but he has heard the summary of what happened on the news. He is worried, wants to know that I am all right, that Richard is looking after me. I assure him, yes, to both these things. I do not tell him Richard is at work. It would give a false impression. Andrew is concerned that Richard might have disowned me and run off to hide behind his parents in Lincoln. A week ago, I might have predicted that would be Richard's reaction myself. But things have changed. In the coming weeks, I will have to think about Andrew and about Richard, but I am not thinking clearly enough to do this now.

When I have showered and dressed, I try to busy myself, tidying together Richard's and my possessions; but of course, we have little with us, and this does not take long.

An hour later, Angela collects me from the hotel and escorts me back to the house. I watch in silence as she gathers Frank's possessions from Jamie's room. She zips them into his bag. It is a final act, marking the ending of a life. Only two people have slept in this room since we moved here and both of them are dead. Angela looks up at me, sees my strained expression. 'The shock will pass,' she tries to reassure me. But she doesn't know the half of it. How could she? She suggests that I might want to collect some more belongings for myself and Richard. She says we should be prepared to stay somewhere else for today and tonight at least. I imagine she means until the police have finished in the kitchen. I presume they are taking photographs and fingerprints. I presume they will not clean the room afterwards, that even when they are done there will be blood stains on the floor at the very least. I gather a few clothes together for myself and a spare suit and a couple of shirts for Richard. This time I also think to take a book for each of us.

When I have finished, Angela asks whether there is a friend I could stay with or whether she should take me back to the hotel. She doesn't like the idea of leaving me on my own, she says, under the circumstances. Apart from the shock, the trauma, she is concerned that I will be hounded by the press, that they will use their invisible radar to detect where I am. If only the police could do the same with criminals, she jokes, trying to make me laugh. I think about where I could stay. I certainly do not want to spend all day alone in the hotel room and neither do I want to walk around town, where I might be recognised, pointed at, stared at. There is always Clare. She is on holiday of course, she is unaware of what has happened. But she gave me the keys to her house back in the summer after Jamie died, said that if I ever felt the need to get away for a few hours her door was always open. I think, at the time, she was referring to my need to vacate my own home when Mrs Blackstock was around. But either way the offer is still open, I still have the keys. I would not want to call her on holiday and ask because then I would have to tell her what has happened and she would worry. But I could spend the day there all the same. On the other hand, Angela is right. I do not want to be alone. I am pondering all this when the landline rings. I pick up the extension beside my bed.

It is Mrs Blackstock. She is glad she caught me in, she says, because she does not like answering machines or mobiles.

She does not say how she knows what has happened, just matter-of-factly comes to the point. She says that she understands that the police are working in the house today, that they may still be here when she is due over herself tomorrow, that providing I am agreeable, she will ask them to contact her when they have finished. She will make the time to come here and see that everything is put right. She will call me when it is done, when it is safe for me to return home.

Dear Mrs Blackstock, how grateful I am to her.

'So where would you like to go?' Angela asks, when I have replaced the phone on the charger. I am about to ask her to fetch Clare's keys for me – which are, unfortunately, kept in a drawer in the kitchen – when, this time my mobile rings. It is Sally. She asks how I am and where I am. She didn't like to ring earlier, she says, in case I was sleeping in. I tell her that I am at the house; that I will go either to Clare's or back to the hotel.

'Don't be silly, you can't do that,' Sally insists. 'Both Pete and I have got the day off because of the baby. You must come over here. In fact, can you come over now?' she encourages me. 'We're going to collect Debbie from the hospital later. You can come with us.'

In something of a daze, I say that I will do this. I ask Angela if she will fetch my car keys – also, of course, in the kitchen drawer - and give her the address where I can be contacted if the police need to speak to me. She brings me the keys but says she would be happier if I didn't drive, under the circumstances. She will drive me over there herself, she insists.

I feel happier once we are out of the house. As we drive through Wollaton, I ask Angela to pull over at a newsagent's so I can buy a card for Debbie and the family. The present will have to wait until later. Back in the car, I text Richard and tell him where I will be spending the day – just in case, when the emergency is over, he returns to the house or the hotel and worries that I am not there. I suggest that Angela may drop me at the end of the road but she insists on taking me to Pete and Sally's house, waiting until she has seen us hug in greeting before she returns to Nottingham.

'We've worried about you,' Sally says, as we draw apart. 'That dreadful business yesterday – it might not have happened if Pete and I had been there like we promised.'

I shake my head. 'It wouldn't have made any difference,' I say, 'except to put you in danger too.'

'Who'd have thought it?' Pete says. 'Saved by the man we were supposed to be protecting you from.'

I shiver, more at the reminder of yesterday than because of the temperature.

'Come on in, love.' Sally puts her arm round me and guides me through the entry to the back door. 'You look like you could do with a cup of tea. We thought we'd have an early lunch before going into Derby.'

I sit at the familiar kitchen table and stroke the dogs as they nuzzle at my ankles.

'Are you sure you'll be all right coming into the hospital with us?' Sally asks as she butters slices of white bread. 'It won't upset you seeing the baby – what with the shock of everything else?'

'Of course not,' I say. 'I'm hoping to return to work soon anyway. I'll be seeing lots of babies.' I pause. 'I truly am pleased for you,' I say.

'I'm that relieved.' Sally opens a can of tuna and distributes it over the bread. 'Only Pete was worried – what with us being grandparents and everything – and for him to think of something like that…'

'I'm coming to terms with everything,' I assure her. 'I'm alive. I'll never take that for granted again. I'm determined to make the most of every good thing that comes along.' I know that what I am saying sounds trite, that it will not be easy. The fact that I have survived will never make up for the fact that Jamie has not, and, if it were possible, I would willingly change places with him, yet, if I do not make the most of my life now, then Frank's death will have been for nothing.

But here we are celebrating a new life. I must not get maudlin. I smile and discreetly sneak each of the dogs a forbidden treat of tuna sandwich while Pete and Sally pretend not to notice.

It feels strange to be in a maternity department where I am not the consultant. I look around me at the new mothers with their babies, delighting in their joy rather than concerning myself with their clinical needs.

Debbie's husband, Steve, is already at the hospital when we arrive. He is a natural at taking on the role of the proud father. He has already changed two nappies, he tells me as he hugs me and kisses me on the cheek. Debbie is dressed but lies back on her bed, propped up on pillows. She looks well, I notice, but, not surprisingly, tired after such a long labour. I pat her hand and ask how she is feeling, trying not to lapse into doctor mode. We talk only about the family and the baby. Debbie and Steve do not know about what happened at my home yesterday and I have asked Sally and Pete not to tell them just yet. Sally pointed out that they will find out soon one way or another and it would be better for her to tell them than for them to read it in the paper or see it on the television. I have agreed that she can tell them when they are back home, when they have seen that I am indeed in one piece. In the meantime, I enjoy the fact that it is no longer the foremost topic of conversation.

I congratulate Debbie and kiss her on the cheek. She lets me hold her daughter. I gather her into my arms and coo at her as she blinks at me with pure blue eyes that do not yet know how to focus. They have decided to call her Katherine, Debbie tells me. I hold her close and breathe in the sweet smell of milk and freshly bathed skin.

I love the way Sally's family works together, the way not just Debbie's husband but also her parents congregate to escort the new baby home. It feels ceremonial, this procession. We will not go into their house though. This is a time when Debbie, Steve and the baby need their own space.

It is only later, when I am settling down to sleep in the hotel bed that night that it occurs to me. Debbie's baby bore no resemblance to the one I saw under hypnosis. But I do not spend long thinking about it. It is a mere detail in a huge drama. It is unimportant. There are other things to think about. I am aware of Richard's arm curled protectively around me as we fall asleep. We have so much catching up to do.

Chapter 32

The next morning, after Richard has left for work, Mrs Blackstock rings me on the hotel phone. Everything is done, she says. Things are put right as much as they can be. She suggests that, as she will be in the house most of the day, as part of her regular hours, it might be an opportunity for me to spend some time there, some time when I will not be alone.

I tell her I will think about this for a few minutes. I have already rung the day centre to let them know I would not be coming in. They were not surprised. The story was on the front page of the local paper yesterday as well as on the television and radio. Now the whole city knows about the drama that has taken place. Apparently, it has captured the public interest.

I pack our belongings, call for a taxi, and check out of the hotel. It is an hour after Mrs Blackstock's call when I arrive home. At first, I am reluctant to go into the kitchen. I smell ground coffee and the spicy aroma of freshly baked fruit cake. I know that Mrs Blackstock is doing her best to tempt me. I peek cautiously round the door, reassure myself that everything is normal, or at least, as normal as it ever will be again. Everything is in its place apart from a sea-grass mat that used to lie between the table and the Aga. This, I notice, has disappeared. I can guess the reason and do not mention it. Mrs Blackstock has attempted to divert my attention with vases of chrysanthemums. She sees me looking at the floor. 'The other one was getting rather worn,' she lies. 'Perhaps something in stripy colours would look nice, maybe it would brighten the place up.'

I nod in agreement.

'I've also taken the liberty of removing the knife rack,' she continues. 'I know you don't use it very often and neither do I. Personally, I prefer an old-fashioned vegetable peeler.'

Again, I suspect she is lying to protect me. But I am grateful.

Despite having Mrs Blackstock for company, I feel uneasy in the house. Eventually, after spending half an hour pacing backwards and forwards from room to room, I turn up the heating in the conservatory. I take a portable radio along with a mug of coffee and attempt to busy myself tending the plants. It is a sunny day and the expanse of glass magnifies the light. As the heating warms the room, I can almost imagine it is spring already.

At mid-day, Angela calls round. As she sits at the kitchen table, Mrs Blackstock discreetly makes an excuse about doing the dusting and leaves us alone.

'I wanted to make sure you were all right,' Angela tells me. 'And also to let you know what's happening with our investigation.' She assures me first that there is no question of my being implicated in the harming of either of the casualties. 'I know it sounds awful that we should even consider it,' she says, 'but the fact is that in many cases of murder or serious assault the first person on the scene is often the perpetrator. So often,' she tells me, 'the last person to see someone alive is also the first one to see them dead. We have to rule out that possibility as a matter of course.'

I nod. I do not like hearing about this, yet, at the same time, it is preferable to have a clear idea in my mind of what happened than to see it forever in a hazy mist, beyond which I might draw my imagined, less favourable version of events.

'Your clothes were soaked in Sykes' blood,' she says. I feel sick at the thought of this. 'And also a little of Ashby's. Sykes' fingerprints were on the knife, as was Ashby's blood and some residues from raw vegetables. Ashby's prints were on the gun. Of course, that could suggest a fight between Ashby and Sykes but that seems unlikely – there is no connection that we can see. The forensic evidence exactly matches what you told us on Sunday night.'

'Frank saved my life,' I say. 'Ashby was going to kill me, and Frank stopped him.'

Angela looks at me searchingly. 'Can you think of any reason why he would be so selfless?' she asks. 'He must have known he was risking his own life defending you.' She pauses. I know what she will ask. 'Were the two of you in love? Having an affair?'

I am horrified at this thought. 'Certainly not,' I say, wishing I could tell her the real reason but knowing I must not.

'Ah well,' Angela continues. 'It may be that he was somehow trying to make recompense for killing his wife. Or he might simply not have considered his own safety. From what you say, it all happened very quickly.'

'I'm lucky to be alive, aren't I?' I ask this in a whisper.

Angela nods. 'I wouldn't have risked upsetting you by saying it quite so definitively but, since you mention it, yes. If Sykes hadn't been there…well it was very lucky for you that he was. Even if the door had been locked, Ashby would have got in easily enough. He was officially licensed to have the gun - it isn't difficult if you're a farmer.'

'How is Ashby?' I venture.

'He's alive but he hasn't regained consciousness. And perhaps, in a way, it would be better if he doesn't. I know I shouldn't say that, but the fact is he didn't want to live. If he does survive he's looking at a long prison sentence for murder – or at the very least manslaughter and attempted murder. And it would be easier for you to move on knowing he could never harm you again. To be honest, a prison sentence can't guarantee that.'

I think about what Angela has said. And I think about Clare and her father. 'He doesn't deserve to die though,' I say. 'He was in turmoil, insane almost. I know it would be – well – neater for everyone if he died, but I'm sure there are people who care for him, whose lives would be devastated if he didn't pull through.'

Angela shrugs. 'It's out of our hands. If it weren't for your neighbour he wouldn't even have made it into hospital. She's quite a remarkable lady. Quite surprising.'

'She certainly surprised me,' I say. I hesitate. There is something else I need to ask about. 'I know it isn't really any of my business,' I begin, 'not being family or anything. But what will happen to Frank?'

'The prison seems to think there's a daughter in Australia. We're trying to contact her but we haven't had any luck as yet. It looks like they lost touch after his mother died. If she can't be traced after a reasonable time then the local authority will arrange a simple funeral.'

'I'd like to do that,' I say. 'To pay for the funeral and to be there for him. I'm sure some of my friends would want to attend too.'

Angela is taken aback. 'That's very generous of you.'

'It's the least I can do,' I say, 'to give him a good send off. After all, he gave me my life.'

Later that week I receive a phone call from Andrew.

'How are you?' he asks. 'I've been worried.'

I tell him that I am coming to terms with everything, that hopefully life will soon begin to return to normal. I hesitate for a moment then I tell him that things are happier with Richard; that we would like to make it work.

'I'm glad,' Andrew says straight away.

'Oh,' I am almost disappointed. 'I was afraid that you might – well, that you might mind.'

'I would mind if you stayed with him out of a sense of duty or because you didn't have the confidence to leave. I would be disappointed if you were settling for second best.'

'You're very generous,' I say.

Andrew explains that, in his Buddhist philosophy, he tries not to rely on attachment. He doesn't mean commitment or loyalty, he assures me, but rather the state of clinging on, to material things, to people. Rather, he aspires to a state of letting go, of letting things be. If Richard and I can be happy together then he can be happy for us.

286

There is another subject he wishes to discuss, he tells me, the circumstances of my adoption and my birth certificate. Technically speaking, he says, one might argue that official documents such as my driving license and national insurance eligibility were fraudulently obtained.

'So what do you suggest I do?' I ask.

'Strictly speaking, I should tell you to consult Richard's solicitor in Nottingham,' he says. 'But, off the record, nobody has challenged you so far and it isn't as though you're intentionally committing a crime. You could simply leave things as they are.'

I nod to myself. So many things have been upset in my life recently. Leaving things as they are seems a very appealing option.

Chapter 33

It is Wednesday morning, ten days after it all happened. When the doorbell rings, I start, tensing my muscles and letting out an involuntary gasp. I wonder, as I stand and walk down the hall, if I will ever be able to relax in this house again. If, what with the trauma of the attack and the memories of Jamie, it wouldn't be better to move, to start afresh somewhere new. But it is early days yet, I remind myself. I peer through the spy-hole in the front door. We had it fitted last week, one of those fish-eye lenses, far easier than trying to guess the identity of callers through the bright distortion of the stained glass. I see the image of a smallish woman so I open the door.

She is little more than a girl, this stranger standing on my step. I say stranger though she looks vaguely familiar.

'Mrs Spencer?' she enquires nervously.

I nod.

'I'm Sarah,' she continues, 'I was a friend of Jamie's, I was at the funeral.'

'Ah yes.' The recognition resolves itself in my mind. I see her now, one of a group who had come up from London. Yet my memories of that day are so hazy. I wonder if I will ever recall it with clarity, wonder if I will ever want to.

'I'm sorry to turn up unannounced,' she says. 'I wrote twice but I wasn't sure if I had the right address.'

For a moment I am puzzled. Then I think of that first note, the one I assumed was from a journalist; with the phone number I almost rang. And the second letter, forgotten in the chaos, still in my desk drawer, unopened.

'May we come in and talk to you?' she asks.

'We?' I notice, then, that beneath her thick winter coat she is bulky, not just with layers of clothes to combat the cold, but with another person, a tiny baby, pressed in a sling against her chest. And even though I can see little of it, swathed as it is in hats and shawls, I realise instantly that it is the baby I saw in the dream, the hypnosis. My heart flutters like a butterfly testing its wings on the first day of summer. I open my door, my arms, my heart.

'Come in!' I say.

I take Sarah through to the kitchen and pull up two chairs by the comfort of the Aga. As I set the kettle on the hotplate Sarah takes off her coat, releasing long dark hair over her bright cardigan. Then she removes the baby from its outer wrappings. It is a girl, no more than four weeks old. It has wisps of dark hair just like Jamie did at that age.

'This is Isabelle,' Sarah says. Then she says the words that I already know she will. 'She's your granddaughter.'

I grip the Aga rail, hang onto it for dear life. I feel heady, faint, euphoric. Like those followers in Pentecostal meetings who, whipped into a frenzy, collapse to the floor in a moment of rapture, overcome by what the rest of us would say is hysteria, what they insist is the presence of the Holy Spirit. And how can we really know, when we are unbelievers? How can we question faith when we have none ourselves?

I take deep breaths; prevent myself from passing out. This is not a test of faith, we have science, there will be a DNA analysis – Richard will insist on it I know. But Sarah knows this too. She wouldn't lie, wouldn't build up my hopes just to see them dashed. And even without my intuition, I can see the likeness, even at this young age. I can see that Isabelle is part of Jamie, part of Richard and part of myself.

Sarah is speaking. I fight against the pressure pounding in my ears, the difficulty in focusing my eyes.

'Would you like to hold her?' she asks.

With one hand still steadying myself on the rail, I lower myself into the chair. Sarah kneels before me and places the baby into my arms, stays close with her arms around both of us so we are all safe. When Isabelle opens her eyes and looks up at me I travel back in time twenty-five years, to the moment when I held Jamie for the first time. I had forgotten what it felt like, his warmth against my breast, his breath tickling my fingers. For six months, I have thought only of the pain, the squalor, the spent needle by his side. I have forgotten everything that really matters.

The kettle breathes steam around us.

'I must get the tea,' I protest, voicelessly.

'I'll do that,' Sarah assures me. 'You look after Isabelle.'

And I do as I am told. For the first time in six months, I am allowed to be truly happy. Not in some exotic escape or a fleeting glimpse of a promise but in a way that is real, that can last forever.

Time passes in a dream. There is exquisite joy. I feel complete as I cuddle Isabelle to me. And there is pain. There are things I need to know. Questions for which Sarah may guard the answers. I ask each question tentatively, my breath held, bracing myself for a reply that I may not want to hear. I hold onto Isabelle for comfort.

What happened to Jamie? What really happened? Was he alone? Unhappy? Did he mean for it to happen? Did he know about Isabelle? Did he realise, as he injected that last fatal dose, that he was going to be a father?

Sarah helps as much as she can but it will take many of these conversations before I feel I understand what happened to my son – as much as that is possible. Sarah was more aware than I was about what was going on, of course. But she could only plead with him, support him, deal him ultimatums. At the end of the day, it was his choice. She feels that she let him down. But she tried. And at the end, she had a choice – to sink with him or to protect Isabelle. And I know she did the only thing she could.

And what of Sarah, my daughter-in-law – for that is how I think of her? She is a doctor too, it seems, a junior doctor. She is taking a year off because of Jamie, because of Isabelle, then she will complete her rotations. She doesn't want to work in a hospital though, she wants to be a GP. She is living with her parents at the moment. They have been very good, very accepting. It has been a difficult time but now she has Isabelle she knows she will get through it.

After lunch, Sarah says she has to go. I urge her to stay. She could stay the night, I suggest, meet Richard. But she insists that she has a train to catch, that her parents are expecting her home in time for dinner. I do not want her to leave. In case I never see her and Isabelle again, in case it all turns out to be a dream. Yet, even if that were to happen, I feel as though I could live on this memory forever, summoning it to me whenever life is hard. I suggest that I could drive her back to London but she will not agree to this. I can tell that she has an independent streak. Eventually, she allows me to give her a lift to the station. I ask her to ring later. I will let Richard take the call. Then he will know that I have not imagined it. And so will I.

Chapter 34

I am alone in the house. Tonight, I will sleep here on my own for the first time since it happened. But I do not mind. In a way, I am looking forward to it.

Richard left a couple of hours ago. He has gone to his parents. He wanted me to go with him but I feel the things he has to say will be better coming from him alone. And in any case, I have matters of my own to attend to.

This morning, we received a card from Andrew. He wishes us well, feels sure that good things will come into our lives. Of course, they already have, I must write and tell him. Andrew says that when his current court case is over he will be going on a retreat, to Nepal probably, or possibly to India. Actually, he uses the words 'extended holiday'. They convey the upper middle class respectability and predictability that Richard will understand. But I know him well enough to understand what he is really saying. I know also that he is telling me that he will leave Richard and myself alone to rebuild our marriage, our lives. Andrew is insistent, however, that, when things are calmer for all of us, we must get together. We must share better things. We must not wait until we have need of his professional services to contact him again.

During the past ten days, everything has been moving fast. We went up to London for the day last weekend and Richard met Sarah and Isabelle. Already he is besotted. Tomorrow, I am going down to Somerset to spend a few days with my mother. I want to tell her, in person, about the baby. I want to ease the surprise, allow it time to gestate in her mind before she meets her great-granddaughter.

I go through to the conservatory. I want to check the plants before I go to Somerset. I will probably stay most of the week. It is my last chance before I start back to work. The sun feels strong and I have no need of a jacket. The room is stuffy and I open one of the windows a few inches. I'm sure it is too early for any birds to be nesting but you never know. The possibility of leaving all this behind, of moving house, moving jobs even, a fresh start somewhere new, drifts in and out of my thoughts, flirting, teasing, tempting me with exotic promises. I look about me, smell the sweetness of a solitary flower that is blooming early on a lemon tree. I would miss this room if we moved. Richard says we should wait a year at least before deciding anything like that. True, the house is large, but perhaps we should use that as an opportunity to entertain more. And of course the attic rooms will be ideal for when Sarah visits with Isabelle.

After lunch, I will drive over to Ilkeston to see Rose. I want to show her the photographs that Sarah sent. Then I will call on Sally and Pete. Debbie and Steve will be round there for the afternoon with Katherine. I haven't seen the baby since that first time in the hospital almost three weeks ago and I have a present to give them. I smile to myself. Already I can see family days out with Katherine and Isabelle playing together.

On the way back from Ilkeston, I drive to Kimberley Place.

Outside, the temperature has dropped even further; the grey gloom is preparing to transform itself into night. I am almost reluctant to get out of the car. As I shut the door behind me, I pull my hat tighter down over my ears and turn up my collar over my scarf. I glance up and down the road but I don't really care whether anyone is looking. I know this will be the last time. I cross the verge and find the hole in the fence. Then I wait.

The garden emerges gradually, like a story unravelling. As the mist clears, the colours clarify, the air warms and the breeze carries the scents of summer. I hear the creaking of the swing on the branch and then I see the girl idling happily, to and fro.

293

ALI COOPER is a musician and music teacher, currently living in rural Devon. She has degrees in psychology and archaeology and both of these subjects feature in her writing. She is published in archaeology non-fiction and is a member of Year Zero Writers.

To contact the author or to join a mailing list for information on new books published by Standing Stone Press please email

standingstonepress@hotmail.co.uk

YEAR ZERO WRITERS are a collective of authors from all over the world, writing mainly in the genre of contemporary literary fiction. To find out more about them and read samples of their work, please see

yearzerowriters.wordpress.com

Books produced by Year Zero Writers and Standing Stone Press are available to purchase from online retailers and can be ordered at high street book stores. However, they rely on word of mouth for advertising. Please help us spread the word. If you enjoyed reading this book, please recommend it to your friends or, better still, buy them a copy.

LaVergne, TN USA
13 July 2010
189379LV00001B/33/P